Anonymous

Lectures on Metaphysics and Logic by William Hamilton Lectures on logic. Vol. 1

Anonymous

Lectures on Metaphysics and Logic by William Hamilton Lectures on logic. Vol. 1

ISBN/EAN: 9783742832153

Manufactured in Europe, USA, Canada, Australia, Japa

Cover: Foto ©Andreas Hilbeck / pixelio.de

Manufactured and distributed by brebook publishing software
(www.brebook.com)

Anonymous

Lectures on Metaphysics and Logic by William Hamilton Lectures on logic. Vol. 1

LECTURES

ON

METAPHYSICS AND LOGIC

BY

SIR WILLIAM HAMILTON, BART.

PROFESSOR OF LOGIC AND METAPHYSICS IN THE
UNIVERSITY OF EDINBURGH

Advocate, A.M. (Oxon.) &c.; Corresponding Member of the Institute of France; Honorary Member of the
American Academy of Arts and Sciences; and of the Latin Society of Jena, &c.

EDITED BY THE

REV. H. L. MANSEL, B.D., LL.D.

WAYNFLETE PROFESSOR OF MORAL AND METAPHYSICAL PHILOSOPHY, OXFORD

AND

JOHN VEITCH, M.A., LL.D.

PROFESSOR OF LOGIC AND RHETORIC IN THE UNIVERSITY OF GLASGOW

IN FOUR VOLUMES

VOL. III.

WILLIAM BLACKWOOD AND SONS
EDINBURGH AND LONDON
MDCCCLXXIV

LECTURES

ON

L O G I C

· BY

SIR WILLIAM HAMILTON, BART.

EDITED BY THE

REV. H. L. MANSEL, B.D., LL.D.

WAYNFLETE PROFESSOR OF MORAL AND METAPHYSICAL PHILOSOPHY, OXFORD

AND

JOHN VEITCH, M.A., LL.D.

PROFESSOR OF LOGIC AND RHETORIC IN THE UNIVERSITY OF GLASGOW

VOL. I.

THIRD EDITION, REVISED

WILLIAM BLACKWOOD AND SONS
EDINBURGH AND LONDON
MDCCCLXXIV

PREFACE.

THE Lectures comprised in the present Volumes form the second and concluding portion of the Biennial Course on Metaphysics and Logic, which was commenced by Sir William Hamilton on his election to the Professorial Chair in 1836, and repeated, with but slight alterations, till his decease in 1856. The Appendix contains various papers, composed for the most part during this period, which, though portions of their contents were publicly taught at least as early as 1840, were only to a very small extent incorporated into the text of the Lectures.

The Lectures on Logic, like those on Metaphysics, were chiefly composed during the session in which they were first delivered (1837-8); and the statements made in the preface to the previous volumes, as regards the circumstances and manner of their composition, are equally applicable to the present course. In this, as in the preceding series, the Author has largely availed himself of the labours of previous writers, many of whom are but little known in this country. To the works of the German logicians of the present century, particularly to those of Krug and Esser, these Lectures are under especial obligations.

In the compilation of the Appendix, some responsibility rests with the Editors; and a few words of explanation may be necessary as regards the manner in which they have attempted to perform this portion of their task. In publishing the papers of a deceased writer, composed at various intervals during a long period of years, and treating of difficult and controverted questions, there are two opposite dangers to be guarded against. On the one hand, there is the danger of compromising the Author's reputation by the publication of documents which his maturer judgment might not have sanctioned; and, on the other hand, there is the danger of committing an opposite injury to him and to the public, by withholding writings of interest and value. Had Sir William Hamilton, at any period of his life, published a systematic treatise on Logic, or had his projected *New Analytic of Logical Forms* been left in a state at all approaching to completeness, the Editors might probably have obtained a criterion by which to distinguish between those speculations which would have received the final *imprimatur* of their Author, and those which would not. In the absence of any such criterion, they have thought it better to run the risk of giving too much than too little; to publish whatever appeared to have any philosophical or historical interest, without being influenced by its coincidence with their own opinions, or by its coherence with other parts of the Author's writings. It is possible that, among the papers thus published, may be found some which are to be considered rather as experimental exercises than as approved results; but no

papers have been intentionally omitted, except such as
were either too fragmentary to be intelligible, or manifestly imperfect sketches of what has been published
here or elsewhere in a more matured form.

The Notes, in these as in the previous volumes, are
divided into three classes. Those printed from the
manuscript of the Lectures appear without any distinctive mark; those supplied from the Author's Com-
monplace-Book and other papers are enclosed within
square brackets without signature; and those added by
the Editors are marked by the signature "ED." These
last, as in the Lectures on Metaphysics, are chiefly confined to occasional explanations of the text and verifica-
tions of references.

In conclusion, the Editors desire to express their ac-
knowledgments to those friends from whom they have
received assistance in tracing the numerous quotations
and allusions scattered through these and the preceding
volumes. In particular, their thanks are due to Hubert
Hamilton, Esq., whose researches among his father's
books and papers have supplied them with many valuable materials; and to H. W. Chandler, Esq., Fellow of
Pembroke College, Oxford, who has aided them from the
resources of a philosophical learning cognate in many
respects to that of Sir William Hamilton himself.

CONTENTS OF VOL. I.

LECTURE XIII

LECTURE XIV.

LECTURE XV.

LECTURE XVI.

LECTURE XVII.

LECTURE XVIII.

LECTURE XIX.

LECTURE XX.

LECTURE XXI.

LECTURE XXII.

LECTURE XXIII.

LECTURES ON LOGIC.

LECTURE I.[a]

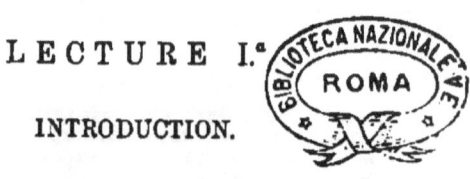

INTRODUCTION.

LOGIC.—I. ITS DEFINITION.

GENTLEMEN,—We are now about to enter on the consideration of one of the most important branches of mental philosophy,—the science which is conversant about the Laws of Thought.[β] But, before commencing the discussion, I would premise a word in regard to the mode in which it ought to be conducted, with a view to your information and improvement. The great end which every instructor ought to propose in the communication of a science, is, to afford the student clear and distinct notions of its several parts, of their relations to each other, and to the whole of which they are the constituents. For unless he accomplish this, it is of comparatively little moment that his information be in itself either new or important; for of what consequence are all the qualities of a doctrine, if that doctrine be not communicated?—and communicated it is not, if it be not understood.

Marginal notes: LECT. I. Logic proper,—mode in which its consideration ought to be conducted. End of instruction.

a The first seven Lectures of the Metaphysical Course, (*Lectures on Metaphysics*, vol. i. p. 1-128), were delivered by Sir W. Hamilton as a General Introduction to the Course of Logic proper.—ED.

β For some remarks on the character and comprehension of Logic, see Appendix I.—ED.

But in the communication of a doctrine, the methods to be followed by an instructor who writes,
and by an instructor who speaks, are not the same.
They are, in fact, to a certain extent, necessarily different : for, while the reader of the one can always
be referred back or forward, can always compare one
part of a book with another, and can always meditate
at leisure on each step of the evolution ; the hearer
of the other, on the contrary, must at every moment
be prepared, by what has preceded, to comprehend at
once what is to ensue. The oral instructor has thus
a much more arduous problem to solve, in accomplishing the end which he proposes. For if, on the
one hand, he avoid obscurity by communicating only
what can easily be understood as isolated fragments,
he is intelligible only because he communicates nothing worth learning ; and if, on the other, he be
unintelligible in proportion as his doctrine is concatenated and systematic, he equally fails in his attempt ;
for as, in the one case, there is nothing to teach, so,
in the other, there is nothing taught. It is, therefore,
evident, that the oral instructor must accommodate his
mode of teaching to the circumstances under which
he acts. He must endeavour to make his audience
fully understand each step of his movement, before
another is attempted ; and he must prepare them for
details by a previous survey of generals. In short,
what follows should always be seen to evolve itself
out of what precedes. It is in consequence of this
condition of oral instruction, that, where the development of a systematic doctrine is attempted in a course
of Lectures, it is usual for the lecturer to facilitate the
labour to his pupils and himself, by exhibiting in a
Manual or Textbook the order of his doctrine and a

summary of its contents. As I have not been able to prepare this useful subsidiary, I shall endeavour, as far as possible, to supply its want. I shall, in the first place, endeavour always to present you with a general statement of every doctrine to be explained, before descending to the details of explanation; and in order that you may be insured in distincter and more comprehensive notions, I shall, where it is possible, comprise the general statements in Propositions or Paragraphs, which I shall slowly dictate to you, in order that they may be fully taken down in writing. This being done, I shall proceed to analyse these propositions or paragraphs, and to explain their clauses in detail. This, I may observe, is the method followed in those countries where instruction by prelection is turned to the best account;—it is the one prevalent on the Continent, more especially in the universities of Germany and Holland.

In pursuance of this plan, I at once commence by giving you, as the first proposition or paragraph, the following. I may notice, however, by parenthesis, that, as we may have sometimes occasion to refer articulately to these propositions, it would be proper for you to distinguish them by sign and number.

The first paragraph, then, is this:—

¶ I. A System of Logical Instruction consists of Two Parts,—1°, Of an Introduction to the science; 2°, Of a Body of Doctrine constituting the Science itself.

These, of course, are to be considered in their order.

¶ II. The Introduction to Logic should afford answers to the following questions;—i. What is Logic.

Logic ? ii. What is its Value ? iii. What are
its Divisions ? iv. What is its History ? and,
v. What is its Bibliography, that is, what are
the best books upon the subject ?

In regard to the first of these questions, it is evident that the answer to it is given in a definition of
Logic. I, therefore, dictate to you the third paragraph.

¶ III. What is Logic ? *Answer*—Logic is the
Science of the Laws of Thought as Thought.

This definition, however, cannot be understood
without an articulate exposition of its several parts.
I, therefore, proceed to this analysis and explanation,
and shall consider it under the three following heads.
In the first, I shall consider the meaning, and history,
and synonyms of the word *Logic*. In the second, I
shall consider the Genus of Logic, that is, explain
why it is defined as a Science. In the third, I
shall consider the Object-matter of Logic, that is,
explain to you what is meant by saying, that it is
conversant about the Laws of Thought as Thought.

First, then, in regard to the signification of the
word. *Logic*, you are aware, is a Greek word, λογική ;
and λογική, like γραμματική, ῥητορική, ποιητική, διαλεκτική, I need hardly tell you, is an adjective, one
or other of the substantives ἐπιστήμη, *science*, τέχνη,
art, or πραγματεία, *study*, or rather *matter of study*,
being understood. The term λογική, in this special
signification, and as distinctly marking out a particular science, is not so old as the constitution of that
science itself. Aristotle did not designate by the
term λογική, the science whose doctrine he first fully

developed. He uses, indeed, the adjective λογικός in LECT.
I.
various combinations with other substantives. Thus
I find in his *Physics* λογικὴ ἀπορία,[a]—in his *Rhetoric*,
λογικαὶ δυσχερείαι,[β]—in his *Metaphysics*, λογικαὶ
ἀποδείξεις,[γ]—in his *Posterior Analytics*, ὄνα λογικά,[δ]
—in his *Topics*, λογικὸν πρόβλημα.[ε] He, likewise, not
unfrequently makes use of the adverb λογικῶς.[ζ] By
whom the term λογικὴ was first applied, as the word
expressive of the science, does not appear. Boethius, Ancient
Peripa-
tetics.
who flourished at the close of the fifth and commence-
ment of the sixth century, says, in his *Commentary
on the Topics of Cicero*,[η] that the name of *Logic* was
first given by the ancient Peripatetics. In the works Alexander
of Aphrodi-
sias.
of Alexander of Aphrodisias, the oldest commentator
we possess on the works of Aristotle, (he flourished
towards the end of the second century), the term
λογικὴ, both absolutely and in combination with
πραγματεία, &c., is frequently employed ;[θ] and the
word is familiar in the writings of all the subsequent
Aristotelians. Previously, however, to Alexander, it Cicero.
is evident that λογικὴ had become a common designation of the science ; for it is once and again thus

a I. iii. c. 3 : Ἔχει Γ ἀπορίαν λογι-
κήν. "Duld(tabionem quas non e rerum
singularium (physicarum) contempla-
tione, sed e ratiocinationes sola orta
est." Waitz, ad Arist. Org., vol. ii.
p. 354. *Logical* and *dialectical* reasoning in Aristotle mean the same
thing,—viz. reasoning founded only
on general principles of probability,
not on necessary truths or on special
experiences.—ED.

β This expression occurs not in the
Rhetoric, but in the *Metaphysics*, L.
iii. (iv.) c. 3, and L. xiii. (xiv.) c. 1.
In the *Rhetoric* we find the expression
λογικοὶ συλλογισμοί, L. I. c. 1.—ED.

γ L. xiii. (xiv.) c. l. Cf. *De Gener.
Anim.*, ii. 8.—ED.

δ L. I. c. 24.—ED.

ε L. v. c. 1.—ED.

ζ E. g., *Anal. Post.*, L. 21, 32 ;
Phys., viii. 8 ; *Metaph.*, vi. 4, 17 ; xi.
1.—ED.

η L. i. sub. init.—ED.

θ See especially his commentary
on the *Prior Analytics*, f. 2, (*Scholia*,
ed. Brandis, p. 141), where he divides ἡ λογικὴ τε καὶ συλλογιστικὴ
πραγματεία into four branches, ἀπο-
δεικτική, διαλεκτική, ῥητορική, and
σοφιστική. Here *Logic* is used in a
wider sense than the adjective and
adverb bear in Aristotle, while the
cognate term *dialectic* retains its original signification.—ED.

LECT.
I.

b. Its deri-
vation and
meaning.

Twofold
meaning of
λόγος.

How ex-
pressed by
Aristotle.

By others.

applied by Cicero.[a] So much for the history of the
word *Logic*, in so far as regards its introduction and
earlier employment. We have now to consider its
derivation and meaning.

It is derived from λόγος, and it had primarily the
same latitude and variety of signification as its original. What then did λόγος signify? In Greek this
word had a twofold meaning. It denoted both thought
and its expression ; it was equivalent both to the *ratio*
and to the *oratio* of the Latins. The Greeks, in order
to obviate the ambiguity thus arising from the confusion of two different things under one expression,
were compelled to add a differential epithet to the
common term. Aristotle, to contradistinguish λόγος,
meaning *thought*, from λόγος, meaning *speech*, calls
the former τὸν ἔσω,—τὸν ἐν τῇ ψυχῇ—*that within,—
that in the mind ;* and the latter, τὸν ἔξω,—*that without.*[β] The same distinction came subsequently to be
expressed by the λόγος ἐνδιάθετος, for *thought*, the
verbum mentis ; and by λόγος προφορικὸς, for *language,* the *verbum oris.*[γ] It was necessary to give you
this account of the ambiguity of the word λόγος,
because the same passed into its derivative λογική ;
and it also was necessary that you should be made
aware of the ambiguity in the name of the science,
because this again exerted an influence on the views
adopted in regard to the object-matter of the science.

a See *De Finibus*, i. 7 ; *Tusc. Quaest.*,
iv. 14. Cicero probably borrowed
this use of the term from the Stoics,
to whose founder, Zeno, Laertius (vii.
39) ascribes the origin of the division
of Philosophy into Logic, Physics,
and Ethics, sometimes erroneously
attributed to Plato.—ED.

β *Anal. Post.*, i. 10.—ED.

γ E. g., Philo, *De Vita Mosis*, p. 672,

edit. Paris, 1640 ; Plutarch, *Philos.
esse cum principibus*, c. 2, (vol. ii. p.
777, C., ed. Francof., 1620) ; Sextus
Empiricus, *Pyrrh. Hyp.*, i. 65 ; Simplicius, *In Categ. Arist.*, p. 7 ; Damas-
cenus, *Fid. Orthod.*, ii. 21. The expressions probably originated with
the Stoics. See Wyttenbach's note
on Plutarch's *Moralia*, p. 44 A, (tom.
vi. pars 1, p. 373, ed. Oxon, 1810.)—ED.

But what, it may be asked, was the appellation of the science before it had obtained the name of *Logic?* for, as I have said, the doctrine had been discriminated, and even carried to a very high perfection, before it received the designation by which it is now generally known. The most ancient name for what was subsequently denominated *Logic*, was *Dialectic.* But this must be understood with certain limitations. By Plato the term *Dialectic* is frequently employed to mark out a particular section of philosophy. But this section is, with Plato, not coextensive with the domain of Logic; it includes, indeed, Logic, but it does not exclude Metaphysic, for it is conversant not only about the form, but about the matter, of our knowledge. (The meaning of these expressions you are soon to learn.)

This word, διαλεκτική (τέχνη, or ἐπιστήμη or πραγματεία, being understood,) is derived, you are aware, from διαλέγεσθαι, *to hold conversation or discourse together; dialectic,* therefore, literally signifies, a *conversation, colloquy, controversy, dispute.* But Plato, who defined thought an internal discourse of the soul with itself,[a] and who explained τὸ διαλέγεσθαι by the ambiguous expression τὸ λόγῳ χρῆσθαι,[b] did not certainly do violence either to the Greek language or to his own opinions, in giving the name of Dialectic to the process, not merely of logical inference, but of metaphysical speculation. In our own times the Platonic signification of the word has been revived, and Hegel has applied it, in even a more restricted meaning, to metaphysical speculation alone.[y]

a Fischaber, p. 10 [*Lehrbuch der Logik,* Einleitung. See *Theaetetus,* p. 189; *Sophistes,* p. 263.—Ed.]

β 1. *Alcib.,* p. 129: 3Ω. Τὸ δὲ διαλέγεσθαι καὶ τὸ λόγῳ χρῆσθαι ταὐ-

τὸν τοῦ καλεῖς: ΑΛ. Πάνυ γε. Cf. Osmundi, *Logica,* Procem. *Opera,* t. L. p. 32.—Ed.

γ See *Encyklopädie,* § 81.—Ed.

But if Plato employed the term Dialectic to denote more than Logic, Aristotle employed it to denote less. With him, *Dialectic* is not a term for the pure science, or the science in general, but for a particular and an applied part. It means merely the Logic of Probable Matter, and is thus convertible with what he otherwise denominates *Topics* (τοπική.)[a] This, I may observe, has been very generally misunderstood, and it is commonly supposed that Aristotle uses the term Dialectic in two meanings, in one meaning for the science of Logic in general, in another for the Logic of Probabilities. This is, however, a mistake. There is, in fact, only a single passage in his writings, on the ground of which it can possibly be maintained that he ever employs *Dialectic* in the more extensive meaning. This is in his *Rhetoric* i. 1,[b] but the passage is not stringent, and *Dialectic* may there be plausibly interpreted in the more limited signification. But at any rate it is of no authority, for it is an evident interpolation,—a mere gloss which has crept in from the margin into the text.[y] Thus it appears that Aristotle possessed no single term by which to designate the general science of which he was the principal author and finisher. *Analytic*, and *Apodeictic* with *Topic*, (equivalent to *Dialectic*, and including *Sophistic*), were so many special names by which he denoted particular parts or particular applications of Logic. I say nothing of the vacillating and various employment of the terms *Logic* and *Dialectic* by the Stoics,

a *Topics*, i. 1: Διαλεκτικὸς δὲ συλλογισμὸς ὁ ἐξ ἐνδόξων συλλογιζόμενος. —ED.

β Περὶ δὲ συλλογισμοῦ ὁμοίως ἅπαντος τῆς διαλεκτικῆς ἐστιν ἰδεῖν, ἢ αὐτῆς ὅλης ἢ μέρους τινός.—ED.

y See Balforeus [R. Balforri Commentarius in Organum Logicum Aristotelis, Burdigalæ, 1618. Qu. 11. [3, p. 12. Muretus in his version omits this passage as an interpolation.—ED.]

Marginal notes:

LECT. L

Aristotle's employment of Dialectic.

Of Analytic, Apodeictic, Topic.

Epicureans, and other ancient schools of philosophy; and now proceed to explain to you the second head of the definition,—viz. the Genus,—class, of Logic, which I gave as Science.

It was a point long keenly mooted by the old logicians, whether Logic were a science, or an art, or neither, or both; and if a science, whether a science practical, or a science speculative, or at once speculative and practical.[a] Plato and the Platonists viewed it as a science;[β] but with them Dialectic, as I have noticed, was coextensive with the Logic and Metaphysics of the Peripatetics taken together. By Aristotle himself Logic is not defined. The Greek Aristotelians, and many philosophers since the revival of letters, deny it to be either science or art.[γ] The Stoics, in general, viewed it as a science;[δ] and the same was done by the Arabian and Latin schoolmen.[ε] In more modern times, however, many Aristotelians, all the Ramists, and a majority of the Cartesians, maintained it to be an art;[ζ] but a considerable party were found who defined it as both art and science.[η] In Germany, since the time of Leibnitz, Logic has been almost universally regarded as a science. The controversy which has been waged on this point is perhaps one of

LECT.
I.

2. Logic,—
its Genus
—whether
Science or
Art.

The question futile.

a See Appendix II.—Ed.

β (Camerarius, *Disputationes Philosophicæ*, p. 30.) [Pars i. qu. 3, ed. Parisiis, 1630. See also qu. 4, p. 44. —Ed.]

γ [See Themistius, *In Anal. Post.*, L. i. c. 24, [*Opera*, p. 6, Venice, 1554. —Ed.] Ammonius Hermiæ, *In Categ.*, Præf. [p. 3, ed. Ald. 1503.—Ed.] Simplicius, *In Categ.*, Præf. [§ 23, p. 5, ed. Basileæ, 1551.—Ed.] Zabarella, *De Natura Logicæ*, [L. i. c. 5, et seq.— Ed.] Smiglecius, *Logica*, Disp. ii. qu. 4, [p. 60, ed. Oxonii, 1658.—Ed.]

Logica Conimbricensis [Tract i. § 1, rubs. 4 et seq., p. 8, ed. 1711.—Ed.] Gerard John Vossius, *De Nat. Artium, sive de Logica*, c. vi.]

δ [See Laertius, *In Vita Zenonis*, L. vii.] [§ 62.—Ed.]

ε [Scotus, *Prædicamenta*, Qu. i. Albertus Magnus, *In De Prædicabilibus*, c. 1.]

ζ [Ramus, *Instit. Dialect.*, L. i. c. 1, Burgersdicius, *Instit. Log.*, L. i. c. 1, § 4.]

η See Smiglecius, as above.—Ed.

the most futile in the history of speculation. In so
far as Logic is concerned, the decision of the question
is not of the very smallest import. It was not in
consequence of any diversity of opinion in regard to
the scope and nature of this doctrine, that philosophers disputed by what name it should be called.
The controversy was, in fact, only about what was
properly an art, and what was properly a science;
and as men attached one meaning or another to these
terms, so did they affirm Logic to be an art, or a
science, or both, or neither. I should not, in fact, have
thought it necessary to say anything on this head,
were it not to guard you against some mistakes of
the respectable author, whose work on Logic I have
recommended to your attention—I mean Dr Whately.

Whately
quoted.

In the opening sentence of his *Elements*, it is said:—
" Logic, in the most extensive sense which the name
can with propriety be made to bear, may be considered
as the Science, and also as the Art, of Reasoning. It
investigates the principles on which argumentation is
conducted, and furnishes rules to secure the mind
from error in its deductions. Its most appropriate
office, however, is that of instituting an analysis of
the process of the mind in reasoning; and in this
point of view it is, as has been stated, strictly a
Science; while considered in reference to the practical
rules above mentioned, it may be called the *Art* of
reasoning. This distinction, as will hereafter appear,
has been overlooked or not clearly pointed out, by
most writers on the subject; Logic having been in
general regarded as merely an art, and its claim to
hold a place among the sciences having been expressly
denied."

Criticised.
This is from first to last erroneous. In the first

place, it is erroneous in what it says of the opinion
prevalent among philosophers in regard to the genus
of Logic. Logic was not, as is asserted, in general
regarded as an art, and its claim to hold a place among
the sciences expressly denied. The contrary would
have been correct; for the immense majority of logicians, ancient and modern, have regarded Logic as a
science, and expressly denied it to be an art. In the
second place, supposing Dr Whately's acceptation of
the terms *art* and *science* to be correct, there is not a
previous logician who would have dreamt of denying
that, on such an acceptation, Logic was both a science
and an art. But in the third place, the discrimination
itself of art and science is wrong. Dr Whately considers
science to be any knowledge viewed absolutely, and
not in relation to practice—a signification in which
every art would, in its doctrinal part, be a science;
and he defines art to be the application of knowledge
to practice, in which sense Ethics, Politics, Religion,
and all practical sciences, would be arts. The distinction of arts and sciences is thus wrong.[a] But in
the fourth place, were the distinction correct, it would
be of no value, for it would distinguish nothing, since
art and science would mark out no real difference
between the various branches of knowledge, but only
different points of view under which the same branch
might be contemplated by us,—each being in different
relations at once a science and an art. In fact, Dr
Whately confuses the distinction of science theoretical
and science practical with the distinction of science
and art. I am well aware that it would be no easy
matter to give a general definition of science as contradistinguished from art, and of art as contradistin-

a Compare *Lectures on Metaphysics*, vol. i. p. 115 et seq.—ED.

LECT.
I.

guished from science; but if the words themselves
cannot validly be discriminated, it would be absurd
to attempt to discriminate anything by them. When
I, therefore, define Logic by the genus *science*, I do
not attempt to give it more than the general denomination of a branch of knowledge; for I reserve the
discrimination of its peculiar character to the differential quality afforded by its object-matter. You will
find, when we have discussed the third head of the
definition, that Logic is not only a science, but a
demonstrative or apodictic science; but so to have
defined it, would have been tautological, for a science
conversant about laws is conversant about necessary
matter, and a science conversant about necessary
matter is demonstrative.

3. Logic,—
its object-
matter.

I proceed, therefore, to the third and last head of
the definition,—to explain what is meant by the
object-matter of Logic,—viz. the Laws of Thought as
Thought. The consideration of this head naturally
divides itself into three questions,—1, What is Thought?
2, What is Thought as Thought? 3, What are the Laws
of Thought as Thought?

a. Thought,
—what.

In the first place, then, in saying that Logic is
conversant about Thought, we mean to say that it is
conversant about thought strictly so called. The term
thought is used in two significations of different extent.

In its wider
and narrow-
er meaning.

In the wider meaning, it denotes every cognitive act
whatever; by some philosophers, as Descartes and his
disciples, it is even used for every mental modification
of which we are conscious, and thus includes the Feelings, the Volitions, and the Desires.[a] In the more

a Descartes, *Principia*, pars i. § 9:
"Cogitationis nomine intelligo illa
omnia quæ nobis consciis in nobis
fiant, quatenus eorum in nobis con-
scientia est. Atque ita non modo
intelligere, velle, imaginari, sed etiam
sentire, idem est hic quod cogitare."
—ED.

limited meaning, it denotes only the acts of the Under- LECT.
standing properly so called, that is, of the Faculty of   L
Comparison, or that which I distinguished as the Elaborative or Discursive Faculty.* It is in this more
restricted signification that thought is said to be the
object-matter of Logic.   Thus Logic does not consider Objects that
the laws which regulate the other powers of mind.   It the sphere
takes no immediate account of the faculties by which   of Logic.
we acquire the rude materials of knowledge; it supposes these materials in possession, and considers only
the manner of their elaboration.   It takes no account,
at least in the department of Pure Logic, of Memory
and Imagination, or of the blind laws of Association,
but confines its attention to connections regulated by
the laws of intelligence.   Finally, it does not consider
the laws themselves of Intelligence as given in the
Regulative Faculty,—Intelligence,—Common Sense;
for in that faculty these laws are data, facts, ultimate
and, consequently, inconceivable; but whatever transcends the sphere of the conceivable transcends the
sphere of Logic.

    Such are the functions about which Logic is not con-
versant, and such, in the limited signification of the
word, are the acts which are not denominated Thought.
We have hitherto found what thought is not, we must
now endeavour to determine generally what it is.

    The contemplation of the world presents to our sub- Thought
sidiary faculties a multitude of objects.   These objects proper.
are the rude materials submitted to elaboration by a
higher and self-active faculty, which operates upon
them in obedience to certain laws and in conformity
to certain ends.   The operation of this faculty is
Thought.   All thought is a comparison, a recognition

    a See *Lectures on Metaphysics*, Lect. xxxiv., vol. ii. p. 277.—ED.

LECT.
L

of similarity or difference; a conjunction or disjunction, in other words, a synthesis or analysis of its objects. In Conception, that is, in the formation of concepts (or general notions), it compares, disjoins or
conjoins attributes; in an act of Judgment, it compares, disjoins or conjoins concepts; in Reasoning, it
compares, disjoins or conjoins judgments. In each
step of this process there is one essential element; to
think, to compare, to conjoin or disjoin, it is necessary
to recognise one thing through or under another, and,
therefore, in defining Thought proper, we may either
define it as an act of comparison, or as a recognition
of one notion as in or under another. It is in performing this act of thinking a thing under a general
notion, that we are said to understand or comprehend
it. For example : An object is presented, say a book;
this object determines an impression, and I am even
conscious of the impression, but without recognising
to myself what the thing is; in that case, there is only
a perception, and not properly a thought. But suppose I do recognise it for what it is, in other words,
compare it with and reduce it under a certain concept,
class, or complement of attributes, which I call *book*;
in that case, there is more than a perception,—there is
a thought.

All this will, however, be fully explained in the
sequel; at present I only attempt to give you a rude
notion of what thinking is, to the end that you may
be able vaguely to comprehend the limitation of Logic
to a certain department of our cognitive functions,
and what is meant by saying that Logic is a science
of thought.

¹ Thought
as thought,
—what.

But Thought simply is still too undetermined; the
proper object of Logic is something still more definite;

it is not thought in general, but thought considered merely as thought, of which this science takes cognisance. This expression requires explanation; we come therefore to the second question,—What is meant by Thought as Thought?

To answer this question, let us remember what has just been said of the act constitutive of thought,—viz. that it is the recognition of a thing as coming under a concept; in other words, the marking an object by an attribute or attributes previously known as common to sundry objects, and to which we have accordingly given a general name. " In this process we are able, by abstraction, to distinguish from each other,—1°, The object thought of; and, 2°, The kind and manner of thinking it. Let us, employing the old and established technical expressions, call the first of these the *matter*, the second the *form*, of the thought. For example, when I think that the book before me is a folio, the matter of this thought is book and folio, the form of it is a judgment. Now it is abundantly evident, that this analysis of thought into two phases or sides is only the work of a scientific discrimination and contrast; for as, on the one hand, the matter of which we think is only cogitable through a certain form, so, on the other, the form under which we think cannot be realised in consciousness, unless in actual application to an object." [a]

Now, when I said that Logic was conversant about thought considered merely as thought, I meant simply to say, that Logic is conversant with the form of thought to the exclusion of the matter. This being understood, I now proceed to show how Logic only proposes,—how Logic only can propose, the form of thought for its object of consideration. It is indeed

(margin notes: Matter and Form of Thought. Logic properly conversant only with the Form of Thought.)

a Esser, *Logik,* § 3, p. 4, 2d edit. Münster, 1830.—Ed.

true, that this limitation of Logic to the form of thought has not always been kept steadily in view by logicians, that it is only gradually that proper views of the science have been speculatively adopted, and still more gradually that they have been carried practically into effect, insomuch that to the present hour, as I shall hereafter show you, there are sundry doctrines still taught as logical, which, as relative to the matter of thought, are in fact foreign to the science of its form.

This shown by a consideration of the nature and conditions of the thing itself.

"But although it is impossible to show by the history of the science, that Logic is conversant with the form, to the exclusion of the matter, of thought; this can, however, be satisfactorily done by a consideration of the nature and conditions of the thing itself. For, if it be maintained that Logic takes not merely the form but the matter of thought into account, (the matter, you will recollect, is a collective expression for the several objects about which thought is conversant), in that case, Logic must either consider all those objects without distinction, or make a selection of some alone. Now the former of these alternatives is manifestly impossible; for if it were required that Logic should comprise a full discussion of all cogitable objects, in other words, if Logic must draw within its sphere all other sciences, and thus constitute itself in fact the one universal science, every one at once perceives the absurdity of the requisition and the impossibility of its fulfilment. But is the second alternative more reasonable? Can it be proposed to Logic to take cognisance of certain objects of thought to the exclusion of others? On this supposition, it must be shown why Logic should consider this particular object and not also that; but as none but an arbitrary answer, that is no answer at all, can be given to this interro-

gation, the absurdity of this alternative is no less
manifest than that of the other. The particular objects, or the matter of thought, being thus excluded,
the form of human thought alone remains as the object-matter of our science; in other words, Logic has
only to do with thinking as thinking, and has no, at
least no immediate, concernment with that which is
thought about. Logic thus obtains, in common parlance, the appellation of a formal science, not indeed
in the sense as if Logic had only a form and not an
object, but simply because the form of human thought
is the object of logic; so that the title *formal science*
is properly only an abbreviated expression." [a]

I proceed now to the third question under this
head,—viz. What is meant by the Laws of Thought
as Thought? in other words, What is meant by the
Formal Laws of Thought?

We have already limited the object of Logic to the
form of thought. But there is still required a last and
final limitation; for this form contains more than
Logic can legitimately consider. "Human thought,
regarded merely in its formal relation, may be considered in a twofold point of view; for, on the one
hand, it is either known to us merely from experience
or observation,—we are merely aware of its phænomena historically or empirically, or, on the other, by
a reflective speculation,—by analysis and abstraction,
we seek out and discriminate in the manifestations of
thought what is contained of necessary and universal.
The empirical or historical consideration of our thinking faculty does not belong to Logic, but to the Phænomenology of Mind,—to Psychology. The empirical

a Esser, *Logik*, § 3, pp. 5, 6. Cf. 17 *et seq.* 2d edit. 1819.—Ed.
Krug, *Denklehre oder Logik*, § 8, p.

LECT.
I.

observation of the phœnomena necessarily, indeed, precedes their speculative analysis. But notwithstanding this, Logic possesses a peculiar province of its own, and constitutes an independent and exclusive science. For where our empirical consideration of the mind terminates, there our speculative consideration commences; the necessary elements which the latter secures from the contingent materials of observation, —these are what constitute the laws of thought as thought."[a]

a Cf. Esser, *Logik*, § 4, pp. 6, 7.—ED.

LECTURE II.

INTRODUCTION.

LOGIC — I. ITS DEFINITION. — HISTORICAL NOTICES OF OPINIONS REGARDING ITS OBJECT AND DOMAIN. — II. ITS UTILITY.

IN my last Lecture I commenced the consideration of Logic,—of Logic properly so denominated,—a science for the cultivation of which every European university has provided a special chair, but which, in this country, in consequence of the misconceptions which have latterly arisen in regard to its nature and its end, has been very generally superseded : insomuch that, for a considerable period, the chairs of Logic in our Scottish universities have in fact taught almost everything except the doctrine which they were established to teach. After some precursory observations in regard to the mode of communication which I should follow in my lectures on this subject, I entered on the treatment of the science itself, and stated to you that a systematic view of Logic would consist of two parts, the one being an Introduction to the doctrine, the other a body of the Doctrine itself. In the introduction were considered certain preparatory points, necessary to be understood before entering on the discussion of the science itself; and I stated that these preparatory points were, in relation to our science, exhausted in five questions and their answers— 1°,

LECT.
II.

Recapitulation.

LECT.
II.
What is Logic? 2°, What is its value? 3°, How is it distributed? 4°, What is its history? 5°, What are its subsidiaries?

I then proceeded to the consideration of the first of these questions; and, as the answer to the question, —what is Logic?—is given in its definition, I defined Logic to be the science conversant about the laws of thought considered merely as thought; warning you, however, that this definition could only be understood after an articulate explanation of its contents. Now this definition, I showed you, naturally fell into three parts, and each of these parts it behoved to consider and illustrate by itself. The first was the word significant of the thing defined,—*Logic*. The second was the genus by which Logic was defined,—science. The third was the object-matter constituting the differential quality of Logic,—the laws of thought as thought. Each of these I considered in its order. I, first of all, explained the original meaning of the term *Logic*, and gave you a brief history of its application. I then stated what was necessary in regard to the genus,— science; and, lastly, what is of principal importance, I endeavoured to make you vaguely aware of that which you cannot as yet be supposed competent distinctly to comprehend, I mean the peculiar character of the object,—object-matter,—about which Logic is conversant. The object of Logic, as stated in the definition, is the laws of thought as thought. This required an articulate explanation; and such an explanation I endeavoured to afford you under three distinct heads; expounding, 1°, What was meant by thought; 2°, What was meant by thought as thought; 3°, What was meant by the laws of thought as thought.

In reference to the first head, I stated that Logic is

conversant about thought taken in its stricter signification, that is, about thought considered as the operation of the Understanding Proper, or of that faculty
which I distinguished as the Elaborative or Discursive,—the Faculty of Relations, or Comparison. I attempted to make you vaguely apprehend what is the
essential characteristic of thought,—viz. the comprehension of a thing under a general notion or attribute.
For such a comprehension enters into every act of the
discursive faculty, in its different gradations of Conception, Judgment, and Reasoning.

But by saying that Logic is conversant about thought
proper, Logic is not yet discriminated as a peculiar
science, for there are many sciences, likewise, *inter alia*,
conversant about the operations and objects of the
Elaborative Faculty.   There is required a further
determination of its object-matter. This is done by
the limitation, that Logic is conversant not merely
about thought, but about thought as thought. The
explanation of this constituted the second head of our
exposition of the object-matter. Thought, I showed,
could be viewed, by an analytic abstraction, on two
sides or phases.   We could either consider the object
thought, or the manner of thinking it; in other words,
we could scientifically distinguish from each other the
matter and the form of thought. Not that the matter
and form have any separate existence ; no object being
cogitable except under some form of thought, and no
form of thought having any existence in consciousness
except some object be thought under it. This, however, formed no impediment to our analysis of these
elements, through a mental abstraction. This is in
fact only one of a thousand similar abstractions we
are in the habit of making ; and if such were impos-

ible, all human science would be impossible. For example, extension is presented to sense only under some modification of colour, and even imagination cannot represent extension except as coloured. We may view it in phantasy as black or white, as translucent or opaque; but represent it we cannot, except either under some positive variety of light, or under the negation of light, which is darkness. But, psychologically considered, darkness or blackness is as much a colour, that is, a positive sensation, as whiteness or redness; and thus we cannot image to ourselves aught extended, not even space itself, out of relation to colour. But is this inability even to imagine extension, apart from some colour, any hindrance to our considering it scientifically apart from all colour? Not in the smallest; nor do Mathematics and the other sciences find any difficulty in treating of extension, without even a single reference to this condition of its actual manifestation. The case of Logic is precisely the same. Logic considers the form apart from the matter of thought; and it is able to do this without any trouble, for though the form is only an actual phænomenon when applied to some matter,—object,—yet, as it is not necessarily astricted to any object, we can always consider it abstract from all objects,—in other words, from all matter. For as the mathematician, who cannot construct his diagrams, either to sense or to imagination, apart from some particular colour, is still able to consider the properties of extension apart from all colour; so the logician, though he cannot concretely represent the forms of thought except in examples of some particular matter, is still able to consider the properties of these forms apart from all matter. The possibility being thus apparent of a consiberation of the form abstractly from the matter of thought, I showed you that such an abstraction was necessary. The objects (the matter) of thought are infinite ; no one science can embrace them all, and, therefore, to suppose Logic conversant about the matter of thought in general, is to say that Logic is another name for the encyclopædia,—the *omne scibile*, —of human knowledge. The absurdity of this supposition is apparent. But if it be impossible for Logic to treat of all the objects of thought, it cannot be supposed that it treats of any ; for no reason can be given why it should limit its consideration to some, to the exclusion of others. As Logic cannot, therefore, possibly include all objects, and as it cannot possibly be shown why it should include only some, it follows that it must exclude from its domain the consideration of the matter of thought altogether ; and as, apart from the matter of thought, there only remains the form, it follows that Logic, as a special science of thought, must be viewed as conversant exclusively about the form of thought.

But the limitation of the object-matter of Logic to the form of thought, (and the expression *form of thought* is convertible with the expression *thought as thought*), is not yet enough to discriminate its province from that of other sciences ; for Psychology, or the Empirical Science of Mind, is, likewise, among the other mental phænomena, conversant about the phænomena of formal thought. A still further limitation is, therefore, requisite ; and this is given in saying, that Logic is the science not merely of Thought as Thought, but of the Laws of Thought as Thought. It is this determination which affords the proximate and peculiar difference of Logic, in contradistinction from

*c. The Laws
of Thought
as Thought.*

LECT.
II.

all other sciences; and the explanation of its meaning
constitutes the third head of illustration demanded by
object-matter in the definition.

The phæno-
mena of
formal
thought are
of two kinds
—contin-
gent and
necessary.

The phænomena of the formal or subjective phases
of thought are of two kinds. They are either such as
are contingent, that is, such as may or may not appear;
or they are such as are necessary, that is, such as cannot but appear. These two classes of phænomena are,
however, only manifested in conjunction; they are
not discriminated in the actual operations of thought;
and it requires a speculative analysis to separate them
into their several classes. In so far as these phænomena are considered merely as phænomena, that is, in
so far as philosophy is observant of them merely as
manifestations in general, they belong to the science
of Empirical or Historical Psychology. But when
philosophy, by a reflective abstraction, analyses the
necessary from the contingent forms of thought, there
results a science, which is distinguished from all others
by taking for its object-matter the former of these
classes; and this science is Logic. Logic, therefore,
is at last fully and finally defined as the science of the
necessary forms of thought. Here terminated our
last Lecture. But though full and final, this definition is not explicit; and it still remains to evolve it
into a more precise expression.

Now when we say that Logic is the science of the
necessary forms of thought, what does the quality of
necessity here imply?

Form of
thought.—
Four con-
ditions of
its necessity.
1. Deter-
mined by
the nature
of the

"In the first place, it is evident that in so far as a
form of thought is necessary, this form must be determined or necessitated by the nature of the thinking
subject itself; for if it were determined by anything
external to the mind, then would it not be a necessary

but a merely contingent determination. The first con- LECT.
II.
dition, therefore, of the necessity of a form of thought
is, that it is subjectively, not objectively, determined. thinking
subject it-
self.

" In the second place, if a form of thought be subjec- 2. Original.
tively necessary, it must be original and not acquired.
For if it were acquired, there must have been a time
when it did not exist; but if it did ever actually not
exist, we must be able at least to conceive the possibility of its not existing now. But if we are so able,
then is the form not necessary; for the criterion of a
contingent cognition is, that we can represent to ourselves the possibility of its non-existence. The second
condition, therefore, of the necessity of a form of
thought is, that it is original, and not acquired.

" In the third place, if a form of thought be neces- 3. Universal.
sary and original, it must be universal; that is, it
cannot be that it necessitates on some occasions, and
does not necessitate on others. For if it did not necessitate universally, then would its necessitation be
contingent, and it would consequently not be an original and necessary principle of mind. The third
condition, therefore, of the necessity of a form of
thought is, that it is universal.

" In the fourth place, if a form of thought be neces- 4. A law.
sary and universal, it must be a law; for a law is
that which applies to all cases without exception, and
from which a deviation is ever, and everywhere, impossible, or, at least, unallowed. The fourth and last
condition, therefore, of the necessity of a form of
thought is, that it is a law."[a] This last condition, like-
wise, enables us to give the most explicit enunciation The Object-
matter of
Logic ex-
plicitly
enounced.
of the object-matter of Logic, in saying that Logic is
the science of the Laws of Thought as Thought, or the

<hr>

a Esser, *Logik*, § 6, pp. 9, 10, with a few original interpolations.—Ed.

science of the Formal Laws of Thought, or the science of the Laws of the Form of Thought; for all these are merely various expressions of the same thing.

General historical retrospect of views in regard to the object and domain of Logic.
Before proceeding further, it may be proper to take a very general retrospect of the views that have prevailed in regard to the object and domain of Logic, from the era when the science received its first grand and distinctive development from the genius of Aristotle to the present time.

Merit of the Author's view of Logic.
I may say, in general, that the view which I have now presented to you of the object and domain of Logic, is the one which concentrates, corrects, and completes the views which have been generally held by logicians of the peculiar province of their science. It is the one towards which they all gravitate.

Aristotle.
It is unfortunate, that by far the greater number of the logical writings of Aristotle have perished, and that those which remain to us exhibit only his views of the science considered in its parts, or in certain special relations. None of the treatises which are now collected in the *Organon*,[a] considers the science from a central point; and we do not even possess a general definition of Logic by its illustrious founder. It would, therefore, be unjust to the mighty master, if, as has usually been done, we estimated his conception of the science only by the partial views contained in the fragmentary or special treatises which have chanced to float ashore from the general wreck of his logical writings. These by themselves are certainly enough to place the Stagirite high above comparison with any subsequent logician; but still if he has done so much in the half-dozen treatises that still remain, what may we not conceive him to have accomplished in the

a See below, p. 34.—ED.

forty which are recorded and seem to have been lost? It is, therefore, not to be attributed to Aristotle, that subsequent logicians, mistaking his surviving treatises of a logical nature,—few in number and written, in general, not in exposition of the pure science, but only of the science in certain modified applications,—for a systematic body of logical doctrine, should have allowed his views of its partial relations to influence their conceptions of the science absolutely and as a whole. By this influence of the Aristotelic treatises, we may explain the singular circumstance, that, while many, indeed most, of the subsequent logicians speculatively held the soundest views in regard to the proper object and end of Logic, few or none of them have attempted by these views to purify the science of those extraneous doctrines, to which the authority of Aristotle seemed to have given a right of occupancy within its domain. I shall not attempt to show you, *in extenso*, how correct, in general, were the notions entertained by the Greek Aristotelians, and even by the Latin schoolmen, for this would require an explanation of the signification of the terms in which their opinions were embodied, which would lead me into details which the importance of the matter would hardly warrant. I shall only say, in general, that, in their multifarious controversies under this head, the diversity of their opinions on subordinate points is not more remarkable than their unanimity on principal. Logic they all discriminated as a science of the form and not of the matter of thought.[a] Those of the schoolmen who held the

a "Logicus solas considerat formas intentionum communes." Albertus Magnus, *In De Anima*, L. I. tract. i. c. 8. For various scholastic theories on the object-matter of Logic, see Scotus, *Super Unic. Porphyrii*, Qu. iii.; Zabarella, *De Natura Logicæ*, lib. I. cap. 19; Smiglecius, *Logica*, Disp. ii. qu. 1; Camerarius, *Disputationes Philosophicæ*, Pars I. qu. 1, p. 2 et sqq. Compare *Discussions*, p. 138.—ED.

LECT.
II.

object of Logic to be things in general, held this, however, under the qualification that things in general
were not immediately and in themselves considered
by the logician, but only as they stood under the
general forms imposed on them by the intellect, ("quatenus secundis intentionibus substabant "),—a mode of
speaking which is only a periphrasis of our assertion,
that Logic is conversant about the forms of thought.[a]
The other schoolmen, again, who maintained that the
object of Logic was thought in its processes of simple
apprehension, judgment, and reasoning, (three, two,
or one,) carefully explained that these operations were
not in their own nature proposed to the logician, for
as such they belonged to Animastic, as they called it,
or Psychology, but only in so far as they were diri-
gible or subject to laws,—a statement which is only a
less simple expression of the fact, that Logic is the
science of the laws of thought.[b] Finally, those schoolmen who held that the object-matter of Logic was
found in second notions as applied to first, only meant
to say that Logic was conversant with conceptions,
judgments and reasonings, not in themselves, but only
as regulators of thought,[y]—a statement which merely
varies and perplexes the expression, that the object of
Logic is the formal laws of thought.

The same views, various in appearance, but, when

---

a [G. J. Vossius, *De Nat. Artium
sive De Logica*, c. iv.} [Compare Alex.
de Ales, *In Arist. Metaph.*, L. iv. t. 5:
"Dialectica est inventa ad regulandum discursum intellectus et rationis;
ideo quædam secundæ intentiones in-
ventæ sunt ad regulandum discursum,
de quibus proprie est Logica." See
also Zabarella and Camerarius, as
above.—Ed.]

β Camerarius, *Disp. Phil.*, P. I.

qu. 1, p. 3. Schuler, *Philosophia*,
p. 307, [L. v., *Logica*, Exerc. i.,
ed. Hagæ Comitis, 1762. — Ed.]
D'Abra de Raconis, [*Tractatio Totius Philosophiæ, Praeludia Logica*,
Post., a. I. p. 48, ed. Parisiis, 1840.—
Ed.]

γ See Zabarella and Camerarius,
as above.—Ed. [Compare Ponclus,
Cursus Philosophicus, Disp. i. qu. alt.,
p. 48, 2d ed. Paris, 1649.]

analysed, essentially the same, and essentially correct, LECT. II.
may be traced through the Leibnitio-Wolfian school ——
into the Kantian; so that, while it must be owned Leibnitio-Wolfian and Kantian Schools.
that they were never adequately carried out into
practical application, it cannot be denied that they
were theoretically not unsound.

The country in which, perhaps, the nature of Logic Bacon,— Locke.
has been most completely and generally misunderstood, is Great Britain. Bacon wholly misconceived
its character in certain respects; but his errors are
insignificant, when compared with the total misapprehension of its nature by Locke. The character of
these mistakes I shall have occasion to illustrate in
the sequel; at present I need only say, that, while
those who, till lately, attempted to write on Logic in
the English language, were otherwise wholly incompetent to the task, they, at the same time, either shared
the misconceptions of its nature with Locke, or only
contributed, by their own hapless attempts, to justify
the prejudices prevalent against the science which
they professed to cultivate and improve.

It would be unjust to confound with other attempts Whately,— general character of his Ele-ments.
of our countrymen in logical science the work of Dr
Whately. The author, if not endowed with any high
talent for philosophical speculation, possesses at least a
sound and vigorous understanding. He unfortunately,
however, wrote his *Elements of Logic* in singular
unacquaintance with all that had been written on the
science in ancient and in modern times, with the
exception apparently of the works of two Oxford
logicians—the *Institutio* of Wallis, and the *Compen-* Wallis.
dium of Aldrich,—both written above a century ago, Aldrich.
neither of them rising above a humble mediocrity, even
at the date of its composition; and Aldrich, whom

LECT.
II.

Whately unfortunately regards as a safe and learned guide, had himself written his book in ignorance of Aristotle and of all the principal authors on the science, — an ignorance manifested by the grossest errors in the most elementary parts of the science. It is not therefore to be wondered at, that the *Elements* of Whately, though the production of an able man, are so far behind the advancement of the science of which they treat; that they are deformed with numerous and serious errors; and that the only recommendation they possess is that of being the best book on the subject in a language which has absolutely no other deserving of notice ![a]

Whately's view of the object-matter and domain of Logic stated and criticised.

I have now, therefore, to call your attention to Dr Whately's account of the object-matter and domain of Logic. "The treatise of Dr Whately," says his Vice-Principal and epitomator Dr Hinds,[β] "displays, and it is the only one that has clearly done so, the true nature and use of Logic; so that it may be approached, no longer as a dark, curious, and merely speculative study, such as one is apt in fancy to class with astrology and alchemy."

Let us try whether this eulogy be as merited as it is unmeasured.

Whately proposes to Logic different and contradictory object-matter.

Now Dr Whately cannot truly be said clearly to display the nature of Logic, because in different passages he proposes to it different and contradictory objects; and he cannot be said to display the true nature of Logic, for of these different objects there is not one which is the true.

In several passages,[γ] he says that "the process or operation of reasoning is alone the appropriate pro-

a See *Discussions*, p. 128, second edition, foot-note.
β *Introduction to Logic*, Preface, p. viii., Oxford, 1827.—ED.
γ See pp. 1, 13, 140, third edition.

vince of Logic." Now this statement is incorrect in two respects. In the first place, it is incorrect, inasmuch as it limits the object-matter of Logic to that part of the Discursive Faculty which is especially denominated Reasoning. In this view Logic is made convertible with Syllogistic. This is an old error, which has been frequently refuted, and into which Whately seems to have been led by his guide Dr Wallis.

In the second place, this statement is incorrect, inasmuch as it makes the process, or, as he also calls it, the operation, of reasoning the object-matter of Logic. Now, a definition which merely affirms that Logic is the science which has the process of reasoning for its object, is not a definition of this science at all; it does not contain the differential quality by which Logic is discriminated from other sciences; and it does not prevent the most erroneous opinions, (it even suggests them,) from being taken up in regard to its nature. Other sciences, as Psychology and Metaphysic, propose for their object, (among the other faculties,) the operation of reasoning, but this considered in its real nature: Logic, on the contrary, has the same for its object, but only in its formal capacity; in fact, it has in propriety of speech nothing to do with the process or operation, but is conversant only with its laws. Dr Whately's definition is, therefore, not only incompetent, but delusive; it would confound Logic and Psychology and Metaphysic, and tend to perpetuate the misconceptions in regard to the nature of Logic which have been so long prevalent in this country.

But Dr Whately is not only wrong as measured by a foreign standard, he is wrong as measured by his own; he is himself contradictory. You have just seen that, in some places, he makes the operation of reason-

The operation of Reasoning not the object-matter of Logic, as Whately affirms.

Whately erroneously and contradictorily makes Language the adequate

ing not only the principal but the adequate object of
Logic. Well, in others he makes this total or adequate
object to be language. But as there cannot be two
adequate objects, and as language and the operation
of reasoning are not the same, there is, therefore, a
contradiction. "In introducing," he says, "the mention of language previously to the definition of logic,
I have departed from established practice, in order
that it may be clearly understood that logic is entirely
conversant about language; a truth which most writers
on the subject, if indeed they were fully aware of it
themselves, have certainly not taken due care to im-
press on their readers." [a]   And again : "Logic is wholly
concerned in the use of language." [β]

In our last Lecture, I called your attention to the
ambiguity of the term λόγος, in Greek, meaning ambiguously either thought or its expression; and this
ambiguity favoured the rise of two counter-opinions
in regard to the object of logic; for while it was
generally and correctly held to be immediately conversant about the internal λόγος, *thought,* some, however,
on the contrary, maintained that it was immediately
conversant about the external λόγος, *language.*   Now,
by some unaccountable illusion, Dr Whately, in different
places, adopts these opposite opinions, and enunciates
them without a word of explanation, or without even
a suspicion that they are contradictory of each other.[γ]

From what I have now said, you may, in some
degree, be able to judge how far credit is to be ac-
corded to the assertion, that Dr Whately is the only
logician who ever clearly displayed the true nature
and use of Logic.   In fact, so far is this assertion from
the truth, that the object-matter and scope of Logic

The true
nature of
Logic more
correctly
understood
by the
scholastic
logicians
than by
Whately.

a Page 56.   β Page 74.   γ Besides most vague.—*Jotting.*

were far more correctly understood even by the scholastic logicians than by Dr Whately ; and I may caution you, by the way, that what you may find stated in the *Elements* of the views of the schoolmen touching the nature and end of Logic, is in general wrong ; in particular, I may notice one most erroneous allegation, that the schoolmen " attempted to employ logic for the purpose of physical discovery."

But if, compared only with the older logicians, the assertion of Dr Hinds is found untenable, what will it be found, if we compare Whately with the logicians of the Kantian and Leibnitian schools, of whose writings neither the Archbishop nor his abbreviator seems ever to have heard ? And here I may observe, that Great Britain is, I believe, the only country of Europe in which books are written by respectable authors upon sciences, of the progress of which, for above a century, they have never taken the trouble to inform themselves.

The second question, to which in the Introduction to Logic an answer is required, is,—What is the Value or Utility of this science ? Before proceeding to a special consideration of this question, it may be proper to observe in general, that the real utility of Logic has been obscured and disparaged by the false utilities which have too frequently been arrogated to it ; for when Logic was found unable to accomplish what its unwise encomiasts had promised, the recoil was natural, and as it failed in performing everything, it was lightly inferred that it could perform nothing. Both of these extremes are equally erroneous. There is that which Logic can, and there is that which Logic cannot, perform ; and, therefore, before attempting to show what it is that we ought to expect from the study of this

LECT. II.

science, it will be proper to show what it is that we ought not. I shall, therefore, in the first place, consider its false utilities, and, in the second, its true.

Utilities falsely attributed to Logic.

The attribution of every false utility to Logic has arisen from erroneous opinions held in regard to the object of the science. So long as it was supposed that logic took any cognisance of the matter of thought,— so long as it was not distinctly understood that the form of thought was the exclusive object of this science, and so long as it was not disencumbered of its extraneous lumber; so long must erroneous opinions have been prevalent as to the nature and comprehension of its end.

As an Instrument of scientific discovery.

It was accordingly, in the first place, frequently supposed that Logic was, in a certain sort, an instrument of scientific discovery. The title of *Organon,—instrument,*—bestowed on the collection we possess of the logical treatises of Aristotle, contributed to this error. These treatises, as I observed, are but a few of the many writings of the Stagirite on Logic, and to him we owe neither the order in which they stand arranged, nor the general name under which they are now comprehended.[a] In later times, these treatises were supposed to contain a complete system of Logic, and Logic was viewed as the organ not only of Philosophy but of the sciences in general. Thus it was that Logic obtained not only the name of *instrument,* or *instrumental philosophy,* but many other high-sounding titles. It was long generally styled the *Art of arts and Science of sciences.*—"Logica," says Scotus, "est ars artium et scientia scientiarum, qua aperta,

a See Brandis, *Aristoteles, seine* Leben. *Elementa Log. Aristot.,* akademischen Zeitgenossen und nach-   p. 38.—ED. sten *Nachfolger,* P. I. p. 140.   Tran-

omnes aliæ aperiuntur; et qua clausa, omnes aliæ
clauduntur; cum qua quælibet, sine qua nulla." [a] In
modern times, we have systems of this science under
the titles of *Via ad Veritatem*[b]—*Cynosura Veritatis*[y]
—*Caput et Apex Philosophia*[ß]—*Heuristica, sive Introductio ad Artem Inveniendi*,[c] &c. But it was not
only viewed as an instrument of discovery, it was
likewise held to be the infallible corrector of our
intellectual vices, the invigorator of our intellectual
imbecility. Hence some entitled their Logics,—*The
Medicine of the Mind*,[f] *The Art of Thinking*,[q] *The
Lighthouse of the Intellect*,[θ] *The Science Teaching the
Right Use of Reason*,[i] &c. &c. Now in all this there
is a mixture of truth and error. To a certain extent,
and in certain points of view, Logic is the organ of
philosophy, the criterion of truth, and the corrector
of error, and in others it is not.

In reference to the dispute whether logic may with
propriety be called the *instrument*, the *organon* of
the other sciences, the question may be at once solved
by a distinction. One science may be styled the
instrument of another, either in a material or in a

a *Mauritii Expositio Quæstionum Doctoris Subtilis in quinque Univer- salia Porphyrii*, Quæst. i. (*Scoti Opera*, Lugd., 1639, tom. i. p. 434). Mauritius refers to St Augustin as his authority for the above quotation. It slightly resembles a passage in the *De Ordine*, L. ii. c. 13.—ED.

ß Gundling, *Via ad Veritatem Mo- ralem*, Halæ, 1713. Darjes, *Via ad Veritatem*, Jenæ, 1764 (2d edit.)— ED.

γ P. Laurembergius, *Cynosura Bonæ mentis i. Logica*, Rostoch, 1633. R. Lossius, *Cynosura Rationis*, Arnhem, 1667.—ED.

δ See Krug, *Logik*, § 9, p. 23, from whom several of the above definitions

were probably taken.—ED.

ε Gunner, *Ars Heuristica Intellec- tualis*, Lipsiæ, 1756. *Trattato di Messer Sebastiano Erizo, dell' Istru- mento et Via Inventrice de gli antichi nelle scienze*, Venice, 1554.—ED.

ζ Tschirnhausen, *Medicina Mentis, sive Artis Inveniendi Praecepta Gene- ralia*, Amst., 1687. Lange, *Medicina Mentis*, Halæ, 1703.—ED.

η *L'Art de Penser*, commonly known as the Port Royal Logic. Several other works have appeared under the same title.—ED.

θ Crousaz, *Pharos Intellectus, sive Logica Electiva*, Lips., 1697.—ED.

ι Watts, *Logic, or the Right Use of Reason*.—ED.

formal point of view. In the former point of view,
one science is the organ of another when one science
determines for another its contents or objects. Thus
Mathematics may be called the material instrument of the various branches of physical science :
Philology,—or study of the languages, Latin, Greek,
Hebrew, Chaldee, &c., with a knowledge of their
relative history,—constitutes a material instrument to
Christian Theology ; and the jurist, in like manner,
finds a material instrument in a knowledge of the
history of the country whose laws he expounds." Thus
also Physiology, in a material point of view, is the
organon of Medicine ; Aristotle has indeed well said
that medicine begins where the philosophy of nature
leaves off.[β] In the latter point of view, one science
is the organon of another, when one science determines
the scientific form of another. Now, as it is generally admitted that Logic stands in this relation to
the other sciences, as it appertains to Logic to consider the general doctrine of Method and of systematic
construction, in this respect Logic may be properly
allowed to be to the sciences an instrument, but only
a formal instrument.[γ]

In regard to the other titles of honour, Logic cannot with propriety be denominated a [Heuretic or]
Art of Discovery. " For discovery or invention is not
to be taught by rules, but is either the free act of an
original genius, or the consequence of a lucky accident,
which either conducts the finder to something unknown, or gives him the impulse to seek it out. Logic
can at best only analytically teach how to discover,
that is, by the development and dismemberment of

α Sen Genovesi, Elementa Artis
Logico-Criticæ, L. i. c. iii. p. 41.
β De Sensu et Sensili, c. i.

γ Krug. Logik, § 9, p. 23; Cf.
Platner, Philosophische Aphorismen,
Part i. p. 23, ed. 1793.—ED.

what is already discovered. By this process there is nothing new evolved, and our knowledge is not amplified; all that is accomplished is a clearer and distincter comprehension of the old;—our knowledge is purified and systematised." [a]   It is well observed by Antonius, in Cicero :—" Nullum est præceptum in hac arte quomodo verum inveniatur, sed tantum est, quomodo judicetur." [β]   Logic is thus not creative; it is only plastic, only formative, in relation to our knowledge.

Again, " Logic cannot with propriety be styled the medicine of the mind, at least without some qualifying adjective, to show that the only remedy it can apply is to our formal errors, while our material errors lie beyond its reach. This is evident. Logic is the science of the formal laws of thought. But we cannot, in limiting our consideration to the laws of formal thinking, investigate the contents,—the matter, of our thought. Logic can, therefore, only propose to purge the understanding of those errors which lie in the confusion and perplexities of an inconsequent thinking. This, however, it must be confessed, is no radical cure, but merely a purification of the understanding. In this respect, however, and to this extent, Logic may justly pretend to be the medicine of the mind, and may, therefore, in a formal relation, be styled, as by some logicians it has in fact been, *Catharticon intellectus.*

" By these observations the value of Logic is not depreciated ; they only prepare us to form an estimate of its real amount. Precisely, in fact, as too much was promised and expected from this study, did it lose in credit and esteem." [γ]

LECT. II.

In what sense Logic can be styled the medicine of the mind.

a Krug, *Logik*, § 9, p. 24.—ED. Cf. [Richter, *Logik*, p. 83 *et seq.*] β *De Oratore*, ii. 38.—ED.

γ Krug, *Logik*, § 9, pp. 24-6.—ED. Cf. [Richter, *Logik*, p. 85.]

LECTURE III.

INTRODUCTION.

LOGIC—II. ITS UTILITY.—III. ITS DIVISIONS—SUBJEC-
TIVE AND OBJECTIVE—GENERAL AND SPECIAL.

LECT.
III.

Recapitula-
tion.

THE last Lecture was occupied with the consideration
of the latter part of the introductory question,—What
is Logic? and with that of the first part of the second,
—What is its Utility?—In the Lecture preceding the
last, I had given the definition of Logic, as the science
of the laws of thought as thought, and, taking the
several parts of this definition, had articulately explained, 1°, What was the meaning and history of the
word *Logic*; 2°, What was the import of the term
science, the genus of Logic; and, 3°, What was signified by laws of thought as thought, the object-matter
of Logic. This last I had considered under three heads,
explaining, 1°, What is meant by *thought*; 2°, What is
meant by *thought as thought*; and, 3°, What is meant
by *laws of thought as thought*. It was under the last
of these heads that the last Lecture commenced. I
had, in the preceding, shown that the form of thought
comprises two kinds of phænomena, given always in
conjunction, but that we are able by abstraction and
analysis to discriminate them from each other. The
one of these classes comprehends what is contingent,
the other what is necessary, in the manifestations of
thought. The necessary element is the peculiar and

exclusive object of Logic ; whereas the phænomena of $\quad$
thought and of mind in general are indiscriminately
proposed to Psychology. Logic, therefore, I said, is
distinguished from the other philosophical sciences by
its definition, as the science of the necessary form of
thought. This, however, though a full and final definition, is capable of a still more explicit enunciation ;
and I showed how we are entitled to convert the term
necessary into the term *laws*, and, in doing so, I took
the opportunity of explaining how, the necessity of a
mental element being given, there is also implicitly
given the four conditions, 1°, That it is subjective;
2°, That it is original; 3°, That it is universal; and,
4°, That it is a law. The full and explicit definition
of Logic, therefore, is,—the science of the Laws of
Thought as Thought ; or, the science of the Laws of
the Form of Thought ; or, the science of the Formal
Laws of Thought :—these being only three various
expressions of what is really the same.

Logic being thus defined, I gave a brief and general retrospect of the history of opinion in regard to
the proper object and domain of Logic, and showed
how, though most logicians had taken speculatively,
and in general, a very correct view of the nature of
their science, they had not carried this view out into
application, by excluding from the sphere of Pure or
Abstract Logic all not strictly relative to the form
of thought, but had allowed many doctrines relative
merely to the matter of thought to complicate and to
deform the science.

I then called attention to the opinions of the author
whom I recommend to your attention, and showed
that Dr Whately, in his statements relative to the
object-matter of Logic, is vague and obscure, errone-

ous and self-contradictory; and that, so far from being entitled to the praise of having been the only logician who has clearly displayed the true nature of the science, on the contrary, in the exposition of this nature, he is far inferior, not only in perspicuity and precision, but in truth, to the logicians of almost every age and country except our own.

Observations interposed relative to the question,—What is Logic?

And here, taking a view of what we have already established, I would interpolate some observations which I ought, in my last Lecture, to have made, before leaving the consideration of the first question, —viz. What is Logic? Logic, we have seen, is exclusively conversant about thought,—about thought considered strictly as the operation of Comparison or the faculty of Relations; and thought, in this restricted signification, is the cognition of any mental object by another in which it is considered as included,—in other words, thought is the knowledge of things under conceptions. By the way, I would here pause to make an observation upon the word *conception*, and to prepare you for the employment of a term which I mean hereafter to adopt. You are aware, from what I have already said, that I do not use *conception* in the signification in which it is applied by Mr Stewart. He usurps it in a very limited meaning, in a meaning which is peculiar to himself,—viz. for the simple and unmodified representation of an object presented in Perception.[a] Reid, again, vacillates in the signification he attaches to this term,—using it sometimes as a synonym for Imagination, sometimes as comprehending not only Imagination, but Understanding and the object of Understanding.[b] It is in the latter relation alone that

The terms *Conception* and *Concept*.

a See *Lectures on Metaphysics*, Lect. xxxiii., vol. ii. p. 261.—ED.   b Ibid.

I ever employ it, and this is its correct and genuine signification, whether we regard the derivation of the word, or its general use by philosophers. *Conception,* in English, is equivalent to *conceptio* and *conceptus* in Latin, and these terms, by the best philosophers and the most extensive schools, have been employed as synonyms for *notion* (*notio*), the act or object of the Understanding Proper or Faculty of Relations. So far, therefore, you are sufficiently prepared not to attribute to the word *conception,* when you hear it from me, the meaning which it bears in the philosophical writings with which you are most likely to be familiar. What is the precise meaning of the term will be soon fully explained in its proper place, when we commence the treatment of Logic itself. But what I principally pause at present to say is,—that, for the sake of perspicuity, I think it necessary, in reference to this word, to make the following distinction. The term *conception,* like *perception, imagination,* &c., means two things, or rather the same thing in two different relations,—relations, however, which it is of great importance to distinguish, and to mark the distinction by the employment of distinct words. *Conception* means both the act of conceiving, and the object conceived ; as *perception,* both the act of perceiving and the thing perceived ; *imagination,* both the act of imagining and what is imagined. Now this is a source of great vagueness in our philosophical discussions ; have we no means of avoiding this inconvenience ? I think we have ; and that too without committing any violence upon language. I would propose the following distinction. For the act of conceiving, the term *conception* should be employed, and that exclusively ; while for the object of concep-

LECT. III.

Author's employment of these terms.

tion, or that which is conceived, the term *concept*
should be used.[a] Concept is the English of the Latin
conceptum,—id quod conceptum est,—and had it no
vested right as an actual denizen of the language, it
has good warrant for its naturalisation. There are a
thousand words in English formed on precisely the
same analogy, as *precept, digest,* &c. &c. But we
have no occasion to appeal to analogy. The term
concept was in common use among the older philosophical writers in English,[b] though, like many other
valuable expressions of these authors, it has been overlooked by our English lexicographers. I may add
that nearly the same fortune has befallen the term
in French. *Concept* was in ordinary use by the old
French philosophers, but had latterly waxed obsolete.
It has, however, I see, been reinstated in its rights
since the reawakening of philosophy in France ; and,
in particular, it is now employed in that language
in translating from the German the term *Begriff.* I
shall, therefore, make no scruple in using the expression *concept* for the object of conception, and *conception* I shall exclusively employ to designate the
act of conceiving. Whether it might not, in like
manner, be proper to introduce the term *percept*
for the object of perception, I shall not at present
inquire.

But to return from this digression. Logic, we have
seen, is exclusively conversant about thought strictly

a See Biel [*In Sent.,* lib. i. dist.
2, qu. 8 ; lib. ii. dist. 3, qu. 2. By
Occam and most others, *conceptus* is
used as "id quod terminat actum in-
telligendi." See Occam, *In Sent.,*
lib. i. dist. 2, q. 8 ; and Biel, lib. i.
dist. 3, q. 4.]

β See Zachary Coke, *Art of Logick,*
London 1654, pp. 11, 101, *et alibi ;*

Gideon Harvey, *Archelogia Philosophica Nova, or New Principles of
Philosophy,* Lond., 1663, P. i., b.
ii., c. 4, p. 22. For several authorities for the use of this term among
the older English logicians, see
Baynes, *New Analytic of Logical
Forms,* pp. 5, 6, note.—ED.

so denominated, and thought proper, we have seen, LECT.
III. is the cognition of one object of thought by another, in or under which it is mentally included,—in other words, thought is the knowledge of a thing through a concept or general notion, or of one notion through another. In thought, all that we think about is considered either as something containing, or as something contained,—in other words, every process of thought is only a cognition of the necessary relations of our concepts. This being the case, it need not move our wonder, that Logic, within its proper sphere, is of such irrefragable certainty, that, in the midst of all the revolutions of philosophical doctrines, it has stood not only unshattered but unshaken. In this respect, Logic and Mathematics stand alone among the sciences, and their peculiar certainty flows from the same source. Both are conversant about the relations of certain *a priori* forms of intelligence :—Mathematics about the necessary forms of Imagination ; Logic about the necessary forms of Understanding ; Mathematics about the relations of our representations of objects, as out of each other in space and time ; Logic about the relations of our concepts of objects, as in or under each other, that is, as, in different relations, respectively containing and contained. Both are thus demonstrative or absolutely certain sciences only as each develops what is given,—what is given as necessary, in the mind itself. The laws of Logic are grounded on the mere possibility of a knowledge through the concepts of the Understanding, and through these we know only by comprehending the many under the one. Concerning the nature of the objects delivered by the Subsidiary Faculties to the Elaborative, Logic pronounces nothing, but restricts its consideration to

the laws according to which their agreement or disagreement is affirmed.[a]

Logic is the negative condition of truth.

It is of itself manifest, that every science must obey
the laws of Logic. If it does not, such pretended
science is not founded on reflection, and is only an
irrational absurdity. All inference, evolution, concatenation, is conducted on logical principles,—principles which are ever valid, ever imperative, ever the
same. But an extension of any science through
Logic is absolutely impossible; for by conforming
to logical canons we acquire no knowledge,—receive
nothing new, but are only enabled to render what is
already obtained more intelligible, by analysis and
arrangement. Logic is only the negative condition
of truth.[b] To attempt by a mere logical knowledge
to amplify a science, is an absurdity as great as if we
should attempt by a knowledge of the grammatical
laws of a language to discover what was written in
this language, without a perusal of the several writings themselves. But though Logic cannot extend,
cannot amplify a science by the discovery of new
facts, it is not to be supposed that it does not contribute to the progress of science. The progress of the
sciences consists not merely in the accumulation of
new matter, but likewise in the detection of the relations subsisting among the materials accumulated;
and the reflective abstraction by which this is effected
must not only follow the laws of Logic, but is most
powerfully cultivated by the habits of logical study.
In these intercalary observations I have, however, in-
sensibly encroached upon the second question,—What
is the Utility of Logic? On this question I now dictate the following paragraph :—

a Cf. Bachmann, *Logik*, Einleitung,
§ 20, edit. 1828.—En.   β [Ancillon, *Essais Philosophiques*,
t. ii. p. 201.]

¶ IV. As the rules of Logic do not regard the matter but only the form of thought, the Utility of Logic must, in like manner, be viewed as limited to its influence on our manner of thinking, and not sought for in any effect it can exert upon what we think about. It is, therefore, in the first place, not to be considered useful as a Material Instrument, that is, as a mean of extending our knowledge by the discovery of new truths ; but merely as a Formal Instrument, that is, as a mean by which knowledge, already acquired, may be methodised into the form accommodated to the conditions of our understanding. In the second place, it is not to be regarded as a Medicine of the mind to the extent of remedying the various errors which originate in the nature of the objects of our knowledge, but merely to the extent of purging the mind of those errors which arise from inconsequence and confusion in thinking.* Logic, however, is still of eminent utility, not only as presenting to us the most interesting object of contemplation in the mechanism of human thought, but as teaching how, in many relations, to discriminate truth from error, and how to methodise our knowledge into system ; while, at the same time, in turning the mind upon itself, it affords to our higher faculties one of their most invigorating exercises. Another utility is, that Logic alone affords us the means requisite to accomplish a rational criticism, and to communicate its results.

What is now summarily stated in the preceding paragraph, I illustrated, in my last Lecture, in detail,—

* Cf. Krug, Logik, § 9.—ED.

LECT. III.

Par. IV. Utility of Logic.

LECT.
III.

in so far as it was requisite to disencumber the real
value of our science from those false utilities which,
in place of enhancing its worth in the opinion of the
world, have, in fact, mainly contributed to reduce the
common estimate of its importance far beneath the
truth. I now proceed to terminate what I have to
say under this head by a few words, in exposition of
what renders the cultivation of Logic,—of genuine
logic, one of the most important and profitable of our
studies.

Logic gives
us, to a cer-
tain extent,
dominion
over our
thoughts.

"Admitting, therefore, that this science teaches nothing new,—that it neither extends the boundaries of
knowledge, nor unfolds the mysteries which lie beyond the compass of the reflective intellect,—and that
it only investigates the immutable laws to which the
mind in thinking is subjected, still, inasmuch as it
develops the application of these laws, it bestows on
us, to a certain extent, a dominion over our thoughts
themselves. And is it nothing to watch the secret
workshop in which nature fabricates cognitions and
thoughts, and to penetrate into the sanctuary of self-
consciousness, to the end that, having learnt to know
ourselves, we may be qualified rightly to understand
all else ? Is it nothing to seize the helm of thought,
and to be able to turn it at our will ? For, through a
research into the laws of thinking, Logic gives us, in
a certain sort, a possession of the thoughts themselves.
It is true, indeed, that the mind of man is, like the
universe of matter, governed by eternal laws, and
follows, even without consciousness, the invariable
canons of its nature. But to know and understand
itself, and out of the boundless chaos of phænomena
presented to the senses to form concepts, through concepts to reduce that chaos to harmony and arrange-

ment, and thus to establish the dominion of intelligence over the universe of existence,—it is this alone which constitutes man's grand and distinctive pre-eminence."[a] "Man," says the great Pascal, "is but a reed,—the very frailest in nature ; but he is a reed that thinks. It needs not that the whole universe should arm to crush him. He dies from an exhalation, from a drop of water. But should the universe conspire to crush him, man would still be nobler than that by which he falls ; for he knows that he dies ; and of the victory which the universe has over him, the universe knows nothing. Thus our whole dignity consists in thought. . . . . Let us labour, then, to think aright; this is the foundation of morality."[β]

In the world of sense, illusive appearances hover around us like evil spirits ; unreal dreams mingle themselves with real knowledge; the accustomed assumes the character of certainty ; and the associations of thought are mistaken for the connections of existence. We thus require a criterion to discriminate truth from error ; and this criterion is, in part at least, supplied to us by Logic. Logic teaches us to analyse the concrete masses of our knowledge into its elements, and thus gives us a clear and distinct apprehension of its parts, it teaches us to think consistently and with method, and it teaches us how to build up our accumulated knowledge into a firm and harmonious edifice.[γ] " The study of logic is as necessary for correct thinking, as the study of grammar is for correct speaking ; were it not otherwise and in itself an interesting study to

Margin note: Supplies in part the criterion of truth from error.

a [Heinrich Richter], [*Über den Gegenstand und den Umfang der Logik*, pp. 3, 4, Leipsic, 1825.—Ed.]
β *Pensées*, P. i. art. iv. § 6, (vol. ii. p. 84, ed. Faugère). Compare *Discussions*, p. 311.—Ed.
γ Cf. Richter, *Logik*, pp. 5, 6, 12. —Ed.

investigate the mechanism of the human intellect in
the marvellous processes of thought. They, at least,
who are familiar with this mechanism, are less exposed
to the covert fallacies which so easily delude those
unaccustomed to an analysis of these processes."[a]

Invigorates
the Under-
standing.
But it is not only by affording knowledge and skill
that Logic is thus useful; it is perhaps equally conducive to the same end by bestowing power. The retor-
sion of thought upon itself,—the thinking of thought,
—is a vigorous effort, and, consequently, an invigorating exercise of the Understanding, and as the understanding is the instrument of all scientific, of all
philosophical, speculation, Logic, by pre-eminently cul-
tivating the understanding, in this respect likewise
vindicates its ancient title to be viewed as the best
preparatory discipline for Philosophy and the sciences
at large.

There is, however, one utility which, though of a
subordinate kind, I must not omit, though I do not
remember to have seen it insisted on by any logical
writer. In reference to this, I give you the following
paragraph :—

Par. V.
Utility of
Logic,—
as affording
a scientific
nomencla-
ture.
¶ V. But Logic is further useful as affording a
Nomenclature of the laws by which legitimate
thinking is governed, and of the violation of these
laws, through which thought becomes vicious or
null.

Illustration.
It is said, in Hudibras,[b]—

> "That all a Rhetorician's rules
> Serve only but to name his tools ;"

and it may be safely confessed that this is one of the
principal utilities of Rhetoric. A mere knowledge of

a Krug, *Logik*, § 9, p. 20.—ED.   b P. L. Cant. i. 89.—ED.

the rules of Rhetoric can no more enable us to compose well, than a mere knowledge of the rules of Logic can enable us to think well. There is required from nature in both the faculty; but this faculty must, in both departments, be cultivated by an assiduous and also a well-directed exercise, that is, in the one, the powers of Comparison must be exercised according to the rules of a sound Rhetoric, in the other, according to the rules of a sound Logic. In so far, therefore, the utility of either science is something more than a mere naming of their tools. But the naming of their tools, though in itself of little value, is valuable as the condition of an important function, which, without this, could not be performed. Words do not give thoughts, but without words thoughts could not be fixed, limited, and expressed. They are, therefore, in general, the essential condition of all thinking worthy of the name. Now, what is true of human thought in general, is true of Logic and Rhetoric in particular. The nomenclature in these sciences is the nomenclature of certain general analyses and distinctions, which express to the initiated, in a single word, what the uninitiated could (supposing,—what is not probable,— that he could perform the relative processes) neither understand nor express without a tedious and vague periphrasis; while, in his hands, it would assume only the appearance of a particular observation, instead of a particular instance of a general and acknowledged rule. To take a very simple example, there is in Logic a certain sophism, or act of illegal inference, by which two things are, perhaps in a very concealed and circuitous manner, made to prove each other. Now, the man unacquainted with Logic may perhaps detect and be convinced of the fallacy; but how will he

LECT. III.

Importance of a scientific nomenclature.

Example.

expose it? He must enter upon a long statement
and explanation, and after much labour to himself
and others, he probably does not make his objection
clear and demonstrative after all. But between those
acquainted with Logic, the whole matter would be
settled in two words. It would be enough to say and
show, that the inference in question involved a *circulus
in concludendo*, and the refutation is at once understood and admitted. It is in like manner that one
lawyer will express to another the *ratio decidendi* of
a case in a single technical expression; while their
clients will only perplex themselves and others in
their attempts to set forth the merits of their cause.
Now, if Logic did nothing more than establish a certain
number of decided and decisive rules in reasoning,
and afford us brief and precise expressions by which
to bring particular cases under those general rules, it
would confer on all who in any way employ their
intellect, that is, on the cultivators of every human
science, the most important obligation. For it is only
in the possession of such established rules, and of such
a technical nomenclature, that we can accomplish,
with facility, and to an adequate extent, a criticism
of any work of reasoning. Logical language is thus
to the general reasoner, what the notation of Arithmetic, and still more of Algebra, is to the mathematician. Both enable us to comprehend and express,
in a few significant symbols, what would otherwise
overpower us by their complexity; and thus it is that
nothing would contribute more to facilitate and extend
the faculty of reasoning, than a general acquaintance
with the rules and language of Logic,—an advantage
extending indeed to every department of knowledge,
but more especially of importance to those professions

which are occupied in inference and conversant with abstract matter,—such as Theology and Law.

I now proceed to the third of the preliminary questions—viz How is Logic divided ? Now, it is manifest that this question may be viewed in two relations ; for in asking how is Logic divided, we either mean how many kinds are there of Logic, or into how many constituent parts is it distributed ?[a] We may consider Logic either as a universal, or as an integrate, whole.

It is necessary to consider the former question first; for before proceeding to show what are the parts of which a logic is made up, it is requisite previously to determine what the logic is of which these parts are the components. Under the former head, I, therefore, give you the following :—

¶ VI. Logic, considered as a Genus or Class, may, in different relations, be divided into different Species. And, in the first place, considered by relation to the mind or thinking subject, Logic is divided into Objective and Subjective, or, in the language of some older authors, into *Logica systematica* and *Logica habitualis*.[b]

By Objective or Systematic Logic is meant that complement of doctrines of which the science of Logic

a Division of Logic into Natural and Artificial, inept.

" He hits each point with native force of mind,
Whilst puzzled Logic struggles far behind "

Cf. Krug, *Logik*, p. 29. Troxler, *Logik*, i. 48.

β See Timpler, p. 877 ; Vossius, p. 217 ; Pacius. [*Logicæ Systema*,

authore M. *Clemente Timplero*, Hanoviæ, 1612. Vossius, *De Natura Artium*, L. iv., *Sive De Logica*, c. ix. Pacius, *In Porphyrii Isagogen*, p. 2, ed. Francof., 1697.—Ed.] On various divisions of Logic, see Timpler, *Logicæ Systema*, L. i. c. 1, q. 13-20, p. 40-56 ; Gisbert ab Isendoorn, *Effata*, *Philosophica*, [Cent. i. § 51-63, p. 95 *et seq.*, ed. Daventriæ, 1643.—Ed.]

is made up; by Subjective or Habitual Logic is meant
the speculative knowledge of these doctrines which
any individual, (as Socrates, Plato, Aristotle), may
possess, and the practical dexterity with which he is
able to apply them.

Both these
Logics ought
to be pro-
posed as the
end of logi-
cal instruc-
tion.
Now, it is evident that both these Logics, or, rather,
Logic considered in this twofold relation, ought to
be proposed to himself by an academical instructor.
We must, therefore, neglect neither. Logic considered as a system of rules, is only valuable as a
mean towards logic considered as a habit of the
mind; and, therefore, a logical instructor ought not
to think that he fulfils his duty,—that he accom-
plishes all that he is called on to perform, if he limit
himself to the mere enouncement of a code of doctrine, leaving his pupils to turn his instructions to
their own account as best they may. On the contrary, he is bound to recollect that he should be
something more than a book; that he ought not
only himself to deliver the one Logic, but to take
care that his pupils acquire the other. The former,
indeed, he must do as a condition of the latter;
but if he considers the systematic logic which he
pronounces, as of any value, except in so far as his
pupils convert it into an habitual logic, he understands nothing of the character of the function which
he attempts to perform. It is, therefore, incumbent
on an academical instructor, to do what in him lies
to induce his pupils, by logical exercise, to digest
what is presented to them as an objective system
into a subjective habit. Logic, therefore, in both
these relations belongs to us, and neither can be neglected without compromising the utility of a course
like the present.

¶ VII. In the second place, by relation to its
application or non-application to objects, Logic
is divided into Abstract or General, and Concrete or Special. The former of these is called
by the Greek Aristotelians, διαλεκτική χωρὶς
πραγμάτων, and by the Arabian and Latin
schoolmen, *Logica docens;* while the latter is
denominated by the Greeks, διαλεκτική ἐν χρήσει
καὶ γυμνασίᾳ πραγμάτων, and by the Arabians
and Latins, *Logica utens.*

LECT.
III.
Par. VII.
Logic, by
relation to
objects, is
Abstract or
General,
and Con-
crete or
Special.

Abstract Logic considers the laws of thought as
potentially applicable to the objects of all arts and
sciences, but as not actually applied to those of any ;
Concrete Logic considers these laws in their actual
and immediate application to the object-matter of
this or that particular art or science. The former of
these is one, and alone belongs to philosophy, whereas
the latter is as multiform as the arts and sciences to
which it is relative.[a]

Explica-
tion.

This division of Logic does not remount to Aristotle, but it is found in his most ancient commentator, Alexander the Aphrodisian, and, after him, in
most of the other Greek Logicians. Alexander illustrates the opposition of the logic divorced from things,
(χωρὶς πραγμάτων—*rebus avulsa*), to the logic applied to things, (ἐν χρήσει καὶ γυμνασίᾳ πραγμάτων—
rebus applicata), by a simile. "The former," he says,
"may be resembled to a geometrical figure, say a
triangle, when considered abstractly and in itself ;
whereas the latter may be resembled to the same
triangle, as concretely existing in this or that particular matter : for a triangle considered in itself is

This divi-
sion of
Logic re-
mounts to
Alexander
the Aphro-
disian.

a See Krug, p. 27 [*Logik,* § 10, Anm. —En.]

LECT.
III.
ever one and the same; but viewed in relation to its
matter, it varies according to the variety of that matter; for it is different as it is of silver, gold, lead, as
it is of wood, of stone, &c.* The same holds good of
Logic. General or Abstract Logic is always one and
the same; but as applied to this or to that object of
consideration, it appears multiform." So far Alexander. This appearance of multiformity I may, however, add, is not real; for the mind has truly only
one mode of thinking, one mode of reasoning, one
mode of conducting itself in the investigation of
truth, whatever may be the object on which it exer-

Illustrated
by com-
parisons.
cises itself. Logic may, therefore, be again well compared to the authority of an universal empire,—of an
empire governing the world by common laws. In
such a dominion there are many provinces, various
regions, and different præfectures. There is one præ-
fect in Asia, another in Europe, a third in Africa, and
each is decorated by different titles; but each governs
and is governed by the common laws of the Empire
confided to his administration. The nature of General Logic may, likewise, be illustrated by another
comparison. The Thames, for instance, in passing
London, is a single river,—is one water, but is there
applied to many and different uses; it is employed

---

a [Isandovrn *Efata*, Cent. i. 55;
Crellius, *Isagoge Logica*, p. 12.] [The
illustration is fully given by Balfo-
rous, *Commentarius in Organum*, p.
23, q. v. § 2. " Alexander Aphrodisiensis Logicam illam abjunctam
similem cum sit figuræ geometricæ,
atque triangulo, dum in se et per
se spectatur; Logicam vero cum rebus conjunctam similem eidem triangulo huic aut illi materiæ impresso.
Nam trianguli in se una est et eadem
ratio; at pro varietate materiæ, varia.

Aliud enim est argenteum, aliud
aureum, aliud ligneum, lapideum aut
plumbeum." The passage referred
to is probably one in the Commentary on the *Prior Analytics*, p. 2, ed.
Ald. The distinction itself, though
not the illustration, is given more
exactly in the language of the text
by some of the later commentators.
See the Introductions of Ammonius
to the *Categoriæ*, and of Philoponus
to the *Prior Analytics.*—Ed.]

for drinking, for cooking, for brewing, for washing, for irrigation, for navigation, &c. In like manner, Logic in itself is one :—as a science or an art, it is single; but, in its applications, it is of various and multiform use in the various branches of knowledge, conversant be it with necessary, or be it with contingent matter. Or further, to take the example of a cognate science, if any one were to lay down different grammars of a tongue, as that may be applied to the different purposes of life, he would be justly derided by all grammarians, indeed by all men; for who is there so ignorant as not to know that there is but one grammar of the same language in all its various applications ?ª Thus, likewise, there is only one method of reasoning, which all the sciences indifferently employ; and although men are severally occupied in different pursuits, and although one is, therefore, entitled a Theologian, another a Jurist, a third a Physician, and so on, each employs the same processes, and is governed by the same laws, of thought. Logic itself is, therefore, widely different from the use,—the application of Logic. For Logic is astricted to no determinate matter, but is extended to all that is the object of reason and intelligence. The use of Logic on the contrary, although potentially applicable to every matter, is always actually manifested by special reference to some one. In point of fact, Logic, in its particular applications, no longer

General Logic is
alone one ;
Special Logic is
manifold,
and part of
the science
in which it
is applied.

ª See Rami Sch., p. 350, [P. Rami Scholæ in Liberales Artes. Basileæ, 1578: "Unus est Latetiæ Sequana, ad multos tamen usus et varios accommodatus, lavandum, aquandum, vehendum, irrigandum, coqaendam: sic una est Logica, varii et multiplicis usus, in propositionibus necessaria, probabili, captiosa; ars tamen una. Si Grammaticas tres aliquis ineptus nobis instituat, unam civilem, alteram agrestem, tertiam de vitis amborum, merito ridestur a Grammaticis omnibus, qui unam Grammaticam norant omnium ejusdem linguæ hominum communem."—Ed.]

LECT.
III.

remains logic, but becomes part and parcel of the art
or science in which it is applied.   Thus Logic, applied
to the objects of geometry, is nothing else than Geometry,—Logic applied to the objects of physics,
nothing else than Natural Philosophy.   We have,
indeed, certain treatises of Logic in reference to different sciences, which may be viewed as something
more than these sciences themselves.   For example,
we have treatises on Legal Logic, &c.   But such
treatises are only introductions,—only methodologies
of the art or science to which they relate.   For such
special logics only exhibit the mode in which a determinate matter or object of science, the knowledge of
which is presupposed, must be treated, the conditions
which regulate the certainty of inferences in that
matter, and the methods by which our knowledge
of it may be constructed into a scientific whole.
Special Logic is thus not a single discipline, not the
science of the universal laws of thought, but a congeries of disciplines, as numerous as there are special
sciences in which it may be applied.   Abstract or
General Logic, on the contrary, in virtue of its universal character, can only and alone be one ; and can
exclusively pretend to the dignity of an independent
science.   This, therefore, likewise exclusively con-
cerns us.

LECTURE IV.

INTRODUCTION.

LOGIC—III. ITS DIVISIONS—PURE AND MODIFIED.

In my last Lecture, after terminating the considera- tion of the second introductory question, touching the Utilities of Logic, I proceeded to the third introduc- tory question,—What are the Divisions of Logic? and stated to you the two most general classifications of this science. Of these, the first is the division of Logic into Objective and Subjective, or Systematic and Habitual; the second is its division into General and Special, or Abstract and Concrete.

To speak only of the latter :—Abstract or General Logic is logic viewed as treating of the formal laws of thought, without respect to any particular matter. Concrete or Special Logic is logic viewed as treating of these laws in relation to a certain matter, and in subordination to the end of some determinate science. The former of these is one, and belongs alone to philo- sophy, that is, to the science of the universal principles of knowledge; the latter is as manifold as the sciences to which it is subservient, and of which it, in fact, constitutes a part,—viz. their Methodology. This division of logic is given, but in different terms, by the Greek Aristotelians and by the Latin schoolmen. The Greek division does not remount to Aristotle, but it is found in his earliest expositor, Alexander of Aphrodisias, and he was probably not the first by whom it was enounced. It is into διαλεκτικὴ χωρὶς πραγμάτων, *Logica rebus avulsa*, that is, Logic merely formal, Logic apart from things, in other words, abstract from all particular matter; and διαλεκτικὴ ἐν χρήσει καὶ γυμνασίᾳ πραγμάτων, *Logica rebus applicata*, that is, Logic as used and exercised upon things, in other words, as applied to certain special objects.

This distinction of Logic by the Greek Aristotelians seems altogether unknown to modern logicians. The division of Logic by the scholastic Aristotelians is the same with the preceding, but the terms in which it is expressed are less precise and unambiguous. This division is into the *Logica docens* and *Logica utens*. The *Logica docens* is explained as logic considered as an abstract theory,—as a preceptive system of rules, —" quæ tradit præcepta ;" the *Logica utens*, as logic considered as a concrete practice, as an application of these rules to use,—" quæ utitur præceptis."[a]

This scholastic division of Logic into *docens* and *utens* has, I see, been noticed by some of the more modern authors, but it has been altogether mistaken, which it would not have been had these authors been aware of the meaning in which the terms were employed, and had they not been ignorant of the more explicit expression of it by the Greeks. Thus the terms *docens* and *utens* are employed by Wolf to mark a distinction not the same as that which they designate in the scholastic logic ; and as the Wolfian distinction will not stand the test of criticism, the terms themselves have been repudiated by those who were not aware, that there was an older and a more

a *Smiglecii Logica*, Disp. ii. q. vi. For scholastic authorities, see Aqui-

nas, *In IV. Metaph.*, lect. iv.; Scotus, *Super Univ. Porphyrii*, q. i.—ED.

valid division which they alone properly expressed." LECT. IV.
Wolf makes the *Logica docens*, the mere knowledge
of the rules : the *Logica utens*, the habit or dexterity
of applying them. This distinction of General and
Special Logic, Wolf and the Wolfian logicians, likewise,
denote by that of Theoretical and Practical Logic.[a]
These terms are in themselves by no means a bad
expression of the distinction, but those by whom they
were employed unfortunately did not limit their
Practical Logic to what I have defined as Special, for
under Practical they included not only Special, but
likewise Modified Logic, of which we are now to speak.

Having explained, then, this primary division of
Logic into General and Special, and stated that General Logic, as alone a branch of philosophy, is alone
the object of our consideration ; I proceed to give
the division of General Logic into two great species
or rather parts,—viz. into Pure or Abstract, and Modified or Concrete.

¶ VIII. In the third place, considered by refer- Par. VIII.
ence to the circumstances under which it can General, di-
come into exercise by us, Logic,—Logic General Pure and
or Abstract, is divided into Pure and Modified ;— Modified.
a division, however, which is perhaps rather the
distribution of a science into its parts than of a
genus into its species. Pure Logic considers the
laws of thought proper, as contained *a priori* in
the nature of pure intelligence itself. Modified

a [As Krug.] [See his *Logik*, § 11,
p. 30. Compare Kant, *Logik*, Einleitung, II.—Ed.]
β Wolf, *Philosophia Rationalis*, §§
8, 9, 10, 12.—Ed. [Cf. Stattler,
Sauter, and Make.](Stattler, *Logica*,

§ 18, p. 12 ; Sauter, *Positiones Logicæ*, P. I. and II., 1778,; *Instit. Log.*,
§ 42, p. 43-4, 1798 ; Paulus Make de
Kerek-Gede, *Comp. Log. Instit.*, § 18,
p. 9, 4th edit., 1773.—Ed.]

LECT.
IV.

Logic, again, exhibits these laws as modified in their actual applications by certain general circumstances external and internal, contingent in themselves, but by which human thought is always more or less influenced in its manifestations.[a]

Pure Logic. Pure Logic considers Thought Proper simply and in itself, and apart from the various circumstances by which it may be effected in its actual application. Human thought, it is evident, is not exerted except by men and individual men. By men, thought is not exerted out of connection with the other constituents of their intellectual and moral character, and, in each individual, this character is variously modified by various contingent conditions of different original genius, and of different circumstances contributing to develop different faculties and habits. Now there **Modified Logic.** may be conceived a science, which considers thought not merely as determined by its necessary and universal laws, but as contingently affected by the empirical conditions under which thought is actually exerted ;— which shows what these conditions are, how they impede, and, in general, modify, the act of thinking, and how, in fine, their influence may be counteracted. **Nomenclature of Modified Logic.** This science is Modified or Concrete Logic. What I have called Modified Logic is identical with what Kant and other philosophers have denominated Applied Logic (*angewandte Logik, Logica applicata.*)[β]

a For distinction of reason in abstracto and reason in concreto, grounding the distinction of an Abstract (or Pure) and a Concrete (or Modified) Logic, see Boyle's *Works,* iv. p. 164. See also Lambert, *Neues Organon,* i. § 444, who says that the sciences in general are only applied logics. Cf. Ploucquet, p. 238 [*Sammlung der*

Schriften welche den logischen Calcul Herrn Prof. Ploucquets betreffen, Tubingen, 1773. — ED.]

β Kant, *Logik,* Einleitung ii. ; Hoffbauer, *Anfangsgründe der Logik,* §§ 17, 406 ; Krug, *Logik,* Einleitung, § 11 ; Fries, *System der Logik,* § 2. — ED.

This expression I think improper. For the term LECT.
IV. *Applied Logic* can only with propriety be used to denote Special or Concrete Logic; and is, in fact, a The term Applied Logic. brief and excellent translation of the terms by which Special Logic was designated by the Greeks, as that ἐν χρήσει καὶ γυμνασίᾳ πραγμάτων. And so, in fact, by the Latin Logicians was the Greek expression rendered. Let us consider the meaning of the term *applied.* Logic, as applied, must be applied to something, and that something can only be an object or matter. Now, Special Logic is necessarily an applied logic; therefore the term *applied,* if given to what I would call Modified Logic, would not distinguish Modified from Special Logic. But further, the term *applied* as given to Modified Logic, considered in itself, is wrong; for in Modified Logic thought is no more considered as actually applied to any particular matter than in Pure Logic. Modified Logic only considers the necessary in conjunction with the contingent conditions under which thought is actually exertible; but it does not consider it as applied to one class of objects more than to another; that is, it does not consider it as actually applied to any, but as potentially applicable to all. In every point of view, How properly em-ployed. therefore, the term *applied,* as given to Modified Logic, is improper; whereas, if used at all, it ought to be used as a synonym for *special;* which I would positively have done, were it not that, having been unfortunately bestowed by high authority on what I have called Modified Logic, the employment of it to designate a totally different distinction might generate confusion. I have, therefore, refrained from making use of the term. I find, indeed, that all logicians who, before Kant, ever employed the expression *Ap-*

LECT.
IV.

plied Logic, employed it as convertible with Special or Concrete Logic." In fine, it is to be observed that the terms *pure* and *applied*, as usually employed in opposition in the Kantian philosophy, and in that of Germany in general, are not properly relative and correlative to each other. For *pure* has its proper correlative in *modified* or *mixed*; *applied* its proper relative in *unapplied*, that is, *divorced from things*, that is, *abstract.*

Modified
Logic not
properly an
essential
part of
Logic.

But passing from words to things, I may observe that it can be questioned whether Modified or Concrete Logic be entitled to the dignity of an essential part of Logic in general, far less of a co-ordinate species as opposed to Pure or Abstract Logic. You are aware, from what I have previously stated under the first introductory question, that Logic, as conversant about a certain class of mental phænomena, is only a part of the general philosophy of mind; but that, as exclusively conversant about what is necessary in the phænomena of thought, that is, the laws of thinking, it is contradistinguished from Empirical Psychology, or that philosophy of mind which is merely observant and inductive of the mental phænomena as facts. But if Modified or Concrete Logic be considered either as a part or as a species of General Logic, this discrimination of Logic, as the Nomology of thought, from Psychology, as the Phænomenology of mind, will not hold. For Modified Logic, presupposing a knowledge of the general and the contingent phænomena of mind, will thus either comprise Psychology within its sphere, or be itself comprised

a See Balforeus, [B. *Balforei Commentarius in Organum*, q. v. § 2, p. 22; "Græci . . . aliam dicunt Logicam abjunctam et a rebus separatam; aliam rebus applicatam et cum iis conjunctam."—ED.]

within the sphere of Psychology. But whichever ^{LECT.} alternative may be preferred, the two sciences are no longer distinct. It is on this ground that I hold, that, in reality, Modified Logic is neither an essential part nor an independent species of General Logic, but that it is a mere mixture of Logic and Psychology, and may, therefore, be called, either Logical Psychology or Psychological Logic." There is thus in truth only one Logic, that is, Pure or Abstract Logic. But while this, I think, must be admitted in speculative rigour, still, as all sciences are only organised for human ends, and as a general consideration of the modifying circumstances which affect the abstract laws of thought in their actual manifestations, is of great practical utility, I trust that I shall not be regarded as deforming the simplicity of the science, if I follow the example of most modern logicians, and add (be it under protest) to Pure or Abstract Logic a part, or an appendix, under the name of Modified Logic. In distributing the science, therefore, into these two principal heads, you will always, I request, keep steadily in mind, that, in strict propriety, Pure Logic is the only science of Logic, Modified Logic being only a scientific accident, ambiguously belonging either to Logic or to Psychology.

This being understood, I now proceed to state to Conspectus you the distribution of the general science into its Course of parts; and as it is of high importance that you now Logic. obtain a comprehensive view of the relation of these parts to each other and to the whole which they constitute, in order that you may clearly understand the point towards which we travel and every stage in our

a [See Richter, p. 67] [Über den Logik, § 17, Leipzig, 1825.—ED.] Orgrasstand und den Umfang der

progress,—I shall comprise this whole statement in the following paragraph, which I shall endeavour to make sufficiently intelligible without much subsequent illustration. That illustration, however, I will give in my next Lecture. As this paragraph is intended to afford you a conspectus of the ensuing Course, in so far as it will be occupied with Logic, I need hardly say that you will find it somewhat long. It is, however, I believe, the only paragraph of any extent which I shall hereafter be obliged to dictate.

¶ IX. GENERAL or ABSTRACT LOGIC, we have seen, is divided into two parts,—PURE and MODIFIED. Of these in their order.

I.—PURE LOGIC may, I think, best be distributed upon the following principles. We may think; and we may think well. On the one hand, the conditions of thinking do not involve the conditions of thinking well; but the conditions of thinking well involve the conditions of thinking. Logic, therefore, as the science of thought, must necessarily consider the conditions of the possibility of thought. On the other hand, the end of thought is not merely to think, but to think well; therefore, as the end of a science must be conformed to the end of its object-matter, Logic, as the science of thought, must display not only the laws of possible, but the laws of perfect, thinking. Logic, therefore, naturally falls into two parts, the one of which investigates the formal conditions of mere thinking; the other, the formal conditions of thinking well.

i.—In regard to the former:—The conditions

of mere thinking are given in certain elemen- LECT.
tary requisites; and that part of Logic which IV.
analyses and considers these may be called its
Stoicheiology, or Doctrine of Elements. These
elements are either Laws or Products.

ii.—In regard to the latter, as perfect thinking
is an end, and as, the elementary means being
supposed, the conditions of an end are the ways
or methods by which it may be accomplished,
that part of Logic which analyses and considers
the methods of perfect thinking, may be called
its Methodology, or Doctrine of Method.

Thus PURE LOGIC is divided into two parts,—
Stoicheiology, or the Doctrine of Elements, and
Methodology, or the Doctrine of Method. Of
these in their order.

Logical Stoicheiology, or the doctrine conversant about the elementary requisites of mere
thought, I shall divide into two parts. The first
of these treats of the fundamental laws of thinking, in other words, of the universal conditions of
the thinkable,—Noetic,—Nomology. The second
treats of the laws of thinking, as governing the
special functions, faculties, or products of thought,
in its three gradations of Conception,—or, as it
is otherwise called, Simple Apprehension,—Judgment, and Reasoning,—Dianoetic—Dynamic.

This second part of Stoicheiology will, therefore, fall into three subordinate divisions corresponding to these several degrees of Conception,
Judgment, and Reasoning. — So much for the
Doctrine of Elements.'

Logical Methodology, or the doctrine conversant about the regulated ways or methods in

which the means of thinking are conducted to their end of thinking well, is divided into as many parts as there are methods, and there are as many methods as there are different qualities in the end to be differently accomplished. Now the perfection of thought consists of three virtues — Clear Thinking, Distinct Thinking, and Connected Thinking; each of these virtues is accomplished by a distinct method; and the three methods will consequently afford the division of Logical Methodology into three parts.

The first part comprises the Method of Clear Thinking, or the Doctrine of Illustration or Definition.

The second part comprises the Method of Distinct Thinking, or the doctrine of Division.

The third part comprises the Method of Concatenated or Connected Thinking, or the doctrine of Proof.

These three parts are only, however, three particular applications of method; they, therefore, constitute each only a Special Methodology. But such special methodology, or union of methodologies, supposes a previous consideration of Method in general, in its notion, its species, and its conditions. Logical Methodology will, therefore, consist of two parts, of a General and of a Special, — the Special being subdivided, as above stated. So much for the distribution of PURE LOGIC.

II.—MODIFIED LOGIC falls naturally into three parts.

The First Part treats of the nature of Truth and Error, and of the highest laws for their discrimination,—Alethiology.

The second treats of the Impediments to think- ing, with the means of their removal. These impediments arise, 1°, From the Mind; 2°, From the Body; or, 3°, From External Circumstances. In relation to the Mind, these impediments originate in the Senses, in Self-consciousness, in Memory, in Association, in Imagination, in Reason, in the faculty of Language, in the Feelings, in the Desires, in the Will. In relation to the Body, they originate in Temperament, or in the state of Health. In relation to External Circumstances, they originate in the diversities of Education, of Rank, of Age, of Climate, of Social Intercourse, &c.

The Third Part treats of the Aids or Subsidiaries of thinking; and thinking is aided either, 1°, Through the Acquisition, or, 2°, Through the Communication, of Knowledge.

The former of these subsidiaries, (the acquisition of knowledge,) consists, 1°, Of Experience, (and that either by ourselves or by others); 2°, Of Generalisation, (and this through Induction and Analogy); and, 3°, Of Testimony, (and this either Oral or Written). Under this last head falls to be considered the Credibility of Witnesses, the Authenticity and Integrity of Writings, the Rules of Criticism, and of Interpretation.

The latter of these subsidiaries, the Communication of Knowledge, is either One - sided or Reciprocal. The former consists of Instruction, either Oral or Written; the latter of Conversation, Conference, Disputation.

So much for the distribution of MODIFIED LOGIC.

The following is a general tabular view of the Divisions of Logic * now given :—

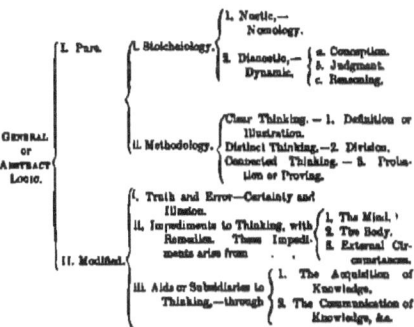

The fourth and fifth questions of the Introduction
would now fall to be considered,—viz. What is the History, and what is the Bibliography, of Logic ? Were
I writing a book, and not giving a course of Lectures
upon Logic, I would certainly consider these questions
in the introduction to the science, but I would do this
with the admonition that beginners should pass these
over, and make themselves first of all familiar with
the doctrines of which the science is itself the complement. For why ? The history of a science is a narrative of the order in which its several parts have been
developed, and of the contributions which have been
made to it by different cultivators ; but such a narrative necessarily supposes a previous knowledge of the
contents of the science,—a knowledge which is identical with a knowledge of the science itself. It is,

       a See further Appendix III.—Ed.

therefore, evident that a history of Logic can only be LECT.
IV. proposed with advantage to those who are already in some degree familiar with Logic itself; and as, in a course like the present, I am bound to presume that you are not as yet conversant with the science, it follows that such a history cannot with any propriety be attempted in the commencement, but only towards the conclusion, of the Lectures.

In regard to the fifth question,—What is the Biblio- V. The graphy or Literature of Logic?—the same is true, in Biblio-
graphy of
Logic. so far as a knowledge of the books written upon a science is correlative to a knowledge of its history. At the same time nothing could be more unprofitable, than for me to recite to you a long series of works to which you have not access, by authors of whom you probably never heard, often in languages which few of you understand. In the present stage of your studies, it is not requisite that you should know of many books, but that you should read attentively a few ;—*non multa sed multum.*—I shall, therefore, adjourn, at least, the consideration of the question,— What in general are the principal books on the science of Logic?—simply recommending to you a few not absolutely the best, but such as you can most easily procure, such as are in languages which most of you can read, and which are of such a character as may be studied with most general advantage.

Of works in our own language, as those most acces- General
notice of
works on
Logic. sible and most intelligible to all, there are unfortunately hardly any which I can recommend to you as exhibiting the doctrines of Logic, either in purity or completeness. The *Logics* of Watts, of Duncan, and others, are worth reading as books, but not as books upon Logic. The *Elements of Logic* by Dr Whately

is, upon the whole, the one best entitled to your attention, though it is erroneous in various respects, and
imperfect in more. The abridgment of this work by
Hinds contains what of the original is most worthy of
study, in the commencement of a logical education.
In French, there are sundry works deserving of your
attention, (Damiron,[a] Delarivière);[b] but the only one
which I would at present earnestly recommend to
your study, is the celebrated Port Royal Art of Thinking,—*L'Art de Penser*,—an anonymous work, but
the authors of which were the two distinguished Jan-
senists, Arnauld and Nicole. It has been frequently
reprinted; and there is a recent stereotyped edition,
by Hachette of Paris, which can easily be procured.
There are more than one translation of the work into
Latin, and at least two English versions, both bad.[c]

In Latin there is a very elegant compend of Logic
by the late illustrious Daniel Wyttenbach of Leyden.
Besides the Dutch editions, which are handsome, there
is a cheap reprint published by Professor Maass of
Halle, who has, however, ventured on the unwarrant-
able liberty of silently altering the text, besides omit-
ting what he did not consider as absolutely indispensable for a text-book. This work can be easily procured.
There is also in Latin a system of Logic by Genovesi,
under the title, *Genuensis Ars Logico-critica*. This
work is, however, extremely rare even in Italy, and it
was many years before I was able to procure a copy.
There was an edition of this work published in Ger-

a *Cours de Philosophie*, t. iv.; *Logique*, Paris, 1837.—Ed.
β *Logique Classique*, Paris, 1829.—
Ed.
γ A third and far superior translation has subsequently appeared by

Mr Baynes, Edinburgh, 1850; 2d
edition, 1851. In the Introduction
to this version will be found an account of the various editions and
translations of the work.—Ed.

many in 1760 at Augsburg, but the impression seems to have been small, for it also is out of print. The Italian Logic of Genovesi has, however, been repeatedly reprinted, and this, with the valuable additions of Romagnosi, is easily obtained. Of the older writers on Logic in Latin, the one I would principally recommend to you is Burgersdyk, — Burgersdicius. His *Institutiones Logicæ* is not a rare work, though, as there are no recent editions, it is not always without trouble to be obtained.[*]

---

* See Appendix IV. for note of treatises on Logic, recommended by the Author to his class. — ED.

LECTURE V.

PURE LOGIC.

PART I.—STOICHEIOLOGY.

SECTION I. NOETIC.—ON THE FUNDAMENTAL LAWS OF THOUGHT—THEIR CONTENTS AND HISTORY.

LECT.
V.
———
Stoicheio-
logy.

HAVING terminated our consideration of the various questions of which the Introduction to Logic is composed, we proceed to the doctrines which make up the science itself, and commence the first great division of PURE LOGIC—that which treats of its elementary or constituent processes,—Stoicheiology. But Stoicheiology was again divided into two parts,—into a part which considered the Fundamental Laws of Thought in general, and into a part which considered these laws as applied to and regulating the special function of Thought in its various gradations of Conception, Judgment, and Reasoning. The title, therefore, of the part of Logic on which we are about to enter is,— *Pure Logic—Part I. Stoicheiology—Section I. Noetic —On the Fundamental Laws of Thought.*

The charac-
ter of
Thought in
general.

Before, however, descending to the consideration of these laws, it is necessary to make one or two preliminary statements touching the character of that thought of which they are the necessary conditions; and, on this point, I give, in the first place, the following paragraph :—

¶ X. Logic considers Thought, not as the oper- LECT.
ation of thinking, but as its product; it does not ——
treat of Conception, Judgment, and Reasoning, Par. X.
but of Concepts, Judgments, and Reasonings.

I have already endeavoured to give you a general Thought as
knowledge of what is meant by *thought*. You are of Logic.
aware that this term is, in relation to Logic, employed
in its strictest and most limited signification,—viz. as
the act or product of the Discursive Faculty, or Faculty of Relations; but it is now proper to consider,
somewhat more closely, the determinate nature of this
process, and the special point of view in which it is
regarded by the logician.

In an act of thinking, there are three things which The subject,
we can discriminate in consciousness,—1°, There is the matter of
thinking subject, that is, the mind or ego, which thought.
exerts or manifests the thought; 2°, There is the
object about which we think, which is called the
matter of thought; and, 3°, There is a relation between subject and object of which we are conscious,
—a relation always manifested in some determinate
mode or manner,—this is the *form* of thought. Now Thought as
of these three, Logic does not consider either the first respectively
or the second. It takes no account, at least no direct logy and of
account, of the real subject, or of the real object, of Logic.
thought, but is limited exclusively to the form of
thought. This has been already stated. But, again,
this form of thought is considered by Logic only in a
certain aspect. The form of thought may be viewed
on two sides or in two relations. It holds, as has been
said, a relation both to its subject and to its object,
and it may accordingly be viewed either in the one of
these relations or in the other. In so far as the form

of thought is considered in reference to the thinking
mind,—to the mind by which it is exerted, it is
considered as an act, or operation, or energy; and in
this relation it belongs to Phænomenal Psychology.
Whereas, in so far as this form is considered in reference to what thought is about, it is considered as the
product of such an act, and, in this relation, it belongs to Logic. Thus Phænomenal Psychology treats
of thought proper as conception, judgment, reasoning;
Logic, or the Nomology of the Understanding, treats
of thought proper as a concept, as a judgment, as a
reasoning. Whately, I have already shown you,
among other errors in his determination of the object-
matter of Logic, confounds or reverses this; for he
proposes to Logic, not thought considered as a product,
but reasoning alone; and that, too, considered as a
producing operation. He thus confounds Logic with
Phænomenal Psychology.

Be it, therefore, observed, that Logic, in treating
of the formal laws of thought, treats of these in reference to thought considered as a product, that is, as
a concept, a judgment, a reasoning; whereas Psychology, as the Phænomenology of mind, considers
thought as the producing act, that is, as conception,
judgment, reasoning. (You here see, by the way,
the utility of distinguishing *concept* and *conception.*
It is unfortunate that we cannot also distinguish
more precisely judgment and reasoning as producing acts, from a judgment and a reasoning as
products.)

¶ XI. Thought, as the knowledge of one thing
in relation to another, is a mediate and complex
cognition.

The distinctive peculiarity of thinking in general LECT. is, that it involves the cognition of one thing by the V. cognition of another. All thinking is, therefore, a Explica- mediate cognition; and is thus distinguished from tion. our knowledge in perception, external and internal, and imagination; in both of which acts we are immediately cognitive of the object, external or internal, presented in the one, and of the object, external or internal, represented in the other. In the Presentative and Representative Faculties, our knowledge is of something considered directly and in itself; in thought, on the contrary, we know one object only through the knowledge of another. Thus in perception, of either kind, and in imagination, the object known is always a single determinate object; whereas in thought,— in thought proper, as one object is only known through another, there must always be a plurality of objects in every single thought. Let us take an example of this, in regard to the simplest act of thought. When I see an individual,—say Bucephalus or Highflyer, or when I represent him in imagination, I have a direct and immediate apprehension of a certain object in and through itself, without reference to aught else. But when I pronounce the term *Horse*, I am unable either to perceive in nature, or to represent in imagination, any one determinate object corresponding to the word. I obtain the notion corresponding to this word, only as the result of a comparison of many perceptions or imaginations of Bucephalus, Highflyer, Dobbin, and other individual horses; it, therefore, contains many representations under it, has reference to many objects, out of relation to which it cannot possibly be realised in thought; and it is in consequence of this necessity of

representing (potentially at least) a plurality of individual objects under the notion *horse*, that it obtains
the denomination *concept*, that is, something taken up
or apprehended in connection with something else.
This, however, requires a further explication. When
we perform an act of thought, of positive thought,
this is done by thinking something, and we can think
anything only by thinking it as existing; while,
again, we cannot think a thing to exist except in
certain determinate modes of existence. On the other
hand, when we perform an act of negative thought,
this is done by thinking something as not existing in
this or that determinate mode, and when we think it
as existing in no determinate mode, we cease to think
it at all; it becomes a nothing, a logical nonentity,
(*non-ens logicum*).

It being thus understood, that thought can only be
realised by thinking something; it being further
understood that this something, as it is thought, must
be thought as existing; and it being still further
understood, that we can think a thing as existing only
by thinking it as existing in this, that, and the other
determinate manner of existence, and that whenever
we cease to think something, something existing, something existing in a determinate manner of existence,
we cease to think at all; this, I say, being understood, it is here proper to make you, once for all,
acquainted with the various terms by which logicians
designate the modes or manners of cogitable existence.
I shall, therefore, comprise these in the following paragraph :—

¶ XII. When we think a thing, this is done by
conceiving it as possessed of certain modes of

being, or qualities, and the sum of these qualities LECT. V.
constitutes its *concept* or *notion*, (νόημα, ἔννοια,
ἐπίνοια, *conceptum, conceptus, notio*).   As these which the modes of cognisable existence are designated.
qualities or modes, (ποιότητες, *qualitates, modi*),
are only identified with the thing by a mental
attribution, they are called *attributes*, (κατηγο-
ρούμενα, *attributa*); as it is only in or through
them that we say or enounce aught of a thing,
they are called *predicates, predicables*, and
predicaments, or *categories*, these words being
here used in their more extensive signification,
(λεγόμενα περί, κατηγορίαι, κατηγορήματα, κατη-
γορούμενα, *prædicata, prædicabilia, prædicamenta*); as it is only in and through them that
we recognise a thing for what it is, they are
called *notes, signs, marks, characters*, (*nota, signa,
characteres, discrimina*); finally, as it is only in
and through them that we become aware that a
thing is possessed of a peculiar and determinate
existence, they are called *properties, differences,
determinations*, (*proprietates, determinationes*).
As consequent on, or resulting from, the existence of a thing, they have likewise obtained the
name of *consequents*, (ἑπόμενα, *consequentia*, &c.)
What in reality has no qualities, has no existence
in thought,—it is a logical nonentity ; hence,
e converso, the scholastic aphorism,—*non-entis
nulla sunt prædicata*.   What, again, has no
qualities attributed to it, though attributable, is
said to be *indetermined*, (ἀδιόριστον, *indeter-
minatum*) ; it is only a possible object of
thought.[*]

* [Scholm, *Logik*, § 13. Bösling. Ulm, 1826. Cf. Krug, *Logik*, § 14.
63.] [*Die Lehren der reinen Logik. —ED.*]

Explica-
tion.
What is
involved in
thinking an
object.

This paragraph, which I have dictated that you might be made once for all acquainted with the relative terms in use among logicians, requires but little explanation. I may state, however, that the mind only thinks an object by separating it from others, that is, by marking it out or characterising it ; and in so far as it does this, it encloses it within certain fixed limits, that is, determines it. But if this discriminative act be expressed in words, I predicate the marks, notes, characters, or determinations of the thing ; and if, again, these be comprehended in one total thought, they constitute its concept or notion. If, for example, I think of Socrates as *son of Sophroniscus,* as *Athenian,* as *philosopher,* as *pug-nosed,* these are only so many characters, limitations, or determinations, which I predicate of Socrates, which distinguish him from all other men, and together make up my notion or concept of him.

The attri-
bution in-
volved in
thought is
regulated
by laws.

What is
meant by
a law as
applicable
to free in-
telligences.

But as thought, in all its gradations of conception, judgment, and reasoning, is only realised by the attribution of certain qualities or characters to the objects of, or about, which we think, so this attribution is regulated by laws, which render a great part of this process absolutely necessary. But when I speak of laws and of their absolute necessity in relation to thought, you must not suppose that these laws and that necessity are the same in the world of mind as in the world of matter. For free intelligences, a law is an ideal necessity given in the form of a precept, which we ought to follow, but which we may also violate if we please ; whereas, for the existences which constitute the universe of nature, a law is only another name for those causes which operate blindly and universally in producing certain inevitable results. By

law of thought, or by *logical necessity*, we do not, there- LECT.
fore, mean a physical law, such as the law of gravi-   V.
tation, but a general precept which we are able certainly to violate, but which if we do not obey, our
whole process of thinking is suicidal or absolutely
null. These laws are, consequently, the primary conditions of the possibility of valid thought, and as the
whole of Pure Logic is only an articulate development
of the various modes in which they are applied, their
consideration in general constitutes the first chapter
in an orderly system of the science. Now, in explain- Order of
ing to you this subject, the method I shall pursue is consideration of the
the following :—I shall, first of all, state in general fundamental laws of
the number and significance of the laws as commonly thought.
received ; I shall then more particularly consider each
of these by itself and in relation to the others; then
detail to you their history ; and, finally, state to you
my own views in regard to their deduction, number,
and arrangement.

¶ XIII. The Fundamental Laws of Thought Par. XIII.
or the conditions of the thinkable, as commonly Fundamental Laws of
received, are four :—1. The Law of Identity ; 2. Thought.
The Law of Contradiction ; 3. The Law of Exclusion or of Excluded Middle ; and, 4. The Law of
Reason and Consequent, or of Sufficient Reason.[a]

Of these in their order.

¶ XIV. The principle of Identity (*principium* Par. XIV.
Identitatis) expresses the relation of total same- Law of
Identity.
ness in which a concept stands to all, and the
relation of partial sameness in which it stands

a See Appendix V.—ED.

to each, of its constituent characters. In other
words, it declares the impossibility of thinking
the concept and its characters as reciprocally
unlike. It is expressed in the formula *A is A*,
or *A = A*; and by *A* is denoted every logical
thing, every product of our thinking faculty,—
concept, judgment, reasoning, &c.[a]

Explica-
tion.
The principle of Identity is an application of the
principle of the absolute equivalence of a whole and
of all its parts taken together, to the thinking of a
thing by the attribution of constituent qualities or
characters. The concept of the thing is a whole, the
characters are the parts of that whole.[β] This law
may, therefore, be also thus enounced,—*Everything is
equal to itself;* for in a logical relation the thing and
its concept coincide; as, in Logic, we abstract altogether from the reality of the thing which the concept
represents. It is, therefore, the same whether we say
that the concept is equal to all its characters, or that
the thing is equal to itself.[γ]

The law has, likewise, been expressed by the formula,—*In the predicate, the whole is contained explicitly, which in the subject is contained implicitly.*
It is also involved in the axiom,—*Nota notæ est nota
rei ipsius.*[δ]

Its logical
importance
—The prin-
ciple of all
logical affir-
mation and
definition.
The logical importance of the law of Identity lies
in this,—that it is the principle of all logical affirmation and definition. An example or two may be
given to illustrate this.

This illus-
trated.
1. In a concept, which we may call Z, the charac-

a [Schulze, *Logik*, § 17. Gerlach
Logik, § 37.] Cf. Krug, *Logik*, § 17.
—ED.

β See Schulze, *Logik*, p. 32-3.—ED.
γ See Krug, *Logik*, p. 40.—ED.
δ See Kant, *Logik*, p. 40.—ED.

ters a, b, and c are thought as its constituents; consequently, the concept, as a unity, is equal to the characters taken together,—$Z = (a + b + c)$. If the former be affirmed, so also is the latter; therefore, Z being $(a + b + c)$ is a, is b, is c. To take a concrete example, —The concept *man* is a complement made up of the characters, 1°, *substance*, 2°, *material*, 3°, *organised*, 4°, *animated*, 5°, *rational*, 6°, *of this earth;* in other words, *man* is *substantial*, is *material*, is *organised*, is *animated*, is *rational*, is *of this earth.* *Being*, as entering into every attribution, may be discharged as affording no distinction.

2. Again, suppose that, in the example given, the character a is made up of the characters l, m, n, it follows, by the same law of Identity, that $Z = a = (l, m, n)$ is l, is m, is n. The concept *man* contains in it the character *animal*, and the character *animal* contains in it the characters *corporeal*, *organised*, *living*, &c.

The second law is the principle of Contradiction or Non-Contradiction, in relation to which I dictate the following paragraph :—

¶ XV. When an object is determined by the affirmation of a certain character, this object cannot be thought to be the same when such character is denied of it. The impossibility of this is enounced in what is called the principle of Contradiction, (*principium Contradictionis seu Repugnantiæ*). Assertions concerning a thing are mutually contradictory, when the one asserts that the thing possesses the character which the other asserts that it does not. This law is logically expressed in the formula,—What is

LECT.
V.

contradictory is unthinkable. $A = not\text{-}A = 0$, *or*
$A - A = 0$.

Its proper
name.

Now, in the first place, in regard to the name of
this law, it may be observed that, as it enjoins the
absence of contradiction as the indispensable condition of thought, it ought to be called, not the Law of
Contradiction, but the Law of Non-Contradiction, or
of *non-repugnantia.*[a]

How
enounced.

This law has frequently been enounced in the formula,—*It is impossible that the same thing can at
once be and not be;* but this is exposed to sundry
objections. It is vague and, therefore, useless. It
does not indicate whether a real or a notional existence
is meant; and if it mean the former, then is it not a
logical but a metaphysical axiom. But even as a
metaphysical axiom it is imperfect, for to the expression *at once* (*simul*) must be added,—*in the same place,
in the same respect,* &c.[β]

This law has likewise been expressed by the formula,—*Contradictory attributes cannot be united in
one act of consciousness.* But this also is obnoxious
to objection. For a judgment expresses as good a
unity of consciousness as a concept. But when I
judge that *round* and *square* are contradictory attributes, there are found in this judgment contradictory
attributes, but yet a unity of consciousness. The formula is, therefore, vaguely and inaccurately expressed.

The prin-
ciple of all
logical nega-
tion and
distinction.

The logical importance of this law lies in its being
the principle of all logical negation and distinction.
The law of Identity and the law of Contradiction
are co-ordinate and reciprocally relative, and neither

a Compare Krug, *Logik,* § 18.—   *Kritik d. r. V.,* p. 134. ed. Rosen-
Ed.   kranz.—Ed.
β Compare the criticism of Kant,

can be educed as second from the other as first; for
in every such attempt at derivation, the supposed
secondary law is, in fact, always necessarily presup-
posed.ᵃ They are, in fact, one and the same law,—
differing only by a positive and negative expression.

In relation to the third law, take the following
paragraph :—

LECT.
V.

> ¶ XVI. The principle of Excluded Third or
> Middle—viz. between two contradictories, (*prin-*
> *cipium Exclusi Medii vel Tertii*), enounces that
> condition of thought, which compels us, of two
> repugnant notions, which cannot both coexist,
> to think either the one or the other as existing.
> Hence arises the general axiom,—Of contradic-
> tory attributions, we can only affirm one of a
> thing ; and if one be explicitly affirmed, the
> other is implicitly denied. *A either is or is*
> *not. A either is or is not B.*ᵝ

Par. XVI.
Law of
Excluded
Middle.

By the laws of Identity and Contradiction, I am
warranted to conclude from the truth of one contradictory proposition to the falsehood of the other, and
by the law of Excluded Middle, I am warranted to
conclude from the falsehood of one contradictory proposition to the truth of the other. And in this lies
the peculiar force and import of this last principle.
For the logical significance of the law of Excluded
Middle consists in this, that it limits or shuts in the
sphere of the thinkable in relation to affirmation ; for
it determines, that, of the two forms given in the laws
of Identity and Contradiction, and by these laws

Logical
significance
of this law.

ᵃ This is shown more in detail by
Hoffbauer, *Anfangsgründe der Logik*,
§ 23.—ED.
ᵝ See Schulze, *Logik*, § 19.—ED.

affirmed as those exclusively possible, the one or the other must be affirmed as necessary.

The principle of Disjunctive Judgments.
The law of Excluded Middle is the principle of Disjunctive Judgments, that is, of judgments in which a plurality of judgments are contained, and which stand in such a reciprocal relation that the affirmation of one is the denial of the other.

I now go on to the fourth law.

Par. XVII.
Law of Sufficient Reason, or of Reason and Consequent.
¶ XVII. The thinking of an object, as actually characterised by positive or by negative attributes, is not left to the caprice of Understanding,—the Faculty of Thought; but that faculty must be necessitated to this or that determinate act of thinking by a knowledge of something different from, and independent of, the process of thinking itself. This condition of our understanding is expressed by the law, as it is called, of Sufficient Reason, (*principium Rationis Sufficientis*); but it is more properly denominated the law of Reason and Consequent, (*principium Rationis et Conseoutionis*). That knowledge by which the mind is necessitated to affirm or posit something else, is called the *logical reason, ground*, or *antecedent;* that something else which the mind is necessitated to affirm or posit, is called the *logical consequent;* and the relation between the reason and consequent, is called the *logical connection,* or *consequence.* This law is expressed in the formula,—Infer nothing without a ground or reason.[a]

Relations between Reason and Consequent.
The relations between Reason and Consequent, when comprehended in a pure thought, are the following :—

a See Schulze, *Logik*, § 19, and Krug, *Logik*, § 20. – ED.

1. When a reason is explicitly or implicitly given, then there must exist a consequent; and, *vice versa*, when a consequent is given, there must also exist a reason.

2. Where there is no reason, there can be no consequent; and, *vice versa*, where there is no consequent, (either implicitly or explicitly,) there can be no reason. That is, the concepts of reason and of consequent, as reciprocally relative, involve and suppose each other.

The logical significance of the law of Reason and Consequent lies in this,—That in virtue of it, thought is constituted into a series of acts all indissolubly connected; each necessarily inferring the other. Thus it is that the distinction and opposition of possible, actual, and necessary matter, which has been introduced into Logic, is a doctrine wholly extraneous to this science.

I may observe that "Reason is something different from Cause, and Consequent something different from Effect; though cause and effect, in so far as they are conceived in thought, stand to each other in the relation of reason and consequent. Cause is thus thought of as a real object, which affords the reason of the existence of another real object, the effect; and effect is thought of as a real object, which is the consequent of another real object, the cause. Accordingly, every cause is recognised in thought as a reason, and every effect is recognised in thought as a consequent; but the converse is not true, that every reason is really considered a cause, and every consequent really considered an effect. We must, therefore, carefully distinguish mere reason and mere consequent, that is, ideal or logical reason and consequent, from the reason which is a cause and the consequent which is an effect, that is, real or metaphysical reason and consequent.

"The expression *logical reason and consequent* refers

Marginal notes:

LECT. V.

Logical significance of this law.

Reason and Consequent, and Cause and Effect.

LECT.
V.

Logical and Metaphysical Reason and Consequent.

to the mere synthesis of thoughts; whereas the expression *metaphysical reason and consequent* denotes the real connection of existences. Hence the axiom of Causality, as a metaphysical principle, is essentially different from the axiom of Reason and Consequent, as a logical principle. Both, however, are frequently confounded with each other; and the law of Reason and Consequent, indeed, formerly found its place in the systems of Metaphysic, while it was not, at least explicitly, considered in those of Logic. The two terms *condition* and *conditioned* happily express at once the relations both of reason and consequent, and of cause and effect. A condition is a thing which determines, [negatively at least,] the existence of another; the conditioned is a thing whose existence is determined in and by another. If used in an ideal or logical signification, *condition* and *conditioned* import only the reason in conjunction with its consequent; if used in a real or metaphysical sense, they express the cause in connection with its effect." [a]

Generality of the terms Condition and Conditioned.

History of the development of the fundamental Laws of Thought.

I have now, in the prosecution of our inquiry into the fundamental laws of logical thinking, to say a few words in regard to their History,—their history being the narration of the order in which, and of the philosophers by whom, they were articulately developed.

a Krug, *Logik*, pp. 62, 63. This exposition of the law of Reason and Consequent does not represent the Author's latest view. In a note to the *Discussions*, p. 160, (where a similar doctrine had been maintained in the article as originally published), he says : "The Logical relation of *Reason and Consequent*, as more than a mere corollary of the law of *Non-contradiction* in its three phases, is, I am confident of proving, erroneous." And again, in the same work, p. 603 : "The principle of *Sufficient Reason* should be excluded from Logic. For, inasmuch as this principle is not material, it is only a derivation of the three formal laws ; and inasmuch as it is material, it coincides with the principle of Causality, and is extra-logical." The Laws of Thought, properly so called, are thus reduced to three,—those of *Identity, Contradiction,* and *Excluded Middle.*—ED.

Of the first three laws, which, from their intimate LECT. cognation, may not unreasonably be regarded as only V. the three sides or phases of a single law, the law of The law of Identity, which stands first in the order of nature, was last devel- oped in the indeed that last developed in the order of time; the order of time. axioms of Contradiction and of Excluded Middle hav- ing been long enounced, ere that of Identity had been discriminated and raised to the rank of a co-ordinate principle. I shall not, therefore, now follow the order in which I detailed to you these laws, but the order in which they were chronologically generalised.

The principles of Contradiction and of Excluded The prin- Middle can both be traced back to Plato, by whom Contradic- they were enounced and frequently applied; though Excluded it was not till long after, that either of them obtained be traced back to a distinctive appellation. To take the principle of Plato. Contradiction first. This law Plato frequently em- ploys, but the most remarkable passages are found in the *Phædo*, in the *Sophista*, and in the fourth and seventh books of the *Republic.*[a]

This law was, however, more distinctively and em- Law of Contradic- phatically enounced by Aristotle. In one place,[β] he tion empha- tically says: "It is manifest that no one can conceive to enounced by himself that the same thing can at once be and not Aristotle. be, for thus he would hold repugnant opinions, and subvert the reality of truth. Wherefore, all who at- tempt to demonstrate, reduce everything to this as the ultimate doctrine; for this is by nature the principle of all other axioms." And in several passages of his *Metaphysics*,[γ] in his *Prior Analytics*,[δ] and in his *Posterior Analytics*,[ε] he observes that "some had

a See *Phædo*, p. 103 ; *Sophista*, p. 252 ; *Republic*, iv. p. 436 ; vii. p. 525.—Ed.

β *Metaph.*, L. iii. (iv.) c. 3.

γ L. iii. c. 4.

δ L. ii. c. 2.

ε L. i. c. 2.

attempted to demonstrate this principle,—an attempt
which betrayed an ignorance of those things whereof
we ought to require a demonstration, and of those
things whereof we ought not : for it is impossible to
demonstrate everything ; as in this case, we must
regress and regress to infinity, and all demonstration
would, on that supposition, be impossible."

With the
Peripatetics
the highest
principle of
knowledge.
Obtained its
name from
the Greek
Aristotel-
ians.
Following Aristotle, the Peripatetics established this
law as the highest principle of knowledge. From the
Greek Aristotelians it obtained the name by which it
has subsequently been denominated, the *principle*, or
law, or *axiom*, *of contradiction*, (ἀξίωμα τῆς ἀντιφάσεως).
This name, at least, is found in the Commentaries of
Ammonius and Philoponus, where it is said to be
" the criterion which divides truth from falsehood

The School-
men,—Sua-
rez.
throughout the universe of existence."• The Schoolmen, in general, taught the same doctrine ; and Suarez
even says, that the law of contradiction holds the
same supremacy among the principles of knowledge which the Deity does among the principles of
existence.β

Controver-
sies respect-
ing the
truth and
character of
this law.
After the decline of the Aristotelian philosophy,
many controversies arose touching the truth, and still
more touching the primitive or axiomatic character,
of this law. Some maintained that it was indemon-

---

a For the name, see Ammonius,
In De Interpret., p. 153 b, ed. Ald.
Venet. 1546. Philoponus, *In Anal.
Pr.*, p. 13 b, 38 b, ed. Venet. 1536 ;
In Anal. Post., p. 30 b, ed. Ald.
Venet. 1534. The language quoted
in the text is nearly a translation of
Ammonius, *In Categ.*, p. 140a: 'Ἡ μὲν
γὰρ κατάφασις καὶ ἀπόφασις ἀεὶ ἀνὶ
πάντων τῶν ὄντων καὶ μὴ ὄντων διαιρεῖ
τὸ ἀληθὲς καὶ τὸ ψεῦδος. Ammonius
is followed by Philoponus, who says :
Τὸ δὲ τῆς ἀντιφάσεως ἀξίωμα ἀνὶ
πάντων μὲν τῶν ὄντων καὶ μὴ ὄντων

διαιρεῖ τὸ ψεῦδος καὶ τὴν ἀλήθειαν.
In Anal. Post., L. i. c. xi. f. 30 h.—
ED. [Cf. Augustinus Niphus Suar-
ensis, *In Anal. Post.*, p. 88, ed.
Paris, 1540.]

β See [Alstedius, *Artium Libera-
lium Systema* (8vo), p. 174 : "Cog-
nitio a priori est principiorum ; inter
quæ agmen ducit hoc, *impossibile est
idem esse et non esse*. . . . Conrale
Metaph. Suarezii : 'Hoc, inquam,
tenet primatum inter principia cognoscendi, sicut Deus inter principia
essendi.' "]

strable; others that it could be proved, but proved
only indirectly by a *reductio ad absurdum;* while
others again held that this could be directly done,
and that, consequently, the law of Contradiction was
not entitled to the dignity of a first principle.[a] In
like manner, its employment was made a further matter of controversy. Finally, it was disputed whether
it were an immediate, native, or *a priori* datum of intelligence; or whether it were an *a posteriori* and ad-
ventitious generalisation from experience. The latter
alternative, that it was only an induction, was main- Locke.
tained by Locke.[β] This opinion was, however, validly
refuted by Leibnitz; who showed that it is admitted Leibnitz.
the moment the terms of its enunciation are understood, and that we implicitly follow it even when we
are not explicitly conscious of its dictate.[γ] Leibnitz,
in some parts of his works, seems to identify the principles of Identity and Contradiction; in others he distinguishes them, but educes the law of Identity out
of the law of Contradiction.[δ] It is needless to pursue the subsequent history of this principle, which in Its truth
latter times has found none to gainsay the necessity denied by
and universality of its truth, except among those absolutists.
philosophers who, in Germany, have dreamt that man
is competent to a cognition of the Absolute: and as
a cognition of the absolute can only be established
through positions repugnant, and, therefore, on logical
principles, mutually exclusive, they have found it necessary to start with a denial of the fundamental
laws of thought; and so, in their effort to soar to a

a Cf. Suarez, *Disputationes Meta-*
physicæ, Disp. iii. § 3.—Ed. [Alste-
dius, *Encyclopædia,* L. iii., *Archelogia,*
c. vii. p. 80.]

β *Essay,* B. i. ch. ii. § 4.—Ed.

γ *Nouveaux Essais,* B. i. ch. i. § 4.

—Ed.

δ Compare *Théodicée,* § 44, *Mona-*
dologie, § 31, with *Nouveaux Essais,*
L. i. ch. i. § 10; L. iv. ch. ii. § 1.—
Ed.

philosophy above logic and intelligence, they have subverted the conditions of human philosophy altogether.
Thus Schelling and Hegel prudently repudiated the
principles of Contradiction and Excluded Middle as
having any application to the absolute ;[a] while again
those philosophers, (as Cousin), who attempt a cognition
of the absolute without a preliminary repudiation of
the laws of Logic, at once involve themselves in contradictions, the cogency of which they do not deny, and
from which they are wholly unable to extricate themselves.[b] But this by the way, and on a subject which
at present you cannot all be supposed to understand.

The law of Excluded Middle between two contradictories remounts, as I have said, also to Plato,
though the *Second Alcibiades*, the dialogue in which
it is most clearly expressed, must be admitted to be
spurious.[γ] It is also in the fragments of Pseudo-
Archytas, to be found in Stobæus.[δ] It is explicitly and
emphatically enounced by Aristotle in many passages

a See Schelling, *Vom Ich als Prin-
cip der Philosophie*, § 10 ; Hegel,
Logik, b. ii. c. 2 ; *Encyklopädie*, §
113, 119. Schelling endeavours to
abrogate the principle of Contradiction in relation to the higher philosophy, by assuming that of Identity ;
the empirical antagonism between
ego and *non-ego* being merged in the
identity of the absolute *ego*. Hegel
regards both principles alike as valid
only for the finite Understanding,
and as inapplicable to the higher
processes of the Reason. This difference between the two philosophers
is pointed out by the latter in his
Geschichte der Philosophie, (*Werke*,
xv. p. 598.)—ED. [On rejection of
the Logical Laws, by Schelling,
Hegel, &c., see Bachmann, *Über die
Philosophie meiner Zeit*, p. 218, ed.
Jena, 1816. Holzaen, *Wissenschafts-*

lehre, iv. *Logik*, § 718. Sigwart,
Logik, § 58, p. 42, ed. 1835. Herbart, *In Principio Logica Exclusi
Medii inter Contradictoria non negli-
genda*, Gotting., 1833. Hartenstein,
*De Methodo Philosophiae Logicae legi-
bus adstringenda, finibus non termi-
nanda*, Lipsiæ, 1835. On the logical
and metaphysical significance of the
principle of Contradiction, see Platner, *Phil. Aph.*, I. § 673, and Kant,
Kritik d. reinen Vernunft, p. 101,
ed. 1790.]

β See the Author's criticism of
Cousin, *Discussions*, p. 1 *et seq.*—ED.
γ *Second Alcibiades*, p. 139. See
also *Sophista*, p. 250.—ED.
δ *Eclogæ*, L. ii. c. 2, p. 158, ed.
Antwerp., 1575 ; Part ii. tom. i. p.
22. ed. Heeren. Cf. Simplicius, *In
Arist. Categ.*, pp. 97, 103, ed. Basil,
155 L—ED.

both of his *Metaphysics*, (L. iii. (iv.) c. 7.), and of his LECT.
Analytics, both *Prior* (L. i. c. 2) and *Posterior*, (L. i. c. 4). ——— V.
In the first of these he says : " It is impossible that
there should exist any medium between contradictory
opposites, but it is necessary either to affirm or to
deny everything of everything." And his expressions
are similar in the other books. Cicero says " that the Cicero.
foundation of Dialectic is, that whatever is enounced
is either true or false." This is from his *Academics*,
(L. ii. c. xxix.), and there are parallel passages in his
Topics, (c. xiv.), and his *De Oratore*, (L. ii. c. xxx.)
This law, though universally recognised as a principle
in the Greek Peripatetic school and in the schools of
the middle ages, only received the distinctive appellation by which it is now known at a comparatively
modern date.[a] I do not recollect having met with Baum-
the term *principium exclusi medii* in any author garten.
older than the Leibnitian Baumgarten,[b] though Wolf[y]
speaks of the *exclusio medii inter contradictoria*.

The law of Identity, I stated, was not explicated Law of
as a co-ordinate principle till a comparatively recent Identity.
period. The earliest author in whom I have found Antonius
this done, is Antonius Andreas, a scholar of Scotus, Andreas.
who flourished at the end of the thirteenth and beginning of the fourteenth century. This schoolman, in
the fourth book of his Commentary on Aristotle's *Metaphysics*,[b]—a commentary which is full of the most in-

a *Lex contradictoriarum, principium contradicentium* (sc. *propositionum*), as used in the schools, included the law of Contradiction and
the law of Excluded Middle. See
Mollenus, *Elementa Logica*, L. ii. c.
14, [p. 172, ed. 1603 : "Contradicentium sensu explicatur nec axiom-
ate :—Contradicentia non possunt de

eodem simul esse vera ; et necessa-
rium est contradicentium alterum
cuilibet rei convenire, alterum non
convenire."—Ed.]
β *Metaphysica*, § 10.—Ed.
γ *Ontologia*, §§ 52, 53.
δ Quæstio v. p. 21 a, ed. Venet.,
1513.—Ed.

genious and original views,—not only asserts to the
law of Identity a co-ordinate dignity with the law of
Contradiction, but, against Aristotle, he maintains,
that the principle of Identity, and not the principle
of Contradiction, is the one absolutely first. The formula in which Andreas expressed it was, *Ens est ens.*
Subsequently to this author, the question concerning
the relative priority of the two laws of Identity and
of Contradiction became one much agitated in the
schools ; though there were also found some who
asserted to the law of Excluded Middle this supreme

Leibnitz. rank.[a] Leibnitz, as I have said, did not always distinguish the principles of Identity and of Contradic-

Wolf. tion. By Wolf the former was styled the principle
of Certainty, (*principium Certitudinis*) ; [b] but he, no
more than Leibnitz himself, sufficiently discriminated
between it and the law of Contradiction. This was,

*Baum-
garten.* however, done by Baumgarten, another distinguished
follower of Leibnitz,[y] and from him it received the
name of the principle of Position, that is, of Affirmation or Identity, (*principium Positionis sive Identi-
talis*),—the name by which it is now universally
known. This principle has found greater favour in
the eyes of the absolutist philosophers, than those of

*Fichte and
Schelling.* Contradiction and Excluded Middle. By Fichte and
Schelling it has been placed as the primary principle

Hegel. of all philosophy.[δ] Hegel alone subjects it, along
with the other laws of thought, to a rigid but fallacious criticism ; and rejects it along with them as be-

---

a [Alex. de Ales, *In Arist. Metaph.,* iv. t. 9.] Compare Suarez,
Disp. Metaph., Disp. iii. § 3. Alexander professes to agree with Aristotle in giving the first place to the
principle of Contradiction, but, in
fact, he identifies it with that of Ex-

cluded Middle, *de quavis affirmatio
vel negatio.*—En.
β *Ontologia,* §§ 55, 288.—En.
y *Metaphysica,* § 11.—En.
δ See Fichte, *Grundlage der ge-
sammten Wissenschaftslehre,* § 1.
Schelling, *Vom Ich,* § 7.—En.

longing to that lower sphere of knowledge, which is LECT.
V. conversant only with the relative and finite.[a]

The fourth law, that of Reason and Consequent, Law of Reason and Consequent. which stands apart by itself from the other three, was, like the laws of Contradiction and Excluded Middle, recognised by Plato.[β] He lays it down as a postu- Recognised by Plato and Aristotle. late of reason, to admit nothing without a cause; and the same is frequently done by his scholar Aristotle.[γ] Both, however, in reference to this principle, employ the ambiguous term cause, (αἰτία, αἴτιον). Aristotle, indeed, distinguishes the law of Reason, as the ideal principle 'Αρχὴ τῆς γνώσεως. of knowledge, (ἀρχὴ τῆς γνώσεως, principium cognos- 'Αρχὴ τῆς γενέσεως. cendi), from the real principle of production, (ἀρχὴ τῆς γενέσεως, principium fiendi, principium essendi).[δ] By Cicero the axiom of reason and consequent was, Cicero. in like manner, comprehended under the formula, nihil sine causa,[ε]—a formula adopted by the school- The Schoolmen. men; although they, after Aristotle, distinguished under it the ratio essendi, and the ratio cognoscendi.

In modern times, the attention of philosophers was Leibnitz called attention to Law of Sufficient Reason. called to this law by Leibnitz, who, on the two prin- ciples of Reason and of Contradiction, founded the whole edifice of his philosophy.[ζ] Under the latter law, as I have mentioned, he comprehended, however, the principle of Identity; and in the former he did not sufficiently discriminate, in terms, the law of Cau- sality, as a real principle, from the law of Reason, properly so called, as a formal or ideal principle. To this axiom he gave various denominations,—now call- ing it the principle of Determining Reason, now the

---

a See above, p. 90 note a.—Ed.
β Philebus, p. 26.—Ed.
γ E. g., Anal. Post., ii. 16; Phys., ii. 3; Metaph., i. l, 3; Rhet., ii. 23. —Ed.

δ Metaph., iv. (γ.) l.—Ed.
ε De Divinatione, ii. c. 25.—Ed.
ζ See Théodicée, § 44. Mondologie, §§ 31, 32.—Ed.

LECT.
V.

principle of Sufficient Reason, and now the principle of Convenience or Agreement, (*convenientia*) ; making it, in its real relation, the ground of all existence, in its ideal, the ground of all positive knowledge. On this subject there was a celebrated controversy between Leibnitz and Dr Samuel Clarke,—a controversy on this, as on other points, eminently worthy of your study. The documents in which this controversy is contained, were published in the English edition under the title, *A collection of Papers which passed between the late learned Mr Leibnitz and Dr Clarke, in the years 1715 and 1716, relating to the Principles of Natural Philosophy and Religion*, London, 1717.[a]

Wolf.

Wolf, the most distinguished follower of Leibnitz, employs the formula,—" Nothing is without a sufficient reason why it is, rather than why it is not; that is, if anything is supposed to be (*ponitur esse*) something also must be supposed, whence it may be understood why the same is rather than is not."[β] He blames the schoolmen for confusing reason (*ratio*) with cause (*causa*) : but his censure equally applies to his master Leibnitz as to them and Aristotle ; for all of these philosophers, though they did not confound the two principles, employed ambiguous terms to denote them.

Discussion regarding the Leibnitian doctrine of the law of Sufficient Reason.

The Leibnitian doctrine of the universality of the law of Sufficient Reason, both as a principle of existence and of thought, excited much discussion among the philosophers, more particularly of Germany. In the earlier half of the last century, some controverted

---

a See especially, Leibnitz's Second Letter, p. 20, in which the principle of Contradiction or Identity is assumed as the foundation of all mathematics, and that of Sufficient Reason as the foundation of natural philosophy.—Ed.

β See Fischer's *Logik*, [§ 59, p. 38, ed. 1838. Compare Wolf, *Ontologia*, §§ 70, 71.—Ed.]

the validity of the principle, others attempted to re-
strict it.[a] Among other arguments, it was alleged, by
the advocates of the former opinion, if the principle
be admitted, that everything must have a sufficient
reason why it is, rather than why it is not,—on this
hypothesis, error itself will have such a reason, and,
therefore, must cease forthwith to be error.[β]

Many philosophers, as Wolf and Baumgarten,
endeavoured to demonstrate this principle by the
principle of Contradiction; while others, with better
success, showed that all such demonstrations were
illogical.[7]

In the more recent systems of philosophy, the universality and necessity of the axiom of Reason has,
with other logical laws, been controverted and rejected
by speculators on the absolute.[8]

α As Feuerlin and Darjes. See
Bachmann, Logik, p. 56, Leipsig,
1828; Cf. Degerando, Hist. Comp.
des Syst. de Phil., t. ii. p. 145, ed.
1804.—Ed.

β See Bachmann, Logik, p. 56.
With the foregoing history of the
laws of Thought compare the same
author, Logik, § 18-31.—Ed.

7 [Kiesewetter, Allgemeine Logik,

P. i. p. 57]; compare Lectures on
Metaphysics, ii. pp. 396, 397, notes.
—Ed.

8 [On principle of Double Nega-
tion as another law of Thought, see
Fries, Logik, § 41, p. 190; Calker,
Denklehre oder Logik und Dialektik,
§ 165, p. 453 ; Beneke, Lehrbuch der
Logik, § 64, p. 41.]

LECTURE VI.

STOICHEIOLOGY.

SECTION I.—NOETIC.

THE FUNDAMENTAL LAWS OF THOUGHT—THEIR
CLASSIFICATION AND IMPORT.

LECT.
VI.

Recapitula-
tion.

HAVING concluded the Introductory Questions, we entered, in our last Lecture, upon our science itself. The first part of Pure Logic is the Doctrine of Elements, or that which considers the conditions of mere or possible thinking. These elements are of two kinds, —they are either the fundamental laws of thought as regulating its necessary products, or they are the products themselves as regulated by those laws. The fundamental laws are four in number,—the law of Identity, the law of Contradiction, the law of Excluded Middle, the law of Reason and Consequent.[a] The products of thought are three,—1°, Concepts or Notions; 2°, Judgments; and 3°, Reasonings. In our last Lecture, we considered the first of these two parts of the doctrine of elements, and I went through the general explanation of the contents and import of the four laws, and their history. Without recapitulating what was then stated, I shall now proceed to certain general observations, which may be suggested in relation to the four laws.

a See, however, above, p. 86, note a.—ED.

And, first of all, I may remark, that they naturally fall into two classes. The first of these classes consists of the three principles of Identity, Contradiction, and Excluded Middle ; the second comprehends the principle of Reason and Consequent alone. This classification is founded both on the different reciprocal connection of the laws, and on the different nature of their results.

In the first place, in regard to the difference of connection between the laws themselves, it is at once evident that the first three stand in a far more proximate relation to each other than to the fourth. The first three are, indeed, so intimately connected, that though it has not even been attempted to carry them up into a higher principle, and though the various and contradictory endeavours that have been made to elevate one or other into an antecedent, and to degrade others into consequents, have only shown, by their failure, the impossibility of reducing the three to one ; still so intimate is their connection, that each in fact supposes the others. They are like the three sides of a triangle ; not the same, not reducible to unity, each pretending with equal right to a prior consideration, and each, if considered first, giving in its own existence the existence of the other two. This intimacy of relation does not subsist between the principle of Reason and Consequent and the three other laws ; they do not, in the same necessary manner, suggest each other in thought. The explanation of this is found in the different nature of their results ; and this is the second subject of our consideration.[a]

In the second place, then, the distinction of the four

LECT.
VI.

General observations in relation to the four fundamental laws of thought. These fall into two classes.

This classification founded, 1°. On the difference of connection between the laws themselves.

---

[a] For a later development of the distinction here indicated, see *Discussions,* p. 602 *et seq.*—ED.

LECT.
VI.

T. On the
difference
of the end
which the
two classes
severally
accomplish.

laws into two classes is not only warranted by the
difference of their mutual dependence in thought, but,
likewise, by the difference of the end which the two
classes severally accomplish. For the first three laws
not only stand apart by themselves, (forming, as it
were, a single principle viewed in three different aspects,) but they necessitate a result very different, both
in kind and in degree, from that determined by the
law of Reason and Consequent. The difference in
their result consists in this,—Whatever violates the
laws, whether of Identity, of Contradiction, or of Excluded Middle, we feel to be absolutely impossible, not
only in thought but in existence. Thus we cannot
attribute even to Omnipotence the power of making
a thing different from itself, of making a thing at once
to be and not to be, of making a thing neither to be
nor not to be. These three laws thus determine to
us the sphere of possibility and of impossibility; and
this not merely in thought but in reality, not only
logically but metaphysically. Very different is the
result of the law of Reason and Consequent. This
principle merely excludes from the sphere of positive
thought what we cannot comprehend; for whatever
we comprehend, that through which we comprehend
it is its reason. What, therefore, violates the law of
Reason and Consequent merely, in virtue of this law
becomes a logical zero; that is, we are compelled to
think it as unthinkable, but not to think it, though
actually non-existent subjectively or in thought, as
therefore necessarily non-existent objectively or in
reality. And why, it may be asked, does the law of
Reason and Consequent not equally determine the
sphere of general possibility, as the laws of Identity,
Contradiction, and Excluded Middle? Why are we

to view the unthinkable in the one case not to be equally impossible in reality, as the unthinkable in the other? Some philosophers have, on the one hand, asserted to the Deity the power of reconciling contradictions;[a] while, on the other, a greater number have made the conceivable in human thought the gauge of the possible in existence. What warrants us, it may be asked, to condemn these opposite procedures as equally unphilosophical? In answer to this, though the matter belongs more properly to Metaphysic than to Logic, I may say a few words, which, however, I am aware, cannot, by many of you, be as yet adequately understood.

To deny the universal application of the first three laws, is, in fact, to subvert the reality of thought; and as this subversion is itself an act of thought, it in fact annihilates itself.

When, for example, I say that A is, and then say that A is not, by the second assertion I sublate or take away what, by the first assertion, I posited or laid down; thought, in the one case, undoing by negation what, in the other, it had by affirmation done. But when it is asserted, that A existing and A non-existing are at once true, what does this imply? It implies that negation and affirmation correspond to nothing out of the mind,—that there is no agreement, no disagreement between thought and its objects; and this is tantamount to saying that truth and falsehood are merely empty sounds. For if we only think by affirmation and negation, and if these are only as they are exclusive of each other, it follows, that unless existence and non-existence be opposed objectively in the same manner as affirmation and negation are

Marginal notes:
LECT. VL.

Two counter opinions regarding the limits of objective possibility.

The respective spheres of the two classes of the laws of thought defined and illustrated.

To deny the universal application of the first three laws is to subvert the reality of thought.

a Compare Le Clerc, *Logica*, part ii. c. 3.—ED.

LECT.
VI.

opposed subjectively, all our thought is a mere illusion. Thus it is, that those who would assert the possibility of contradictories being at once true, in fact annihilate the possibility of truth itself, and the whole significance of thought.

But this is not involved in the denial of the universal application of the law of Reason and Consequent.

But this is not the case when we deny the universal, the absolute, application of the law of Reason and Consequent. When I say that a thing may be, of which I cannot conceive the possibility, (that is, by conceiving it as the consequent of a certain reason,) I only say that thought is limited; but within its limits, I do not deny, I do not subvert, its truth. But how, it may be asked, is it shown that thought is thus limited? How is it shown that the inconceivable is not an index of the impossible, and that those philosophers who have employed it as the criterion of the absurd, are themselves guilty of absurdity? This is a matter which will come under our consideration at another time and in its proper place; at present it will be sufficient to state in general, that the hypothesis which makes the thinkable the measure of the possible brings the principle of Reason and Consequent at once into collision with the three higher laws, and this hypothesis itself is thus reduced at once to contradiction and absurdity. For if we take a comprehensive view of the phænomena of thought, we shall find that all that we can positively think, that is, all that is within the jurisdiction of the law of Reason and Consequent, lies between two opposite poles of thought, which, as exclusive of each other, cannot, on the principles of Identity and Contradiction, both be true, but of which, on the principle of Excluded Middle, the one or the other must. Let us take, for example, any of the general objects of our knowledge. Let us take

This law shows in general not to be the measure of objective possibility.

body, or rather, since body as extended is included under extension, let us take extension itself, or space. Now extension alone will exhibit to us two pairs of contradictory inconceivables, that is, in all, four incomprehensibles, but of which, though all are equally unthinkable, and, on the hypothesis in question, all, therefore, equally impossible, we are compelled, by the law of Excluded Middle, to admit some two as true and necessary.

LECT.
VI.

Extension, then, may be viewed either as a whole or as a part; and, in each aspect, it affords us two incogitable contradictories. ' 1', Taking it as a whole : —space, it is evident, must either be limited, that is, have an end, a circumference; or unlimited, that is, have no end, no circumference. These are contradictory suppositions; both, therefore, cannot, but one must, be true. Now let us try positively to comprehend, positively to conceive, the possibility of either of these two mutually exclusive alternatives. Can we represent or realise in thought extension as absolutely limited ? in other words, can we mentally hedge round the whole of space, conceive it absolutely bounded, that is, so that beyond its boundary there is no outlying, no surrounding space ? This is impossible. Whatever compass of space we may enclose by any limitation of thought, we shall find that we have no difficulty in transcending these limits. Nay, we shall find that we cannot but transcend them; for we are unable to think any extent of space except as within a still ulterior space, of which, let us think till the powers of thinking fail, we can never reach the circumference. It is thus impossible for us to think space as a totality, that is, as absolutely bounded, but all-containing. We may, therefore, lay down this first

By reference to Extension, 1°, As a Whole.

Space or extension as absolutely bounded unthinkable.

extreme as inconceivable. We cannot think space as limited.

Space as limited inconceivable, as contradictory.

Let us now consider its contradictory; can we comprehend the possibility of infinite or unlimited space? To suppose this is a direct contradiction in terms; it is to comprehend the incomprehensible. We think, we conceive, we comprehend, a thing, only as we think it as within or under something else; but to do this of the infinite is to think the infinite as finite, which is contradictory and absurd.

Objection from the name and notion of the Infinite obviated.

Now here it may be asked, how have we then the word *infinite?* How have we the notion which this word expresses? The answer to this question is contained in the distinction of positive and negative

Distinction of positive and negative thought and notion.

thought. We have a positive concept of a thing, when we think it by the qualities of which it is the complement. But as the attribution of qualities is an affirmation, as affirmation and negation are relatives, and as relatives are known only in and through each other, we cannot, therefore, have a consciousness of the affirmation of any quality, without having at the same time the correlative consciousness of its negation. Now, the one consciousness is a positive, the other consciousness is a negative notion. But, in point of fact, a negative notion is only the negation of a notion; we think only by the attribution of certain qualities, and the negation of these qualities and of this attribution, is simply, in so far, a denial of our thinking at all. As affirmation always suggests negation, every positive notion must likewise suggest a negative notion; and as language is the reflex of thought, the positive and negative notions are expressed by positive and negative names. Thus it is with the infinite. The finite is the only object of real

or positive thought; it is that alone which we think
by the attribution of determinate characters; the
infinite, on the contrary, is conceived only by the
thinking away of every character by which the finite
was conceived; in other words, we conceive it only
as inconceivable. This relation of the infinite to the
finite is shown, indeed, in the terms by which it is
expressed in every language. Thus in Latin, *infinitum;*
in Greek, ἄπειρον; in German, *unendlich;* in all of
which original tongues the word expressive of the
infinite is only a negative expression of the finite or
limited. Thus the very objection from the existence
of a name and notion of the infinite, when analysed,
only proves more clearly that the infinite is no object
of thought; that we conceive it, not in itself, but only
in correlation and contrast to the finite.

The indefinite is, however, sometimes confounded
with the infinite; though there are hardly two notions
which, without being contradictory, differ more widely.
The indefinite has a subjective, the infinite an objective relation. The one is merely the negation of the
actual apprehension of limits, the other the negation
of the possible existence of limits.

But to return whence we have been carried, it is
manifest that we can no more realise the thought or
conception of infinite, unbounded, or unlimited space,
than we can realise the conception of a finite or absolutely bounded space. But these two inconceivables
are reciprocal contradictories, and if we are unable to
comprehend the possibility of either, while, however,
on the principle of Excluded Middle one or other must
be admitted, the hypothesis is manifestly false, that proposes the subjective or formal law of Reason and Consequent as the criterion of real or objective possibility.

This further
shows by
reference to
Extension,
F, As a
Part.

It is needless to show that the same result is given by the experiment made on extension considered as a part, as divisible. Here, if we attempt to divide extension in thought, we shall neither, on the one hand, succeed in conceiving the possibility of an absolute minimum of space, that is, a minimum *ex hypothesi* extended, but which cannot be conceived as divisible into parts, nor, on the other, of carrying on this division to infinity. But as these are contradictory opposites, they again afford a similar refutation of the hypothesis in question.

F, By reference to the Law of Reason and Consequent itself.

But the same conclusion is reached by simply considering the law of Reason and Consequent in itself. This law enjoins,—Think nothing without a reason why we must think it, that is, think nothing except as contained in, as evolved out of, something else which we already know. Now this reason,—this something else,—in obedience to this very law, must, as itself known, be itself a consequent of some other antecedent; and this antecedent be again the consequent of some anterior or higher reason; and so on, *ad infinitum.* But the human mind is not possessed of infinite powers, or of an infinite series of reasons and consequents; on the contrary, its faculties are very limited, and its stock of knowledge is very small. To erect this law, therefore, into a standard of existence, is, in fact, to bring down the infinitude of the universe to the finitude of man,—a proceeding than

The laws of Reason and Consequent, &c. reducible to a higher principle.

which nothing can be imagined more absurd. The fact is, that the law of Reason and Consequent can, with the law of Cause and Effect, the law of Substance and Phœnomenon, &c., be, if I am not mistaken, all reduced to one higher principle; a principle which explains from the very limitation of the human

mind, from the very imbecility of its powers, a great
variety of phænomena, which, from the liberality of
philosophers, have obtained for their solution a number of positive and special principles. This, however,
is a discussion which would here be out of place.[a]
What, however, has been said may suffice to show,
that, while the first three laws of thought are of an
absolute and universal cogency, the fourth is only of
a cogency relative and particular; that while the former determine the possibility, not only of all thought
but of all real knowledge, the latter only regulates the
validity of mediate or reflective thought. The laws
of Identity, Contradiction, and Excluded Middle are,
therefore, not only logical but metaphysical principles,
the law of Reason and Consequent a logical principle
alone; a doctrine which is, however, the converse of
what is generally taught.

I proceed, now, to say a few words on the general
influence which these laws exert upon the operations
of thinking. These operations, however various and
multiform they may seem, are so governed in all their
manifestations by the preceding laws, that no thought
can pretend to validity and truth which is not in
consonance with, which is not governed by, them.
For man can recognise that alone as real and assured,
which the laws of his understanding sanction; and
he cannot but regard that as false and unreal, which
these laws condemn. From this, however, it by no
means follows that what is thought in conformity
to these laws is, therefore, true; for the sphere of
thought is far wider than the sphere of reality, and
no inference is valid from the correctest thinking of
an object to its actual existence. While these laws.

a See *Discussions*, p. 609.—ED.

therefore, are the highest criterion of the non-reality of an object, they are no criterion at all of its reality; and they thus stand to existence in a negative and not in a positive relation. And what I now say of the fundamental principles of thought in general, holds equally of all their proximate and special applications, that is, of the whole of Logic. Logic, as I have already explained, considering the form alone of thought to the exclusion of its matter, can draw no conclusion from the correctness of the manner of thinking an object to the reality of the object itself.

The true relations of Logic overlooked in two ways:— 1. Logic erroneously held to be the positive standard of truth.

Yet among modern, nay recent, philosophers, two opposite doctrines have sprung up, which, on opposite sides, have overlooked the true relations of Logic. "One party of philosophers defining truth in general, —the absolute harmony of our thoughts and cognitions,—divide truth into formal (or logical) and

The division of truth into formal and material,— criticised.

material (or metaphysical), according as that harmony is in consonance with the laws of formal thought, or, over and above, with the laws of real knowledge." The criterion of formal truth they place in the principles of Contradiction and of sufficient Reason, enouncing that what is non-contradictory and consequent is formally true. This criterion, which is positive and immediate of formal truth, (inasmuch as what is non-contradictory and consequent can always be thought as possible), they style a negative and mediate criterion of material truth: as what is self-contradictory and logically inconsequent is in reality impossible; at the same time, what is not self-contradictory and not logically inconsequent is not, however, to be regarded as having an actual existence.

a See Kant, Logik, Einleitung, vii.; Krug, Logik, § 22; Fries, Lo- gik, § 42.—ED.

But here the foundation is treacherous; the notion of truth is false. When we speak of truth, we are not satisfied with knowing that a thought harmonises with a certain system of thoughts and cognitions; but, over and above, we require to be assured that what we think is real, and is as we think it to be. Are we satisfied on this point, we then regard our thoughts as true; whereas if we are not satisfied of this, we deem them false, how well soever they may quadrate with any theory or system. It is not, therefore, in any absolute harmony of mere thought that truth consists, but solely in the correspondence of our thoughts with their objects. The distinction of formal and material truth is thus not only unsound in itself, but opposed to the notion of truth universally held, and embodied in all languages. But if this distinction be inept, the title of Logic, as a positive standard of truth, must be denied; it can only be a negative criterion, being conversant with thoughts and not with things, with the possibility and not with the actuality of existence.[*]

The preceding inaccuracy is, however, of little moment compared with the heresy of another class of philosophers, to whose observations on this point I can, however, only allude. Some of you may, perhaps, find a difficulty in believing the statement, that there is a considerable party of philosophers, illustrious for the highest speculative talent, and whose systems, if not at present, were, a few years ago, the most celebrated, if not the most universally accredited, in Europe, who establish their metaphysical theories on the subversion of all logical truth.[β] I refer to those philosophers who hold that man is capable of

α Esser, *Logik*, p. 63-6.—ED.   β See above, p. 90, note a.—ED.

more than a relative notion of existence,—that he
is competent to a knowledge of absolute or infinite
being, (for these terms they use convertibly,) in an
identity of knowledge and existence, of himself and
the Divinity. This doctrine, which I shall not now
attempt to make you understand, is developed in very
various schemes, that is, the different philosophers
attempt, by very different and contradictory methods,
to arrive at the same end; all these systems, however, agree in this,—they are all at variance with the
four logical laws. Some, indeed, are established on
the express denial of the validity of these laws; and
others, without daring overtly to reject their authority, are still built in violation of their precept. In
fact, if contradiction remain a criterion of falsehood,
if Logic and the laws of thought be not viewed as
an illusion, the philosophy of the Absolute, in all its
forms, admits of the most direct and easy refutation.
But on this matter I only now touch, in order that
you may not be ignorant, that there are philosophers,
and philosophers of the highest name, who, in pursuit
of the phantom of absolute knowledge, are content to
repudiate relative knowledge, logic, and the laws of
thought. This hallucination is, however, upon the
wane, and as each of these theorists contradicts his
brother, Logic and Common Sense will at length re-
fute them all.

Mistake of
Reid in
regard to
Conception.
Before leaving the consideration of this subject, it
is necessary to notice a mistake of Dr Reid, which it
is not more remarkable that he should have committed, than that others have been found to follow and
applaud it, as the correction of a general error. In
the fourth *Essay on the Intellectual Powers,* and in
the third chapter, entitled *Mistakes concerning Con-*

ception," there is the following passage, which at once LECT.
VI. exhibits not only his own opinion, but the universality of the doctrine to which it is opposed :—

"There remains," he says, "another mistake con- Reid
quoted. cerning conception, which deserves to be noticed. It is—That our conception of things is a test of their possibility, so that, what we can distinctly conceive, we may conclude to be possible ; and of what is impossible, we can have no conception.

"This opinion has been held by philosophers for more than a hundred years, without contradiction or dissent, as far as I know ; and, if it be an error, it may be of some use to inquire into its origin, and the causes that it has been so generally received as a maxim whose truth could not be brought into doubt."

I may here observe that this limitation of the prevalence of the opinion in question to a very modern period is altogether incorrect ; it was equally prevalent in ancient times, and as many passages could easily be quoted from the Greek logicians alone as Dr Reid has quoted from the philosophers of the century prior to himself. Dr Reid goes on :—

"One of the fruitless questions agitated among the scholastic philosophers in the dark ages was—What is the criterion of truth? as if men could have any other way to distinguish truth from error, but by the right use of that power of judgment which God has given them.

"Descartes endeavoured to put an end to this controversy, by making it a fundamental principle in his system, that whatever we clearly and distinctly perceive, is true."

"To understand this principle of Descartes, it must

a Collected Works, p. 376-8.—ED.

LECT.
VI.

be observed, that he gave the name of *perception* to
every power of the human understanding; and in
explaining this very maxim, he tells us that sense,
imagination, and pure intellection, are only different
modes of perceiving, and so the maxim was understood by all his followers.

"The learned Dr Cudworth seems also to have
adopted this principle. 'The criterion of true knowledge,' says he, ' is only to be looked for in our knowledge and conceptions themselves: for the entity of
all theoretical truth is nothing else but clear intel-
ligibility, and whatever is clearly conceived is an
entity and a truth; but that which is false, Divine
power itself cannot make it to be clearly and distinctly understood. A falsehood can never be clearly
conceived or apprehended to be true.' (*Eternal and
Immutable Morality*, p. 172, &c.)

"This Cartesian maxim seems to me to have led
the way to that now under consideration, which seems
to have been adopted as the proper correction of the
former. When the authority of Descartes declined,
men began to see that we may clearly and distinctly
conceive what is not true, but thought, that our conception, though not in all cases a test of truth, might
be a test of possibility.

"This indeed seems to be a necessary consequence
of the received doctrine of ideas; it being evident
that there can be no distinct image, either in the mind
or anywhere else, of that which is impossible. The
ambiguity of the word *conceive*, which we observed,
Essay i. chap. i., and the common phraseology of
saying, *we cannot conceive such a thing*, when we would
signify that we think it impossible, might likewise
contribute to the reception of this doctrine.

" But whatever was the origin of this opinion, it
seems to prevail universally, and to be received as a maxim.

" 'The bare having an idea of the proposition proves the thing not to be impossible; for of an impossible proposition there can be no idea.'—Dr Samuel Clarke.

" 'Of that which neither does nor can exist we can have no idea.'—Lord Bolingbroke.

" 'The measure of impossibility to us is inconceivableness, that of which we can have no idea, but that reflecting upon it, it appears to be nothing, we pronounce to be impossible.'—Abernethy.

" 'In every idea is implied the possibility of the existence of its object, nothing being clearer than that there can be no idea of an impossibility, or conception of what cannot exist.'—Dr Price.

" 'Impossibile est cujus nullam notionem formare possumus; possibile e contra, cui aliqua respondet notio.'—Wolfii *Ontologia*.

" 'It is an established maxim in metaphysics, that whatever the mind conceives, includes the idea of possible existence, or, in other words, that nothing we imagine is absolutely impossible.'—D. Hume.

" It were easy to muster up many other respectable authorities for this maxim, and I have never found one that called it in question.

" If the maxim be true in the extent which the famous Wolfius has given it in the passage above quoted, we shall have a short road to the determination of every question about the possibility or impossibility of things. We need only look into our own breast, and that, like the Urim and Thummim, will give an infallible answer. If we can conceive the

thing, it is possible; if not, it is impossible. And,
surely, every man may know whether he can conceive
what is affirmed, or not.

"Other philosophers have been satisfied with one
half of the maxim of Wolfius. They say, that whatever we can conceive is possible; but they do not
say, that whatever we cannot conceive is impossible."

On this I may remark, that Dr Reid's criticism of
Wolf must be admitted in so far as that philosopher
maintains our inability to conceive a thing as possible,
to be the rule on which we are entitled to pronounce
it impossible. But Dr Reid now advances a doctrine
which I cannot but regard as radically erroneous.

"I cannot help thinking even this to be a mistake which philosophers have been unwarily led into,
from the causes before mentioned. My reasons are
these :—

"1. Whatever is said to be possible or impossible
is expressed by a proposition. Now, what is it to
conceive a proposition? I think it is no more than
to understand distinctly its meaning. I know no
more that can be meant by simple apprehension or
conception, when applied to a proposition. The
axiom, therefore, amounts to this :—Every proposition, of which you understand the meaning distinctly, is possible. I am persuaded that I understand as distinctly the meaning of this proposition,
*Any two sides of a triangle are together equal to the
third*, as of this, *Any two sides of a triangle are together greater than the third;* yet the first of these is
impossible."

Criticised. Now this is a singular misunderstanding of the
sense in which it has been always held by philosophers, that what is contradictory is conceived as

inconceivable and impossible.* No philosopher, I
make bold to say, ever dreamt of denying that we
can distinctly understand the meaning of the proposition, the terms of which we recognise to be contradictory, and, as contradictory, to annihilate each
other. When we enounce the proposition, A *is not-*
A, we clearly comprehend the separate meaning of the
terms *A* and *not-A*, and also the import of the assertion of their identity. But this very understanding
consists in the consciousness that the two terms are
contradictories, and that as such it is impossible to
unite them in a mental judgment, though they stand
united in a verbal proposition. If we attempt this,
the two mutually exclusive terms not only cannot be
thought as one, but in fact annihilate each other;
and thus the result, in place of a positive judgment,
is a negation of thought. So far Dr Reid is wrong.
But he is not guilty of the absurdity attributed
to him by Dr Gleig; he does not say, as by that
writer he is made to say, that "any two sides of
a triangle may be conceived to be equal to the third,
as distinctly as any two sides of a triangle may be
conceived to be greater than the third." ᵖ These are
not Dr Reid's words, and nothing he says warrants the
attribution of such expressions to him, in the sense in
which they are attributed. He is made to hold, not
merely that we can understand two terms as contradictory, but that we are able to combine them in the
unity of thought. After the passage already quoted,
Reid goes on to illustrate, in various points of view,
the supposed error of the philosophers; but as all he

says on this head originates in the misconception already shown of the opinion he controverts, it is needless to take any further notice of his arguments.

Postulates of Logic.
We have thus considered the conditions of Logic, in so far as certain laws or principles are prescribed; we have now to consider its conditions, in so far as certain postulates are demanded. Of these there are more than one, but one alone it is here requisite to signalise; for although it be necessarily supposed in the science, strange to say, it has, by logical writers, not only been always passed over in silence, but frequently and inconsistently violated. This postulate I comprise in the following paragraph :—

Par. XVIII.
The logical postulate.
¶ XVIII. The only postulate of Logic which requires an articulate enouncement is the demand, that before dealing with a judgment or reasoning expressed in language, the import of its terms should be fully understood; in other words, Logic postulates to be allowed to state explicitly in language all that is implicitly contained in the thought."

This postulate cannot be refused.
This postulate cannot be refused. In point of fact, as I have said, Logic has always proceeded on it, in overtly expressing all the steps of the mental process in reasoning,—all the propositions of a syllogism; whereas, in common parlance, one at least of these steps or propositions is usually left unexpressed. This postulate, as we shall have occasion to observe in the sequel, though a fundamental condition of Logic, has not been consistently acted on by logicians

a See Appendix VI.—Ed.

in their development of the science; and from this omission have arisen much confusion and deficiency and error in our present system of Logic. The illustration of this postulate will approprintely find its place on occasion of its applications. I now articulately state it, because it immediately follows in order the general axioms of the science; and, at present, I only beg that you will bear it in mind. I may, however, before leaving the subject, observe, (what has already, I believe, been mentioned), that Aristotle states of Syllogistic, and, of course, his statement applies to Logic in general, that the doctrine of syllogism deals, not with the external expression of reasoning, in ordinary language, but with the internal reasoning of the mind itself." But of this again and more fully, in the proper places.

In like manner, we might here, as is done in Mathematics, premise certain definitions; but these it will be more convenient to state as they occur in the progress of our development. I, therefore, pass on to the Second Section of the Doctrine of Elements, which is occupied with the products of thought; in other words, with the processes regulated by the previous conditions.

LECT. VI.

This postulate implied in the doctrine of Syllogism, according to Aristotle.

a *Anal. Post.*, i. 10.—ED.

LECTURE VII.

STOICHEIOLOGY.

SECTION II.—OF THE PRODUCTS OF THOUGHT.

I. ENNOEMATIC—OF CONCEPTS OR NOTIONS.

A. OF CONCEPTS IN GENERAL.

LECT.
VII.

I CONCLUDED, in my last Lecture, all that I think it necessary to say in regard to the Fundamental Laws of Thought, or the necessary conditions of the thinkable. The discussion, I am aware, must have been found somewhat dry, and even abstruse; not that there is the smallest difficulty in regard to the apprehension of the laws themselves, for these are all self-evident propositions, but because, though it is necessary in a systematic view of Logic to commence with the elementary principles of thought, it is impossible, in speaking of these and their application, not to employ expressions of the most abstract generality, and even not to suppose a certain acquaintance with words and things, which, however, only find their explanation in the subsequent development of the science.

The Products of Thought,—Concepts, Judgments, and Reasonings.

Having considered, therefore, the four Laws of Thought, with the one Postulate of Logic, which constitute the First Section of the Doctrine of Logical Elements, I now proceed to the Second,—that which is conversant about Logical Products. These pro-

ducts, though identical in kind, are of three different
degrees ; for while Concepts, Judgments, and Reasonings, are all equally the products of the same Faculty
of Comparison, they still fall into three classes, as
the act, and, consequently, the result of the act, is
of a greater or a less simplicity. These three degrees
are all in fact, strictly, only modifications of the
second, as both concepts and reasonings may be reduced to judgments ; for the act of judging, that is,
the act of affirming or denying one thing of another
in thought, is that in which the understanding or
Faculty of Comparison is essentially expressed. By
anticipation :—A concept is a judgment ; for, on the
one hand, it is nothing but the result of a foregone
judgment, or series of judgments, fixed and recorded
in a word,—a sign, and it is only amplified by the
annexation of a new attribute, through a continuance
of the same process. On the other hand, as a concept
is thus the synthesis or complexion, and the record, I
may add, of one or more prior acts of judgment, it
can, it is evident, be analysed into these again ; every
concept is, in fact, a judgment or a fasciculus of judgments,—these judgments only not explicitly developed
in thought, and not formally expressed in terms.

Again, a reasoning is a judgment ; for a reasoning
is only the affirmation of the connection of two things
with a third, and, through that third, with each other.
It is thus only the same function of thought which is
at work in Conception, Judgment, and Reasoning ; and
these express no real, no essential, distinction of operation, but denote only the different relations in which
we may regard the indivisible act of thought. Thus,
the consideration of concepts cannot be effected out of
all relation to, and without even some anticipation of,

LECT.
VII.

These are
all products
of Compari-
son, and all
modifica-
tions of
judgment.

the doctrine of judgments. This being premised, I now proceed to the consideration of the Products of Thought, viewed in the three relations or the three degrees, of Concepts, Judgments, and Reasonings.

Under the Second Section of Stoicheiology, Concepts or Notions form the First Chapter.

1 Of Concepts or Notions, order of discussion.

Now in treating of Concepts, the order I shall follow is this,—I shall, in the first place, treat of them in general ; in the second, treat of them in special. Under the former, or general, head, will be considered, 1°, What they are ; 2°, How they are produced. Under the latter, or special, head, they will be considered under their various relations. And here, I may observe, that as you obtain no information from Dr Whately in regard to the primary laws of thought,—these laws being in fact apparently unknown to every British logician old or new,—so you will find but little or no aid from his *Elements* towards an understanding of the doctrine of concepts. His omission, in this respect, cannot be excused by his error in regard to the object-matter of Logic ; that object, you will recollect, being on his view, or rather one of his views, not thought in general or the products of the comparative faculty in their three degrees, but reasoning or argumentation alone ; for even on the hypothesis that Logic is thus limited, still as the doctrine of reasoning can only be scientifically evolved out of the doctrine of concepts, the consideration of the latter forms the indispensable condition of a satisfactory treatment of the former. But not only is

Whately's omission of the doctrine of Concepts.

α [Hume, *Treatise of Human Nature*, Bk. I. part iii. § 7. Jac. Thomasius, *Physica*, p. 285] [c. xliii. § 112, where he holds that simple apprehension is impossible without judgment. Compare also Krug, *Logik*, § 23, Anm. ii. p. 70. —ED.]

Whately's doctrine of concepts, or, in his language, of LECT.
"the process of simple apprehension," meagre and ────
imperfect, it is even necessary to forewarn you, that it
leads to confusion and error. There is a fundamental
distinction of what is called the *Extension* and the
Comprehension of notions,—a distinction which, in
fact, as you will find, forms the very cardinal point on
which the whole theory of Logic turns. But not only
is this distinction not explained, it is not even articulately stated, nay, the very words which logicians
have employed for the expression of this contrast, are
absolutely used as synonymous and convertible. Instead, therefore, of referring you for information in
regard to our present object of consideration to Dr
Whately, I am sorry to be compelled to caution you
against putting confidence in his guidance. But to
return. The following I dictate as the title of the
first head to be considered.

A. Of Concepts or Notions in General: What are
    they?

In answering this question, let us, first, consider the
meaning of the expressions ; and, secondly, the nature
of the thing expressed.

¶ XIX. *Concept* or *notion*, (ἔννοια, ἐννόημα,
νόημα, ἐπίνοια,[a] *conceptio, notio*), are terms em-

a In Greek, the terms ἔννοια (ἐννοη-
τικός), ἐννόημα (ἐννοηματικός), ἐπίνοια
(ἐπινοηματικός), νόημα, to say nothing
of ἐνθύμημα (ἐνθυμηματικός), are all
more or less objectionable, as all
more or less ambiguously used for
the object or product of thought, in
an act of Conception, or, as it has
been usually called by the logicians,

Simple Apprehension. See Blemmidas, *Epitome Logica* (c. v. Περὶ
Ἐννοίας, p. 31, ed. 1605.—ED.);
Eugenios, *Logica* (Λογική, c. ii. p.
170, Leipsic, 1766.—ED.) Stephanus, *Thesaurus*, v. Νοῦς; Hocker,
Clavis Phil. Arist., v. Νόημα, p.
227 et seq. ; Micraelius, *Lexicon Philosophicum*, v. Νόημα, p. 890, and p.

LECT.
VII.

a. Mean-
ing of the
terms.

ployed as convertible, but while they denote the same thing, they denote it in a different point of view. *Conception*, the act of which *concept* is the result, expresses the act of comprehending or grasping up into unity the various qualities by which an object is characterised; *Notion* (*notio*), again, signifies either the act of apprehending, signalising, that is, the remarking or taking note of the various notes, marks, or characters of an object, which its qualities afford; or the result of that act.

Illustrated
—employ-
ment of the
terms animo
vel mente
concipere,
and animi
conceptus.

In Latin, the word *concipere*, in its many various applications, always expresses, as the etymology would indicate, the process of *embracing or comprehending the many into the one*, as could be shown by an articulate analysis of the phrases in which the term occurs. It was, accordingly, under this general signification, that this word and its derivatives were analogically applied to the operation of mind. *Animo vel mente concipere*, as used by Cicero, Pliny, Seneca, and other Roman writers, means to *comprehend* or *understand*, that is, to embrace a multitude of different objects by their common qualities in one act of thought; and *animi conceptus* was, in like manner, applied by the ancient writers to denote this operation,

Of conci-
pere, con-
ceptus, and
conceptio,
without ad-
junct.

or its result. The employment of *concipere*, *conceptus*, and *conceptio*, as technical terms, in the philosophy of mind, without the explanatory adjunct, was of a later

80 [v. Αἰσθήματα. Cf. p. 310, v. *Conceptus*; p. 833, v. *Intenlio.*—ED.] On νοήματα, see Aristotle, *De Interp.*, c. 1, and Waitz, *Commentarius*, p. 327. In Aristotle, *De Anima*, L. iii. cc. 6 (7), 7 (8), 8 (9), etc., νοήματα are clearly equivalent

to *concepts* in our meaning; [c. 6, Ἡ μὲν οὖν τῶν ἀδιαιρέτων νόησις ἐν τούτοις, περὶ ἃ οὐκ ἔστι τὸ ψεῦδος· ἐν οἷς δὲ καὶ τὸ ψεῦδος καὶ τὸ ἀληθές, σύνθεσίς τις ἤδη νοημάτων, ὥσπερ ἓν ὄντων. κ.τ.λ.—ED.]

introduction,—was, indeed, only possible after they had been long familiarly used in a psychological relation. But when so introduced, they continued to be employed by philosophers in general in their proper signification as convertible with *thought* or *comprehension*, and as opposed to the mere *apprehension* of Sense or Imagination. Not, indeed, that examples enough may not be adduced of their abusive application to our immediate cognitions of individual objects, long before Mr Stewart formally applied the term *conception* to a certain accidental form of representation,—to the simple reproduction or repetition of an act of perception in imagination.[a] In using the terms *conception* and *concept* in the sense which I have explained, I, therefore, employ them not only in strict conformity to their grammatical meaning, but to the meaning which they have generally obtained among philosophers.

The term *notion*, like *conception*, expresses both an act and its product. I shall, however, as has commonly been done, use it only in this latter relation. This word has, like *conception*, been sometimes abusively applied to denote not only our knowledge of things by their common characters, but, likewise, to include the mere presentations of Sense and representations of Phantasy. This abusive employment has, however, not been so frequent in reference to this term as to the term *conception;* but it must be acknowledged, that nothing can be imagined more vague and vacillating than the meaning attached to *notion* in the writings of all British philosophers, without exception. So much for the expressions *concept* and *notion*. I now go on to that which they express.

a See *Lectures on Metaphysics,* vol. ii. p. 261.—Ed.

LECT.
VII.

Par. XX.
Concepts,—
b. Nature of
the thing.

¶ XX.[a]—In our consciousness,—apprehension, of an individual object, there may be distinguished the two following cognitions :—1°, The immediate and irrespective knowledge we have of the individual object, as a complement of certain qualities or characters, considered simply as belonging to itself; 2°, The mediate and relative knowledge we have of this object, as comprising qualities or characters common to it with other objects.

The former of these cognitions is that contained in the Presentations of Sense, external and internal, and Representations of Imagination. They are only of the individual or singular. The latter is that contained in the Concepts of the Understanding, and is a knowledge of the common, general, or universal.

The conceiving an object is, therefore, its recognition mediately through a concept; and a Concept is the cognition or idea of the general character or characters, point or points, in which a plurality of objects coincide.

Concepts,—
their nature
illustrated
by reference
to the his-
tory of our
knowledge.

Objects are
originally
presented in
confused
and imper-
fect percep-
tions.

This requires some illustration, and it will be best afforded by considering the history of our knowledge. Our mental activity is not first exerted in an apprehension of the common properties of things. On the contrary, objects are originally presented to us in confused and imperfect perceptions. The rude materials furnished by Sense, retained in Memory, reproduced by Reminiscence, and represented in Imagination, the Understanding elaborates into a higher knowledge,

---

a On this and three following paragraphs apply Leibnitz's distinction of Intuitive and Symbolical Knowledge, see *Opera* II. i. p. 14 *et seq.*— [*Meditationes de Cognitione, Veritate, et Ideis.*—Ed.]

simply by means of Comparison and Abstraction. The LECT.
VII.
primary act of Comparison is exerted upon the individual objects of Perception and Imagination alone.
In the multitude and complexity of these objects,
certain attributes are found to produce similar, others
to produce dissimilar, impressions. The observation
of this fact determines a reflective consideration of
their properties. Objects are intentionally compared
together for the purpose of discovering their similarities and differences. When things are found to agree
or to disagree in certain respects, the consciousness is,
by an act of volition, concentrated upon the objects
which thus partially agree, and, in them, upon those
qualities in or through which they agree ; and by
this concentration,—which constitutes the act called
Attention,—what is effected ? On the objects and
qualities, thus attentively considered, a strong light
is shed ; but precisely in proportion as these are
illuminated in consciousness, the others, to which
we do not attend, are thrown into obscurity.
The result of Attention, by concentrating the mind
upon certain qualities, is thus to withdraw or abstract
it from all else. In technical language, we are said *to
prescind* the phænomena which we exclusively consider. *To prescind, to attend,* and *to abstract,* are
merely different but correlative names for the same
process ; and the first two are nearly convertible.
When we are said *to prescind* a quality, we are merely
supposed to attend to that quality exclusively ; and
when we abstract, we are properly said *to abstract
from,* that is, to throw other attributes out of account.
I may observe that the term *abstraction* is very often
abusively employed. By Abstraction we are frequently
said to attend exclusively to certain phænomena,—

those, to wit, which we abstract; whereas, the term *abstraction* is properly applied to the qualities which we abstract from, and by abstracting from some, we are enabled to consider others more attentively. Attention and Abstraction are only the same process viewed in different relations. They are, as it were, the positive and negative poles of the same act.[a]

By Comparison, the points of resemblance among things being thus discovered, and by Attention constituted into exclusive objects; by the same act they are also reduced in consciousness from multitude to unity. What is meant by this will be apparent from the following considerations.

The reduction of objects from multitude to unity,—explained and illustrated.
We are conscious to ourselves that we can repeat our acts of consciousness,—that we can think the same thought over and over. This act, or this thought, is always in reality the same, though manifested at different times: for no one can imagine that in the repetition of one and the same thought, he has a plurality of thoughts; for he is conscious, that it is one and the same thought which is repeated, so long as its contents remain identical.

Thought is one and the same, while its contents are identical.

Objects are to be the same when we are unable to distinguish their cognitions.
Now this relation of absolute similarity which subsists between the repetitions of the same thought, is found to hold between our representations of the resembling qualities of objects. Two objects have similar qualities only as these qualities afford a similar presentation in sense or a similar representation in imagination, and qualities are to us completely similar, when we are unable to distinguish their cognitions. But what we cannot distinguish, is, to us, the same; therefore, objects which determine undistinguishable

a See *Lectures on Metaphysics*, vol. *Logik*, § 49.—En. [Schulze, *Logik*, ii. p. 292, and Bachmann, *Logik*, § § 28; Drobisch, *Logik*, § 14, p. 11 et 44. Compare Kant, *Logik*, § 6; Krug, sq.]

impressions upon us, are perceived and represented in the same mental modification, and are subjectively to us precisely as if they were objectively identical.

But the consciousness of identity is not merely the result of the indiscernible similarity of total objects, it is equally the result of the similarity of any of their parts,—partial characters. For by abstracting observation from the points in which objects differ, and limiting it to those in which they agree, we are able to consider them as identical in certain respects, however diverse they may appear to be in others, which, for the moment, we throw out of view. For example, let B, C, and D represent a series of individual objects, which all agree in possessing the resembling attributes of *y, y, y,* and severally differ in each respectively possessing the non-resembling attributes *i, o, u.* Now, in so far as we exclusively attend to the resembling qualities, we, in the first place, obscure or remove out of view their non-resembling characters, *i, o, u,* while we remain exclusively conscious of their resembling qualities, *y, y, y.* But in the second place, the qualities expressed by *y, y, y,* determine in us cognitive energies which we are unable to distinguish, and which we, therefore, consider as the same. We, therefore, view the three similar qualities in the three different objects as also identical; we consider the *y* in this, the *y* in that, and the *y* in the third object, as one, and in so far as the three objects participate in this oneness or identity, we regard them also as the same. In other words, we classify B, C, and D under *y; y* is the genus, B, C, and D are its individuals or species, severally distinguished from each other by the non-resembling properties, *i, o, u.* Now it is the points of similarity thus discovered and identified in the unity of consciousness, which constitute Concepts or Notions.

Generalisation.
It is evident that the same process of Comparison and Abstraction may be again performed on the concepts thus formed. They are, in like manner, compared together, and their points of resemblance noted, exclusively considered, and reduced to one in the synthesis of thought. This process is called *Generalisation*; that is, the process of evolving the general or one, out of the individual and manifold. Notions and concepts are also sometimes designated by the style of *general notions,—general conceptions.* This is superfluous, for, in propriety of speech, notions and concepts are, in their very nature, general; while the other cognitive modifications to which they are opposed,—perceptions and imaginations,—have, in like manner, their essence in their individuality.

Concepts or notions superfluously styled general.

Idea,— reason why not regularly employed, and sense in which it is occasionally used, by the Author.
By the way, you may have noticed that I never use the term *idea.* The reason of my non-employment of that word is this:—There is no possible diversity of meaning in which that term has not been usurped, and it would only confuse you, were I to attempt to enumerate and explain them. I may, however, occasionally not eschew the word, but if you ever hear it from me, I beg you to observe, that I apply it, in a loose and general signification, to comprehend the presentations of Sense, the representations of Phantasy, and the concepts or notions of the Understanding. We are in want of a generic term to express these; and the word *representation (representatio)*, which, since the time of Leibnitz, has been commonly used by the philosophers of the Continent, I have restricted to denote what only it can in propriety express, the immediate object or product of Imagination. We

arc, likewise, in want of a general term to express what is common to the presentations of Perception, and the representations of Phantasy, that is, their individuality and immediacy. The Germans express this by the term *Anschauung*, which can only be translated by *intuition*, (as it is in Latin by Germans), which literally means *a looking at.* This expression has, however, been preoccupied in English to denote the apprehension we have of self-evident truths, and its application in a different signification would, therefore, be, to a certain extent, liable to ambiguity. I shall, therefore, continue, for the present at least, to struggle on without such a common term, though the necessity thus imposed of always opposing presentation and representation to concept is both tedious and perplexing.

¶ XXI.—A Concept or Notion thus involves— 1°, The representation of a part only of the various attributes or characters of which an individual object is the sum; and, consequently, affords only a one-sided and inadequate knowledge of the things which are thought under it.

General Characters of Concepts.

Par. XXI. 1. A Concept affords only inadequate knowledge.

This is too simple to require any commentary. It is evident that when we think Socrates by any of the concepts,—*Athenian, Greek, European, man, biped, animal, being,*—we throw out of view the far greater number of characters of which Socrates is the complement, and those, likewise, which more proximately determine or constitute his individuality. It is, likewise, evident, that in proportion as we think him by a more general concept, we shall represent him by a smaller bundle of attributes, and, consequently, repre-

Explication.

sent him in a more partial and one-sided manner.
Thus, if we think him as *Athenian*, we shall think
him by a greater number of qualities than if we think
him by *Greek*; and, in like manner, our representation
will be less and less adequate, as we think him by
every higher concept in the series,—*European, man,
biped, animal, being*.

Par. XXII.
b. A Con-
cept affords
no absolute
object of
knowledge.
¶ XXII.—2°, A concept or notion, as the result
of a comparison, necessarily expresses a relation.
It is, therefore, not cognisable in itself, that is,
it affords no absolute or irrespective object of
knowledge, but can only be realised in consciousness by applying it, as a term of relation, to one
or more of the objects which agree in the point
or points of resemblance which it expresses.

This para-
graph con-
tains a key
to the mys-
tery of Ge-
neralisation
and Gene-
ral Terms.
In this paragraph, (if I may allude to what you may
not all be aware of,) is contained a key to the whole
mystery of Generalisation and General Terms; for the
whole disputes between the Conceptualists and Nominalists, (to say nothing of the Realists,) have only
arisen from concepts being regarded as affording
an irrespective and independent object of thought.[a]
This illusion has arisen from a very simple circumstance. Objects compared together are found to possess certain attributes, which, as producing indiscernible modifications in us, are to us absolutely similar.
They are, therefore, considered the same. The relation
of similarity is thus converted into identity, and the
real plurality of resembling qualities in nature is
factitiously reduced to a unity in thought; and this

[a] For a full account of this dis-   vol. ii. p. 296 et seq.—ED.
pute, see *Lectures on Metaphysics.*

unity obtains a name in which its relativity, not being
expressed, is still further removed from observation.
But the moment we attempt to represent to ourselves any of those concepts, any of these abstract
generalities, as absolute objects, by themselves, and
out of relation to any concrete or individual realities,
their relative nature at once reappears; for we find it
altogether impossible to represent any of the qualities
expressed by a concept, except as attached to some
individual and determinate object; and their whole
generality consists in this, that though we must
realise them in thought under some singular of the
class, we may do it under any.   Thus, for example,
we cannot actually represent the bundle of attributes
contained in the concept *man*, as an absolute object,
by itself, and apart from all that reduces it from a
general cognition to an individual representation.
We cannot figure in imagination any object adequate
to the general notion or term *man;* for the man to be
here imagined must be neither tall nor short, neither
fat nor lean, neither black nor white, neither man nor
woman, neither young nor old, but all and yet none
of these at once.   The relativity of our concepts is
thus shown in the contradiction and absurdity of the
opposite hypothesis.

LECTURE VIII.

STOICHEIOLOGY.

SECT. II.—OF THE PRODUCTS OF THOUGHT.

I.—ENNOEMATIC.

A. OF CONCEPTS IN GENERAL; B. IN SPECIAL—I. THEIR OBJECTIVE RELATION—QUANTITY.

LECT.
VIII.

Recapitula-
tion, with
further ex-
planation
and illustra-
tion.

IN our last Lecture, we began the Second Section of Stoicheiology,—the consideration of the product of Thought. The product of thought may be considered as Concepts, as Judgments, and as Reasonings; these, however, are not to be viewed as the results of different faculties, far less as processes independent of each other, for they are all only the product of the same energy in different degrees, or rather in simpler or more complex application to its objects.

In treating of Concepts, which form the subject of the First Chapter of this Second Section, I stated that I should first consider them in general, and then consider them in special; and, in my last Lecture, I had nearly concluded all that I deem it requisite under the former head to state in regard to their peculiar character, their origin, and their general accidents. I, first of all, explained the meaning of the two terms *concept* and *notion*, words convertible with each other, but still severally denoting a different aspect of the simple operation which they equally express; *notion* being relative to and expressing the apprehension—

the remarking—the taking note of the resembling attributes in objects; *concept*, the grasping up or synthesis of these in the unity of thought.

Having shown what was properly expressed by the terms *notion* and *concept* or *conception*, I went on to a more articulate explanation of that which they are employed to denote. And here I again stated what a Concept or Notion is in itself, and in contrast to a Presentation of Perception, or Representation of Phantasy. Our knowledge through either of the latter, is a direct, immediate, irrespective, determinate, individual, and adequate cognition; that is, a singular or individual object is known in itself, by itself, through all its attributes, and without reference to aught but itself. A concept, on the contrary, is an indirect, mediate, relative, indeterminate, and partial cognition of any one of a number of objects, but not an actual representation either of them all, or of the whole attributes of any one object.

Though it be not strictly within the province of Logic to explain the origin and formation of our notions, the logician assuming, as data, the laws and products of thought, as the mathematician assumes, as data, extension and number and the axioms by which their relation is determined, both leaving to the metaphysician the inquiry into their grounds;—this notwithstanding, I deemed it not improper to give you a very brief statement of the mode and circumstances in which our concepts are elaborated out of the presentations and representations of the subsidiary faculties. Different objects are complements partly of similar, partly of different, attributes. Similar qualities are those which stand in similar relation to our organs and faculties, and where the similarity

is complete, the effects which they determine in us
are, by us, indiscernible.   To us, they are, therefore,
virtually the same, and the same we, accordingly, consider them to be, though in different objects; precisely as we consider the thought of the same object
to be itself the same, when repeated at intervals,—at
different times, in consciousness.   This by way of
preface being understood, I showed that in the formation of a concept or notion the process may be
analysed into four moments.   In the first place, we
must have a plurality of objects presented or represented by the subsidiary faculties.   These faculties
must furnish the rude material for elaboration.   In
the second place, the objects thus supplied are, by an
act of the Understanding, compared together, and their
several qualities judged to be similar or dissimilar.
In the third place, an act of volition, called Attention,
concentrates consciousness on the qualities thus recognised as similar; and that concentration, by attention on them, involves an abstraction of consciousness
from those which have been recognised and thrown
aside as dissimilar; for the power of consciousness is
limited, and it is clear or vivid precisely in proportion to the simplicity or oneness of its object.   Attention and abstraction are the two poles of the same
act of thought; they are like the opposite scales in a
balance, the one must go up as the other goes down.
In the fourth place, the qualities, which by comparison are judged similar and by attention are constituted into an exclusive object of thought,—these are
already, by this process, identified in consciousness;
for they are only judged similar, inasmuch as they
produce in us indiscernible effects.   Their synthesis
in consciousness may, however, for precision's sake, be

stated as a fourth step in the process; but it must be LECT.
remembered, that at least the three latter steps are VIII.
not, in reality, distinct and independent acts, but are
only so distinguished and stated, in order to enable
us to comprehend and speak about the indivisible
operation, in the different aspects in which we may
consider it. In the same way, you are not to suppose that the mental sentence which must be analysed
in order to be expressed in language, has as many
parts in consciousness, as, it has words, or clauses,
in speech; for it forms, in reality, one organic and
indivisible whole. To repeat an illustration I have
already given:—The parts of an act of thought stand
in the same relation to each other as the parts of a
triangle,—a figure which we cannot resolve into any
simpler figure, but whose sides and angles we may
consider apart, and, therefore, as parts; though these
are, in reality, inseparable, being the necessary conditions of each other.—But this by the way.

The qualities of different individual things, thus
identified in thought, and constituting concepts, under
which, as classes, these individual things themselves
are ranged;—these primary concepts may themselves
be subjected to the same process, by which they were
elaborated from the concrete realities given in Perception and Imagination. We may, again, compare different concepts together, again find in the plurality of attributes which they comprehend, some like, some unlike;
we may again attend only to the similar, and again
identify these in the synthesis of consciousness; and this
process of evolving concepts out of concepts we may
go on performing, until the generalisation is arrested
in that ultimate or primary concept, the basis itself
of all attributes,—the concept of Being or Existence.

Having thus endeavoured to give you a general view of what concepts are, and by what process they are formed, I stated by way of corollary, some of their general characteristics. The first of these I mentioned is their partiality or inadequacy,—that is, they comprehend only a larger or smaller portion of the whole attributes belonging to the things classified or contained under them.

The second is their relativity. Formed by comparison, they express only a relation. They cannot, therefore, be held up as an absolute object to consciousness, —they cannot be represented, as universals, in imagination. They can only be thought of in relation to some one of the individual objects they classify, and, when viewed in relation to it, they can be represented in imagination; but then, as so actually represented, they no longer constitute general attributions, they fall back into mere special determinations of the individual object in which they are represented. Thus it is, that the generality or universality of concepts is potential, not actual. They are only general, inasmuch as they may be applied to any of the various objects they contain; but while they cannot be actually elicited into consciousness, except in application to some one or other of these, so, they cannot be so applied without losing, *pro tanto*, their universality. Take, for example, the concept *horse*. In so far as by *horse* we merely think of the word, that is, of the combination formed by the letters, *h, o, r, s, e*,—this is not a concept at all, as it is a mere representation of certain individual objects. This I only state and eliminate, in order that no possible ambiguity should be allowed to lurk. By *horse*, then, meaning not merely a representation of the word, but a concept relative to

certain objects classed under it;—the concept *horse*,
I say, cannot, if it remain a concept, that is, a universal attribution, be represented in imagination; but, except it be represented in imagination, it cannot be applied to any object, and, except it be so applied, it cannot be realised in thought at all. You may try to escape the horns of the dilemma, but you cannot. You cannot realise in thought an absolute or irrespective concept, corresponding in universality to the application of the word ; for the supposition of this involves numerous contradictions. An existent horse is not a relation, but an extended object possessed of a determinate figure, colour, size, &c. ; horse, in general, cannot, therefore, be represented, except by an image of something extended, and of a determinate figure, colour, size, &c. Here now emerges the contradiction. If, on the one hand, you do not represent something extended and of a determinate figure, colour, and size, you have no representation of any horse. There is, therefore, on this alternative, nothing which can be called the actual concept or image of a horse at all. If, on the other hand, you do represent something extended and of a determinate figure, colour, and size, then you have, indeed, the image of an individual horse, but not a universal concept coadequate with horse in general. For how is it possible to have an actual representation of a figure, which is not a determinate figure ? but if of a determinate figure, it must be that of some one of the many different figures under which horses appear ; but then, if it be only of one of these, it cannot be the general concept of the others, which it does not represent. In like manner, how is it possible to have the actual representation of a thing coloured, which is

not the representation of a determinate colour, that
is, either white, or black, or grey, or brown, &c.? but if
it be any one of these, it can only represent a horse
of this or that particular colour, and cannot be the
general concept of horses of every colour.   The same
result is given by the other attributes; and what I
originally stated is thus manifest,—that concepts have
only a potential, not an actual, universality, that is,
they are only universal, inasmuch as they may be
applied to any of a certain class of objects, but as
actually applied they are no longer general attributions, but only special attributes.

But it does not from this follow that concepts are
mere words, and that there is nothing general in
thought itself.   This is not indeed held in reality by
any philosopher; for no philosopher has ever denied
that we are capable of apprehending relations, and in
particular the relation of similarity and difference; so
that the whole controversy between the conceptualist
and nominalist originates in the ambiguous employment of the same terms to express the representations
of Imagination and the notions or concepts of the
Understanding.   This is significantly shown by the
absolute non-existence of the dispute among the philosophers of the most metaphysical country in Europe.
In Germany the question of nominalism and conceptualism has not been agitated, and why?   Simply because the German language supplies terms by which
concepts, (or notions of thought proper), have been
contradistinguished from the presentations and representations of the subsidiary faculties.[a]   But this is
not a subject on which I ought at present to have

But con-
cepts are
not, there-
fore, mere
words.

a See the Author's note, *Reid's*   *taphysics*, vol. ii. p. 296 *et seq.*—
Works, p. 412; and *Lectures on Me-*   ED.

touched, as it is, in truth, foreign to the domain of Logic; and I have only been led now to recur to it at all, in consequence of some difficulties expressed to me by members of the class.—All that I wish you now to understand is,—that concepts, as the result of comparison, that is, of the apprehension and affirmation of a relation, are, necessarily, in their nature relative, and, consequently, not capable of representation as absolute attributes.

I shall terminate the consideration of concepts in general by the following paragraph, in which is stated, besides their inadequacy and relativity, their dependence on language :—

¶ XXIII. The concept thus formed by an abstraction of the resembling from the non-resembling qualities of objects, would again fall back into the confusion and infinitude from which it has been called out, were it not rendered permanent for consciousness, by being fixed and ratified in a verbal sign.   Considered in general, thought and language are reciprocally dependent; each bears all the imperfections and perfections of the other; but without language there could be no knowledge realised of the essential properties of things, and of the connection of their accidental states.

This also is not a subject of which the consideration properly belongs to Logic, but a few words may not be inexpedient to make you aware, in general, of the intimate connection of thought and its expression, and of the powerful influence which language exerts upon our mental operations.   Man, in fact, only obtains the use of his faculties in obtaining the use of speech, for language is the indispensable mean of the

LECT.
VIII.

Language
not necessarily
in certain
mental
operations.

development of his natural powers, whether intellectual or moral.

For Perception, indeed, for the mere consciousness
of the similarities and dissimilarities in the objects
perceived, for the apprehension of the causal connection of certain things, and for the application of this
knowledge to the attainment of certain ends, no language is necessary; and it is only the exaggeration
of a truth into an error, when philosophers maintain
that language is the indispensable condition of even
the simpler energies of knowledge. Language is the
attribution of signs to our cognitions of things. But
as a cognition must have been already there, before it
could receive a sign; consequently, that knowledge
which is denoted by the formation and application of
a word, must have preceded the symbol which denotes
it. Speech is thus not the mother, but the godmother,
of knowledge. But though, in general, we must hold
that language, as the product and correlative of
thought, must be viewed as posterior to the act
of thinking itself; on the other hand, it must be
admitted, that we could never have risen above the
very lowest degrees in the scale of thought, without
the aid of signs. A sign is necessary, to give stability
to our intellectual progress,—to establish each step in
our advance as a new starting-point for our advance
to another beyond.

Mental
operations
to which
language
is indispen-
sable, and
its relation
to them.

A country may be overrun by an armed host, but
it is only conquered by the establishment of fortresses.
Words are the fortresses of thought. They enable us
to realise our dominion over what we have already
overrun in thought; to make every intellectual conquest the basis of operations for others still beyond.—
Or another illustration :—You have all heard of the

process of tunnelling, of tunnelling through a sand-
bank. In this operation it is impossible to succeed,
unless every foot, nay almost every inch in our progress, be secured by an arch of masonry, before we
attempt the excavation of another. Now, language is
to the mind precisely what the arch is to the tunnel.
The power of thinking and the power of excavation
are not dependent on the word in the one case, on the
mason-work in the other; but without these subsidiaries, neither process could be carried on beyond its
rudimentary commencement. Though, therefore, we
allow that every movement forward in language must
be determined by an antecedent movement forward in
thought; still, unless thought be accompanied at each
point of its evolution, by a corresponding evolution of
language, its further development is arrested. Thus
it is, that the higher exertions of the higher faculty of
Understanding,—the classification of the objects presented and represented by the subsidiary powers in
the formation of a hierarchy of notions, the connection
of these notions into judgments, the inference of one
judgment from another, and, in general, all our consciousness of the relations of the universal to the particular, consequently all science strictly so denominated, and every inductive knowledge of the past and
future from the laws of nature :—not only these, but
all ascent from the sphere of sense to the sphere
of moral and religious intelligence, are, as experience
proves, if not altogether impossible without a language,
at least possible only to a very low degree. Admitting even that the mind is capable of certain elementary concepts without the fixation and signature
of language, still these are but sparks which would
twinkle only to expire, and it requires words to give

them prominence, and, by enabling us to collect and elaborate them into new concepts, to raise out of what would otherwise be only scattered and transitory scintillations a vivid and enduring light.

B. Of Concepts or Notions in special.
I here terminate the General and proceed to the Special consideration of Concepts—that is, to view them in their several Relations. Now, in a logical point of view, there are, it seems to me, only three possible relations in which concepts can be considered; for the only relations they hold are to their objects, to their subject, or to each other. In relation to their objects,—they are considered as inclusive of a greater or smaller number of attributes, that is, as applicable to a greater or smaller number of objects; this is technically styled their *Quantity.* In relation to their subject, that is, to the mind itself, they are considered as standing in a higher or a lower degree of consciousness,—they are more or less clear, more or less distinct; this, in like manner, is called their *Quality.* In relation to each other, they are considered as the same or different, co-ordinated or subordinated to each other; this is their *Relation,* strictly so called.[a] Under these three heads, I now, therefore, proceed to treat them; and, first, of their Quantity.

Par. XXIV.
Quantity of Concepts &c
¶ XXIV. As a concept, or notion, is a thought in which an indefinite plurality of characters is

---

[a] On their relation to their origin as direct or indirect, see *Esser,* [*System der Logik*, § 49, p. 96.—Ed.] Metn.—N. B. Notions may be thus better (?) divided:—

1°, By relation to themselves they have the quantity of comprehension.

2°, By relation to their objects they have the quantity of extension. These two thus quantity in general.

3°, By relation to each other they have relation strictly so called.

4°, By relation to their subject they have clearness and distinctness. (This last had better be relegated to Methodology.)—*Memorundo.*

bound up into a unity of consciousness, and applicable to an indefinite plurality of objects, a
concept is, therefore, necessarily a quantity, and
a quantity varying in amount according to the
greater or smaller number of characters of which
it is the complement, and the greater or smaller
number of things of which it may be said. This
quantity is thus of two kinds ; as it is either Intensive or Extensive. The Internal or Intensive
Quantity of a concept is determined by the greater
or smaller number of constituent characters contained in it. The External or Extensive Quantity
of a concept is determined by the greater or
smaller number of classified concepts or realities
contained under it. The former (the Intensive
Quantity) is called by some later Greek logicians
depth, (βάθος) ; by the Latin logical writers *comprehension*, (*comprehensio, quantitas compre-
hensionis, complexus*, or *quantitas complexus*).
The latter (the Extensive Quantity) is called by
the same later Greek Logicians the *breadth*,
(πλάτος) ; by Aristotle, ἡ περιοχή, τὸ περιέχειν,
τὸ περιέχεσθαι ;[a] by the logical writers of the
western or Latin world, the *extension* or *circuit*,
(*extensio, quantitas extensionis, ambitus, quantitas ambitus*) and likewise the *domain* or *sphere*
of a notion, (*regio, sphæra*).[β]

a See *Lectures on Metaphysics*, vol.
ii. p. 290 n. Aristotle does not use
περιοχή as a substantive, though
the verb, both active and passive,
is employed in this signification,
e.g. *Anal. Prior.*, i. 27 ; *Rhet.*, iii. 5.
—ED.

β [Cf. *Porphyrii, Isagoge*, cc. i. ii.
viii. ; Cajetan, *In Porphyrii Prædi-

cabilia*, cc. i. ii.} [p. 37 ed. 1579 ;
prefixed to his Commentary on the
Categories, first published in 1496 :
"Ad hoc breviter dicitur, quod esse
magis collectivum multorum potest
intelligi dupliciter : uno modo intensive, et sic species magis est collec-
tiva, quia magis unit adunata ; alio
modo extensive, et sic genus est magis

The Internal Quantity of a notion,—its Intention or Comprehension, is made up of those different attributes of which the concept is the conceived sum; that is, the various characters connected by the concept itself into a single whole in thought. The External Quantity of a notion or its Extension is, on the other hand, made up of the number of objects which are thought mediately through a concept. For example, the attributes, *rational, sensible, moral*, &c., go to constitute the intention, or internal quantity, of the concept *man;* whereas the attributes *European, American, philosopher, tailor,* &c., go to make up a concept of this or that individual man.

These two quantities are not convertible. On the contrary, they are in the inverse ratio of each other; the greater the depth or comprehension of a notion the less its breadth or extension, and *vice versâ.*

You will observe, likewise, a distinction which has been taken by the best logicians. Both quantities are said *to contain :* but the quantity of extension is said to contain *under* it; the quantity of comprehension is said to contain *in* it. By the intension, comprehension, or depth of a notion, we think the most qualities of the fewest objects; whereas by the extension or breadth

collectivum, quia multo plura sub sua ambitione cadunt, quam sub speciei ambitu. Unde species et genus so habent sicut duo duces, quorum alter habet exercitum parvum, sed valde unanimum, alter exercitum magnum, sed diversarum factionum. Ille enim magis colligit intensive, hic extensive. Porphyrius autem loquebatur hic de extensiva collectione, idea dixit, genus esse magis collectivum." Quoted by Stahl, *Regulæ Philosophicæ,* tit. xii., reg. 5, p. 381. Cf. reg. 0, ed. London, 1658. -- ED.]

[*Port-Royal Logic,* P. i. c. 6, p. 74, ed. 1718. Boethius, *Introductio ad Syllogismos, Opera,* p. 592; *In Topica Ciceronis Commentarii,* lib. i., *Opera,* p. 765, ed. Basileæ, 1570. Reuschius, *Systema Logicum,* pp. 11, 92; Baumgarten, *Acroasis Logica,* §§ 56, 67, ed. Halæ Magdeburgæ, 1773. Krug, *Logik,* § 26; Schulze, *Logik,* § 30; Esser, *Logik,* § 34 *et seq.;* Nagenios, p. 194 *et seq.*] [Aσγκή, c. iv., Περὶ Ἑρμηνείας Βόθων τε καὶ Πλάτωνς.—ED.]

of a concept, we think the fewest qualities of the most
objects. In other words, by the former, we say the
most of the least; by the latter, the least of the most.

Again; you will observe the two following distinctions: the first,—the exposition of the Comprehension
of a notion is called its *Definition*; (a simple notion
cannot, therefore, be defined); the second,—the exposition of the Extension of a notion is called its
Division; (an individual notion cannot be divided.)

What follows is in further illustration of the paragraph. Notions or concepts stand in a necessary relation to certain objects, thought through them; for
without something to think of, there could exist no
thought, no notion, no concept. But in so far as we
think an object through a concept, we think it as
part of, or as contained under, that concept: and in
so far as we think a concept of its object or objects,
we think it as a unity containing, actually or potentially, in it a plurality of attributions. Out of the
relation of a concept to its object, it necessarily results, that a concept is a quantum or quantity; for
that which contains one or more units by which it may
be measured, is a quantity.

But the quantity of a concept is of two, and two
opposite kinds. Considered internally, that is, as a
unity which may, and generally does, contain in it a
plurality of parts or component attributes, a concept
has a certain quantity, which may be called its *internal*
or *intensive* quantity. This is generally called its
comprehension, sometimes its *depth*, βάθος, and its
quantitas complexus. Here the parts, that is, the
several attributes or characters, which go to constitute
the total concept, are said to be contained *in* it. For
example, the concept *man* is composed of two con-

stituent parts or attributes, that is, of two partial
concepts,—*rational* and *animal*; for the characters
rational and *animal* are only an analytical expression
of the synthetic unity of the concept *man*.   But each
of these partial concepts, which together make up the
comprehension of the total concept *man*, are themselves wholes, in like manner made up of parts.   To
take only the concept *animal*;—this comprehends in
it, as parts, *living* and *sensitive* and *organised*, for a
living and sentient organism may be considered as an
analytical development of the constituents of the synthetic unity *animal*.   But each of these, again, is a concept, comprehending and made up of parts; and these
parts, again, are relative wholes, divisible into other
constituent concepts ; nor need we stop in our analysis till we reach attributes which, as simple, stand as
a primary or ultimate element, into which the series
can be resolved.   Now, you will observe, that as the
parts of the parts are parts of the whole, the concept
man, as immediately comprehending the concepts
rational and *animal*, mediately comprehends their
parts, and the parts of their parts, to the end of the
evolution.   Thus we can say, not only that *man* is
an *animal*, but that he is a *living being*, a *sentient
being*, &c.   The logical axiom, *Nota notæ est nota rei
ipsius*, or, as otherwise expressed, *Prædicatum prædicati est prædicatum subjecti*,[a]—is only a special
enunciation of the general principle, that the part of a
part is a part of the whole.   You will, hereafter, see
that the Comprehension of notions affords one of the
two great branches of reasoning which, though marvellously overlooked by logicians, is at least of equal

a A translation of Aristotle's first   ὧσα καὶ κατὰ τοῦ ἐκατηγορίου ῥηθή-
antipredicamental rule, *Categ.* iti. 1,   σιται.— Ed.
°Όσα κατὰ τοῦ κατηγορουμένου λέγεται

importance with that which they have exclusively developed, and which is founded on the other kind of quantity exhibited by concepts, and to which I now proceed.

But a concept may also be considered externally, that is, as a unity which contains under it a plurality of classifying attributes or subordinate concepts, and, in this respect, it has another quantity which may be called its *external* or *extensive* quantity. This is commonly called its *extension;* sometimes its *sphere* or *domain,* (*sphæra, regio, quantitas, ambitus*); and, by the Greek Logicians, its *breadth* or *latitude,* (πλά-τος.)[a] Here the parts which the total concept contains, are said to be contained *under* it, because, holding the relation to it of the particular to the general, they are subordinated or ranged under it. For example, the concepts *man, horse, dog,* &c., are contained under the more general concept *animal,*—the concepts *triangle, square, circle, rhombus, rhomboid,* &c., are contained under the more general concept *figure;* inasmuch as the subordinate concepts can each or any be thought through the higher or more general. But as each of these subordinate concepts is itself a whole or general, which contains under it parts or more particular concepts, it follows, again, on the axiom or self-evident truth, that a part of a part is a part of the whole,—an axiom which, you will hereafter see, constitutes the one principle of all Deductive reasoning,—it follows, on this axiom, that whatever is contained under the partial or more particular concept is contained under the total or more general concept. Thus, for example, *triangle* is contained under *figure;* all, therefore, that is contained under

a See above. p. 141, notes a, β.—ED.

2 Exten-
sive.

triangle, as *rectangled triangle, equilateral triangle*, &c., will, likewise, be contained under *figure*, by which we may, accordingly, think and describe them.

Such, in general, is what is meant by the two Quantities of concepts,—their Comprehension and Extension.

But these quantities are not only different, they are opposed, and so opposed, that though each supposes the other as the condition of its own existence, still, however, within the limits of conjunct, of correlative existence, they stand in an inverse ratio to each other, —the maximum of the one being necessarily the minimum of the other. On this I give you the following paragraph :—

Intensive
and Exten-
sive quan-
tities are
opposed to
each other.

Par. XXV.
Law regu-
lating the
mutual re-
lations of
Extension
and Com-
prehension.

¶ XXV. A notion is intensively great in proportion to the greater number, and intensively small in proportion to the smaller number, of determinations or attributes contained in it. Is the Comprehension of a concept a minimum, that is, is the concept one in which a plurality of attributes can no longer be distinguished, it is called *simple;* whereas, inasmuch as its attributes still admit of discrimination, it is called *complex* or *compound.*[a]

A notion is extensively great in proportion to the greater number, and extensively small in proportion to the smaller number, of determinations or attributes it contains under it. When the Extension of a concept becomes a minimum, that is, when it contains no other notions under it, it is called an *individual.*[b]

These two quantities stand always in an inverse

a Krug, *Logik,* § 28.—Ed.   b Krug, *ibid.,* § 29.—Ed.

ratio to each other : For the greater the Comprehension of a concept the less is its Extension, and the greater its Extension the less its Comprehension.[a]

To illustrate this :—When I take out of a concept, that is, abstract from one or more of its attributes, I diminish its comprehension. Thus, when from the concept *man*, equivalent to *rational animal*, I abstract from the attribute or determination *rational*, I lessen its internal quantity. But by this diminution of its comprehension I give it a wider extension, for what remains is the concept *animal*, and the concept *animal* embraces under it a far greater number of objects than the concept *man*.

Illustration.

Before, however, proceeding further in illustrating the foregoing paragraph, it may be proper to give you also the following :—

¶ XXVI. Of the logical processes by which these counter quantities of concepts are amplified,—the one which amplifies the Comprehension is called *Determination*, and sometimes called *Concretion*, the other which amplifies the Extension is called *Abstraction* or *Generalisation*. *Definition* and *Division* are severally the resolution of the Comprehension and of the Extension of notions, into their parts. A Simple notion cannot be defined ; an Individual notion cannot be divided.[β]

Par. XXVI. Processes by which the Comprehension and Extension of Notions are amplified and resolved.

a Krug, *Logik*, § 27. — En. ; [Schulze, *Logik*, § 33. Cf. Porphyry, *Isagoge*, c. viii. §§ 9, 10.] [Ἔτι τὸ μὲν γένος πλεονάζει τῇ τῶν ὑπ᾽ αὐτὸ εἴδων τομῇ· τὸ δὲ εἶδος τῶν γενῶν πλεονάζει ταῖς οἰκείαις διαφοραῖς. Ἔτι οὔτε τὸ εἶδος γένοιτ᾽ ἂν γενικώτατον οὔτε τὸ γένος εἰδικώτατον.—En.]

β [Synonyms of Abstraction :—1, Analysis (of Comprehension); 2, Synthesis ; 3, Generification ; 4, Induction ; 5, Amplification.

Synonyms of Determination or Concretion :—1, Analysis (of Extension); 2, Synthesis ; 3, Specification ; 4, Restriction ; 5, Individuation.]

LECT.
VIII.

Illustration
of the two
foregoing
paragraphs.

Comprehen-
sion and
Extension
are opposed
in an in-
verse ratio
to each
other.

The reason of this opposition of the two quantities
is manifest in a moment, from the consideration of
their several natures. The comprehension of a concept is nothing more than a sum or complement
of the distinguishing characters, of which the concept is made up; and the extension of a concept
is nothing more than the sum or complement of
the objects themselves, whose resembling characters
were abstracted to constitute the concept. Now, it
is evident, that the more distinctive characters the
concept contains, the more minutely it will distinguish
and determine, and that if it contain a plenum of
distinctive characters, it must contain the distinctive,
—the determining, characters of some individual object. How do the two quantities now stand? In
regard to the comprehension or depth, it is evident,
that it is here at its maximum, the concept being a
complement of the whole attributes of an individual
object, which, by these attributes, it thinks and dis-
criminates from every other. On the contrary, the
extension or breadth of the concept is here at its
minimum; for, as the extension is great in proportion to the number of objects to which the concept
can be applied, and as the object is here only an
individual, it is evident it could not be less,
without ceasing to exist at all. Again, to reverse
the process;—throwing out of the comprehension of
the concept, that is, abstracting from those attributes, which belonging exclusively to, exclusively
distinguish, the individual, we at once diminish
the comprehension, by reducing the sum of its attributes, and amplify the extension of the concept,
by bringing within its sphere all the objects, which
the characteristics, now thrown out of the comprehen-

sion, had previously excluded from the extension. Continuing the process, by abstraction we throw out of the sum of qualities constituting the comprehension, other discriminating attributes, and forthwith the extension is proportionally amplified, by the entrance into its sphere of all those objects which had previously been debarred by the determining characteristics last discarded. Thus proceeding, and at each step ejecting from the comprehension those characters which are found the proximate impediments to the amplification of the extension of the concept, we at each step diminish the former quantity precisely as we increase the latter; till, at last, we arrive at that concept which is the necessary constituent of every other,—at that concept which all comprehension and all extension must equally contain, but in which comprehension is at its minimum, extension at its maximum,—I mean the concept of *Being* or *Existence.*[a]

We have thus seen, that the maximum of comprehension and the minimum of extension are found in the concept of an individual,—that the maximum of extension and the minimum of comprehension are found in the concept of the absolutely simple, that is, in the concept of *existence.* Now comprehension and extension, as quantities, are wholes; for wholes are only the complement of all their parts, and as wholes are only by us clearly comprehended as we distinctly comprehend their parts, it follows:—1°, That comprehension and extension may each be analysed into its parts; and, 2°, That this analysis will afford the mean by which each of these quantities can be clearly and distinctly understood. But as the two quantities

Definition
and Divi-
sion,—are
the pro-
cesses by
which Com-
prehension
and Exten-
sion of Con-
cepts are
resolved.

---

a This, like other logical relations, [See below, p. 162.—Ed.]
may be typified by a sensible figure.

are of an opposite nature, it is manifest that the two processes of analysis will, likewise, be opposed. The analysis of the intensive or comprehensive quantity of concepts, that is, their depth, is accomplished by Definition; that of their extensive quantity or breadth, by Division. On Definition and Division I at present touch, not to consider them in themselves or on their own account, that is, as the methods of clear and of distinct thinking, for this will form the matter of a special discussion in the Second Part of 'Logic or Methodology, but simply in so far as it is requisite to speak of them in illustration of the general nature of our concepts.

Definition illustrated.
The expository or explanatory analysis of a concept, considered as an intensive whole or quantum, if properly effected, is done by its resolution into two concepts of which it is proximately compounded, that is, into the higher concept under which it immediately stands, and the concept which affords the character by which it is distinguished from the other co-ordinate concepts under that higher concept. This is its Definition ; that is, in logical language, its exposition by an analysis into its Genus and Differential Quality ;—the genus being the higher concept, under which it stands ; the differential quality the lower concept, by which it is distinguished from the other concepts subordinate to the genus, and on a level or co-ordinate with itself, and which, in logical language, are called *Species*. For example, if we attempt an expository or explanatory analysis of the concept *man*, considered as an intensive quantity or complexus of attributes, we analyse it into *animal*, this being the higher concept or genus under which it stands, and *rational*, the attribute of reason being the character-

istic or differential quality by which *man* is dis- LECT.
tinguished from the other concepts or species which VIII.
stand co-ordinated with itself, under the genus *animal*,
—that is, *irrational animal* or *brute*.

Here you will observe, that though the analysis be
of the comprehension, yet it is regulated by the extension ; the extension regulating the order in which
the comprehension is resolved into its parts.

The expository analysis of a concept, an extensive Division.
whole or quantum, is directly opposed to the preceding,
to which it is correlative. It takes the higher concept, and, if conducted aright, resolves it into its proximately lower concepts, by adding attributes which
afford their distinguishing characters or differences.
This is division :—Thus, for example, taking the highest concept, that of *ens* or *existence*, by adding to it the
differential concepts *per se* or *substantial*, and *non per
se* or *accidental*, we have *substantial existence* or *existence per se*, equivalent to *substance*, and *accidental
existence* or *existence non per se*, equivalent to *accident*. We may then divide substance by *simple* and
not-simple, equivalent to *compound*, and again simple
by *material* and *non-material*, equivalent to *immaterial*, equivalent to *spiritual* ;—and matter or material
substance by *organised* and *not-organised*, equivalent
to *brute matter*. Organised matter we may divide by
sentient or *animal*, and *non-sentient* or *vegetable*.
Animal we may divide by *rational* and *irrational*,
and so on, till we reach a concept which, as that of
an individual object, is, in fact, not a general concept,
but only in propriety a singular representation.

Thus it is manifest, that as Definition is the analysis The Inde-
of a complex concept into its component parts or at- Indivisible.
tributes, if a concept be simple, that is, if it contain in

it only a single attribute, it must be indefinable; and again, that as Division is the analysis of a higher or more general concept into others lower and less general, if a concept be an individual, that is, only a bundle of individual qualities, it is indivisible, is, in fact, not a proper or abstract concept at all, but only a concrete representation of the Imagination.

Diagram representing Extension and Comprehension of Concepts.   * The following Diagram represents Breadth and Depth, with the relations of Affirmation and Negation to these quantities.

SCHEME OF THE TWO QUANTITIES.

Line of Breadth.   Aff.   Neg.

Ground of Reality.

Explanation.   In the preceding Table there are represented :—by A, A, &c., the highest genus or widest attribute; by Y, the lowest species or narrowest attribute; whilst the other four horizontal series of vowels typify the subaltern genera and species, or the intermediate attributes. The *vowels* are reserved exclusively for classes, or common qualities; whereas the *consonants* z, z′, z″, (and which to render the contrast more ob-

a The Diagram and relative text   the Editors from the Author's *Dis-*
to end of Lecture are extracted by   *cussions*, p. 699-701.—Ed.

trusive are not capitals,) represent individuals or sin-
gulars. Every higher class or more common attribute
is supposed (in conformity with logical precision) to
be dichotomised,—to be divided into two by a lower
class or attribute, and its contradictory or negative.
This contradictory, of which only the commencement
appears, is marked by an italic vowel, preceded by a
perpendicular line (|) signifying *not* or *non*, and
analogous to the minus (−) of the mathematicians.
This being understood, the Table at once exhibits the
real identity and *rational* differences of Breadth and
Depth, which, though denominated *quantities*, are, in
reality, one and the same quantity, viewed in counter
relations and from opposite ends. Nothing is the
one, which is not, *pro tanto*, the other.

In *Breadth :* the supreme genus (A, A, &c.) is, as
it appears, absolutely the greatest whole ; an individual (z) absolutely the smallest part ; whereas the
intermediate classes are each of them a relative part
or species, by reference to the class or classes above
it ; a relative whole or genus, by reference to the class
or classes below it.—In *Depth :* the individual is absolutely the greatest whole, the highest genus is absolutely the smallest part ; whilst every relatively lower
class or species, is relatively a greater whole than the
class, classes, or genera, above it.—The two quantities
are thus, as the diagram represents, precisely the inverse of each other. The greater the Breadth, the
less the Depth ; the greater the Depth, the less the
Breadth : and each, within itself, affording the correlative differences of whole and part, each, therefore, in
opposite respects, *contains* and *is contained.* But, for
distinction's sake, it is here convenient to employ a
difference, not altogether arbitrary, of expression.

We should say :—" containing and contained *under*,"
for Breadth ; " containing and contained *in*," for
Depth. This distinction, which has been taken by
some modern logicians, though unknown to many
of them, was not observed by Aristotle. We find
him, (to say nothing of other ancient logicians), using
the expression ἐν ὅλῳ εἶναι or ὑπάρχειν, for either
whole. Though different in the order of thought
(*ratione*), the two quantities are identical in the
nature of things (*re*). Each supposes the other ; and
Breadth is not more to be distinguished from Depth,
than the relations of the sides, from the relations of
the angles, of a triangle. In effect it is precisely the
same reasoning, whether we argue in Depth,—" z′ is
(*i.e.* as subject, contains *in* it the inherent attribute)
some Y ; all Y is some U ; all U is some O ; all O
is some I ; all I is some E ; all E is some A ;—therefore, z′ is some A :" or whether we argue in Breadth,—
" Some A is (*i.e.* as class, contains *under* it the subject
part) all E ; some E is all I ; some I is all O ; some O
is all U ; some U is all Y ; some Y is z′ ;—therefore,
some A is z′." The two reasonings, internally identical, are externally the converse of each other ; the
premise and term, which in Breadth is major, in
Depth is minor. In syllogisms also, where the contrast of the two quantities is abolished, there, with
the difference of figure, the differences of major and
minor premise and term fall likewise. In truth, however, common language in its enouncement of propositions, is here perhaps more correct and philosophical than the technical language of logic itself.
For as it is only an *equation*—only an *affirmation of
identity* or *its negation*, which is, in either quantity,
proposed ; therefore the substantive verb, (*is, is not*,)

used in both cases, speaks more accurately, than the
expressions, *contained*, (or *not contained*) *in* of the
one, *contained*, (or *not contained*) *under* of the other.
In fact, the *two quantities* and the *two quantifications*
have by logicians been neglected *together*.

This Table, (the principle of which becomes more
palpably demonstrative, when the parts of the table
are turned into the parts of a circular machine[a]),
exhibits all the mutual relations of the counter quantities.—1°, It represents the classes, as a series of
resemblances thought as one, (by a repetition of the
same letter in the same series,) but as really distinct,
(by separating lines). Thus, A is only A, not A, A, A,
&c.; some Animal is not some Animal; one class of
Animals is not all, every, or any other; this Animal
is not that; Socrates is not Plato; z is not z'. On
the other hand, E is E A; and Y is Y U O I E A;
every lower and higher letter in the series coalescing
uninterruptedly into a series of reciprocal subjects and
predicates, as shown by the absence of all discriminating lines. Thus, Socrates (z'), is Athenian (Y),
Greek (U), European (O), Man (I), Mammal (E), Animal (A). Of course the series must be in grammatical and logical harmony. We must not collate
notions abstract and notions concrete.—2°, The Table
shows the inverse correlation of the two quantities in
respect of amount. For example : A, (*i.e.* A, A, &c.),
the highest genus, is represented as having six times the
Breadth of Y ; whilst Y, (*i.e.* Y—A), the lowest species,
has six times the Depth of A.—3°, The Table manifests all the classes, as in themselves unreal, subjective,

a A machine of this kind was constructed by the Author, and used in
the class-room to illustrate the doctrine of the text. For a description
of it see *Memoir of Sir W. Hamilton*,
p. 249-252.—Ed.

ideal ; for these are merely fictions or artifices of the
mind, for the convenience of thinking. Universals
only exist in nature, as they cease to be universal in
thought ; that is, as they are reduced from general
and abstract attributes to individual and concrete
qualities. A—Y are only truly objective as distributed through z, z', z'', &c. ; and in that case they
are not universals. As Boëthius expresses it :—
" Omne quod est, eo quod est, singulare est."—4°, The
opposition of class to class, through contradictory
attributes, is distinguished by lines different from
those marking the separation of one part of the same
class from another. Thus, Animal, or Sentiently-
organised, (A), is contrasted with Not-animal, or Not-
sentiently - organised, (| A), by lines thicker than
those which merely discriminate one animal (A), from
another (A).[a]

a See further in *Discussions*, p. 701 et seq.—ED.

LECTURE IX.

STOICHEIOLOGY.

SECT. II.—OF THE PRODUCTS OF THOUGHT.

I.—ENNOEMATIC.

B. OF CONCEPTS IN SPECIAL.—II. THEIR SUBJECTIVE

RELATION—QUALITY.

HAVING concluded the consideration of the relation LECT. of concepts to their objects,—the relation in which ${IX.}$ their Quantity is given, I now proceed to consider Relation of Concepts to their relation to their conceiving subject—the relation ject. in which is given their Quality. This consideration of the quality of concepts does not, in my opinion, belong to the Doctrine of Elements, and ought, in scientific rigour, to be adjourned altogether to the Methodology, as a virtue or perfection of thought. As logicians, however, have generally treated of it likewise under the former doctrine, I shall do so too, and commence with the following paragraph.

¶ XXVII. A concept or notion is the unity in Par. XXVII. consciousness of a certain plurality of attributes, The Quality of Concepts and it, consequently, supposes the power of think-consists in its logical ing these, both separately and together. But as Perfection or Imper- there are many gradations in the consciousness fection. with which the characters of a concept can be thought severally and in conjunction, there will consequently be many gradations in the actual

Perfection or Imperfection of a notion. It is this
perfection or imperfection which constitutes the
logical Quality of a concept.[a]

It is thus the greater or smaller degree of consciousness which accompanies the concept and its object,
that determines its quality, and according to which it
is called logically perfect or logically imperfect. Now
there may be distinguished two degrees of this logical
perfection, the nature of which is summarily expressed
in the following paragraph.

Par. XXVIII.
The two
degrees of
the logical
Perfection
and Imper-
fection of
Concepts,—
their Clear-
ness and
Distinct-
ness, and
their Ob-
scurity and
Indistinct-
ness.

¶ XXVIII. There are two degrees of the logical
perfection of concepts,—viz. their *Clearness* and
their *Distinctness*, and, consequently, two opposite
degrees of their corresponding imperfection,—viz.
their *Obscurity* and their *Indistinctness*. These
four qualities express the perfection and imperfection of concepts in extremes; but between
these extremes, there lie an indefinite number of
intermediate degrees.

A concept is said to be *clear* (*clara*), when
the degree of consciousness is such as enables us
to distinguish it as a whole from others; and
obscure (*obscura*), when the degree of consciousness is insufficient to accomplish this. A concept
is said to be *distinct* (*distincta, perspicua*), when
the degree of consciousness is such, as enables
us to discriminate from each other the several
characters, or constituent parts of which the concept is the sum; and *indistinct* or *confused*
(*indistincta, confusa, imperspicua*), when the
amount of consciousness requisite for this is

a Krug. *Logik*, § 30. Cf. Reser, *Logik*, § 45 *et seq.*—ED.

wanting. *Confused (confusa)* may be employed
as the genus including *obscure* and *indistinct.*[a]

The expressions *clearness* and *obscurity,* and *distinctness* and *indistinctness,* as applied to concepts, originally denote certain modifications of vision ; from vision they were analogically extended to the other senses, to imagination, and finally to thought. It may, therefore, enable us the better to comprehend their secondary application, to consider their primitive. To Leibnitz[β] we owe the precise distinction of concepts into clear and distinct, and from him I borrow the following illustration. In darkness,—in the complete obscurity of night,—we see nothing,—there is no perception—no discrimination of objects. As the light dawns, the obscurity diminishes, the deep and uniform sensation of darkness is modified,—we are conscious of a change,—we see something, but are still unable to distinguish its features,—we know not what it is. As the light increases, the outlines of wholes begin to appear, but still not with a distinctness sufficient to allow us to perceive them completely ; but when this is rendered possible, by the rising intensity of the light, we are then said to see clearly. We then recognise mountains, plains, houses, trees, animals, &c., that is, we discriminate these objects as wholes, as unities, from each other. But their parts,—the manifold of which these unities are the sum,—their parts still lose themselves in each other, they are still but

LECT.
IX.

Original application of the expressions *clearness, obscurity,* &c.

Illustrated by reference to vision.

---

a Compare Krug, *Logik,* 31 *et seq.* —ED. [Buffier, *Logique,* § 345 *et seq.* Kant, *Kr. d. r. Vernunft,* B. ii. Trans. Dial., art. i. p. 414, 3d ed., 1790.]

β See his *Meditationes de Cognitione, Veritate, et Ideis,* (*Opera,* ed. Erdmann, p. 79), *Nouveaux Essais,* L. ii., ch. xxix. The illustration, however, does not occur in either of these passages. It was probably borrowed from Krug, *Logik,* § 31, and attributed to Leibnitz by an oversight.—ED.

LECT.
IX.

indistinctly visible. At length when the daylight has
fully sprung, we are enabled likewise to discriminate
their parts ; we now see distinctly what lies around
us. But still we see as yet only the wholes which lie
proximately around us, and of these, only the parts
which possess a certain size. The more distant wholes,
and the smaller parts of nearer wholes, are still seen
by us only in their conjoint result, only as they con-
cur in making up that whole which is for us a visible
minimum. Thus it is, that in the distant forest or
the distant hill, we perceive a green surface ; but we
see not the several leaves, which in the one, nor the
several blades of grass, which in the other, each con-
tributes its effect to produce that amount of impression which our consciousness requires. Thus it is,
that all which we do perceive is made up of parts
which we do not perceive, and consciousness is itself
a complement of impressions, which lie beyond its
apprehension.* Clearness and distinctness are thus
only relative. For between the extreme of obscurity
and the extreme of distinctness, there are in vision an
infinity of intermediate degrees. Now the same thing
occurs in thought. For we may either be conscious
only of the concept in general, or we may also be
conscious of its various constituent attributes, or both
the concept and its parts may be lost in themselves to
consciousness, and only recognised to exist by effects
which indirectly evidence their existence.

Clearness
and ob-
scurity as
in Concepts.

The perfection of a notion, as I said, is contained in
two degrees or in two virtues,—viz. in its clearness
and in its distinctness ; and, of course, the opposite
vices of obscurity and indistinctness afford two degrees or two vices, constituting its imperfection. "A

* See *Lectures on Metaphysics*, vol. I. p. 348 *et seq.*—ED.

concept is said to be *clear*, when the degree of consciousness by which it is accompanied is sufficient to
discriminate what we think in and through it, from
what we think in and through other notions; whereas
if the degree of consciousness be so remiss that this
and other concepts run into each other, in that case,
the notion is said to be *obscure*. It is evident that
clearness and obscurity admit of various degrees;
each being capable of almost infinite gradations, according as the object of the notion is discriminated
with greater or less vivacity and precision from the
objects of other notions. A concept is *absolutely*
clear, when its object is distinguished from all other
objects; a concept is *absolutely obscure*, when its object can be distinguished from no other object. But
it is only the absolutely clear and the absolutely obscure which stand opposed as contradictory extremes;
for the same notion can at once be relatively or comparatively clear, and relatively or comparatively obscure. Absolutely obscure notions, that is, concepts
whose objects can be distinguished from nothing else,
exist only in theory;—an absolutely obscure notion
being, in fact, no notion at all. For it is of the very
essence of a concept, that its object should, to a certain degree at least, be comprehended in its peculiar,
consequently, in its distinguishing, characteristics.
But, on the other hand, of notions absolutely clear,
that is, notions whose objects cannot possibly be confounded with aught else, whether known or unknown,
—of such notions a limited intelligence is possessed
of very few, and, consequently, our human concepts
are, properly, only a mixture of the opposite qualities;
—*clear* or *obscure* as applied to them, meaning only
that the one quality or the other is the preponderant.

In a logical relation, the illustration of notions consists in the raising them from a preponderant obscurity to a preponderant clearness—or from a lower degree of clearness to a higher."[a] So much for the quality of clearness or obscurity considered in itself.

The Distinctness and Indistinctness of Concepts.

But a Clear concept may be either Distinct or Indistinct; the distinctness and indistinctness of concepts are, therefore, to be considered apart from their clearness and obscurity.

Historical notice of this distinction.

But before entering upon the nature of the distinction itself, I may observe that we owe the discrimination of Distinct and Indistinct from Clear and Obscure

Due to Leibnitz.

notions to the acuteness of the great Leibnitz. By the Cartesians the distinction had not been taken ; though the authors of the *Port Royal Logic* come so near, that we may well marvel how they failed explicitly to enounce

Locke.

it.[b] Though Locke published his *Essay Concerning Human Understanding* some five years subsequent to the paper in which Leibnitz—then a very young man—had, among other valuable observations, promulgated this distinction, Locke did not advance beyond the limit already reached by the Cartesians ;—indeed, the praises that are so frequently lavished on this philosopher for his doctrine concerning the distinctions of Ideas,—the conditions of Definition, &c., —only prove that his encomiasts are ignorant of what had been done, and, in many respects, far better done, by Descartes and his school :—in fact, with regard to the Cartesian Philosophy in general, it must be confessed, that Locke has many errors to expiate, arising

a Essay, pp. 91, 92, [*Logik*, § 46.— ED.]
β Part 1. ch. ix. —For a comparison of this statement with those of Descartes and

Leibnitz, see the Appendix to Mr Baynes's translation of the *Port Royal Logic*, p. 423 (second edition.) —ED.

partly from oversight, and partly from the most un-
almost needless to say, that those who, in this country,
have written on this subject, posterior to Locke, have
not advanced a step beyond him; for though Leibnitz be often mentioned, and even occasionally quoted,
by our British philosophers, I am aware of none who
possessed a systematic acquaintance with his philosophy, of none, I might almost say, who were even
superficially versed, either in his writings, or in those
of any of the illustrious thinkers of his school.

But to consider the distinction in itself.—We have   The dis-
seen that a concept is clear, when we are able to re-   tinction in
cognise it as different from other concepts. But we   itself.
may discriminate a whole from other wholes, we may
discriminate a concept from other concepts, though
we have only a confused knowledge of the parts of
which that whole, of the characters of which that
concept, is made up. This may be illustrated by the   Illustrat-
analogy of our Perceptive and Representative Faculties.   ed by the
We are all acquainted with many, say a thousand,   analogy of
individuals; that is, we recognise such and such a   Perception
                                                        and Repre-
countenance as the countenance of John, and as not   sentation.
the countenance of James, Thomas, Richard, or any of
the other 999. This we do with a clear and certain
knowledge. But the countenances, which we thus
distinguish from each other, are, each of them, a complement made up of a great number of separate traits
or features; and it might, at first view, be supposed
that, as a whole is only the sum of its parts, a clear
cognition of a whole countenance can only be realised
through a distinct knowledge of each of its constituent
features. But the slightest consideration will prove
that this is not the case. For how few of us are able

LECT.
IX.

to say of any, the most familiar face, what are the particular traits which go to form the general result; and yet, on that account, we hesitate, neither in regard to our own knowledge of an individual, nor in regard to the knowledge possessed by others.—Suppose a witness be adduced in a court of justice to prove the identity or non-identity of a certain individual with the perpetrator of a certain crime, the commission of which he had chanced to see,—would the counsel be allowed to invalidate the credibility of the witness by, first of all, requiring him to specify the various elements of which the total likeness of the accused was compounded, and then by showing that, as the witness either could not specify the several traits, or specified what did not agree with the features of the accused, he was, therefore, incompetent to prove the identity or non-identity required ? This would not be allowed. For the court would hold that a man might have a clear perception and a clear representation of a face and figure, of which, however, he had not separately considered, and could not separately image to himself, the constituent elements. Thus, even the judicial determination of life and death supposes, as real, the difference between a clear and a distinct knowledge : for a distinct knowledge lies in the knowledge of the constituent parts; while a clear knowledge is only of the constituted whole.

Continuing our illustrations from the human countenance,—we all have a clear knowledge of any face which we have seen, but few of us have distinct knowledge even of those with which we are familiar ; but the paintr, who, having looked upon a countenance, can retire and reproduce its likeness in detail, has necessarily both a clear and a distinct know-

ledge of it. Now, what is thus the case with perceptions and representations, is equally the case with
notions. We may be able clearly to discriminate one
concept from another, although the degree of consciousness does not enable us distinctly to discriminate the various component characters of either concept from each other. The Clearness and the Distinctness of a notion are thus not the same; the former
involves merely the power of distinguishing the total
objects of our notions from each other; the latter involves the power of distinguishing the several characters, the several attributes, of which that object is the
sum. In the former, the unity, in the latter, the multiplicity, of the notion is called into relief.

The Distinctness of a concept supposes, however, the
Clearness; and may, therefore, be regarded as a higher
degree of the same quality or perfection. "To the
distinctness of a notion, over and above its general
clearness, there are required three conditions,—1°, The
clear apprehension of its several characters or component
parts; 2°, The clear contrast or discrimination of these;
and, 3°, The clear recognition of the nexus by which
the several parts are bound up into a unity or whole.

"As the clearness, so the distinctness, of a notion
is susceptible of many degrees. A concept may be
called *distinct*, when it involves the amount of consciousness required to discriminate from each other its
principal characters; but it is so much the more distinct, 1°, In proportion to the greater number of the
characters apprehended; 2°, In proportion to the
greater clearness of their discrimination; and, 3°, In
proportion to the precision with which the mode of
their connection is recognised. But the greater distinctness is not exclusively or even principally deter-

LECT.
IX.

mined by the greater number of the clearly apprehended characters; it depends still more on their
superior importance. In particular, it is of moment,
whether the characters be positive or negative, internal or external, permanent or transitory, peculiar or
common, essential or accidental, original or derived.
From the mere consideration of the differences subsisting between attributes, there emerge three rules to
be attended to in bestowing on a concept its requisite
distinctness.

"In the first place, we should endeavour to discover
the positive characters of the object conceived; as it
is our purpose to know what the object is, and not
what it is not. When, however, as is not unfrequently
the case, it is not at once easy to discover what the
positive attributes are, our endeavour should be first
directed to the detection of the negative; and this
not only because it is always an advance in knowledge,
when we ascertain what an object is not, but, likewise,
because the discovery of the negative characters conducts us frequently to a discovery of the positive.

"In the second place, among the positive qualities
we should seek out the intrinsic and permanent before
the extrinsic and transitory; for the former give us a
purer and more determinate knowledge of an object,
though this object may likewise at the same time
present many external relations and mutable modifications. Among the permanent attributes, the proper
or peculiar always merit a preference, if for no other
reason, because through them, and not through the
common qualities, can the proper or peculiar nature
of the object become known to us.

"In the third place, among the permanent characters we ought first to hunt out the necessary or essen-

tial, and then to descend from them to the contingent or accidental; and this not only because we thus give order and connection to our notions, but, likewise, because the contingent characters are frequently only to be comprehended through the necessary." [a]

LECT. IX.

But before leaving this part of our subject, it may be proper to illustrate the distinction of Clear and Distinct notions by one or two concrete examples. Of many things we have clear but not distinct notions. Thus we have a clear, but not a distinct, notion of colours, sounds, tastes, smells, &c. For we are fully able to distinguish red from white, to distinguish an acute from a grave note, the voice of a friend from that of a stranger, the scent of roses from that of onions, the flavour of sugar from that of vinegar; but by what plurality of separate and enunciable characters is this discrimination made? It is because we are unable to do this, that we cannot describe such perceptions and representations to others.

The distinction of Clear and Distinct notions illustrated by concrete examples.

" If you ask of me," said St Augustin, " what is Time, I know not; if you do not ask me, I know." [b] What does this mean? Simply that he had a clear, but not a distinct, notion of Time.

Of a triangle we have a clear notion, when we distinguish a triangle from other figures, without specially considering the characters which constitute it what it is. But when we think it as a portion of space bounded by three lines, as a figure whose three angles are equal to two right angles, &c., then we obtain of it a distinct concept.

We now come to the consideration of the question,— How does the Distinctness of a concept stand affected

How the Distinctness of a Concept

LECT.
IX.

is affected
by the two
quantities of
a Concept.

Par. XXIX.
Distinct-
ness, Inter-
nal and
External.

Explication.

by the two quantities of a concept?—and in reference
to this point I would, in the first place, dictate to you
the following paragraph:—

¶ XXIX. As a concept is a plurality of characters bound up into unity, and as that plurality
is contained partly in its Intensive, partly under
its Extensive, quantity; its Distinctness is, in
like manner, in relation to these quantities, partly
an Internal or Intensive, partly an External or
Extensive Distinctness.*

In explanation of this, it is to be observed, that, as
the distinctness of a concept is contained in the clear
apprehension of the various attributes of which it is
the sum, as it is the sum of these attributes in two
opposite relations, which constitute, in fact, two opposite quantities or wholes, and as these wholes are
severally capable of illustration by analysis,—it follows,
that each of these analyses will contribute its peculiar
share to the general distinctness of the concept. Thus,
if the distinctness of a notion bears reference to that
plurality which constitutes its comprehension, in other
words, to that which is contained *in* the concept, the
distinctness is denominated an *internal* or *intensive*
distinctness, or distinctness of *comprehension*. On the
other hand, if the distinctness refers to that plurality
which constitutes the extension of the notion, in other
words, to what is contained *under* it, in that case, the
distinctness is called an *external* or *extensive* distinctness, a distinctness of *extension*. It is only when a
notion combines in it both of these species of distinctness, it is only when its parts have been analysed in

* Krug, *Logik*, § 34 ; Esser, *Logik*, § 48.—ED.

reference to the two quantities, that it reaches the
highest degree of distinctness and of perfection.

LECT.
IX.

The Internal Distinctness of a notion is accomplished by Definition, that is, by the enumeration of
the characters or partial notions contained in it; the
External Distinctness, again, of a notion is accomplished through Division, that is, through the enumeration of the objects which are contained under it.
Thus the concept *man* is rendered intensively more
distinct, when we declare that man is a *rational animal*; it is rendered extensively more distinct, when
we declare that man is partly *male*, partly *female
man.* In the former case, we resolve the concept
man into its several characters,—into its partial or
constituent attributes; in the latter, we resolve it
into its subordinate concepts, or inferior genera. In
simple notions, there is thus possible an extensive,
but not an intensive, distinctness; in individual
notions, there is possible an intensive, but not an
extensive, distinctness.β Thus the concepts *existence,
green, sweet,* &c., though as absolutely or relatively
simple, their comprehension cannot be analysed into
any constituent attributes, and they do not, therefore,
admit of definition; still it cannot be said that they
are incapable of being rendered more distinct. For
do we not analyse the pluralities of which these concepts are the sum, when we say, that existence is
either ideal or real, that green is a yellowish or a
bluish green, that sweet is a pungent or a mawkish
sweet?—and do we not, by this analysis, attain a
greater degree of logical perfection than when we
think them only clearly and as wholes?[7] "A con-

α Krug, p. 96, [*Logik*, § 34.—Ed.]   γ Krug, *Logik*, § 84, Anmerk., i.
β Esser, *Logik*, § 43.—Ed.   pp. 95, 96.—Ed.

cept has, therefore, attained its highest point of distinctness, when there is such a consciousness of its characters that, in rendering its comprehension distinct, we touch on notions which, as simple, admit of no definition, and in rendering its extension distinct, we touch on notions which, as individual, admit of no ulterior division. It is true, indeed, that a distinctness of this degree is one which is only ideal; that is, one to which we are always approximating, but which we never are able actually to reach. In order to approach as near as possible to this ideal, we must always inquire, what is contained in, and what under, a notion, and endeavour to obtain a distinct consciousness of it in both relations. What, in this research, first presents itself we must again analyse anew, with reference always both to comprehension and to extension; and descending from the higher to the lower, from the greater to the less, we ought to stop only when our process is arrested in the individual or in the simple." [a]

a Esser, *Logik*, § 48, p. 96.—Ed.

LECTURE X.

STOICHEIOLOGY.

SECT. II.—OF THE PRODUCTS OF THOUGHT.

I.—ENNOEMATIC.

IMPERFECTION OF CONCEPTS.

I⊤ is now necessary to notice an Imperfection to which
concepts are peculiarly liable, and in the exposition
of which I find it necessary to employ an expression,
which, though it has the highest philosophical authority for its use, I would still, in consequence of its ambiguity in English, have avoided, if this could have been
done without compromising the knowledge of what it
is intended to express. The expression I mean, is
intuitive, in the particular signification in which it is
used by Leibnitz[a] and the continental philosophers in
general, to denote what is common to our direct and
ostensive cognition of individual objects, in Sense or
Imagination, (Presentation or Representation), and in
opposition to our indirect and symbolical cognition of
general objects, through the use of signs or language,
in the Understanding. But, on this head, I would,
first of all, dictate to you the following paragraph.

¶ XXX. As a notion or concept is the factitious whole or unity made up of a plurality of

LECT.
X.

Imperfec-
tion of Con-
cepts.

Par. XXX.
Imperfec-
tion of Con-
cepts.

a *Meditationes de Cognitione, Veri-*   p. 80.—ED.
tate, et Ideis, Opera, ed. Erdmann,

attributes,—a whole too often of a very complex multiplicity; and as this multiplicity is only mentally held together, inasmuch as the concept is fixed and ratified in a sign or word; it frequently happens, that, in its employment, the word does not suggest the whole amount of thought for which it is the adequate expression, but, on the contrary, we frequently give and take the sign, either with an obscure or indistinct consciousness of its meaning, or even without an actual consciousness of its signification at all.

This liability to the vices of Obscurity and Indistinctness arises, 1°, From the very nature of a concept, which is the binding up of a multiplicity in unity; and, 2°, From its dependence upon language, as the necessary condition of its existence and stability. .In consequence of this, when a notion is of a very complex and heterogeneous composition, we frequently use the term by which it is denoted, without a clear or distinct consciousness of the various characters of which the notion is the sum; and thus it is, that we both give and take words without any, or, at least, without the adequate complement of thought. I may exemplify this;—You are aware, that in countries where bank-notes have not superseded the use of the precious metals, large payments are made in bags of money, purporting to contain a certain number of a certain denomination of coin, or, at least, a certain amount in value. Now, those bags are often sealed up and passed from one person to another, without the tedious process, at each transference, of counting out their contents, and this upon the faith, that, if examined, they will be found actually to contain the number of pieces for which they are marked, and for which they pass current. In this state of matters, it is, however, evident, that many errors or frauds may be committed, and that a bag may be given and taken in payment for one sum, which contains another, or which, in fact, may not even contain any money at all. Now the case is similar in regard to notions. As the scaled bag or *rouleau* testifies to the enumerated sum, and gives unity to what would otherwise be an unconnected multitude of pieces, each only representing its separate value; so the sign or word proves and ratifies the existence of a concept, that is, it vouches the tying up of a certain number of attributes or characters in a single concept,—attributes which would otherwise exist to us only as a multitude of separate and unconnected representations of value. So far the analogy is manifest; but it is only general. The bag, the guaranteed sum, and the constituent coins, represent in a still more proximate manner the term, the concept, and the constituent characters. For in regard to each, we may do one of two things. On the one hand, we may test the bag, that is, open it, and ascertain the accuracy of its stated value, by counting out the pieces which it purports to contain; or we may accept and pass the bag, without such a critical enumeration. In the other case, we may test the general term, prove that it is valid for the amount and quality of thought of which it is the sign, by spreading out in consciousness the various characters of which the concept professes to be the complement; or we may take and give the term without such an evolution.[a]

a A hint of this illustration is to vol. i. chap. viii. p. 200.—Ed.
be found in Degerando, *Des Signes*,

LECT.
X.

It is evident from this, that notions or concepts are peculiarly liable to great vagueness and ambiguity, and that their symbols are liable to be passed about without the proper kind, or the adequate amount, of thought.

The liability to ambiguity and vagueness of concepts noticed by British philosophers.

This interesting subject has not escaped the observation of the philosophers of this country, and by them it has, in fact, with great ingenuity been illustrated; but as they are apparently ignorant, that the matter had, before them, engaged the attention of sundry foreign philosophers, by whom it has been even more ably canvassed and expounded, I shall, in the exposition of this point, also do justice to the illustrious thinkers to whom is due the honour of having originally and most satisfactorily discussed it.

Stewart quoted on this subject.

The following passage from Mr Stewart will afford the best foundation for my subsequent remarks. "In the last section I mentioned Dr Campbell as an ingenious defender of the system of the Nominalists, and I alluded to a particular application which he has made of their doctrine. The reasonings which I had then in view, are to be found in the seventh chapter of the second book of his *Philosophy of Rhetoric*, in which chapter he proposes to explain how it happens, 'that nonsense so often escapes being detected, both by the writer and the reader.' The title is somewhat ludicrous in a grave philosophical work, but the disquisition to which it is prefixed, contains many acute and profound remarks on the nature and power of signs, both as a medium of communication, and as an instrument of thought.

Refers to Hume.

"Dr Campbell's speculations with respect to language as an instrument of thought, seem to have been suggested by the following passage in Mr Hume's

Treatise of Human Nature :[a]—' I believe every one who examines the situation of his mind in reasoning, will agree with me, that we do not annex distinct and complete ideas to every term we make use of; and that in talking of Government, Church, Negotiation, Conquest, we seldom spread out in our minds all the simple ideas of which these complex ones are composed. It is, however, observable, that notwithstanding this imperfection, we may avoid talking nonsense on these subjects, and may perceive any repugnance among the ideas, as well as if we had a full comprehension of them. Thus if, instead of saying, that in war the weaker have always recourse to negotiation, we should say, that they have always recourse to conquest; the custom which we have acquired, of attributing certain relations to ideas, still follows the words, and makes us immediately perceive the absurdity of that proposition.'

"In the remarks which Dr Campbell has made on this passage, he has endeavoured to explain in what manner our habits of thinking and speaking gradually establish in the mind such relations among the words we employ, as enable us to carry on processes of reasoning by means of them, without attending in every instance to their particular signification. With most of his remarks on this subject I perfectly agree; but the illustrations he gives of them are of too great extent to be introduced here, and I would not wish to run the risk of impairing their perspicuity, by attempting to abridge them. I must, therefore, refer such of my readers as wish to prosecute the speculation, to his very ingenious and philosophical treatise.

"'In consequence of these circumstances,' says Dr

a Part i. § 7.—Ed.

Campbell, ' it happens that, in matters which are perfectly familiar to us, we are able to reason by means
of words, without examining, in every instance, their
signification. Almost all the possible applications of
the terms (in other words, all the acquired relations
of the signs) have become customary to us. The consequence is, that an unusual application of any term
is instantly detected ; this detection breeds doubt,
and this doubt occasions an immediate recourse to
ideas. The recourse of the mind, when in any degree puzzled with the signs, to the knowledge it has
of the things signified, is natural, and on such subjects
perfectly easy. And of this recourse the discovery of
the meaning, or of the unmeaningness of what is said,
is the immediate effect. But in matters that are by
no means familiar, or are treated in an uncommon .
manner, and in such as are of an abstruse and intricate
nature, the case is widely different.' The instances in
which we are chiefly liable to be imposed on by words
without meaning, are (according to Dr Campbell), the
three following :—

    " *First*, Where there is an exuberance of metaphor.

    " *Secondly*, When the terms most frequently occur-
ring denote things which are of a complicated nature,
and to which the mind is not sufficiently familiarised.
Such are the words—Government, Church, State, Constitution, Polity, Power, Commerce, Legislature, Jurisdiction, Proportion, Symmetry, Elegance.

    " *Thirdly*, When the terms employed are very
abstract, and consequently of very extensive signification.

    " ' The more general any word is in its signification,
it is the more liable to be abused by an improper or
unmeaning application. A very general term is appli-

cable alike to a multitude of different individuals, a LECT. X.
particular term is applicable but to a few.   When the
rightful applications of a word are extremely numerous, they cannot all be so strongly fixed by habit, but
that, for greater security, we must perpetually recur
in our minds from the sign to the notion we have of
the thing signified ; and for the reason aforemen-
tioned, it is in such instances difficult precisely to
ascertain this notion.   Thus the latitude of a word,
though different from its ambiguity, hath often a
similar effect.' "[a]

Now, on this I would, in the first place, observe, Locke an-ticipated
that the credit attributed to Hume by Dr Campbell Hume in remarking
and Mr Stewart, as having been the first by whom the employ-
the observation had been made, is, even in relation to ment of terms with-
British philosophers, not correct.   Hume has stated out distinct meaning.
nothing which had not, with equal emphasis and an
equal development, been previously stated by Locke,
in four different places of his *Essay*.[β]

Thus, to take only one out of at least four passages
directly to the same effect, and out of many in which
the same is evidently maintained, he says, in the
chapter entitled—*Of the Abuse of Words :*—" Others Locke quoted.
there be who extend this abuse yet farther, who take
so little care to lay by words which, in their primary
notation, have scarce any clear and distinct ideas
which they are annexed to, that by an unpardonable
negligence they familiarly use words which the propriety of language · has affixed to very important
ideas, without any distinct meaning at all.   *Wisdom,
glory, grace,* &c., are words frequent enough in every

<hr>

a *Elements,* vol. i., chap. iv. § 4,   § 7 ; ii., xxix. 9 ; ii., xxxi. 8 ; iii.,
Works, vol. ii., p. 193-196.   ix. 6 ; iii., x. 2.—ED.
β Compare *Essay,* B. ii., ch. xxii.,

man's mouth; but if a great many of those who use
them should be asked what they mean by them, they
would be at a stand, and not know what to answer:
a plain proof, that though they have learned those
sounds, and have them ready at their tongue's end,
yet there are no determined ideas laid up in their
minds, which are to be expressed to others by them.
Men having been accustomed from their cradles to
learn words, which are easily got and retained, before
they knew or had framed the complex ideas to which
they were annexed, or which were to be found in the
things they were thought to stand for, they usually
continue to do so all their lives; and without taking
the pains necessary to settle in their minds determined
ideas, they use their words for such unsteady and
confused notions as they have, contenting themselves
with the same words other people use; as if their
very sound necessarily carried with it constantly the
same meaning. This though men make a shift with
in the ordinary occurrences of life, where they find it
necessary to be understood, and therefore they make
signs till they are so; yet this insignificancy in their
words, when they come to reason concerning either
their tenets or interest, manifestly fills their discourse
with abundance of empty unintelligible noise and jar-
gon, especially in moral matters, where the words, for
the most part, standing for arbitrary and numerous collections of ideas, not regularly and permanently united
in nature, their bare sounds are often only thought
on, or at least very obscure and uncertain notions
annexed to them. Men take the words they find in
use among their neighbours, and that they may not
seem ignorant what they stand for, use them confi-
dently, without much troubling their heads about a

certain fixed meaning : whereby, besides the case of it,
they obtain this advantage, that as in such discourses they seldom are in the right, so they are as seldom to be convinced that they are in the wrong; it being all one to go about to draw those men out of their mistakes who have no settled notions, as to dispossess a vagrant of his habitation, who has no settled abode. This I guess to be so ; and every one may observe in himself and others, whether it be or no." [a]

From a comparison of this passage with those which I have given you from Stewart, Campbell, and Hume, it is manifest that, among British philosophers, Locke is entitled to the whole honour of the observation : for it could easily be shown, even from the identity of expression, that Hume must have borrowed it from Locke; and of Hume's doctrine the two other philosophers profess only to be expositors.

This curious and important observation was not, however, first made by any British philosopher; for Leibnitz had not only anticipated Locke, in a publication prior to the *Essay*, but afforded the most precise and universal explanation of the phænomenon, which has yet been given.

The distinction of Intuitive and Symbolical knowledge first taken by Leibnitz.

To him we owe the memorable distinction of our knowledge into Intuitive and Symbolical, in which distinction is involved the explanation of the phænomenon in question. It is the establishment of this distinction, likewise, which has superseded in Germany the whole controversy of Nominalism and Conceptualism,—which, in consequence of the non-establishment of this distinction, and the relative imperfection of our philosophical language, has idly

This distinction has superseded the controversy of Nominalism and Conceptualism in Germany.

a Essay concerning Human Under-   x. §§ 3, 4.—ED.]
standing, vol. i. p. 226; [B. III., ch.

agitated the psychology of this country and of France.

That the doctrines of Leibnitz, on this and other cardinal points of psychology, should have remained apparently unknown to every philosopher of this country, is a matter not less of wonder than of regret, and is only to be excused by the mode in which Leibnitz gave his writings to the world. His most valuable thoughts on the most important subjects were generally thrown out in short treatises or letters, and these, for a long time, were to be found only in partial collections, and sometimes to be laboriously sought out, dispersed as they were in the various scientific Journals and Transactions of every country of Europe; and even when his works were at length collected, the attempt of his editor to arrange his papers according to their subjects (and what subject did Leibnitz not discuss?) was baffled by the multifarious nature of their contents. The most important of his philosophical writings,—his *Essays* in refutation of Locke,—were not merely a posthumous publication, but only published after the collected edition of his Works by Dutens; and this treatise, even after its publication, was so little known in Britain, that it remained absolutely unknown to Mr Stewart, (the only British philosopher, by the way, who seems to have had any acquaintance with the works of Leibnitz), until a very late period of his life. The matter, however, with which we are at present engaged, was discussed by Leibnitz in one of his very earliest writings; and in a paper entitled *De Cognitione, Veritate, et Ideis*, published in the *Acta Eruditorum* of 1684, we have, in the compass of two quarto pages, all that has been advanced of principal

importance in regard to the peculiarity of our cognitions LECT.
by concept, and in regard to the dependence of our X.
concepts upon language. In this paper, besides estab-
lishing the difference of Clear and Distinct knowledge,
he enounces the memorable distinction of Intuitive
and Symbolical knowledge,—a distinction not certainly unknown to the later philosophers of this country, but which, from their not possessing terms in
which precisely to embody it, has always remained
vague and inapplicable to common use. Speaking of
the analysis of complex notions, he says—"For the
most part, however, especially in an analysis of any
length, we do not view at once (*non simul intuemur*)
the whole characters or attributes of the thing, but
in place of these we employ signs, the explication
of which into what they signify, we are wont, at the
moment of actual thought, for the sake of brevity,
to omit, knowing or believing that we have this explication always in our power. Thus, when I think a
chiliogon, (or polygon of a thousand equal sides), I do
not always consider the various attributes, of the side,
of the equality, and of the number a thousand, but
use these words, (whose meaning is obscurely and imperfectly presented to the mind), in lieu of the notions
which I have of them, because I remember, that I
possess the signification of these words, though their
application and explication I do not at present deem
to be necessary. This kind of thinking I am used to
call *blind* or *symbolical*. We employ it in Algebra and
in Arithmetic, and in fact universally. And certainly,
when the notion is very complex, we cannot think at
once all the ingredient notions; but where this is possible,—at least, inasmuch as it is possible,—I call the
cognition *intuitive*. Of the primary elements of our

Leibnitz
quoted on
Intuitive
and Symbo-
lical know-
ledge.

LECT.
X.

notions, there is given no other knowledge than the
intuitive; as of our composite notions, there is, for
the most part, possible only a symbolical. From these
considerations it is also evident, that of the things
which we distinctly know we are not conscious of the
ideas, except in so far as we employ an intuitive cognition. And, indeed, it happens that we often falsely
believe that we have in our mind the ideas of things,
erroneously supposing that certain terms which we
employ had been applied and explicated; and it is
not true,—at least it is ambiguously expressed, what
some assert,—that we cannot speak concerning anything, understanding what we say, without having
an idea of it actually present. For we frequently
apply any kind of meaning to the several words, or we
merely recollect us that we have formerly understood
them, but because we are content with this blind
thinking, and do not follow out the resolution of the
notions, it happens, that contradictions are allowed to
lie hid, which perchance the composite notion involves.
.   .   .   .   Thus, at first sight, it must seem, that we
could form an idea of a maximum velocity (*motus
celerrimus*), for in using the terms we understand what
we say; we shall find, however, that it is impossible,
for the notion of a quickest motion is shown to be contradictory, and, therefore, inconceivable. Let us suppose, that a wheel is turned with a velocity absolutely
at its maximum; every one perceives that if one of
its spokes be produced, its outer end will be moved
more rapidly than the nails in the circumference of
the wheel; the motion, therefore, of these is not a
maximum, which is contrary to the hypothesis, and,
therefore, involves a contradiction."

This quotation will suffice to show you how cor-

rectly Leibnitz apprehended the nature of concepts,
as opposed to the presentations and representations
of the subsidiary faculties; and the introduction of
the term *Symbolical* knowledge, to designate the
former, and the term *Intuitive* knowledge to comprehend the two latter,—terms which have ever since
become classical in his own country,—has bestowed
on the German language of philosophy, in this respect, a power and precision to which that of no other
nation can lay claim. In consequence of this, while
the philosophers of this country have been all along
painfully expounding the phænomenon as one of the
most recondite arcana of psychology, in Germany it
has, for a century and a half, subsided into one of the
elementary doctrines of the science of mind. It was
in consequence of the establishment of this distinction
by Leibnitz, that a peculiar expression, (*Begriff, conceptus*), was appropriated to the symbolical notions of
the Understanding, in contrast to the intuitive presentations of Sense and representations of Imagination,
which last also were furnished with the distinctive
appellation of *intuitions, (Anschauungen, intuitus).*
Thus it is, that, by a more copious and well-appointed
language, philosophy has, in Germany, been raised
above various controversies, which, merely in consequence of the poverty and vagueness of its English
nomenclature, have idly occupied our speculations.
But to return to the mere logical question.

The doctrine of Leibnitz in regard to this natural
imperfection of our concepts was not overlooked by his
disciples, and I shall read to you a passage from the
Lesser Logic of Wolf,—a work above a century old,
and which was respectably translated from German
into English in the year 1770. This translation is

now rarely to be met with, which may account for its being apparently totally unknown to our British philosophers; and yet, upon the whole, with all its faults and imperfections, it is perhaps the most valuable work on Logic, (to say nothing of the *Port Royal Logic*), in the English language.

Wolf quoted. Words or terms,— what.

"By Words, we usually make known our thoughts to others. And thus they are nothing but uttered articulate signs of our thoughts for the information of others. For example, if one asks me, what I am thinking of, and I answer, the sun; by this word I acquaint him what object my thoughts are then employed about.

"If two persons, therefore, are talking together, it is requisite, in order to be understood, first, that he who speaks shall join some notion or meaning to each word; secondly, that he who hears shall join the very same notion that the speaker does.

"Consequently, a certain notion or meaning must be connected with, and therefore something be signified by, each word.

"Now, in order to know whether we understand what we speak, or that our words are not mere empty sound, we ought, at every word we utter, to ask ourselves what notion or meaning we join therewith.

In speaking or thinking, the meaning of words not always attended to.

"For it is carefully to be observed, that we have not always the notion of the thing present to us or in view, when we speak or think of it; but are satisfied, when we imagine we sufficiently understand what we speak, if we think we recollect that we have had at another time the notion which is to be joined to this or the other word; and thus we represent to ourselves, as at a distance only, or obscurely, the thing denoted by the term.

" Hence it usually happens, that when we combine words together, to each of which apart a meaning or notion answers, we imagine we understand what we utter, though that which is denoted by such combined words be impossible, and, consequently, can have no meaning ; for that which is impossible is nothing at all, and of nothing there can be no idea. For instance, we have a notion of gold, as also of iron : but it is impossible that iron can, at the same time, be gold, consequently neither can we have any notion of iron-gold ; and yet we understand what people mean when they mention *iron-gold.*

" In the instance alleged, it certainly strikes every one at first that the expression *iron-gold* is an empty sound ; but yet there are a thousand instances in which it does not so easily strike. For example, when I say a rectilineal two-lined figure, contained under two right lines, I am equally well understood as when I say a right-lined triangle, a figure contained under three right-lines : and it should seem we had a distinct notion of both figures. However, as we show in geometry that two right-lines can never contain a space, it is also impossible to form a notion of a rectilineal two-lined figure ; and, consequently, that expression is an empty sound. Just so it holds with the vegetable soul of plants, supposed to be a spiritual being, whereby plants are enabled to vegetate or grow. For though those words taken apart are intelligible, yet in their combination they have no manner of meaning. Just so if I say that the Attractive Spirit, or Attractive Cord, as Linus calls it, or the Attractive Force, as some philosophers at this day, is an immaterial principle superadded to matter, whereby the attractions in nature are performed ; no

LECT.
X.

notion or meaning can possibly be joined with these
words. To this head also belong the Natural Sym-
pathy and Antipathy of Plants; the Band of Right
or law (*vinculum juris*), used in the definition of
Obligation, by Civilians; the Principle of Evil of the
Manicheans," &c."

a *Logic or Rational Thoughts on*   mers *of Baron Wolfius*, c. ii., p. 54-
the *Powers of the Human Under-*   57; London, 1770.—ED.
standing. *Translated from the Ger-*

LECTURE XI.

STOICHEIOLOGY.

SECT. I.—OF THE PRODUCTS OF THOUGHT.

I.—ENNOEMATIC.

III. RECIPROCAL RELATIONS OF CONCEPTS.

A. QUANTITY OF EXTENSION—SUBORDINATION AND CO-ORDINATION.

I NOW proceed to the third and last Relation of Con- LECT.
cepts,—that of concepts to each other. The two ___XI.___
former relations of notions,—to their objects and to
their subject,—gave their Quantity and Quality. This,
the relation of notions to each other, gives what is
emphatically and strictly denominated their *Relation.*
In this rigorous signification, the Relation of Concepts
may be thus defined.

¶ XXXI. The Relation proper of notions con- Par. XXXI.
sists in those determinations or attributes which Reciprocal
belong to them, not viewed as apart and in them- of Concepts.
selves, but as reciprocally compared. Concepts can
only be compared together with reference, either,
1°, To their Extension ; or, 2°, To their Comprehension.   All their relations are, therefore, dependent
on the one or on the other of these quantities.[a]

¶ XXXII. As dependent upon Extension, con- Par. XXXII.
cepts stand to each other in the five mutual Under Ex-
                                                tension.

[a] Cf. Krug, *Logik,* § 36.—ED.

relations, 1°, Of Exclusion ; 2°, Of Coextension ;
3°, Of Subordination ; 4°, Of Co-ordination ; and,
5°, Of Intersection.

1. One concept excludes another, when no part
of the one coincides with any part of the other.
2. One concept is coextensive with another, when
each has the same number of subordinate concepts
under it. 3. One concept is subordinate to another, (which may be called the *Superordinate*),
when the former is included within, or makes a
part of, the sphere or extension of the latter. 4.
Two or more concepts are co-ordinated when each
excludes the other from its sphere, but when
both go immediately to make up the extension
of a third concept, to which they are co-subordi-
nate. 5. Concepts intersect each other, when
the sphere of the one is partially contained in
the sphere of the other.[a]

Of Exclusion, *horse, syllogism,* are examples. There
is, however, no absolute exclusion.

As examples of Coextension,—the concepts, *living
being,* and *organised being,* may be given. For, using
the term *life* as applicable to plants as well as to
animals, there is nothing living which is not organised, and nothing organised which is not living. This
reciprocal relation will be represented by two circles
covering each other, or by two lines of equal length
and in positive relation.

As examples of Subordination and Co-ordination,
man, dog, horse, stand, as correlatives, in subordination to the concept *animal,* and, as reciprocal correlatives, in co-ordination with each other.

a Cf. Krug, *Logik,* § 41.—Ed.

What I would call the reciprocal relation of In- LECT.
XI. tersection, takes place between concepts, when their spheres cross or cut each other, that is, fall partly within, partly without, each other. Thus, the concepts *black* and *heavy* mutually intersect each other, for some black things are heavy, some not, and some heavy things are black, some not.

CONCEPTS, THEIR RELATIONS PROPER: TO WIT OF

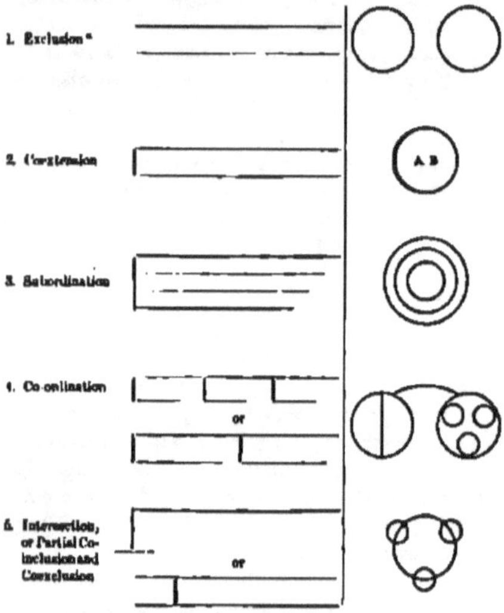

1. Exclusion*

2. Coextension

3. Subordination

4. Co-ordination

        or

5. Intersection, or Partial Co-inclusion and Coexclusion

        or

Of these relations those of Subordination and Co- Subordina-
tion and
Co-ordina- ordination are of principal importance, as on them

<hr>

* The notation by straight lines   1848.—ED.
was first employed by the Author in

LECT.
XL.

tion of
principal
Importance.

Terms ex-
pressive of
the different
modes of the
relation of
Subordina-
tion.
reposes the whole system of classification; and to
them alone it is, therefore, necessary to accord a more
particular consideration.

Under the Subordination of notions, there are various terms to express the different modes of this relation; these it is necessary that you should now learn
and hereafter bear in mind, for they form an essential
part of the language of Logic, and will come frequently, in the sequel, to be employed in considering
the analysis of Reasonings.

Par. XXXIII.
Superior and
Inferior,
Broader and
Narrower,
notions.
¶ XXXIII. Of notions which stand to each
other in the relation of Subordination,—the one
is the *Higher* or *Superior*, (*notio, conceptus, superior*), the other the *Lower* or *Inferior*, (*notio, conceptus, inferior*). The superior notion is likewise
called the *Wider* or *Broader* (*latior*), the inferior
is likewise called the *Narrower* (*angustior*).[a]

Explication.
The meaning of these expressions is sufficiently
manifest. A notion is called the *higher* or *superior*,
inasmuch as it is viewed as standing over another in
the relation of subordination,—as including it within
its domain or sphere; and a correlative notion is called
the *lower* or *inferior*, as thus standing under a superior. Again the higher notion is called the *wider* or
broader, as containing under it a greater number of
things; the lower is called the *narrower*, as containing under it a smaller number.

Par. XXXIV.
Universal
and Particu-
lar notions.
¶ XXXIV. The higher or wider concept is
also called, in contrast to the lower or narrower,
a *Universal* or *General Notion*, (νόημα καθόλου,

a Cf. Krug, *Logik*, § 42.—Ed.

notio, conceptus, universalis, generalis); the lower or narrower concept, in contrast to the higher or wider, a *Particular Notion*, (νόημα μερικόν, *notio, conceptus, particularis*).[a]

The meaning of these expressions, likewise, requires no illustration. A notion is called *universal*, inasmuch as it is considered as binding up a multitude of parts or inferior concepts into the unity of a whole; for *universus* means *in unum versus* or *ad unum versus*, that is, *many turned into one*, or *many regarded as one*, and *universal* is employed to denote the attribution of this relation to objects. A notion is called *particular*, inasmuch as it is considered as one of the parts of a higher concept or whole.

¶ XXXV. A superior concept, inasmuch as it constitutes a common attribute or character for a number of inferior concepts, is called a *General Notion*, (νόημα καθόλου, *notio, conceptus, generalis*), or, in a single word, a *Genus*, (γένος, *genus*). A notion, inasmuch as it is considered as at once affording a common attribution for a certain complement of inferior concepts or individual objects, and as itself an inferior concept, contained under a higher, is called a *Special Notion*, (νόημα εἰδικόν, *notio, conceptus, specialis*), or in a single word, a *Species*, (εἶδος, *species*). The abstraction which carries up species into genera, is called, in that respect, *Generification*, or, more loosely, *Generalisation*. The determination which

a [See Ammonius, *In De Interpret.*, l. 72 b, (Brandis, *Scholia in Aristot.*, p. 113; Facciolati, *Rudimenta Logica*, p. 39] [*Logica*, tom. I., P. I., c. iv., § 8, 4th edit., Venice, 1772. Cf. Krug, *Logik*, § 42.—Ed.]

divides a genus into its species is called, in that
respect, *Specification.* Genera and Species are
both called *Classes;* and the arrangement of
things under them is, therefore, denominated
Classification.[*]

It is manifest that the distinction into Genera and
Species is a merely relative distinction; as the same
notion is, in one respect, a genus, in another respect,
a species. For except a notion has no higher notion,
that is, except it be itself the widest or most universal
notion, it may always be regarded as subordinated to
another; and, in so far as it is actually thus regarded,
it is a species. Again, every notion except that which
has under it only individuals, is, in so far as it is thus
viewed, a genus. For example, the notion *triangle,* if
viewed in relation to the notion of *rectilineal figure,*
is a species, as is likewise *rectilineal figure* itself, if
viewed in relation to *figure* simply. Again, the concept *triangle* is a genus, when viewed in reference to
the concepts,—*right-angled triangle, acute-angled
triangle,* &c. A right-angled triangle is, however,
only a species, and not possibly a genus, if under it be
necessarily included individuals alone. But, in point
of fact, it is impossible to reach in theory any lowest
species; for we can always conceive some difference
by which any concept may be divided *ad infinitum.*
This, however, as it is only a speculative curiosity,
like the infinitesimal divisibility of matter, may be
thrown out of view in relation to practice; and,
therefore, the definition, by Porphyry and logicians in
general, of the lowest species, (of which I am immediately to speak), is practically correct, even though

* Krug, *Logik,* § 43.—Ed.

it cannot bo vindicated against theoretical objections. On the other hand, we soon and easily reach the highest genus, which is given in τὸ ὄν, ens aliquid, being, thing, something, &c., which are only various expressions of the same absolute universality. Out of these conditions there arise certain denominations of concepts, which it is, likewise, necessary that you bo made aware of.

In regard to the terms *Generification* and *Specification*, these are limited expressions for the processes of Abstraction and Determination, considered in a particular relation. Abstraction and Determination, you will recollect, we have already spoken of in general;[a] it will, therefore, be necessary to say only a very few words in reference to them, as the several operations by which out of species we evolve genera, and out of genera we evolve species. And first, in regard to Abstraction and Generification. In every complex notion, we can limit our attention to its constituent characters, to the exclusion of some one. We thus think away from this one,—we abstract from it. Now, the concept which remains, that is, the fasciculus of thought *minus* the one character which we have thrown out, is, in relation to the original,—the entire, concept, the next higher,—the proximately superior notion. But a concept and a next higher concept are to each other as species and genus. The process of Abstraction, therefore, by which out of a proximately lower we evolve a proximately higher concept, is, when we speak with logical precision, called the process of *Generification*.

Take, for example, the concept *man*. This concept is proximately composed of the two concepts or con-

a See above, p. 122 *et seq.*—Ed.

VOL. I.   N

stituent characters,—*animal* and *rational being*. If
we think either of these characters away from the
other, we shall have in that other a proximately higher
concept, to which the concept *man* stands in the
relation ·of a species to its genus. If we abstract
from *animal*, then *man* will stand as a species in
subordination to the genus *rational being*, and the
concept *animal* will then afford only a difference to
distinguish *man* as a co-ordinate species from *immaterial intelligences*. If, on the other hand, we abstract
from *rational being*, then *man* will stand as a species
in subordination to the genus *animal*, having for a
co-ordinate species *irrational animal*. Such is the
process of Generification. Now for the converse process of Specification.

Specifica-
tion.
Every series of concepts which has been obtained
by. abstraction, may be reproduced in an inverted
order, when, descending from the highest notion, we,
step by step, add on the several characters from which
we had abstracted in our ascent. This process, as
you remember, is called *Determination* ;—a very appropriate expression, inasmuch as by each character
or attribute which we add on, we limit or determine
more and more the abstract vagueness or extension of
the notion ; until at last, if every attribute be annexed,
the sum of attributes contained in the notion becomes
convertible with the sum of attributes of which some
concrete individual or reality is the complement.
Now, when we determine any notion by adding on a
subordinate concept, we divide it ; for the extension
of the higher concepts is precisely equal to the extension of the added concept *plus* its negation. Thus, if
to the concept *animal* we add on the next lower concept *rational*, we divide its extension into two halves ;

the one equal to *rational animal*, the other equal to its negation, that is, to *irrational animal.* Thus au added concept and its negation always constitute the immediately lower notion, into which a higher notion is divided. But as a notion stands to the notions proximately subordinate to it, in the immediate relation of a genus to its species, the process of Determination, by which a concept is thus divided, is, in logical language, appropriately denominated *Specification.*

So much in general for the Subordination of notions, considered as Genera and Species. There are, however, various gradations of this relation, and certain terms by which these are denoted, which it is requisite that you should learn and lay up in memory. The most important of these are comprehended in the following paragraph :—

¶ XXXVI. A Genus is of two degrees,—a high- est and a lower. In its highest degree, it is called the *Supreme* or *Most General Genus*, (γένος γενικώτατον, *genus summum* or *generalissimum*) and is defined, "that which being a genus cannot become a species." In its lower degree, it is called a *Subaltern* or *Intermediate*, (γένος ὑπάλληλον, *genus subalternum* or *medium*), and is defined, "that which being a genus can also become a species." A Species also is of two degrees,—a lowest and a higher. In its lowest degree, it is called a *Lowest* or *Most Special Species*, (εἶδος εἰδικώτατον, *species infima, ultima,* or *specialissima*"), and is defined, "that which being a species cannot become a genus." In its higher

a Vide Timpler, p. 253. [*Logicæ Systema*, L. ii. c. l. q. 16.—ED.]

degree it is called a *Subaltern* or *Intermediate
Species*, (εἶδος ὑπάλληλον, *species subalterna,
media*), and is defined, " that which being a
species may also become a genus." Thus a Subaltern Genus and a Subaltern Species are convertible.

Explica-
tion.

The distinctions and definitions in this paragraph
are taken from the celebrated *Introduction*[a] of Porphyry to the *Categories* of Aristotle, and they have
been generally adopted by logicians. It is evident,
that the only absolute distinction here established, is
that between the Highest or Supreme Genus and the
Lowest Species, for the other classes, to wit, the Subaltern or Intermediate, are, all and each, either genera
or species, according as we regard them in an ascending or a descending order; the same concept being a
genus, if considered as a whole containing under it
inferior concepts as parts, and a species, if considered
as itself the part of a higher concept or whole. The
distinction of concepts into Genus and Species, into
Supreme and Intermediate Genus, into Lowest and
Intermediate Species, is all that Logic takes into
account; because these are all the distinctions of
degree that are given necessarily in the form of
thought, and as abstracted from all determinate
matter.

Categories
of Aristotle.

It is, however, proper here to say a word in regard
to the Categories or Predicaments of Aristotle. These
are ten classes into which Existence is divided,—viz.
1, Substance; 2, Quantity; 3, Quality; 4, Relation;
5, Action; 6, Passion; 7, Where; 8, When; 9, Posture;
and 10, Habit. (By this last is meant the relation of

a C. ii., §§ 23, 28, 29.

a containing to a contained.) They are comprehended
in the two following verses :—

> Arbor sex servos fervore refrigerat ustos,
> Ruri cras stabo, nec tunicatus ero.[a]

In regard to the meaning of the word *category*, it is a term borrowed from the courts of law, in which it literally signifies an *accusation*. In a philosophical application, it has two meanings, or rather it is used in a general and in a restricted sense. In its general sense, it means, in closer conformity to its original application, simply a *predication* or *attribution;* in its restricted sense, it has been deflected to denote predications or attributions of a very lofty generality, in other words, certain classes of a very wide extension. I may here notice, that, in modern philosophy, it has been very arbitrarily, in fact very abusively, perverted from both its primary and its secondary signification among the ancients. Aristotle first employed the term, (for the supposition that he borrowed his categories, name and thing, from the Pythagorean Archytas is now exploded,—the treatise under the name of this philosopher being proved to be a comparatively recent forgery[β]),—I say, Aristotle first employed the term to denote a certain classification, *a posteriori*, of the modes of objective or real existence;[γ] and the word was afterwards employed and applied in the same manner by Plotinus,[δ] and other of the older philosophers. By Kant,[ε] again, and, in conformity to his example, by many other recent philoso-

[margin note: Original meaning and employment of the term category.]

[margin note: Kant's employment of the term.]

---

a Marmellii *Isagoge*, c. i. Vide Micraelius [*Lex. Phil.* v. *Prædicamenta.*—Ed.] p. 1085. Facciolati, *Logica*, [t. i., *Rudimenta Logica*, P. I. c. iii. p. 32.—Ed.]

β See *Discussions*, p. 140.—Ed.

γ See especially *Metaph.*, iv. 7.

In the treatise specially devoted to them, the Categories are viewed rather in a grammatical than in a metaphysical aspect.—Ed.

δ *Enn.* VI., L. i. c. i.—Ed.

ε *Kritik d. r. V.*, p. 78 (ed. Rosenkranz), *Prolegomena*, § 39.—Ed.

LECT.
XI.

Transcendent and Transcendental,—their original employment and use by Kant.

phers, the word has been usurped to denote the *a priori* cognitions, or fundamental forms of thought. Nor did Kant stop here; and I may explain to you the genealogy of another of his expressions, of which I see many of his German disciples are unaware. By the Schoolmen, whatever, as more general than the ten categories, could not be contained under them, was said to rise beyond them,—*to transcend* them; and, accordingly, such terms as *being, one, whole, good, &c.*, were called *transcendent* or *transcendental* (*transcendentia* or *transcendentalia*).[a] Kant, as he had twisted the term *category*, twisted also these correlative expressions from their original meaning. He did not even employ the two terms *transcendent* and *transcendental* as convertible. The latter he applied

---

a [See Facciolati, *Rud.*, p. 39; and *Inst.*, p. 26.] [*Logica*, L. I., *Rudimenta Logica*, P. I. c. iv., § 7: "Aliud est categoricum, quod significat certam quamdam rem categoriâ comprehensam: aliud rerum, quod nulla categoria continetur, sed per omnes vagatur, cujusmodi sunt *ens, res, bonitas ordo*, et similia multa." *Logica*, L. II., *Institutiones Logicæ*, P. I. c. ii.: "Sunt quaedam vocabula, quae *vaga* et *transcendentia* dicuntur; quod genus quodlibet exaequarent in omni categoriâ. Hujusmodi sunt *res, aliquid, res, unum, verum, bonum*." Cf. *Reid's Works*, pp. 687 note §, 782 b. —ED.]

Excluded from the Aristotelic Categories, all except the following:—

Ex parte vocis—"Vox una et simplex, rebus omnibus servanda."

Ex parte rei—"Entia per sese, finita, realia, tota."

See others in Maruzellius, *Isagoge*, c. I.; Sanderson, p. 20. [Maruzellius gives as his own the terms—

Complexum, Consignificans, Fictum, Polymerum,

Vox logica, Deus, Exemhens, Privatio, Parvque,

Hinc, studiose, categoriis non scriptum ...

And Sanderson, (*Logica*, L. I. c. viii.), after citing the mnemonic of the Categories themselves, adds, "In aliqua istarum classium quicquid aspiam rerum est collocatur; modo sit unum quid, reale, completum, limitatumque ac *finita natura*. Exulant ergo his aedibus *Intentiones Secundæ, Privationes*, et *Ficta*, quia non sunt realia; *Concreta, Reuicum*, et *Complexa*, quia non sunt una; *Pars*, quia non est completum quid; *Dens*, quia non est finite; *Transcendens*, quia non est limitate natura. Hinc versiculi:

Complexum, Consignificans, Privatio, Fictum,

Pars, Deus, Æquivocum, Transcendens, Ens ratione;

Sunt exclusa decem classibus ista uno verso."—ED.]

[That the Categories of Aristotle are not applicable to God, see (Pseudo) Augustin, *De Cognitione Veræ Vitæ*, c. iii.]

as a synonym for *a priori*, to denote those elements
of thought which were native and necessary to the
mind itself, and which, though not manifested out of
experience, were still not contingently derived from
it by an *a posteriori* process of generalisation. The
term *transcendent*, on the contrary, he applied to all
pretended knowledge that transcended experience,
and was not given in an original principle of the
mind. *Transcendental* he thus applied in a favourable, *transcendent* in a condemnatory, acceptation.[*]
—But to return from this digression.

The *Categories* of Aristotle do not properly constitute a logical, but a metaphysical, treatise; and they
are, accordingly, not overlooked in the Aristotelic
books on the First Philosophy, which have obtained
the name of *Metaphysics* (τὰ μετὰ τὰ φυσικά). Their
insertion in the series of the surviving treatises of
Aristotle on a logical argument, is, therefore, an
error.[β]

But looking at these classes as the highest genera
into which simple being is divided, they are, I think,
obnoxious to various objections. Without pausing
to show that in other respects they are imperfect, it
is manifest that the supreme genus or category *Being*
is not immediately divided into these ten classes, and
that they neither constitute co-ordinate nor distinct
species. For *Being* (τὸ ὄν, *ens*) is primarily divided
into *Being by itself* (*ens per se*), and *Being by accident* (*ens per accidens*). *Being by itself* corresponds
to the first Category of Aristotle, equivalent to Substance ; *Being by accident* comprehends the other

LECT.
XI.

Categories
of Aristotle
Metaphysi-
cal.

Categories
criticised
as a classi-
fication of
Being.

---

a *Kritik d. r. V.*, p. 240, edit. Rosenkranz.—ED.

β [That the Categories of Aristotle
are not logical but metaphysical, see

C. Carleton ;] [Thomas Compton Carleton, *Philosophia Universa*, Disp.
Met. d. vi. § 1.—ED.]

nine, but is, I think, more properly divided in the following manner :—*Being by accident* is viewed either as absolute or as relative. As absolute, it flows either from the matter, or from the form of things. If from the matter, it is *Quantity*, Aristotle's second category ; if from the form, it is *Quality*, Aristotle's third category. As relative, it corresponds to Aristotle's fourth category, *Relation* ; and to Relation all the other six may be reduced. For the category *Where* is the relation of a thing to other things in space ; the category *When* is the relation of a thing to other things in time ; *Action* and *Passion* constitute a single relation,—the relation of the agent and the patient ; *Posture* is the relation of the parts of a body to each other ; finally, *Habit* is the relation of a thing containing and a thing contained.[a] The little I have now said in regard to the categories of Aristotle is more, perhaps, than I was strictly warranted to say, considering them, as I do, as wholly extralogical, and I have merely referred to them as exhibiting an example of the application of the doctrine of classification.[β]

---

[a] This classification of the Categories is given by Pacius, *In Arist. Categ.*, c. 3, p. 40, ed. 1597. Cf. Aquinas, *In Arist. Metaph.*, L. v. lect. 9 ; Suarez, *Disputationes Metaphysicæ*, Disp. xxxix. § 12, 16.—ED.

[β] There is nothing in regard to which a greater diversity of opinion has prevailed, even among Logicians, than the number of the Categories. For some allow only two—Substance and Mode ; others three—Substance, Mode, and Relation ; others four—Mind, Space, Matter, and Motion ; others seven, which are comprehended in the following distich :—

> *M..s, Mensura, Quies, Motus, Positura, Figura,*

Cræumque Materia, dederunt exordia rebus."

Second line better—

" Sunt, cum Materia, cunctarum exordia rerum."

Reid's *Account of Aristotle's Logic*, c. ii. §§ 1, 2, *Works*, p. 685 *et seq*. See Facciolati, *Logica*, t. i., *Rudimenta Logicæ*, P. I. c. iii. p. 32. Purchot, *Instit. Philos.*, t. i. *Logica*, p. 82, ed. 1716. Chauvin, *Lexicon Philosophicum* v. *Categorema*. [For various attempts at reduction and classification of the categories, see Plotinus, *Enneads*, VI. L. ii. c. 8 *et seq*. (Tennemann, *Gesch. der Phil.*, vi. p. 173 *et seq*.] ; David the Arme-

I may, likewise, notice, by the way, that in the
physical sciences of arrangement, the best instances
of which are seen in the different departments of
Natural History, it is found necessary, in order to
mark the relative place of each step in the ascending
and descending series of classes, to bestow on it a
particular designation. Thus *kingdom, class, order,
tribe, family, genus, subgenus, species, subspecies, variety,* and the like, are terms that serve conveniently
to mark out the various degrees of generalisation, in
its application to the descriptive sciences of nature.
With such special applications and contingent differences, Logic has, however, no concern. I, therefore,
proceed to the last relative denomination of concepts
under the head of Subordination in Extension. It is
expressed in the following paragraph :—

¶ XXXVII. A genus as containing under it
species, or a species as containing under it individuals, is called a *Logical,* or *Universal,* or
Subject, or *Subjective,* or *Potential Whole ;* while
species as contained under a genus, and individuals as contained under a species, are called
Logical, or *Universal,* or *Subject,* or *Subjective,*
or *Potential Parts. E converso,*—an individual
as containing in it species, or a species as containing in it genera, is called a *Metaphysical,* or

Marginal notes:
LECT. XL.
Names for the different steps in the series of classes in the physical sciences of arrangement.

PAR. XXXVII. Logical and Metaphysical Wholes and Parts.

nian, in Brandis, *Scholia ad Aristot.,*
p. 49; Ramus, *Animad. Aristot.,* [L.
iv. p. 80 *et seq.,* ed. 1850.—Ed.] ; Jo.
Picus Mirandulanus, *Conclusiones,
Opera,* p. 90, ed. Basil., 1572 ; Laurentius Valla, [*Dialecticæ Disputationes,* cc. i. ii.—Ed.] ; Eugenios,
Λογική, p. 225 *et seq.* On categoric
tables of various authors, see Denzinger, *Inst. Log.,* ii. § 608, p. 53.

On history of categories in antiquity,
see Petersen, *Chrysippax Phil. Fun-
damenta,* p. 1 *et seq.* For the doctrines of the Platonists and Stoics
on the subject of the Categories, see
Facciolati, *Instit. Log.,* [*Logica,* t. ii.
p. ii., p. 84 *et seq.* Cf. Trendelenburg, *Geschichte der Kategorienlehre,*
pp. 231, 257.—Ed.]

Formal, or *Actual Whole*; while species as contained in an individual, and genera as contained in species, are called *Metaphysical*, or *Formal*, or *Actual Parts*.[a] This nomenclature, however, in so far as metaphysical is opposed to logical, is inept; for we shall see that both these wholes and parts are equally logical, and that logicians have been at fault in considering one of them, in their doctrine of reasoning, to the exclusion of the other.

A whole is that which contains parts; a part is that which is contained in a whole. But as the relation of a whole and parts is a relation dependent on the point of view from which the mind contemplates the objects of its knowledge, and as there are different points of view in which these may be considered, it follows that there may also be different wholes and parts. Philosophers have, accordingly, made various enumerations of wholes; and, without perplexing you with any minute discussion of their various divisions, it may be proper, in order to make you the better aware of the two wholes with which Logic is conversant,—(and that there are two logical wholes, and, consequently, two grand forms of reasoning, and not one alone, as all logicians have hitherto taught, I shall hereafter endeavour to convince you),—to this end, I say, it may be expedient to give you a general view of the various wholes into which the human mind may group up the objects of its speculation.

Wholes may be first divided into two genera,—into

a See Timpler, *Logica*, [p. 232 *et seq.*—Ed.] Facciolati, [*Logica*, l. i., *Rudimenta Logica*, P. II. c. vi., p. 51-52.—Ed.] Derodon, p. 447, [*Logica Restituta*, P. III., c. ii. § 2, ed. Geneva, 1668.—Ed.] Burgersdyk, [*Institutiones Logicæ*, p. 51.—Ed.]

a Whole by itself (*totum per se*), and a Whole by accident (*totum per accidens*). A Whole *per se* is that which the parts of their proper nature necessarily constitute; thus body and soul constitute the man. A Whole *per accidens* is that which the parts make up contingently; as when man is considered as made up of the poor and the rich. A whole *per se* may, again, be subdivided into five kinds, into a Logical, a Metaphysical, a Physical, a Mathematical, and a Collective. 1°, A Logical, styled also a Universal, a Subject or Subjective, a Potential Whole; and 2°, A Metaphysical, styled also a Formal or an Actual Whole,—these I have defined in the paragraph. It is manifest that the logical and metaphysical wholes are the converse of each other. For as the logical whole is the genus, the logical parts the species and individual; in the metaphysical, *e contra*, an individual is the whole of which the species, a species the whole of which the genera, are the parts. A metaphysical whole is thus manifestly the whole determined by the comprehension of a concept, as a logical whole is that whole determined by its extension; and if it can be shown that the whole of comprehension affords the conditions of a process of reasoning equally valid, equally useful, equally easy, and, to say the least of it, equally natural, as that afforded by the whole of extension, it must be allowed that it is equally well entitled to the name of a logical whole, as the whole which has hitherto exclusively obtained that denomination. 3°, A Physical, or, as it is likewise called, an Essential Whole, is that which consists of matter and form, in other words, of substance and accident, as its essential parts. 4°, A Mathematical, called likewise a Quantitative, an Integral,

LECT.
XL.

Whole per
se, and
Whole per
accidens.

Whole per
se divided
into, 1°,
Logical;
2°, Metaphysical.

3°, Physical.

4°, Mathematical.

more properly an Integrate, Whole, (*totum integratum*),
is that which is composed of integral, or, more properly,
of integrant, parts, (*partes integrantes*).   In this
whole every part lies out of every other part, whereas,
in a physical whole, the matter and form, the substance and accident, permeate and modify each other.
Thus in the integrate whole of a human body, the
head, body, and limbs, its integrant parts, are not contained in, but each lies out of, each other.   5°, A Collective, styled also 'a Whole of Aggregation, is that
which has its material parts separate and accidentally
thrown together, as an army, a heap of stones, a pile
of wheat, &c.[a]

5°, Collec-
tive.

But to proceed now to an explanation of the terms
in the paragraph last dictated.   Of these, none seem
to require any exposition, save the words *subjective*
and *potential*, as synonyms applied to a Logical or
Universal whole or parts.

The terms
subject and
subjective
as applied
to Logical
whole and
parts.
The former of these,—the term *subjective*, or more
properly *subject*, as applied to the species as parts subjacent to, or lying under, a genus,—to the individuals,
as parts subjacent to, or lying under, a species, is a
clear and appropriate expression.   But as applied to
the genus or species, considered as wholes, the term
subject is manifestly improper, and the term *subjective*
hardly defensible.   In like manner, the term *universal*,
as applied to genus or species, considered as logical
wholes, is correct ; but as applied to individuals, considered as logical parts, it is used in opposition to its
proper meaning.   The desire, however, to obtain
epithets common both to the parts and to the whole,
and thus to indicate at once the relation in general,
has caused logicians to violate the proprieties both of

a See above, p. 202, note.—Ed.

language and of thought. But as the terms have LECT.
XL
been long established, I think it sufficient to put you
on your guard by this observation.

In regard to the term *potential*,—I shall, before
saying anything, read to you a passage from the
Antient Metaphysics of the learned Lord Monboddo.[a]
" In the first place, it is impossible, by the nature of
things, that the genus should contain the species as a
part of it, and the species should likewise contain the
genus, in the same respect. But, in different respects,
it is possible that each of them may contain the other,
and be contained by it. We must, therefore, try to
distinguish the different manners of containing, and
being contained. And there is a distinction that runs
through the whole of ancient philosophy, solving many
difficulties that are otherwise insurmountable, and
which, I hope, will likewise solve this difficulty. The
distinction I mean is the distinction betwixt what
exists δυνάμει, or potentially only, and that which exists ἐνεργείᾳ, or actually. In the first sense, everything exists in its causes; and, in the other sense,
nothing exists but what is actually produced. Now,
in this first sense, the whole species exists in the
genus; for the genus virtually contains the whole
species, not only what actually exists of it, but what
may exist of it in any future time. In the same
manner, the lowest species, below which there is nothing but individuals, contains virtually all those individuals, present and future. Thus, the species *man*,
comprehends all the individuals now existing, or
that shall hereafter exist; which, therefore, are said
to be parts of the species *man*. On the other
hand, the genus is actually contained in the species ;

a Vol. i. p. 479.

and the species, likewise, in each of the individuals under it. Thus, the genus *animal* is actually contained in the species *man*, without which it could not be conceived to exist. And, for the same reason, the species *man* is actually contained in each individual.—It is a piece of justice which I think I owe to an author, hardly known at all in the western parts of Europe, to acknowledge that I got the hint of the solution of this difficulty from him. The author I mean is a living Greek author, Eugenius Diaconus, at present Professor, as I am informed, in the Patriarch's University at Constantinople, who has written an excellent system of logic, in very good Attic Greek."

Stewart's strictures on this passage considered.
This, or rather a similar passage at p. 73 of the fourth volume of the *Antient Metaphysics*, affords Mr Stewart an opportunity of making sundry unfavourable strictures on the technical language of Logic, in regard to which he asserts, "the adepts are not, to this day, unanimously agreed;" and adds, that "it is an extraordinary circumstance, that a discovery on which, in Lord Monboddo's opinion, *the whole truth of the syllogism depends*, should be of so very recent a date."[a] Now this is another example which may serve to put you on your guard against any confidence in the assertions and arguments even of learned men. You may be surprised to hear, that so far is Eugenius from being the author of this observation, and of the term *potential* as applied to a logical whole, that both are to be found, with few exceptions, in all the older systems of Logic. To quote only one, but one of the best and best known, that of Burgersdyk,—he says, speaking of the logical whole: "Et quia universale subjectas species et individua *non actu* continet sed

a *Elements*, vol. ii., c. iii., § 1; *Works*, vol. iii., p. 199 and p. 200, note.

potentia; factum est, ut hoc totum dictum sit *totum*
potentiale, cum ceteræ species totius dicantur *totum*
actuale, quia partes suas actu continent."[a]   Aristotle
notices this difference of the two wholes.[β]

Having thus terminated the consideration of concepts as reciprocally related in the perpendicular line
of Subordination, and in the quantity of Extension,
in so far as they are viewed as containing classes,—I
must, before proceeding to consider them under this
quantity in the horizontal line of Co-ordination, state
to you two terms by which characters or concepts are
denominated, in so far as they are viewed as differences by which a concept is divided into two subordinate parts.

¶ XXXVIII. The character, or complement of
characters, by which a lower genus or species is
distinguished, both from the genus to which it is
subordinate, and from the other genera or species
with which it is co-ordinated, is called the *Generic*
or the *Specific Difference*, (διαφορὰ γενική, and
διαφορὰ εἰδική, *differentia generica*, and *differentia specifica*).   The sum of characters, again, by
which a singular or individual thing is discriminated from the species under which it stands,
and from other individual things along with
which it stands, is called the *Individual* or
Singular or *Numerical Difference*, (*differentia
individualis* vel *singularis* vel *numerica*).[γ]

Two things are thus said to be generically different, inasmuch as they lie apart in two different
genera; specifically different, inasmuch as they lie

Par. XXXVIII.
Generic,
Specific,
and Indivi-
dual Differ-
ence.

Explica-
tion.

a Lib. I. c. xiv., p. 43, ed. 1660.   a. l. *De Toto et Parte.*— En.]
—En.   γ Krug, *Logik*, § 45.—En.
β Vide Timpler, *Logica*, [L. II.

Generic
and Specific
Difference.

apart in two different species; individually or numerically different, inasmuch as they do not constitute
one and the same reality. Thus *animal* and *stone*
may be said to be generically different; *horse* and *ox*
to be specifically different; *Highflyer* and *Eclipse* to
be numerically or individually different. It is evident, however, that as all genera and species, except
the highest of the one and the lowest of the other,
may be styled indifferently either genera or species;
generic difference and *specific difference* are in general only various expressions of the same thing, and,
accordingly, the terms *heterogeneous* and *homogeneous*, which apply properly only to the correlation of
genera, are usually applied equally to the correlation
of species.

Individual
or Singular
Difference.

"Individual existences can only be perfectly discriminated in Perception, external or internal, and their
numerical differences are endless; for of all possible
contradictory attributes the one or the other must,
on the principles of Contradiction and Excluded
Middle, be considered as belonging to each individual
thing. On the other hand, species and genera may be
perfectly discriminated by one or few characters. For
example, *man* is distinguished from every genus or
species of animal by the one character of *rationality*;
triangle, from every other class of mathematical
figure, by the single character of *trilaterality*. It is,
therefore, far easier adequately to describe a genus or
species than an individual existence; as in the latter
case, we must select, out of the infinite multitude of
characters which an individual comprises, a few of
the most prominent, or those by which the thing may
most easily be recognised." [a] But as those which we

a Krug, *Logik*, § 46, p. 134-5.—Ed.

thus select are only a few, and are only selected with
reference to our faculty of apprehension and our capacity of memory, they always constitute only a petty,
and often not the most essential, part of the numerical differences by which the individuality of the object
is determined.

Having now terminated the consideration of the
Subordination of concepts under Extension, it is only
necessary to observe that their Co-ordination under
that quantity affords nothing which requires explanation, except what is contained in the following paragraph :—

¶ XXXIX. Notions, in so far as they are
considered the co-ordinate species of the same
genus, may be called *Conspecies;* and in so far
as Conspecies are considered to be different but
not contradictory, they are properly called *Discrete* or *Disjunct Notions* (*notiones discretæ* vel
disjunctæ). The term *Disparate* (*notiones disparatæ*) is frequently applied to this opposition
of notions, but less properly ; for this ought to
be reserved to denote the corresponding opposition of notions in the quantity of Comprehension.

I conclude the consideration of concepts, as dependent on Extension, by a statement of the two general
laws, by which both Subordination and Co-ordination
of notions, under this quantity, are regulated.

¶ XL. The whole classification of things by
Genera and Species is governed by two laws.
The one of these, the law of *Homogeneity* (*prin-
cipium Homogeneitatis*), is,—That how different

LECT.
XI.

under Ex-
tension, are
regulated,—
viz. of Ho-
mogeneity
and Hetero-
geneity.

soever may be any two concepts, they both still stand subordinated under some one higher concept; in other words, things the most dissimilar must, in certain respects, be similar. The other, the law of *Heterogeneity* (*principium Heterogeneitatis*), is,—That every concept contains other concepts under it; and, therefore, when divided proximately, we descend always to other concepts, but never to individuals; in other words, things the most homogeneous,—similar,—must, in certain respects, be heterogeneous,—dissimilar.

Explica-
tion.
Generifica-
tion and
Specifica-
tion.

Of these two laws, the former, as the principle which enables, and in fact compels, us to rise from species to genus, is that which determines the process of Generification; and the latter, as the principle which enables, and in fact compels, us to find always species under a genus, is that which regulates the process of Specifica-

tion. The second of these laws, it is evident, is only true ideally, only true in theory. The infinite divisibility of concepts, like the infinite divisibility of space and time, exists only in speculation. And that it is theoretically valid, will be manifest, if we take two similar concepts, that is, two concepts with a small difference : let us then clearly represent to ourselves this difference, and we shall find that how small soever it may be, we can always conceive it still less, without being nothing, that is, we can divide it *ad infinitum* ; but as each of these infinitesimally diverging differences affords always the condition of new species, it is evident that we can never end, that is, never reach the individual, except *per saltum.*[a]

There is another law, which Kant promulgates in

a Cf. Krug, *Logik,* § 45, p. 135, and pp. 136, 137.—Ed.

the *Critique of Pure Reason*,[a] and which may be called
the law of Logical Affinity, or the law of Logical Con-
tinuity. It is this,—That no two co-ordinate species
touch so closely on each other, but that we can conceive other or others intermediate. Thus *man* and
orang-outang, *elephant* and *rhinoceros*, are proximate
species, but still how great is the difference between
them, and how many species can we not imagine to
ourselves as possibly interjacent?

This law I have, however, thrown out of account,
as not universally true. For it breaks down when
we apply it to mathematical classifications. Thus
all angles are either acute or right or obtuse. For
between these three co-ordinate species or genera no
others can possibly be interjected, though we may
always subdivide each of these, in various manners,
into a multitude of lower species. This law is also
not true when the co-ordinate species are distinguished
by contradictory attributes. There can in these be
no interjacent species, on the principle of Excluded
Middle. For example:—In the Cuvierian classification
the genus *animal* is divided into the two species of
vertebrata and *invertebrata*, that is, into animals with
a backbone,—with a spinal marrow, and animals
without a backbone,—without a spinal marrow. Is
it possible to conceive the possibility of any intermediate class ?[β]

LECT.
XI.

Law of Lo-
gical Af-
nity.

Grounds on
which this
law must be
rejected.

a P. 510, ed. Rosenkranz. Cf.   102, 103. [Compare Fries, *Logik*,
Krug. *Logik*, p. 138.—Ed.   § 21.—Ed.]
β Bachmann, [*Logik*, § 61, pp.

LECTURE XII.

STOICHEIOLOGY.

SECT. II.—OF THE PRODUCTS OF THOUGHT.

I.—ENNOEMATIC.

III. RECIPROCAL RELATIONS OF CONCEPTS.

B. QUANTITY OF COMPREHENSION.

LECT.
XII.

Reciprocal
Relation of
notions in
Compre-
hension.

HAVING now concluded the consideration of the Reciprocal Relation of Concepts as determined by the
quantity of Extension, I proceed to treat of that
relation as regulated by the counter quantity of
Comprehension. On this take the following paragraph :—

Par. XLI.
Identical
and Differ-
ent notions.

" XLI. When two or more concepts are compared together according to their Comprehension, they either coincide or they do not ; that
is, they either do or do not comprise the same
characters. Notions are thus divided into *Identical* and *Different*, (*conceptus identici et diversi*).
The Identical are either absolutely or relatively
the same. Of notions *Absolutely Identical*
there are actually none ; notions *Relatively
Identical* are called, likewise, *Similar* or *Cognate*, (*notiones similes, affines, cognatæ*) ; and if
the common attributes, by which they are allied,

be proximate and necessary, they are called *Re-* ciprocating *or* Convertible, (notiones reciprocæ, convertibiles.)[a]

LECT.
XII.

In explanation of this paragraph, it is only neces- Explica- sary to say a word in regard to notions absolutely Identical. That such are impossible is manifest. " For, it being assumed that such exist, as absolutely identical they necessarily have no differences by which they can be distinguished : but what are indiscernible can be known, neither as two concepts, nor as two identical concepts; because we are, *ex hypothesi*, unable to discriminate the one from the other. They are, therefore, to us as one. Notions absolutely identical can only be admitted, if, abstracting our view alto-gether from the concepts, we denominate those notions *identical*, which have reference to one and the same object, and which are conceived either by different minds, or by the same mind, but at different times. Their difference is, therefore, one not intrinsic and necessary, but only extrinsic and contingent. Taken in this sense, *Absolutely Identical* notions will be only a less correct expression for *Reciprocating* or *Convertible* notions." [β]

Absolutely Identical notions impossible

¶ XLII. Considered, again, under their Com-prehension, concepts, in relation to each other, are said to be either *Congruent* or *Agreeing*, inas-much as they may be connected in thought ; or *Conflictive*, inasmuch as they cannot. The con-fliction constitutes the *Opposition* of notions, (τὸ ἀντικεῖσθαι, *oppositio*). This is twofold ;—1°,

Par. XLII. Opposition of Concepts.

a [Esser, *Logik*, § 36.]
β [Esser, *Logik*, § 36, p. 79.] Cf.
Krug, *Logik*, § 37, and Anm. i.—
Ed.

Immediate or *Contradictory Opposition,* called
likewise *Repugnance,* (τὸ ἀντιφατικῶς ἀντικεῖσθαι, ἀντίφασις, *oppositio immediata* sive *contradictoria, repugnantia*) ; and, 2°, *Mediate* or *Contrary Opposition,* (τὸ ἐναντίως ἀντικεῖσθαι, ἐναντιότης, *oppositio mediata* vel *contraria*). The
former emerges when one concept abolishes (*tol-
lit*) directly or by simple negation, what another
establishes (*ponit*) ; the latter, when one concept
does this not directly or by simple negation, but
through the affirmation of something else."

Explica-
tion.
Identity and
Agreement,
Diversity
and Conflic-
tion.

" Identity is not to be confounded with Agreement
or Congruence, nor Diversity with Confliction. All
identical concepts are, indeed, congruent; but all
congruent notions are not identical. Thus, *learning*
and *virtue, beauty* and *riches, magnanimity* and *sta-
ture,* are congruent notions, inasmuch as, in thinking
a thing, they can easily be combined in the notion
we form of it, although in themselves very different
from each other. In like manner, all conflictive notions are diverse or different notions, for unless different, they could not be mutually conflictive. But, on
the other hand, all different concepts are not conflictive ; but those only whose difference is so great that
each involves the negation of the other ; as, for example, *virtue* and *vice, beauty* and *deformity, wealth*
and *poverty.* Thus these notions are by pre-eminence — κατ᾿ ἐξοχὴν — said to be *opposed,* although
it is true, that in thinking we can oppose, or place
in antithesis, not only different, but even identical,
concepts."

" To speak now of the distinction of Contradictory

a [Cf. Drobisch, *Logik,* p. 17, § 25 *et seq.*]

and Contrary Opposition, or of Contradiction and LECT. XII.
Contrariety ;—of these the former,—Contradiction,— Contradictory and Contrary Opposition.
is exemplified in the opposites,—*yellow, not yellow,*
walking, not walking. Here each notion is directly,
immediately, and absolutely, repugnant to the other,
—they are reciprocal negatives. This opposition is,
therefore, properly called that of *Contradiction* or of
Repugnance ; and the opposing notions themselves
are *contradictory* or *repugnant* notions, in a single
word, *contradictories.* The latter, or Contrary Opposition, is exemplified in the opposites, *yellow, blue,*
red, &c., walking, standing, lying, &c."

"In the case of Contradictory Opposition, there are
only two conflictive attributes conceivable ; and of
these one or other must be predicated of the object
thought In the case of Contrary Opposition, on the
other hand, more than two conflictive characters are
possible, and it is not, therefore, necessary, that if
one of these be not predicated of an object any one
other must. Thus, though I cannot at once sit and
stand, and consequently *sitting* and *standing* are attributes each severally incompatible with the other ;
yet I may exist neither sitting nor standing.—I may
lie ; but I must either sit or not sit, I must either
stand, or not stand, &c. Such, in general, are the
oppositions of Contradiction and Contrariety."

"It is now necessary to say a word in regard to Logical sig-nificance of Contradic-tory and Contrary opposition.
their logical significance. Immediate or Contradictory
Opposition constitutes, in Logic, affirmative and negative notions. By the former something is posited or
affirmed (*ponitur, affirmatur*) ; by the latter, something is sublated or denied (*tollitur, negatur*). This,
however, is only done potentially, in so far as concepts
are viewed apart from judgments, for actual affirma-

tion and actual negation suppose an act of judgment ; but, at the same time, in so far as two concepts afford the elements, and, if brought into relation, necessitate the formation, of an affirmative or negative proposition, they may be considered as in themselves negative and affirmative."

"Further, it is evident that a notion can be logically denied only by a contradiction. For when we abstract from the matter of a notion, as Logic does, it is impossible to know that one concept excludes another, unless the one be supposed the negation of the other. Logically considered, all positive or affirmative notions are congruent, that is, they can, as far as their form is concerned, be all conceived or thought together ; but whether in reality they can coexist,—that cannot be decided by logical rules. If, therefore, we would, with logical precision and certainty, oppose things, we must oppose them not as contraries, (*A. B. C.*), but as contradictories, (*A.—not A. B.—not B. C.—not C.*)—Hence it also follows, that there is no negation conceivable without the concomitant conception of an affirmation, for we cannot deny a thing to exist, without having a notion of the existence which is denied." [a]

There are also certain other relations subsisting between notions, compared together in reference to their Comprehension.

¶ XLIII. Notions, as compared with each other in respect of their Comprehension, are further distinguished into *Intrinsic* and *Extrinsic*. The former are made up of those attributes which are essential, and, consequently, necessary to the

a Krug, *Logik*, p. 118-120.—Ed.

object of the notion : these attributes, severally   LECT.
considered, are called *Essentials* or *Internal De-*   XII.
nominations, (οὐσιώδη, *essentialia, denominati-*
ones internæ, intrinsicæ), and, conjunctly, the
Essence (οὐσία, *essentia*). The latter, on the contrary, consist of those attributes which belong to
the object of the notion only in a contingent
manner, or by possibility ; and which are, therefore, styled *Accidents,* or *Extrinsic Denomina-*
tions, (συμβεβηκότα, *accidentia, denominationes*
externa or *extrinsicæ.*) *

Having thus given you the distinctions of notions, Involu-
as founded on their more general relations under the Co-ordina-
quantity of Comprehension, I now proceed to con- cepts under
sider them under this quantity in their proximate sion, --these
relations ; that is, in the relation of Involution and glected by
the relation of Co-ordination. These relations have logicians.
been, I may say, altogether neglected by logicians :
who, in consequence, have necessarily overlooked Hence
one of the two great divisions of all reasoning ; for in compre-
all our reasoning is either from the whole to the parts overlooked
and from the parts to the whole, in the quantity of by logicians.
extension, or from the whole to the parts and from
the parts to the whole, in the quantity of comprehension.   In each quantity there is a deductive, and in
each quantity there is an inductive, inference ; and if
the reasoning under either of these two quantities
were to be omitted, it ought, perhaps, to have been
the one which the logicians have exclusively cultivated.
For the quantity of extension is a creation of the
mind itself, and only created through, as abstracted
from, the quantity of comprehension ; whereas the

α Krug, *Logik,* § 39.—ED.

LECT.
XII.
quantity of comprehension is at once given in the very nature of things. The former quantity is thus secondary and factitious, the latter primary and natural.

But probably contemplated by Aristotle.
That logicians should have neglected the process of reasoning which is competent between the parts and the whole of the quantity of comprehension, is the more remarkable, as, after Aristotle, they have in general articulately distinguished the two quantities from each other, and, after Aristotle, many of them have explicitly enounced the special law on which the logic of comprehension proceeds. This principle established, but not applied, is expressed in the axiom,—The character of the character is the character of the thing; or, The predicate of the predicate is the predicate of the subject, (*Nota notæ est nota rei ipsius; Prædicatum prædicati est prædicatum subjecti*). This axiom is enounced by Aristotle ;[a] and its application, I have little doubt, was fully understood by him. In fact I think it even possible to show in detail, that his whole analysis of the syllogism has reference to both quantities, and that the great abstruseness of his *Prior Analytics*, the treatise in which he develops the general forms of reasoning, arises from this,—that he has endeavoured to rise to formulæ sufficiently general to express at once what was common to both kinds ;—an attempt so far beyond the intelligence of subsequent logicians, that they have wholly misunderstood and perverted his doctrine. They understood this doctrine, only as applied to the reasoning in extensive quantity ; and in relation to this kind of reasoning, they have certainly made palpable and easy what in Aristotle is abstract and difficult. But then

a *Categ.*, c. iii.—ED.

they did not observe that Aristotle's doctrine applies to two species, of which they only consider one. It was certainly proper to bring down the Aristotelic logic from its high abstraction, and to deliver its rules in proximate application to each of the two several species of reasoning. This would have been to fill up the picture of which the Stagirite had given the sketch. But by viewing his *Analytic* as exclusively relative to the reasoning in extension, though they simplified the one-half of syllogistic, they altogether abolished the other. This mistake,—this partial conception of the science,—is common to all logicians, ancient and modern : for in so far as I am aware, no one has observed, that of the quantities of comprehension and extension, each affords a reasoning proper to itself; and no one has noticed that the doctrine of Aristotle has reference indifferently to both; although some, I know, having perceived in general that we do reason under the quantity of comprehension, have on that founded an objection to all reasoning under the quantity of extension, that is, to the whole science of Logic as at present constituted. I have, in some degree, at present spoken of matters which properly find their development in the sequel; and I have made this anticipation, in order that you should attend particularly to the relation of concepts, under the quantity of comprehension, as containing and contained, inasmuch as this affords the foundation of one, and that not the least important, of the two great branches, into which all reasoning is divided.

¶ XLIV. We have seen that of the two quan- tities of notions each affords a logical Whole and Parts; and that, by opposite errors, the one of

these has, through over inclusion, been called the
logical, whilst the other has, through over exclusion, been called the *metaphysical*. Thus, in
respect of their Comprehension, no less than of
their Extension, notions stand to each other in a
relation of Containing and Contained ; and this
relation, which in the one quantity (extension)
is styled that of *Subordination*, may in the other
(comprehension), for distinction's sake, be styled
that of *Involution. Co-ordination* is a term which
may be applied in either quantity."

In the quantity of comprehension, one notion
is involved in another, when it forms a part of
the sum total of characters, which together constitute the comprehension of that other; and
two notions are in this quantity co-ordinated,
when, whilst neither comprehends the other, both
are immediately comprehended in the same lower
concept.

Explica
tion.
From what has been formerly stated, you are aware
that the quantity of comprehension, belonging to a
notion, is the complement of characters which it contains in it ; and that this quantity is at its maximum
in an individual. Thus the notion of the individual
Socrates, contains in it, besides a multitude of others,
the characters of *Son of Sophroniscus, Athenian,
Greek, European, man, animal, organised being,* &c.
But these notions, these characters, are not all equally
proximate and immediate; some are only given in
and through others. Thus the character *Athenian* is
applicable to Socrates only in and through that of *Son
of Sophroniscus,*—the character of *Greek*, only in and

a [Cf. Drobisch, *Logik*, §§ 22, 23; Fischer, *Logik*, § 49.]

through that of *Athenian*,—the character of *Europe-*
an, only in and through that of *Greek*,—and so forth ;
in other words, Socrates is an Athenian only as the
son of Sophroniscus, only a Greek as an Athenian,
only a European as a Greek, only a man as a European, only an animal as a man, only an organised
being as an animal. Those characters, therefore, that
are given in and through others, stand to these others
in the relation of parts to wholes ; and it is only
on the principle,—*Part of the part is a part of the
whole,—*that the remoter parts are the parts of the
primary whole. Thus, if we know that the individual
Socrates comprehends the character *son of Sophroniscus*, and that the character *son of Sophroniscus*
comprehends the character *Athenian ;* we are then
warranted in saying that *Socrates* comprehends *Athenian*, in other words, that *Socrates* is an *Athenian*.
The example here taken is too simple to show in what
manner our notions are originally evolved out of the
more complex into the more simple, and that the progress of science is nothing more than a progressive
unfolding into distinct consciousness of the various
elements comprehended in the characters, originally
known to us in their vague or confused totality.

It is a famous question among philosophers,—
Whether our knowledge commences with the general or with the individual,—whether children first
employ common, or first employ proper, names. In
this controversy, the reasoners have severally proved
the opposite opinion to be untenable ; but the question is at once solved, by showing that a third opinion
is the true,—viz., that our knowledge commences
with the confused and complex, which, as regarded
in one point of view or in another, may easily be

mistaken either for the individual, or for the general.
The discussion of this problem belongs, however, to
Psychology, not to Logic.[a] It is sufficient to say in
general, that all objects are presented to us in complexity; that we are at first more struck with the
points of resemblance than with the points of contrast; that the earliest notions, and, consequently,
the earliest terms, are those that correspond to this
synthesis, while the notions and the terms arising from
an analysis of this synthesis into its parts, are of a
subsequent formation. But though it be foreign to
the province of Logic to develop the history of this
procedure; yet, as this procedure is natural to the
human mind, Logic must contain the form by which
it is regulated. It must not only enable us to reason
from the simple and general to the complex and individual; it must, likewise, enable us to reverse the
process, and to reason from the complex and individual to the simple and the general. And this it
does by that relation of notions as containing and
contained, given in the quantity of comprehension.
The nature of this reasoning can indeed only be
shown, when we come to treat of syllogism; at present, I only request that you will bear in mind the
relations of Involution and Co-ordination, in which
notions stand to each other in the whole or quantity
of comprehension. In this quantity the involving
notion or whole is the more complex notion; the
involved notion or part is the more simple. Thus
pigeon as comprehending *bird*, *bird* as comprehending *feathered*, *feathered* as comprehending *warm-
blooded*, *warm-blooded* as comprehending *heart with
four cavities*, *heart with four cavities* as comprehend-

In Compre-
hension, the
involving
notion is the
more com-
plex; the
involved,
the more
simple.

a See *Lectures on Metaphysics,* Lect. xxxvi., vol. ii. p. 319-327.—Ed.

ing *breathing by lungs*, are severally to each other
as notions involving and involved.   Again, notions,
in the whole of comprehension, are co-ordinated, when
they stand together as constituting parts of the notion
in which they are both immediately comprehended.
Thus the characters *oviparous* and *warm-blooded*,
heart with four cavities, and *breathing by lungs*, as
all immediately contributing to make up the comprehension of the notion *bird*, are, in this respect, severally considered as its co-ordinate parts.   These characters are not relative and correlative,—not containing
and contained.   For we have oviparous animals which
are not warm-blooded, and warm-blooded animals
which are not oviparous.   Again, it is true, I believe,
that all warm-blooded animals have hearts with four
cavities (two auricles and two ventricles), and that
all animals with such hearts breathe by lungs and
not by gills.   But then, in this case, we have no
right to suppose that the first of these characters
comprehends the second, and that the second comprehends the third.   For we should be equally entitled
to assert, that all animals breathing by lungs possessed hearts of four cavities, and that all animals
with such hearts are warm-blooded.   They are thus
thought as mutually the conditions of each other;
and whilst we may not know their reciprocal dependence, they are, however, conceived by us, as on an
equal footing of co-ordination.   (This at least is true
of the two attributes *heart with four cavities* and
breathing by lungs; for these must be viewed as co-
ordinate, but, taken together, they may be viewed
as jointly necessitating the attribute of *warm-blooded*,
and, therefore, may be viewed as comprehending it.)
On this I give you the following paragraph.

LECT.
XII.

Co-ordina-
tion in
Compre-
hension.

LECT.
XII.

Par. XLV.
Co-ordina-
tion of
notions in
Compre-
hension.

" XLV. Notions co-ordinated in the whole of comprehension, are, in respect of the discriminating characters, different without any similarity. They are thus, *pro tanto*, absolutely different ; and, accordingly, in propriety are called *Disparate Notions* (*notiones disparatæ*). On the other hand, notions co-ordinated in the quantity or whole of extension, are, in reference to the objects by them discriminated, different (or diverse) ; but, as we have seen, they have always a common attribute or attributes in which they are alike. Thus they are only relatively different (or diverse) ; and, in logical language, are properly called *Disjunct* or *Discrete Notions* (*notiones disjunctæ, discretæ*)."

a [Drobisch, *Logik*, §§ 23, 24. Cf. Fischer, *Logik*, § 49 *et seq*.]

LECTURE XIII.

STOICHEIOLOGY.

SECT. II.—OF THE PRODUCTS OF THOUGHT.

II. APOPHANTIC, OR THE DOCTRINE OF JUDGMENTS.

JUDGMENTS.—THEIR NATURE AND DIVISIONS.

HAVING terminated the Doctrine of Concepts, we now proceed to the Doctrine of Judgments. Concepts and Judgments, as I originally stated, are not to be viewed as the results of different operations, for every concept, as the product of some preceding act of Comparison, is in fact a judgment fixed and ratified in a sign. But in consequence of this acquired permanence, concepts afford the great means for all subsequent comparisons and judgments, and as this now forms their principal relation, it behoved, for convenience, throwing out of view their original genealogy, to consider Notions as the first product of the Understanding, and as the conditions or elements of the second. A concept may be viewed as an implicit or undeveloped judgment; a judgment as an explicit or developed concept. But we must now descend to articulate statements.

LECT. XIII.

Doctrine of Judgments.

¶ XLVI. To Judge (κρίνειν,[a] judicare) is to recognise the relation of congruence or of con-

Par. XLVI. Judgment, what.

---

[a] The verb κρίνειν, to judge, and still more the substantive, κρίσις, judgment, are rarely used by the Greeks — (never by Aristotle) — as technical terms of Logic or of Psychology.

fliction, in which two concepts, two individual
things, or a concept and an individual, compared
together, stand to each other. This recognition,
considered as an internal consciousness, is called
a *Judgment*, (λόγος ἀποφαντικός, *judicium*); considered as expressed in language, it is called a
Proposition or *Predication*, (ἀπόφανσις, πρότασις,[a] διάστημα, *propositio*, *prædicatio*, *pronun-
ciatum*, *enunciatio*, *effatum*, *profatum*, *axioma*[b]).

*Explica-
tion, — what
is implied
in Judg-
ment.*

As a judgment supposes a relation, it necessarily
implies a plurality of thoughts, but conversely a plurality of thoughts does not necessarily imply a judgment. The thoughts whose succession is determined
by the mere laws of Association, are, though manifested
in plurality, in relation, and, consequently, in connection, not, however, so related and so connected as
to constitute a judgment. The thoughts *water*, *iron*,
and *rusting*, may follow each other in the mental
train ; they may even be viewed together in a simultaneous act of consciousness, and this without our
considering them in an act of Comparison, and without, therefore, conjoining or disjoining them in an act
of judgment. But when two or more thoughts are
given in consciousness, there is in general an endeavour
on our part to discover in them, and to develop, a
relation of congruence or of confliction ; that is, we
endeavour to find out whether these thoughts will or
will not coincide,—may or may not be blended into

a [Aristotle uses the term πρότασις
merely for the premise of a syllogism,
especially the major (he has no other
word for premise) ; whereas ἀπόφανσις he employs always for an enunciation considered not as merely syllogistic. See Ammonius, *In De In-*
terpret., f. 4 a. Gr. p. 4. Lat ; Facciolati, *Rudimenta Logica*, P. ii. c.
i. p. 59 ; Waitz, *Commentarius in
Organon*, I. p. 368 ; *Organon Pacii*,
pp. 92, 127, 240 et seq., 416, 417.]
β By Stoics and Ramists.

one. If they coincide, we judge, we enounce, their congruence or compatibility; if they do not coincide, we judge, we enounce, their confliction or incompatibility. Thus, if we compare the thoughts,—*water, iron,* and *rusting,*—find them congruent, and connect them into a single thought, thus—*water rusts iron*—in that case we form a Judgment.[*]

But if two notions be judged congruent, in other words, be conceived as one, this their unity can only be realised in consciousness, inasmuch as one of these notions is viewed as an attribute or determination of the other. For, on the one hand, it is impossible for us to think as one two attributes, that is, two things viewed as determining, and yet neither of them determining or qualifying the other; nor, on the other hand, two subjects, that is, two things thought as determined, and yet neither of them determined or qualified by the other. For example, we cannot think the two attributes *electrical* and *polar* as a single notion, unless we convert the one of these attributes into a subject to be determined or qualified by the other; but if we do,—if we say, *what is electrical is polar,* we at once reduce the duality to unity, we judge that *polar* is one of the constituent characters of the notion *electrical,* or that what is *electrical* is contained under the class of things marked out by the common character of *polarity.* In like manner, we cannot think the two subjects *iron* and *mineral* as a single notion, unless we convert the one of these subjects into an attribute by which the other is determined or qualified; but if we do,—if we say *iron is a mineral,* we again reduce the duality to unity, we judge that one of the attributes of the subject *iron* is,

Condition under which notions are judged congruent.

a Cf. Krug, *Logik*, § 61, Anm. i. p. 149-150.

that it is a *mineral*, or that *iron* is contained under the class of things marked out by the common character of *mineral*.

A judgment must contain three notions.
From what has now been said, it is evident that a judgment must contain and express three notions, which, however, as mutually relative, constitute an indivisible act of thought. It must contain, 1°, The notion of something to be determined ; 2°, The notion of something by which another is determined ; and, 3°, A notion of the relation of determination between the two. This will prepare you to understand the following paragraph.

Par. XLVII.
Subject,
Predicate,
and Copula.
¶ XLVII. That which, in the act of Judging, we think as the determined or qualified notion, is technically called the *Subject*, (ὑποκείμενον, *subjectum*) ; that which we think as the determining or qualifying notion, the *Predicate*, (κατηγορούμενον, *prædicatum*) ; and the relation of determination, recognised as subsisting between the subject and the predicate, is called the *Copula*. With Aristotle, the predicate includes the copula ;[a] and, from a hint by him, the latter has, by subsequent Greek logicians, been styled the *Appredicate*, (προσκατηγορούμενον, *apprædicatum*).[b] The Subject and Predicate of a proposition together are, after Aristotle, called its *Terms* or *Extremes*,[y]

a See *De Interp.*, c. 3, where the ῥῆμα, or verb, includes the predicate and copula united.—ED.

b See *De Interpretatione*, c. 10, § 4 : *Ὅταν δὲ τὸ ἐστὶ τρίτον προσκατηγορῆται*,—an expression to which may be traced the scholastic distinction between *secundi* and *tertii adjacentis*. For the term προσκατη-

γορούμενον to denote the predicate of a proposition, see Ammonius on *De Interp.*, p. 110 b, ed. Ald., Venetiis, 1546. See below, p. 230.— ED. [For the origin of this distinction see Blemmidas (after Aristotle), *Logica*, p. 186.]

y *Anal. Prior.*, l. i, 4.—ED.

($\H{o}\rho\check{o}\iota$, $\H{a}\kappa\rho\alpha$, $\pi\acute{e}\rho\alpha\tau\alpha$, *termini*); as a proposition is by him sometimes called an *Interval*, ($\delta\iota\acute{a}$-$\sigma\tau\eta\mu\alpha$),ᵃ being, as it were, a line stretched out between the extremes or terms. We may, therefore, articulately define a judgment or proposition to be the product of that act in which we pronounce, that of two notions thought as subject and as predicate, the one does or does not constitute a part of the other, either in the quantity of Extension, or in the quantity of Comprehension.

Thus in the proposition, *iron is magnetic,* we have Illustration. *iron* for the Subject, *magnetic* for the Predicate, and the substantive verb *is* for the Copula. In regard to this last, it is necessary to say a few words. " It is not always the case, that in propositions the copula is expressed by the substantive verb *is* or *est*, and that the copula and predicate stand as distinct words. In adjective verbs the copula and predicate coalesce, as in the proposition, *the sun shines, sol lucet,* which is equivalent to *the sun is shining, sol est lucens.* In existential propositions, that is, those in which mere existence is predicated, the same holds good. For when I say *I am, Ego sum,* the *am* or *sum* has here a far higher and more emphatic import than that of the mere copula or link of connection. For it expresses, *I am existent, Ego sum existens.* It might seem that, in negative propositions, when the copula is affected by the negative particle, it is converted into a non-copula. But if we take the word *copula* in a wider meaning, for that through which the subject and predicate are connected in a mutual relation, it

ᵃ *Anal. Prior.,* I. 15, 16, 25.—ED.

will apply not only to affirmative but to negative, not only to categorical but to hypothetical and disjunctive, propositions." [a]

I may notice that propositions with the subject, predicate, and copula, all three articulately expressed, have been called by the schoolmen those of the *third adjacent*, (*propositiones tertii adjacentis*, or *tertii adjecti*), inasmuch as they manifestly contain three parts. This is a barbarous expression for what the Greeks, after Aristotle, called προτάσεις ἐκ τρίτου (ἐστὶ) κατηγορουμένου. For the same reason, propositions with the copula and predicate in one were called those of the *second adjacent.*[β]

"What has now been said will enable you to perceive how far concepts and judgments coincide, and how far they differ. On the one hand, they coincide in the following respects:—In the first place, the concept and the judgment are both products; the one the product of a remote, the other the product of an immediate, act of comparison. In the second place, in both, an object is determined by a character or attribute. Finally, in the third place, in both, things relatively different in existence are reduced to a relative identity in the unity of thought. On the other hand, they differ in the following respects:—In the first place, the determination of an object by an attribute is far more express in the judgment than in the concept; for in the one it is developed, in the other only implied. In the second place, in the concept the unity of thought is founded only on a similarity of quality; in the judgment, on the other hand, it is

a Krug, *Logik*, § 52, Anm. ii. p. 74; Crakanthorpe, *Logica*, pp. 183-184. — En. [Compare Bachmann, *Logik*, p. 127; Schulze, *Logik*, 160, 167.] β See above, p. 228, note β.—En.

founded on a similarity of relation. For in the
notion, an object and its characters can only be conceived as one, inasmuch as they are congruent and
not conflictive, for thus only can they be united into
one total concept. But in the judgment, as a subject
and predicate are not necessarily thought under a
similarity of quality, the judgment can comprehend
not only congruent, but likewise conflictive, and even
contradictory, notions; for two concepts which are
compared together can be recognised as standing in
the relation either of congruence or of repugnance.
Such is the sameness, and such is the diversity, of
concept and judgment." [a]

We have thus seen that a judgment or proposition
consists of three parts or correlative notions,—the
notion of a subject, the notion of a predicate, and the
notion of the mutual relation of these as determined
and determining.

Judgments may, I think, be primarily divided in
two ways,—the divisions being determined by the
general dependencies in which their component parts
stand to each other,—and the classes afforded by these
divisions, when again considered, without distinction,
in the different points of view given by Quantity,
Quality, and Relation, will exhaust all the possible
forms in which judgments are manifested.

¶ XLVIII. The first great distinction of Judgments is taken from the relation of Subject and
Predicate, as reciprocally whole and part. If the
Subject or determined notion be viewed as the
containing whole, we have an Intensive or Comprehensive proposition; if the Predicate or de-

a Esser, *Logik*, § 56, p. 111.

termining notion be viewed as the containing
whole, we have an Extensive proposition.

Explica-
tion,—this
distinction
founded on
the Com-
prehension
and Exten-
sion of Con-
cepts.
This distinction of propositions is founded on the
distinction of the two quantities of concepts,—their
Comprehension and their Extension. The relation of
subject and predicate is contained within that of
whole and part, for we can always view either the
determining or the determined notion as the whole
which contains the other. The whole, however, which
the subject constitutes, and the whole which the predicate constitutes, are different, being severally determined by the opposite quantities of comprehension
and of extension; and as subject and predicate necessarily stand to each other in the relation of these
inverse quantities, it is manifestly a matter of indiffer-
ence, in so far as the meaning is concerned, whether
we view the subject as the whole of comprehension,
which contains the predicate, or the predicate as the
whole of extension, which contains the subject. In
point of fact, in single propositions it is rarely apparent which of the two wholes is meant; for the copula
is, est, &c., equally denotes the one form of the relation
as the other. Thus, in the proposition *man is two-
legged,*—the copula here is convertible with *comprehends* or *contains in it,* for the proposition means
man contains in it two-legged, that is, the subject
man, as an intensive whole or complex notion, comprehends as a part the predicate *two-legged.* Again,
in the proposition *man is a biped,* the copula corresponds to *contained under,* for this proposition is
tantamount to, *man is contained under biped,* that
is, the predicate *biped,* as an extensive whole or class,
contains under it as a part the subject *man.* But, in

point of fact, neither of the two propositions unam- LECT.
XIII. biguously shows whether it is to be viewed as of an intensive or of an extensive purport; nor in a single proposition is this of any moment. All that can be said is, that the one form of expression is better accommodated to express the one kind of proposition, the other better accommodated to express the other. It is only when propositions are connected into syllogism, that it becomes evident whether the subject or the predicate be the whole in or under which the other is contained; and it is only as thus constituting two different, two contrasted, forms of reasoning,— forms the most general, as under each of these every other is included,—that the distinction becomes necessary in regard to concepts and propositions. The distinction of propositions into Extensive and Intensive, it is needless to say, is, therefore, likewise the most general; and, accordingly, it is only in subordination to this distinction that the other distinctions, of which we are about to treat, are valid.

I now proceed to the second division of Judgments, and commence with the following paragraph.

¶ XLIX. The second division of Judgments Par. XLIX.
Second
division of
Judgments,
—Categori-
cal and Con-
ditional,—
the latter
of which is
subdivided
into Hypo-
thetical,
Disjunctive,
and Dilem-
matic. is founded on the different mode in which the relation of determination may subsist between the subject and predicate of a proposition. This relation is either *Simple* or *Conditional*, (*propositio simplex, propositio conditionalis*). On the former alternative, the proposition is called *Categorical;*[a] on the latter, inasmuch as the condition lies either

a [Categorical had better be called *Absolute*, as is done by Gassendi, *Logica*, p. 287, ed. Oxon.; or *Perfect*, as by Mocenicus, who has also *Absolute*. See *Contemplationes Peripateticæ*, ll. c. 2, p. 39 et seq.]

in the subject, or in the predicate, or in both the subject and predicate, there are three species of proposition. In the first case, the proposition is *Hypothetical*, in the second, *Disjunctive*, in the third, *Dilemmatic* or *Hypothetico-disjunctive*.[a]

Explica-
tion,—1.
Categorical
Judgments.
The term
Categorical.

I shall consider these in their order; and, first, of Categorical propositions. But here it is proper, before proceeding to expound what is designated by the term *categorical*, to commence with an explanation of the term itself. This word, as far as is now known, was first employed by Aristotle in a logical signification. I have already explained the meaning of the term *category*;[b] but you are not to suppose that *categorical* has any reference to the ten *summa genera* of the Stagirite. By Aristotle the term κατηγορικὸς is frequently employed, more especially in the books of the *Prior Analytics*,—and in these books alone it occurs, if I am correct in my estimate, eighty-seven times.

Now you will observe, that in no single instance is this word applied by Aristotle except in one unambiguous signification, that is, the signification of *affirmative;* and it is thus by him used as a term convertible with καταφατικὸς, and as opposed to the two synonyms of negation he indifferently employs,—ἀποφατικὸς and στερητικὸς.[γ] Such is the meaning of the

Its meaning
in the writ-
ings of his
disciples.

word in Aristotelic usage. Now you will observe, that it obtained a totally different meaning in the writings of his disciples. This new meaning it probably obtained from Theophrastus, the immediate disciple of Aristotle, for by him and Eudemus we know that it

---

a Cf. Krug, *Logik*, § 57.—ED.
[Mocenicus, *loc. cit.*; Schulze, *Logik*,
§§ 45, 52, 50-69.]

β See above, p. 197.—ED.
γ Compare *Discussions*, p. 152.—
ED.

was so employed;—and in this new meaning it was
exclusively applied by all the Greek and Latin expositors of the Peripatetic philosophy, in fact, by all
subsequent logicians without exception. In this
second signification, the term *categorical*, as applied
to a proposition, denotes a judgment in which the
predicate is simply affirmed or denied of the subject,
and in contradistinction to those propositions which
have been called *hypothetical* and *disjunctive*. In this
change of signification there is nothing very remarkable. But it is a singular circumstance that, though
the Aristotelic employment of the word be in every
instance altogether clear and unambiguous, no one,
either in ancient or in modern times, should ever have
made the observation, that the word was used in two
different meanings; and that in the one meaning it
was used exclusively by Aristotle, and in the other
exclusively by all other logicians. I find, indeed, that
the Greek commentators on the *Organon* do, in reference to particular passages, sometimes state that καττ-
γορικὸς is there used by Aristotle in the signification
of *affirmative*; but, in so far as I have been able to
ascertain, no one has made the general observation,
that the word was never applied by Aristotle in the
sense in which alone it was understood by all other
logical writers. So much for the meaning of the
term *categorical*; as now employed for *simple* or
absolute, and as opposed to *conditional*, it is used
in a sense different from its original and Aristotelic
meaning.

In regard to the nature of a Categorical Judgment
itself, it is necessary to say almost nothing. For, as
this judgment is that in which the two terms stand
to each other simply in that relation which every

This differ-
ence of sig-
nification
not hitherto
observed.

Nature of a
Categorical
Judgment.

judgment implies, to the exclusion of all extrinsic conditions, it is evident, that what we have already said of the essential nature of judgment in general, affords all that can be said of categorical judgments in particular. A categorical proposition is expressed in the formulæ, A *is* B, A *is not* B. I proceed, therefore, to the genus of propositions as opposed to categorical,—viz., the Conditional,—Conditioned.

This genus, as stated in the paragraph, comprises two species, according as the condition lies more proximately in the subject, or in the predicate; to which is to be added, either as a third species, or as a compound of these two, those propositions in which there is a twofold condition,—the one belonging to the subject, the other to the predicate. The first of these, as stated, forms the class of Hypothetical, the second that of Disjunctive, the third that of Dilem-

matic, propositions. I may notice, by the way, that there is a good deal of variation in the language of logicians in regard to the terms *Conditional* and *Hypothetical*. You are aware that *conditionalis*, in Latin, is commonly applied as a translation of ὑπο- θετικός in Greek; and by Boethius, who was the first among the Latins who elaborated the logical doctrine of hypotheticals, the two terms are used convertibly with each other.[a] By many of the schoolmen, how- ever, the term *hypothetical* (*hypotheticus*) was used to denote the genus, and the term *conditional*, to denote the species, and from them this nomenclature has passed into many of the more modern compends of logic,—and, among others, into those of Aldrich and Whately. This latter usage is wrong. If either

[a] Compare *Discussions*, p. 150. *Syllogismo Hypothetico*, L. i.—ED. For Boethius, see his treatise *De*

term is to be used in subordination to the other, *con-*   LECT.
ditional, as the more extensive term, ought to be   XIII.
applied to designate the genus; and so it has accordingly been employed by the best logicians. But to
pass from words to things.

I said that Hypothetical propositions are those in 1. Hypo-
which the condition qualifying the relation between thetical.
the subject and predicate lies proximately in the
subject. In the proposition, B *is* A, the subject B is
unconditionally thought to exist, and it thus constitutes a categorical proposition. But if we think the
subject B existing only conditionally, and under this
conditional existence enunciate the judgment, we shall
have the hypothetical proposition, *If* B *is,* A *is,*—
or, in a concrete example,—*Rainy weather is wet
weather,* is a categorical proposition—*If it rains, it
will be wet,* is an hypothetical. In an hypothetical
proposition the objects thought stand in such a mutual
relation, that the one can only be thought in so far
as the other is thought; in other words, if we think
the one, we must necessarily think the other. They
thus stand in the relation of Reason and Consequent.
For a reason is that which, being affirmed, necessarily
entails the affirmation of something else; a consequent is that which is only affirmed, inasmuch as
something previous is affirmed. The relation between
reason and consequent is necessary. For a reason
followed by nothing, would not be the reason of anything, and a consequent which did not proceed from
a reason, would not be the consequent of anything.
An hypothetical proposition must, therefore, contain
a reason and its consequent, and it thus presents the
appearance of two members or clauses. The first
clause,—that which contains the reason,—is called the

Antecedent, also the *Reason*, the *Condition*, or the *Hypothesis*, (*hypothesis, conditio, ratio, antecedens*,—*i.e.*, *membrum sive propositio*); the second, which contains the consequent necessitated by this ground, is called the *Consequent*, also the *Thesis*, (*consequens, thesis, rationatum, conditionatum*). The relation between the two clauses is called the *Consequence*, (*consequentia*), and is expressed by the particles *if* on the one hand, and *then, so, therefore,* &c., on the other, which are, therefore, called the *Consecutive particles*, (*particulæ consecutivæ*).* These are frequently, however, not formally expressed.

"This consequence (*if is—then is*) is the copula in hypothetical propositions; for through it the concepts are brought together, so as to make up, in consciousness, but a single act of thought; consequently, in it lies that synthesis, that connection, which constitutes the hypothetical judgment. Although, therefore, an hypothetical judgment appear double, and may be cut into two different judgments, it is nevertheless not a composite judgment. For it is realised through a simple act of thought, in which *if* and *then*, the antecedent and the consequent, are thought at once and as inseparable. The proposition *if* B *is, then* A *is*, is tantamount to the proposition, A *is through* B. But this is as simple an act as if we categorically judged B *is* A, that is, B *is under* A. Of these two, neither the one,—*If the sun shines*, nor the other,—*then it is day*,—if thought apart from the other, will constitute a judgment, but only the two in conjunction. But if we think,—*The sun shines*, and *it is day*, each by itself, then the whole connection between the two thoughts is abolished, and we have nothing more than

* Krug, *Logik*, § 57, Anm. 2, p. 168.—ED.

two isolated categorical judgments. The relatives *if* and *then*, in which the logical synthesis lies, constitute thus an act one and indivisible.

"For the same reason, an Hypothetical judgment cannot be converted into a Categorical. For the thought, A *is through* B, is wholly different from the thought, A *is in* B. The judgment,—*If God is righteous, then will the wicked be punished*, and the judgment,—*A righteous God punishes the wicked*, are very different, although the matter of thought is the same. In the former judgment, *the punishment of the wicked* is viewed as a consequent of *the righteousness of God*; whereas the latter considers it as an attribute of *a righteous God*. But as the consequent is regarded as something dependent from,—the attribute, on the contrary, as something inhering in, it is from two wholly different points of view that the two judgments are formed. The hypothetical judgment, therefore, A *is through* B, is essentially different from the categorical judgment, A *is in* B; and the two judgments are regulated by different fundamental laws. For the Categorical judgment, as expressive of the relation of subject and attribute, is determined by the laws of Identity and Contradiction; the Hypothetical, as expressive of the relation of Reason and Consequent, is regulated by the principle of that name." [a] So much for Hypotheticals.

Not convertible into a Categorical.

"Disjunctive judgments are those in which the condition qualifying the relation between the subject and predicate, lies proximately in the predicate, as in the proposition, D *is either* B, *or* C, *or* A. In this class

2. Disjunctive.

a Krug, *Logik*, § 57, p. 168, Anm. 2.—ED. [Hypotheticals take account not of the correctness of the two clauses, but only of their connection, (*consequentia*.) Hence the logical rule, *Propositio Conditionalis nihil ponit in esse.* Christian Weiss, *Lehrbuch der Logik*, p. 109, ed. 1801.]

of judgments a certain plurality of attributes is predicated of the subject, but in such a manner that this
plurality is not predicated conjunctly, but it is only
judged that, under conditions, some one, and only
some one, of this bundle of attributes appertains to
the subject. When I say that *Men are either Black,
or White, or Tawny,*—in this proposition, none of
these three predicates is unconditionally affirmed; but
it is only assumed that one or other may be affirmed,
and that, any one being so affirmed, the others must,
eo ipso, be denied. The attributes thus disjunctively
predicable of the subject, constitute together a certain
sphere or whole of extension ; and as the attributes
mutually exclude each other, they may be regarded
as reciprocally reason and consequent. A disjunctive
proposition has two forms, according as it is regulated
by a contradictory, or by a contrary, opposition. A
is either B *or not* B,—*This mineral is either a metal
or not,*—are examples of the former ; A *is either* B,
or C, *or* D,—*This mineral is either lead, or tin, or
zinc,*—are examples of the latter. The opposite attributes or characters in a disjunctive proposition are
called the *Disjunct Members (membra disjuncta)* ; and
their relation to each other is called the *Disjunction,*
(disjunctio), which in English is expressed by the relative particles *either, or, (aut, vel),* in consequence of
which these words constitute the *Disjunctive particles,*
(particulæ disjunctivæ). In propositions of this class
the copula is formed by *either is,—or is,* for hereby
the concepts are brought together so as to constitute
a single object of consciousness, and thus a synthesis
or union of notions is effected.

"Now, although in consequence of the multiplicity
of its predicates, a disjunctive proposition may be

resolved into a plurality of judgments, still it is not LECT. XIII. on that account a complex or composite judgment. For it is realised by one simple energy of thought, in reality composite, and not convertible into a Categorical. which the two relatives,—the *either* and the *or*,—are thought together as inseparable, and as binding up the opposite predicates into a single sphere. In consequence of this, a disjunctive proposition cannot be converted into a categorical. For in a categorical judgment a single predicate is simply affirmed or denied of a subject; whereas in a disjunctive judgment there is neither affirmation nor negation, but the opposition of certain attributes in relation to a certain subject constitutes the thought. Howbeit, therefore, that a disjunctive and a categorical judgment may have a certain resemblance in respect of their object-matter; still in each the form of thought is wholly different, and the disjunctive judgment is, consequently, one essentially different from the categorical."[a]

Dilemmatic propositions are those in which a condi- a. Dilemmatic. tion is found both in the subject and in the predicate, and, as thus a combination of an hypothetical form and of a disjunctive form, they may also appropriately be denominated *Hypothetico-disjunctive*. *If X is A, it is either B or C—If an action be prohibited, it is prohibited either by natural or by positive law—If a cognition be a cognition of fact, it is given either through an act of external perception or through an act of self-consciousness.* In such propositions, it is not necessary that the disjunct predicates should be limited to two; and besides what are strictly called *dilemmatic judgments*, we may have others that would properly obtain the names of *trilemmatic, tetralem-*

a Krug, *Logik*, pp. 170, 171. Compare Kant, *Logik*, § 29.—ED.

matic, *polylemmatic*, &c. But in reference to propositions, as in reference to syllogisms, *dilemma* is a word
used not merely to denote the cases where there are
only two disjunct members, but is, likewise, extended
to any plurality of opposing predicates. There remains here, however, always an ambiguity; and perhaps, on that account, the term *hypothetico-disjunctive*
might with propriety be substituted for *dilemmatic*.

A Dilem-
matic judg-
ment indi-
visible, and
not redu-
cible to a
plurality
of categori-
cal proposi-
tions.
A proposition of this class, though bearing both an
hypothetical and a disjunctive form, cannot, however,
be analysed into an hypothetical and a disjunctive
judgment. It constitutes as indivisible a unity of
thought as either of these; and can as little as these
be reduced without distinction to a plurality of categorical propositions.

Every form of Judgments which we have hitherto
considered, has its corresponding form of Syllogism;
and it is as constituting the foundations of different
kinds of reasoning, that the consideration of these
different kinds of propositions is of principal import-

Judgments
considered
in reference
to Quantity.
ance. These various kinds of propositions may, however, be considered in the different points of view of
Quantity, Quality, and Relation. And first of Quantity; in reference to which I give you the following
paragraph.

Par. L.
1°. The
common
doctrine of
the division
of Judg-
ments ac-
cording to
their Quan-
tity.
2°. The doc-
trine of the
Author on
this point.
¶ L. The Quantity of Judgments has reference to the whole of Extension, to the number
of the objects concerning which we judge. On
this I shall state articulately, 1°, The doctrine of
the Logicians; and, 2°, The doctrine which I conceive to be the more correct.

1°. (The doctrine of the Logicians.) The
common doctrine, which, in essentials, dates from

Aristotle,[a] divides Propositions according to their
Quantity into four classes; viz., (A), the *Universal*
or *General* (*pr. universales, generales, προτάσεις αἱ
καθόλου*) ; (B), the *Particular* (*pr. particulares,
προτάσεις μερικαί, αἱ ἐν μέρει*) ; (C), the *Individual* or *Singular* (*pr. individuales, singulares,
expositoriæ, προτάσεις αἱ καθ' ἕκαστον, τὰ ἄτομα*) ;
(D), the *Indefinite* (*pr. impræfinitæ, indefinitæ,
προτάσεις ἀδιόριστοι, ἀπροσδιόριστοι*). They
mean by *universal propositions*, those in which
the subject is taken in its whole extension ;
by *particular propositions*, those in which the
subject is taken in a part, indefinitely, of its
extension ; by *individual propositions*, those
in which the subject is at a minimum of extension ; by *indefinite propositions*, those in
which the subject is not articulately or overtly
declared to be either universal, particular, or
individual.

2°. (The doctrine I prefer.) This division appears to me untenable, and I divide Propositions according to their Quantity in the following manner :—In this respect their differences
arise either (A), as in Judgments, from the
necessary condition of the Internal Thought ;
or (B), as in Propositions, merely from the
accidental circumstances of its External Expression.

Under the former head (A), Judgments are
either (a) of Determinate or Definite Quantity,
according as their sphere is circumscribed, or (b)
of Quantity Indeterminate or Indefinite, according as their sphere is uncircumscribed.—Again,

a *De Interp.*, c. 7; *Anal. Prior.*, i. 1.—ED.

Judgments of a Determinate Quantity (a) are either (1) of a Whole Undivided, in which case they constitute a *Universal* or *General Proposition;* or (2) of a Unit Indivisible, in which case they constitute an *Individual* or *Singular Proposition.*—A Judgment of an Indeterminate Quantity (b) constitutes a *Particular Proposition.*

Under the latter head (B), Propositions have either, as propositions, their quantity (determinate or indeterminate) marked out by a verbal sign, or they have not; such quantity being involved in every actual thought. They may be called in the one case (a) *Predesignate;* in the other (b) *Preindesignate.*

Again, the common doctrine, remounting also to Aristotle,[a] takes into view only the Subject, and regulates the quantity of the proposition exclusively by the quantity of that term. The Predicate, indeed, Aristotle and the logicians do not allow to be affected by quantity; at least they hold it to be always Particular in an Affirmative, and Universal in a Negative, Proposition.

This doctrine I hold to be the result of an incomplete analysis; and I hope to show you that the confusion and multiplicity of which our present Logic is the complement, is mainly the consequence of an attempt at synthesis, before the ultimate elements had been fairly reached by a searching analysis, and of a neglect, in this instance, of the fundamental postulate of the science.

a *De Interp.,* c. 7.—ED.

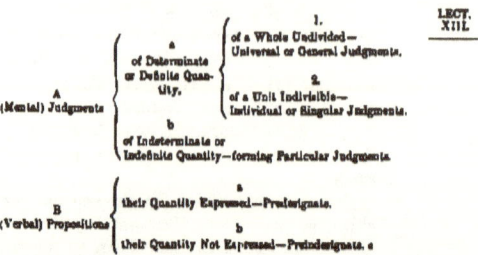

Universal Judgments are those in which the whole number of objects within a sphere or class are judged of,—as *All men are mortal,* or *Every man is mortal;* the *all* in the one case defining the whole collectively, the *every* in the other defining it discretively. In such judgments the notion of a determinate wholeness or totality, in the form of omnitude or allness, is involved.

*Explication.
Universal
Judgments.*

Individual Judgments are those in which, in like manner, the whole of a certain sphere is judged of, but in which sphere there is found only a single object, or collection of single objects,—as *Catiline is ambitious,*—*The twelve apostles were inspired.* In such judgments the notion of determinate whole-

*Singular or
Individual
Judgments,
what.*

a Vide Th. of. Am. apud Am. *In de Int.*, 8vo, ff. 72, 111-113. [In the first of these passages Ammonius, proceeding on a merely arithmetical calculation, enumerates sixteen varieties of the Proposition, any one of four quantities in the subject (*all — not all, some — not some or none*) being capable of combination with any one of four quantities in the predicate.

But of these some are but verbal varieties of the same judgment, and others are excluded on material grounds, so that his division finally coincides with Aristotle's. In the second passage Theophrastus is cited in illustration of a very obscure statement concerning the opposition of indesignate propositions.—ED.]

ness or totality in the form of oneness, indivisible
unity, is involved."

Particular
Judgments,
what.

Particular Judgments are those in which, among
the objects within a certain sphere or class, we judge
concerning some indefinite number less than the whole,
—as *Some men are virtuous*—*Many boys are courage-
ous*—*Most women are compassionate;* the indefinite
plurality, within the totality, being here denoted by
Words
which serve
to mark out
quantity in
Universal,
Individual,
and Parti-
cular Pro-
positions.
the words *some, many, most.* There are certain words
which serve to mark out the quantity in the case
of Universal, Individual, and Particular propositions.
The words which designate universality are *all, the
whole of, every, both, each, none, no one, neither, always,
everywhere,* &c. The words which mark out particularity are *some, not all, one, two, three,* &c., *sometimes,
somewhere,* &c. There are also terms which, though
they do not reach to an universal whole, approximate
to it, as *many, most, almost all, the greatest part,* &c.,
few, very few, hardly any, &c., which, in the common
employment of language, and in reference to merely
probable matter, may be viewed as almost tantamount
to marks of universality.

Distinction
of Universal
and Indivi-
dual from
Particular
Judgments.
By logicians in general it is stated, that in a logical
relation, an Individual is convertible with an Universal
proposition ; as in both something is predicated of a
whole subject, and neither admits of any exception.
But a Particular Judgment, likewise, predicates something of a whole subject, and admits of no exception ;
for it embraces all that is viewed as the subject, and
excludes all that is viewed as not belonging to it.
The whole distinction consists in this,—that, in Uni-

α *Individuum (proprium) signatum,*
and *individuum vagum.* So *particulare signatum,* and *particulare va-*
gum. The former of each, and the
latter of each, corresponding.—*Me-
moranda.*

versal and in Individual Judgments, the number of the objects judged of is thought by us as definite; whereas, in Particular Judgments, the number of such objects is thought by us as indefinite. That Individual Judgments do not correspond to Universal Judgments, merely in virtue of the oneness of their subject, is shown by this,—that, if the individual be rendered indefinite, the judgment at once assumes the character of particularity. For example, the propositions,—*A German invented the art of printing,—An Englishman generalised the law of gravitation,—*are to be viewed as particular propositions. But, if we substitute for the indefinite expressions *a German* and *an Englishman*, the definite expressions *Fust* and *Newton*, the judgment obtains the form of an universal.

With regard to quantity, it is to be observed, say the logicians, that Categorical Judgments are those alone which admit of all the forms. "Hypothetical and Disjunctive propositions are always universal. For in hypotheticals, by the position of a reason, there is posited every consequent of that reason; and in disjunctives the sphere or extension of the subject is so defined, that the disjunct attributes are predicated of the whole sphere. It may, indeed, sometimes seem as if in such propositions something were said of some, and, consequently, that the judgment is particular or indefinite. For example, as an hypothetical,—*If some men are learned, then others are unlearned ;* as a disjunctive,—*Those men who are learned are either philosophers or not.* But it is easily seen that these judgments are essentially of a general character. In the first judgment, the real consequent is,—*then all others are unlearned ;* and in the second, the true subject is,—*all learned men,*

Categorical Judgments alone, according to the logicians, admit of all the forms of quantity.

for this is involved in the expression—*Those men
who are learned, &c.*" [a]

This doc-
trine erro-
neous.

Such is the doctrine of the Logicians. This I cannot
but hold to be erroneous ; for we can easily construct
propositions, whether hypothetical or disjunctive, which
cannot be construed either as universal or singular.
For example, when we say, hypothetically,—*If some
Dodo is, then some animal is;* or, disjunctively,—
Some men are either rogues or fools :—in either case,
the proposition is indefinite or particular, and no ingenuity can show a plausible reason why it should be
viewed as definite,—as general or individual.

a Krug, *Logik*, § 57, Anm. 4, p.
171 *et seq.*—Ed. [Cf. Hoffbauer,
Anfangsgründe der Logik, § 243; Sigwart, *Logik*, § 164 *et seq.*, ed. 1835 ;
Kiesewetter, *Grundriss einer allge-
meinen Logik*, i. § 122; Schulze, *Logik*, § 60. *Contra :*—Esser, *Logik*, §
92, p. 177.—See below, pp. 333,
334, note a.—Ed.]

LECTURE XIV.

STOICHEIOLOGY.

SECTION II.—OF THE PRODUCTS OF THOUGHT.

II.—APOPHANTIC.

JUDGMENTS—THEIR QUALITY, OPPOSITION, AND CONVERSION.

THE first part of our last Lecture was occupied with the doctrine of Judgments, considered as divided into Simple and Conditional; Simple being exclusively Categorical, Conditional, either Hypothetical, Disjunctive, or Hypothetico-disjunctive. We then proceeded to treat of the Quantity of propositions, and, in this respect, I stated that they are either Definite or Indefinite; the Definite comprising the two subordinate classes of General or Universal, and of Singular or Individual propositions, while the Indefinite are correspondent to Particular propositions alone. In regard to the terms *definite* and *indefinite*, I warned you that I do not apply them in the sense given by logical writers. With them, Indefinite propositions denote those in which the quantity is not explicitly declared by one of the designatory terms, *all, every, some, many, &c.* Such propositions, however, ought to be called *preindesignate* (*præindesignatæ, ἀπροσδιόριστοι*), that is, *not marked out by a prefix,*—a term better adapted to indicate this external accident of their enunciation; for, in point of fact, these preindesignate propositions

LECT. XIV.

Recapitulation.

250 LECTURES ON LOGIC.

LECT.
XIV.

Second
division
of Judg-
ments, or
that accord-
ing to their
Quality.

are either definite or indefinite, and quite as definite
or indefinite in meaning, as if their quantity had been
expressly marked out by the predesignatory terms.

This being premised, I now go on to the next division of Judgments,—the division proceeding on that
ground which by Logicians has been called the *Quality* of Judgments. In itself the term *quality* is here
a very vague and arbitrary expression, for we might,
with equal propriety, give the name of *quality* to
several other of the distinguishing principles of propositions. For example, the truth or falsehood of propositions has been also called their *quality;* and some
logicians have even given the name of *quality* to the
ground of the distinction of judgments into categorical,
hypothetical, and disjunctive. What, however, has
been universally, if not always exclusively, styled the
quality of propositions, both in ancient and modern
times, is that according to which they are distributed
into Affirmative and Negative.

Par. LI.
Judgments,
in respect of
their Qua-
lity, are Af-
firmative
and Nega-
tive.

¶ LI. In respect of their Quality, Judgments
are divided into two classes. For either the
Subject and Predicate may be recognised as reciprocally containing and contained, in the opposite
quantities of Extension and Comprehension ; or
they may be recognised as not standing in this
relation. In the former case, the subject and
predicate are affirmed of each other, and the
proposition is called an *Affirmative,* (πρότασις
καταφατική or κατηγορική, *judicium affirmati-
vum* or *positivum*) ; in the latter case, they are
denied of each other, and the proposition is called
a *Negative,* (πρότασις ἀποφατική or στερητική,
judicium negativum).

In this paragraph, I have enounced more generally than is done by logicians the relation of predication, in its affirmative and negative phases.   For their defi- nitions only apply either to the subject or to the predi- cate, taken as a whole ; whereas, since we may indiffer- ently view either the subject as the whole in relation to the predicate, or the predicate as the whole in rela- tion to the subject, according as we consider the pro- position to express an intensive or to express an exten- sive judgment,—it is proper in our definition, whether of predication in general, or of affirmation and negation in particular, to couch it in such terms that it may indifferently comprehend both these classes,—both these phases, of propositions.

As examples of Affirmative and Negative proposi- tions, the following may suffice :—A *is* B—A *is not* B —*God is merciful*—*God is not vindictive.*   In an Affirmative judgment, there is a complete inclusion of the subject within the predicate as an extensive whole, or of the predicate within the subject as an intensive whole.   In Negative judgments, on the contrary, there is a total exclusion of the subject from the sphere of the predicate (extensively), or of the predicate from the comprehension of the subject (intensively).   In affirmative propositions there is also distinctly enounced through what predicate the notion of the subject is to be thought, that is, what predicate must be annexed to the notion of the subject ; in negative propositions, in like manner, it is distinctly enounced through what predicate the notion of the subject is not to be thought, that is, what predicate must be shut out from the notion of the subject.   In negative judgments, therefore, the negation essentially belongs to the Copula ; for otherwise all propositions

without distinction would be affirmative. This, however, has been a point of controversy among modern
logicians; for many maintain that the negation belongs

*That nega-
tion does
not belong
to the Cop-
ula, held by
some logi-
cians.*

to the predicate, on the following grounds :—If the
negation pertained to the copula, there could be no
synthesis of the two terms,—the whole act of judgment
would be subverted ; while at the same time a non-
connecting copula, a non-copulative, is a contradiction
in terms. But a negative predicate, that is, a predicate
by which something is taken away or excluded from
the subject, involves nothing contradictory ; and, therefore, a judgment with such a predicate is competent."

*The oppo-
site doctrine
maintained
by the
Author.*

The opposite doctrine is, however, undoubtedly the
more correct. For if we place the negation in the predicate, negative judgments, as already said, are not
different in form from affirmative, being merely affir-
mations that the object is contained within the sphere
of a negative predicate, or that a negative predicate
forms one of the attributes of the subject. This, however, the advocates of the opinion in question do not
venture to assert. The objection from the apparent
contradiction of a non-connecting copula is valid only
if the literal, the grammatical, meaning of the term
copula be coextensive with that which it is applied
logically to express. But this is not the case. If literally taken, it indicates only one side of its logical

*True import
of the logi-
cal copula.*

meaning. What the word *copula* very inadequately
denotes, is the form of the relation between the subject
and predicate of a judgment. Now, in negative judgments, this form essentially consists in the act of tak-

a Krug, *Logik*, § 55, Anm. 3.—
F.n. [Compare, on the same side,
Buffier, *Logique*, i. § 75 et seq.; Bolzano, *Wissenschaftslehre*, *Logik*, vol.
ii. § 127, 129, 136 ; Schulze, *Logik*,
§ 50, p. 74 ; Bardili, *Grundriss der*

eratra Logik, § 12 ; Derodon, *Logica*,
p. 642 ; cf. p. 615 et seq. *Contra* :
—Kant, *Logik*, § 72, Anm. 3 ; Bachmann, *Logik*, § 84, p. 127 ; Esser,
Logik, § 59, p. 115.]

ing a part out of a whole, and is as necessary an act of LECT. thought as the putting it in. The notion of the one ―XIV― contradictory in fact involves the notion of the other.[a]

The controversy took its origin in this,—that every negative judgment can be expressed in an affirmative form, when the negation is taken from the copula, and placed in the predicate. Thus, A *is not* B may be changed into,—A *is not*-B. The contrast is better expressed in Latin, A *non est* B—A *est non*-B. In fact, we are compelled in English to borrow the Latin *non* to make the difference unambiguously apparent, saying, A *is non*-B, instead of A *is not*-B. But this proves nothing; for by this transposition of the negation from the copula to the predicate, we are also enabled to express every affirmative proposition through a double negation. Thus, A *is* B, in the affirmative form is equivalently enounced by A *is not non*-B—A *non est non*-B, in the negative.

This possibility of enunciating negative propositions in an affirmative, and affirmative propositions in a negative, form, has been the occasion of much perverse refinement among logicians. Aristotle[β] denominated the negative terms, such as *non* B, *non homo*, *non albus*, &c., ὀνόματα ἀόριστα, literally, *indefinite nouns*. Boethius,[γ] however, unhappily translated Aristotle's Greek term ἀόριστος by the Latin *infinitus*, reserving the term *indefinitus* to render ἀδιόριστος as applied to propositions, but of which the notion is more appropriately expressed, as we have seen, by the word *indesignate* (*indesignatus*), or better *preindesignate* (*præindesignatus*). The Schoolmen, following Boethius, thus called the ὀνόματα ἀόριστα of Aristotle *no*-

Origin of the controversy regarding the place of negation.

Negative terms, how designated by Aristotle.

By Boethius.

By the Schoolmen.

a Bachmann, *Logik*, p. 127.—Ed.
β *De Interpretatione*, c. 2.—Ed.
γ *In De Interpretatione*, L. ii. § 1. *Opera*, p. 280.—Ed.

mina infinita: and the *non* they styled the *particula infinitans.* Out of such elements they also constructed *Propositiones Infinita;* that is, judgments in which either the subject or the predicate was a negative notion, as *non homo est viridis,* and *homo est nonviridis,* and these they distinguished from the simple negative, *homo—non est—viridis.* Herein Boethius and the schoolmen have been followed by Kant,[a] through the Wolfian logicians; for he explains Infinite Judgments as those which do not simply indicate, that a subject is not contained under the sphere of a predicate, but that it lies out of its sphere, somewhere in the infinite sphere. He has thus considered them as combining an act of negation and an act of affirmation, inasmuch as one thing is affirmed in them through the negation of another. In consequence of this view, he gave them, after some Wolfians, the name of *Limitative,* which he constituted as a third form of judgments under quality,—all propositions being thus either Affirmative, Negative, or Limitative. The whole question touching the validity of the distinction is of no practical consequence; and consists merely in whether a greater or less latitude is to be given to certain terms. I shall not, therefore, occupy your attention by entering on any discussion of what may be urged in refutation or defence. But if what I have already stated of the nature of negation and its connection with the copula, be correct, there is no ground for regarding Limitative propositions as a class distinct in form, and co-ordinate with Affirmative and Negative judgments.[b]

If we consider the quantity and quality of judg-

Margin notes:
LECT. XIV.

Propositiones Infinitæ of the schoolmen,—what.

On this point followed by Kant.

Kant's three-fold division of Propositions unfounded.

---

a *Logik,* § 22. Compare Wolf, *Philos. Ration.,* § 209.—Ed.

β Compare Krug, *Logik,* § 55. Anm. 2.—Ed. [Against the distinction, see Bachmann, *Logik,* § 94, p. 128; Schulze, *Logik,* § 50; Drobisch, *Logik,* § 42.]

ments as combined, there emerges from this juncture four separate forms of propositions, for they are either Universal Affirmative, or Universal Negative, Particular Affirmative, or Particular Negative. These forms, in order to facilitate the statement and analysis of the syllogism, have been designated by letters, and as it is necessary that you should be familiar with these symbols, I shall state them in the following paragraph.

¶ LII. In reference to their Quantity and Quality together, Propositions are designated by the vowels A, E, I, O. The *Universal Affirmative* are denoted by A; the *Universal Negative* by E; the *Particular Affirmative* by I; the *Particular Negative* by O. To aid the memory, these distinctions have been comprehended in the following lines :—

> Asserit A, negat E, sed universaliter ambæ,
> Asserit I, negat O, sed particulariter ambo.[a]

I may here, likewise, show you one, and perhaps the best, mode, in which these different forms can be expressed by diagrams.

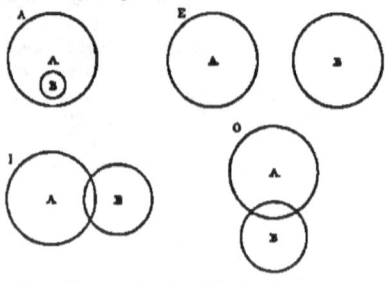

The invention of this mode of sensualising by
circles the abstractions of Logic is generally given to
Euler, who employs it in his *Letters to a German
Princess on different matters of Physics and Philosophy.*[a] But, to say nothing of other methods, this by
circles is of a much earlier origin. For I find it in
the *Nucleus Logicæ Weisianæ*, which appeared in
1712; but this was a posthumous publication, and
the author, Christian Weise, who was Rector of Zit-
tau, died in 1708. I may notice, also, that Lambert's
method of accomplishing the same end, by parallel
lines of different lengths, is to be found in the *Logic*
of Alstedius, published in 1614, consequently above a
century and a half prior to Lambert's *Neues Organon.*[β] Of Lambert's originality there can, however,
I think, be no doubt; for he was exceedingly curious
about, and not over-learned in, the history of these
subsidia, while in his philosophical correspondence
many other inventions of the kind, of far inferior interest, are recorded, but there is no allusion whatever
to that of Alstedius.

Before leaving this part of the subject, I may take
notice of another division of Propositions made by
all logicians,—viz., into *Pure* and *Modal.* Pure propositions are those in which the predicate is categorically affirmed or denied of the subject, simply, without
any qualification; Modal, those in which the predicate
is categorically affirmed or denied of the subject, under
some mode or qualifying determination. For example,
—*Alexander conquered Darius*, is a pure,—*Alexander*

The first
employ-
ment of
circular
diagrams
in logic
improperly
ascribed to
Euler.
To be found
in Christian
Weise.

Lambert's
method to
be found in
Alstedius.

Distinction
of Proposi-
tions into
Pure and
Modal.

---

a Partie ii. Lettre xxxv., ed.
Cournot.—ED.

β A very imperfect diagram of
this kind, with the lines of equal
length, in illustration of the first syl-

logistic figure, is given in the *Logica
Systema Harmonicum* of Alstedius
(1614), p. 395. Lambert's diagrams
(*Neues Organon*, vol. i. p. 111 *et seq.*)
are much more complete.—ED.

conquered Darius honourably, is a modal proposi- LECT. XIV.
tion.[a] Nothing can be more futile than this distinction. The mode in such propositions is nothing more
than a part of the predicate. The predicate may be
a notion of any complexity, it may consist of any
number of attributes, of any number even of words,
and the mere circumstance that one of these attributes
should stand prominently out by itself, can establish
no difference in which to originate a distinction of the
kind. Of the examples adduced,—the pure proposition, *Alexander conquered Darius*, means, being resolved, *Alexander was the conqueror of Darius*,—
Alexander being the subject, *was* the copula, and *the
conqueror of Darius* the predicate. Now, if we take
the modal,—*Alexander conquered Darius honourably*,
and resolve it in like manner, we shall have *Alexander
was the honourable conqueror of Darius*; and here the
whole difference is, that in the second the predicate is
a little more complex, being *the honourable conqueror
of Darius*, instead of *the conqueror of Darius*.

But logicians, after Aristotle,[b] have principally considered as modal propositions those that are modified
by the four attributions of Necessity, Impossibility,
Contingence, and Possibility. But in regard to these,
the case is precisely the same; the mode is merely a
part of the predicate, and if so, nothing can be more
unwarranted than on this accidental, on this extralogical, circumstance to establish a great division of
logical propositions. This error is seen in all its fla-
grancy when applied to practice. The discrimination

[a] These modals are not acknowledged by Aristotle, who allows only
the four mentioned below. They appear, however, in his Greek commentators, and from them were adopted
by the Schoolmen. Compare Ammonius, *In De Interp.*, p. 148 b, ed.
1546.—ED.

[b] *De Interp.*, c. 12. Compare
Anal. Prior., i. 2.—ED.

of propositions into Pure and Modal, and the discrimination of Modal propositions into Necessary, Impossible, Contingent, Possible, and the recognition of
these as logical distinctions, rendered it imperative
on the logician, as logician, to know what matter was
necessary, impossible, contingent, and possible. For
rules were laid down in regard to the various logical
operations to which propositions were subjected, according as these were determined by a matter of one
of these modes or of another, and this too when the
modal character itself was not marked out by any
peculiarity or form of expression. Thus, to take one of
many passages to the same effect in Whately. Speaking
of the quality of propositions, he says :—"When the
subject of a proposition is a Common-term, the *universal signs* ('all, no, every') are used to indicate that
it is distributed, (and the proposition consequently
is universal); the *particular signs* (' some, &c.') the
contrary. Should there be *no sign* at all to the common term, the quantity of the proposition (which is
called an *Indefinite* proposition) is ascertained by the
matter : i.e. the nature of the connection between the
extremes : which is either Necessary, Impossible, or
Contingent. In necessary and in impossible matter,
an Indefinite is *understood as a universal:* e. g., birds
have wings ; i. e. *all :* birds are not quadrupeds ; i. e.
none : in contingent matter, (i. e. where the terms
partly (i. e. sometimes) agree, and partly not) an
Indefinite is understood as a particular ; e. g., food is
necessary to life ; i.e. *some* food ; birds sing ; i. e.
some do ; birds are not carnivorous : i. e. *some* are
not, or, all are not."[a]

Now, all this proceeds upon a radical mistake of
the nature and domain of Logic. Logic is a purely

[a] *Elements of Logic,* book ii. chap. ii. § 2, pp. 63, 64.

formal science, it knows nothing of, it establishes
nothing upon, the circumstances of the matter, to
which its form may chance to be applied. To be able
to say that a thing is of necessary, impossible, or contingent matter, it is requisite to generalise its nature
from an extensive observation; and to make it incumbent on the logician to know the modality of all
the objects to which his science may be applied, is at
once to declare that Logic has no existence; for this
condition of its existence is in every point of view
impossible. It is impossible—1°, Inasmuch as Logic
would thus presuppose a knowledge of the whole cycle
of human science; and it is impossible—2°, Because
it is not now, and never will be, determined what
things are of necessary or contingent, of possible or
impossible existence. Speaking of things impossible
in nature, Sir Thomas Brown declared, that it is impossible that a quadruped could lay an egg, or that a
quadruped could possess the beak of a bird; and, in
the age of Sir Thomas Brown, these propositions would
have shown as good a title to be regarded as of impossible matter as some of the examples adduced by
Dr Whately. The discovery of New Holland, and of
the Ornithorhynchus, however, turned the impossible
into the actual; for, in that animal, there is found a
quadruped which at once lays an egg and presents
the bill of a duck. On the principle, then, that Logic
is exclusively conversant about the forms of thought,
I have rejected the distinction of propositions and
syllogisms into pure and modal, as extra-logical.
Whatever cannot be stated by A, B, C, is not of logical import; and A, B, C, know nothing of the necessary, impossible, and contingent.[a]

LECT.
XIV.

On the sup-
position
that Logic
takes cog-
nisance of
the modality
of objects,
this science
can have no
existence.

a See *Discussions*, p. 145 et seq.   72, and § 23, p. 79; Schulze, *Logik*,
—En. [Compare Bachmann, *Logik*,   § 82, p. 78.]
§ 73, p. 115; Richter, *Logik*, § 19, p.

LECT.
XIV.
It may be proper, however, to explain to you the meaning of three terms which are used in relation to

Explana-
tion of three
terms used
in reference
to Pure and
Modal Pro-
positions.
Pure and Modal propositions. A proposition is called *Assertory*, when it enounces what is known as actual; *Problematic*, when it enounces what is known as possible; *Apodeictic* or *Demonstrative*, when it enounces what is known as necessary.[a]

Third Divi-
sion of Judg-
ments—Re-
lation to
each other.
The last point of view in which judgments are considered, is their Relation to each other. In respect of these relations, propositions have obtained from Logicians particular names, which, however, cannot be understood without at the same time regarding the matter which the judgments contain. As the distinctions of Judgments and of Concepts are, in this respect, in a great measure analogous, both in name and nature, it will not be necessary to dictate them.

Judgments,
Identical.
When the matter and form of two judgments are considered as the same, they are called *Identical, Convertible, Equal* or *Equivalent (propositiones identicæ, pares, convertibiles, æquipollentes)*; on the opposite

Different.
alternative, they are called *Different (pr. diversæ)*. If considered in certain respects the same, in others dif-

Relatively
Identical.
ferent, they are called *Relatively Identical, Similar*, or *Cognate (pr. relative identicæ, similes, affines, cognatæ)*. This resemblance may be either in the subject and comprehension, or in the predicate and extension.

Disparate.
If they have a similar subject, their predicates are *Disparate (disparata)*; if a similar predicate, their

Disjunct.
subjects are *Disjunct (disjuncta)*.

When two judgments differ merely in their quantity of extension, and the one is, therefore, a particular, the other a general, they are said to be subordinated, and their relation is called *Subordination*

a Kant, *Logik*, § 30.—Ed.

(*subordinatio*). The subordinating (or, as it might, perhaps, be more properly styled, the *superordinate*) judgment is called the *Subalternant* (*subalternans*) ; the subordinate judgment is called the *Subalternate* (*subalternatum*).

When, of two or more judgments, the one affirms, the other denies, and when they are thus reciprocally different in quality, they are said to be *Opposed* or *Conflictive* (*pr. opposita, ἀντικείμεναι*), and their relation, in this respect, is called *Opposition* (*oppositio*). This opposition is either that of *Contradiction* or *Repugnance* (*contradictio, ἀντίφασις*), or that of *Contrariety* (*contrarietas, ἐναντιότης*).

If neither contradiction nor contrariety exists, the judgments are called *Congruent* (*pr. congruentes, consonantes, consentientes*). In regard to this last statement, you will find in logical books, in general,[a] that there is an opposition of what are called *Subcontraries* (*subcontraria*), meaning by these particular propositions of different quality, as, for example, *Some A are B, some A are not B*, or, *Some men are learned, some men are not learned ;* and they are called *Subcontraries*, as they stand subordinated to the universal contrary propositions,—*All A are B, no A is B*, or, *All men are learned, no man is learned.* But this is a mistake, there is no opposition between Subcontraries ; for both may at once be maintained, as both at once must be true if the *some* be a negation of *all.* (They cannot, however, both be false.) The opposition in this case is only apparent ;[β] and it was probably only

---

a *Elements of Logic*, by Dr Whately, part ii. chap. ii. § 3, p. 68, 3d edit. But see Scheibler, *Opera Logica*, Pars iii. c. xi. p. 487, ed. 1665; Ulrich, [*Instit. Log. et Met.* § 183, p. 190.—Ed.]

β For which reason Aristotle describes it as an opposition in language, but not in reality. *Anal. Prior.*, ii. 15.—Ed. [Compare Fonseca, *In-*

LECT.
XIV.

laid down from a love of symmetry, in order to make
out the opposition of all the corners in the square of
Opposition, which you will find in almost every work
on Logic.

Conversion
of Proposi-
tions.

Finally, various relations of judgments arise from
what is called their *Conversion.* When the subject
and predicate in a categorical proposition, (for to this
we now limit our consideration), are transposed, the
proposition is said to be converted; the proposition
given and its product are both called the *judicia conversa;* the relation itself in which the judgments
stand is called *Conversion* or *Reciprocation,* sometimes
Obversion or *Transposition* (*conversio, reciprocatio,
obversio, transpositio, μετάθεσις, μεταβολή, ἀντιστροφή*).

Terms em-
ployed to
denote the
original and
converted
proposition.

The given proposition is called the *Converted* or *Converse,* (*judicium, conversum, præjacens, propositio
conversa*); the other, into which it is converted, the
Converting, (*jud., prop., convertens, subjacens*). There
is, however, much ambiguity, to say the least of it, in
the terms commonly employed by Logicians to designate the two propositions,—that given, and that the
product of the logical elaboration. The *præjacent* and
subjacent may pass, but they have been very rarely
employed. The term *propositio conversa,* the converse or converted judgment, specially for the original
proposition, is worse than ambiguous; it is applied
generally to both judgments; it may, in fact, more
appropriately denote the other,—its product,—to which
indeed it has, but through a blunder, been actually

stit. Dialect., L. iii. c. 6, p. 129, ed.
1604; *Conimbricense Nova Logica,*
Tract. iii. Disp. iii. § 2, p. 124, ed.
1711. Kant expressly rejects Sub-
contrariety, *Logik,* § 50, Anm. Compare Krug, *Logik,* § 64, Anm. 4;
Bruniam, *Grundriss der Logik,* p. 105;

Derringer, *Institutionem Logicæ,* vol.
ii. § 713, p. 139; Caramuel, p. 33.]
[*Rationalis et Realis Philosophia,
authore Joanne Caramuel Lobkowitz,
S. Th. Lovaniensi Doctore, Abbate
Melrosensi.* Lovanii, 1642.—ED.]

applied by Aldrich,[a] and he is followed, of course, by
Whately. The original proposition ought to be called
the *Convertend* or *Convertible* (*pr. convertenda, con-*
vertibilis).[β] The term *Converting* (*convertens*), employed for the proposition, the product of conversion,
marks out nothing of its peculiar character. The expression *pr. exposita* applied to this judgment by
Aldrich,[γ] without a word of comment, is only another
instance of his daring ignorance ; for the phrase *pr. ex-*
posita had nothing to recommend it in this relation, and
was employed in a wholly different meaning by logicians and mathematicians.[δ] In this error Aldrich is
followed by Whately, who, like his able predecessor, is
wholly unversed in the literature and language of Logic.

    The logicians after Aristotle have distinguished two,
or, as we may take it, three, or even four, species of
Conversion.

    1. The first, which is called *Simple* or *Pure Con-*
version (*conversio simplex, ἀντιστροφὴ ἁπλῆ, τοῖς ὅροις*
πρὸς ἑαυτήν, Aristotle, *i.e., cum terminis reciprocatis*),[ε]
is when the quantity and quality of the two judgments

Propositio exposita—its use by Aldrich erroneous.

Species of Conversion distinguish-ed by logi-cians.

a *Rudimenta Logica*, L. i. c. ii.
β [So Noldius, p. 263,] [*Logica Re-cognita*, Hafniæ, 1766.—Ed.]
γ Crakanthorpe, Sanderson, and Wallis [denominate the original pro-position *pr. conversa*, its product *pr. convertens*. See Crakanthorpe, *Logi-ca*, L. iii. c. 10, p. 179, ed. 1677; Sanderson, *Logica*, L. ii. c. 7, p. 76, ed. 1741; Wallis, *Institutio Logicæ*, L. ii. c. 7, p. 113, edit. 1729. Wallis also uses *pr. conversa* as a syno-nym for *pr. conversa.*—Ed.]
δ The term *exposition* (ἔκθεσις) is employed by Aristotle, and by most subsequent logicians, to denote the selection of an individual instance whose qualities may be perceived by sense (ἐκτιθέναι, *exponere, objicere*

sensui), in order to prove a general relation between notions apprehend-ed by the intellect. This method is used by Aristotle in proving the con-version of propositions and the reduc-tion of syllogisms. See *Anal. Prior.*, i. 2; i. 6; i. 8. The instance se-lected is called the *expositum*, (τὸ ἐκτεθέν); and hence singular propo-sitions and syllogisms are called *ex-pository*. Compare Pacius on *Anal. Pr.*, i. 2, and Sir W. Hamilton's note, *Reid's Works*, p. 696.—Ed.
ε Τοῖς ὅροις ἀντιστρέφειν, *Anal. Pr.*, i. 2, *i.e.*, when each term is the exact equivalent of the other. See Trendel-enburg, *Elementa Log. Arist.*, § 14; *In De Anima*, p. 408; Waitz, *In Arist. Org.*, vol. i. p. 373.—Ed.

are the same. It holds in Universal Negative and Particular Affirmative propositions.

2. The second, which is called *Conversion by Accident* (c. per accidens, ἀντιστροφὴ ἐν μέρει, κατὰ μέρος, Aristotle), is when, the quality remaining unaltered, the quantity is reduced. It holds in Universal Affirmatives. These two are the species of the conversion of propositions acknowledged by all; they are evolved by Aristotle, not, as might have been expected, in his treatise *On Enouncement*, but in the second chapter of the first book of his *Prior Analytics*.[a]

3. The third, which is called *Conversion by Contraposition* (c. per oppositionem, c. per contrapositionem, both by Boethius,[β] contrapositio, ἀντιστροφὴ σὺν ἀντιθέσει, Alexander[γ]), is when, instead of the subject and predicate, the quantity and quality remaining the same, there is placed the contradictory of each. This holds in Universal Affirmatives, and most logicians allow it in Particular Negatives. It is commemorated by Aristotle in the eighth chapter of the second book of his *Topics*: it is there called the *inverse consecution from contradictions*.

Mnemonic verses expressing conversion.

I shall here mention some mnemonic verses in which the doctrine of conversion is expressed.

1°. Regarding conversion as limited to the Simple

---

a [Boethius seems the first who gave the name of *Conversio per Accidens*. With him it is properly both Ampliative and Restrictive. (So Rüdiger, *De Sensu Veri et Falsi*, pp. 250, 303, 2d edit. 1722; Fischer, *Logik*, p. 108). It is opposed as a conspecies to c. *generalis*; and both are species of c. *simplex*, which is opposed to Contraposition. See Opera, *De Syllogismo Categorico*, L. i. p. 587. Thus conversio is divided primarily into c. *simplex* and c. *per con-*trapositionem. Aristotle does not use ἀντιστροφὴ ἐν μέρει, as subsequent logicians, for c. *diminuta*. He uses it merely for particular in opposition to universal. (See *Anal. Prior.*, i. 2, § 4.) They are thus wrong in their use of the words *accidental* and *partial*.]

β *Introductio ad Syllogismos Categoricos*, and *De Syllogismo Categorico*, L. i.—Ed.

γ *In Anal. Prior.*, f. 10 b, edit. Ald. 1520.—Ed.

and Accidental, and excluding altogether Contraposi- LECT. XIV.
tion, we have the doctrine contained in the two following verses.

> E, I, *simpliciter vertendo, signa manebunt* ;
> Ast A cum vertis, signa minora cape.[a]

O is not convertible.

2°. Admitting Contraposition as a legitimate species
of conversion, the whole doctrine is embodied in the
following verses by Petrus Hispanus.

> F E c I (F E s I) *simpliciter,* convertitur E v A (E p A) per *Accid.*
> Ast O (A c O) per *Contrap.* ; sic fit conversio tota.[β]

Or to condense the three kinds of conversion with
all the propositions, prejacent and subjacent, in a
single line.

> "Ecce, tibi, *Simp.* ; Armi—orros, *Acc.* ; Arma, bono, *Contr.*"

It may be proper now to make you acquainted with Distinction of Proposi-
certain distinctions of judgments and propositions, tions not
which, though not strictly of a logical character, it is strictly lo- gical.
of importance that you should be aware of. " Consi-
dered in a material point of view, all judgments are,
in the first place, distinguished into *Theoretical* and Theoretical
Practical. Theoretical are such as declare that a cer- and Practi- cal.
tain character belongs or does not belong to a certain
object; Practical, such as declare that something can
be or ought to be done,—brought to bear.

" Theoretical, as well as practical, judgments are Indemon-
either *Indemonstrable,* when they are evident of strable and Demon-
themselves,—when they do not require and when strable.

---

a [Given by Chauvin, *Lex. Phil.,* v. *Conversio;* Denzinger, *Institutiones Logica,* ii. 140.]

β See Petrus Hispanus, p. 9[*Sum- mula,* Tract. i. partie. 4, f. 9, ed.

1505. Cf. Petrus Tataretus, *Expo- sitio in Summulas Petri Hispani,* Tract. i., f. 9 b.—Ed.]

γ[Hispanus, *Summula,* l.c. ; Chau- vin, l.c.]

LECT.
XIV.

they are incapable of proof; or they are *Demonstrable*, when they are not immediately apparent as true or false, but require some external reason to establish their truth or falsehood.

"Indemonstrable propositions are absolute principles (ἀρχαί, *principia*); that is, from which in the construction of a system of science cognitions altogether certain not only are, but must be, derived. Demonstrable propositions, on the other hand, can at best constitute only relative principles; that is, such as, themselves requiring a higher principle for their warrant, may yet afford the basis of sundry other propositions.

Axioms and Postulates.

"If the indemonstrable propositions be of a theoretical character, they are called *Axioms*; if of a practical character, *Postulates*. The former are principles of immediate certainty; the latter, principles of immediate application.

Theorems and Problems.

"Demonstrable propositions, if of a theoretical nature, are called *Theorems* (*theoremata*); if of a practical, *Problems* (*problemata*). The former, as propositions of a mediate certainty, require proof; they, therefore, consist of a *Thesis* and its *Demonstration*; the latter, as of mediate application, suppose a *Question* (*quæstio*) and its *Solution* (*resolutio*).

Corollaries.

"As species of the foregoing, there are, likewise, distinguished *Corollaries* (*consectaria, corollaria*), that is, propositions which flow without a new proof out of theorems or postulates previously demonstrated.

Experimental Propositions.

Propositions whose validity rests on observation or experiment are called *Experiential, Experimental* propositions (*empiremata, experientiæ, experimenta*).

Hypotheses.

Hypotheses, that is, propositions which are assumed with probability, in order to explain or prove some-

thing else which cannot otherwise be explained or LECT. XIV.
proved. *Lemmata*, that is, propositions borrowed
from another science in order to serve as subsidiary Lemmata.
propositions in the science of which we treat. Finally,
Scholia, that is, propositions which only serve as illus- Scholia.
trations of what is considered in chief. The clearest
and most appropriate examples of these various kinds
of propositions are given in mathematics." [a]

[a] Esser, *Logik*, § 79, pp. 147, 148.—ED. [Compare Krug, *Logik*, §§ 67, 68.]

LECTURE XV.

STOICHEIOLOGY.

SECTION II.—OF THE PRODUCTS OF THOUGHT.

III.—THE DOCTRINE OF REASONINGS.

REASONING IN GENERAL — SYLLOGISMS — THEIR DIVISIONS ACCORDING TO INTERNAL FORM.

LECT.
XV.

The act of
Reasoning,
—what.

IN my last Lecture, I terminated the Doctrine of Judgments, and now proceed to that of Reasonings.

"When the necessity of the junction or separation of a certain subject-notion and a certain predicate-notion is not manifest from the nature of these notions themselves, but when, at the same time, we are desirous of knowing whether they must be thought as inclusive, or as exclusive, of each other,—in this case, we find ourselves in a state of doubt or indecision, from our ignorance of which of the two contradictory predicates must be affirmed or denied of the subject. But this doubt can be dissipated,—this ignorance can be removed, only in one way,—only by producing in us a necessity to connect with, or disconnect from, the subject one of the repugnant predicates. And since, *ex hypothesi*, this necessity does not, at least does not immediately, arise from the simple knowledge of the subject in itself, or of the predicate in itself, or of both together in themselves; it follows

that it must be derived from some external source,
and derived it can only be, if derived from some other
knowledge which affords us, as its necessary consequence, the removal of the doubt originally harboured.
But if this knowledge has for its necessary consequence the removal of the original doubt, it must
stand to the existing doubt in the relation of a general
rule; and, as every rule is a judgment, it will constitute a general proposition. But a general rule does
not simply and of itself reach to the removal of doubt
and indecision; there is required, and necessarily
required, over and above, this further knowledge,—
that the rule has really an application, or, what is
the same thing, that the doubt really stands under
the general proposition, as a case which can be decided by it as by a general rule. But when the
general rule has been discovered, and when its application to the doubt has likewise been recognised,
the solution of the doubt immediately follows, and
therewith the determination of which of the contradictory predicates must or must not be affirmed of the
subject; and this determination is accompanied with
a consciousness of necessity or absolute certainty."[a] A Illustrated
simple example will place the matter in a clearer light. by an example.
When the notion of the subject *man* is given along
with the contradictory predicates *free agent* and *necessary agent*, there arises the doubt,—with which of
these contradictory predicates the subject is to be connected; for, as contradictory, they cannot both be
affirmed of the subject, and, as contradictory, the one
or the other must be so affirmed; in other words, I
doubt whether *man* be a *free agent* or *not*. The notion *man*, and the repugnant notions *free agent* and

a Esser, *Logik*, § 82, p. 153.

necessary agent, do not, in themselves, afford a solution of the doubt; and I must endeavour to discover some other notion which will enable me to decide. Now, taking the predicate *free agent,* this leads me to the closely connected notion *morally responsible agent,* which let it be supposed that I otherwise know to be necessarily a free agent. I thus obtain the proposition,—*Every morally responsible agent is a free agent.* But this proposition does not of itself contain the solution of the doubt, for it may still be asked, does the notion *morally responsible agent* constitute a predicate which appertains to the notion of *man,* the subject? This question is satisfied, if it is recognised that the notion *man* involves in it the notion of a *morally responsible agent.* I can then say,—*Man is a morally responsible agent.* These two propositions being thus formed, and applied to the subsisting doubt, the removal of this doubt follows of itself; and in place of the previous indecision, whether man be a free agent or not, there follows, with the consciousness of necessity or absolute certainty, the connected judgment that, *Man is also a free agent.* The whole process,—the whole series of judgments,—will stand thus :—

> *Every morally responsible agent is a free agent ;*
> *Man is a morally responsible agent ;*
> *Therefore, man is a free agent.*

The example given in a Remarking in the whole of Extension, and may be represented by three circles.
Let us consider in what relation the different constituent parts of this process stand to each other. It is evident that the whole process consists of three notions and their mutual relations. The three notions are, *free agent, responsible agent,* and *man.* Their mutual relations are all those of whole and part, —and whole and part in the quantity of exten-

sion; for the notion *free agent* is seen to contain under it the notion *responsible agent*, and the notion *responsible agent* to contain under it the notion *man*. Thus, these three notions are like three circles of three various extensions, severally contained one within another; and it is evident, that the process by which we recognise that the narrowest notion, *man*, is contained under the widest notion, *responsible agent*, is precisely the same by which we should recognise the inmost circle to be contained in the outmost, if we were only supposed to know the relation of these together by their relation to the middle circle. Let A B C denote the three circles. Now, *ex hypothesi*, we know, and only know, that A contains B, and that B contains C; but as it is a self-evident principle that a part of the part is a part of the whole, we cannot, with our knowledge that B contains C, and is contained in A, avoid recognising that C is contained in A. This is precisely the case with the three notions,—*free agent*,—*responsible agent*,—*man*; not knowing the relation between the notions *free agent* and *man*, but knowing that *free agent* contains under it *responsible agent*, and that *responsible agent* contains under it *man*, we, upon the principle that the part of a part is a part of the whole, are compelled to think, as a necessary consequence, that *free agent* contains under it *man*. It is thus evident, that the process shown in the example adduced is a mere recognition of the relation of three notions in the quantity of extension; our knowledge of the relation of two of these notions to each other being not given immediately, but obtained through our knowledge of their relation to the third.

But let us consider this process a little closer. The relations of the three notions, in the above example, are those given in the quantity of Breadth or Extension. But every notion has not only an Extensive, but likewise an Intensive quantity, — not only a quantity in breadth, but a quantity in depth ; and these two quantities stand to each other, as we have seen,* always in a determinate ratio,—the ratio of inversion. It would, therefore, appear *a priori*, to be a necessary presumption, that if notions bear a certain relation to each other in the one quantity, they must bear a counter relation to each other in the other quantity ; consequently, that if we are able, under the quantity of extension, to deduce from the relations of two notions to a third their relation to each other, a correspondent evolution must be competent of the same notions, in the quantity of comprehension. Let us try whether this theoretical presumption be warranted *a posteriori* and by experiment, and whether, in the example given, the process can be inverted, and the same result obtained with the same necessity. That example, as in extension, was :—

> *All responsible agents are free agents ;*
> *But man is a responsible agent ;*
> *Therefore, man is a free agent.*

In other words,—the notion *responsible agent* is contained under the notion *free agent ;* but the notion *man* is contained under the notion *responsible agent ;* therefore, on the principle that the part of a part is a part of the whole, the notion *man* is also contained under the notion *free agent.* Now, on the general doctrine of the relation of the two quantities, we must,

a See above, p. 146.—ED.

if we would obtain the same result in the comprehensive which is here obtained under the extensive
quantity, invert the whole process, that is, the notions
which in extension are wholes become in comprehension parts, and the notions which in the former are
parts become in the latter wholes. Thus the notion
free agent, which, in the example given, was the greatest whole, becomes, in the counter process, the smallest
part, and the notion *man*, which was the smallest part,
now becomes the greatest whole. The notion *responsible agent* remains the middle quantity or notion in
both, but its relation to the two other notions is reversed; what was formerly its part being now its
whole, what was formerly its whole being now its
part. The process will, therefore, be thus explicitly
enounced :—

*The notion man comprehends in it the notion responsible agent ;
But the notion responsible agent comprehends in it the notion free
agent ;
Therefore, on the principle, that the part of a part is a part of
the whole, the notion man also comprehends in it the notion
free agent.*

Or, in common language :—

*Man is a responsible agent ;
But a responsible agent is a free agent ;
Therefore, man is a free agent.*

This reversed process, in the quantity of comprehension, gives, it is evident, the same result as it gave in
the quantity of extension. For, on the supposition,
that we did not immediately know that the notion
man comprehends *free agent*, but recognised that
man comprehends *responsible agent*, and that *responsible agent* comprehends *free agent*, we necessarily
are compelled to think, in the event of this recogni-

tion, that the notion *man* comprehends the notion
free agent.

The copula
in extension
and comprehension of a
counter
meaning.

It is only necessary further to observe, that in the
one process,—that, to wit, in extension, the copula *is*
means *is contained under*, whereas in the other, it
means *comprehends in.* Thus the proposition,—*God
is merciful,* viewed as in the one quantity, signifies
God is contained under merciful, that is, the notion
God is contained under the notion *merciful;* viewed
as in the other, means *God comprehends merciful,*
that is, the notion *God comprehends in it* the notion
merciful.

Now, this process of thought, (of which I have endeavoured to give you a general notion), is called
Reasoning; but it has, likewise, obtained a variety of
other designations. The definition of this process,
with its principal denominations, I include in the following paragraph :—

Par. LIII.
Definition
of the pro-
cess of
Reasoning
with the
principal
denomina-
tions of pro-
cess and
product.

¶ LIII. Reasoning is an act of mediate comparison or Judgment ; for to reason is to recognise that two notions stand to each other in the
relation of a whole and its parts, through a
recognition, that these notions severally stand
in the same relation to a third. Considered as
an act, Reasoning or Discourse of Reason, (τὸ
λογίζεσθαι, λογισμός, διάνοια, τὸ διανοεῖσθαι), is,
likewise, called the act or process of *Argumentation (argumentationis),* of *Ratiocination (ratio-
cinationis),* of *Inference* or *Illation (inferendi),*
of *Collecting (colligendi),* of *Concluding (con-
cludendi),* of *Syllogising (τοῦ συλλογίζεσθαι,*
barbarously *syllogisandi).* The term *Reasoning*
is, likewise, given to the product of the act ; and

a reasoning, in this sense, (*ratiocinatio, ratiocinium*), is, likewise, called an *Argumentation* (*argumentatio*) ; also frequently an *Argument* (*argumentum*), an *Inference* or *Illation* (*illatio*), a *Collection* (*collectio*), a *Conclusion* (*conclusio*, συμπέρασμα); and, finally, a *Syllogism* (συλλογισμὸς).

A few words in explanation of these will suffice ; and, first, of the thing and its definition, thereafter of its names.

In regard to the act of Reasoning, nothing can be more erroneous than the ordinary distinction of this process, as the operation of a faculty different in kind from those of Judgment and Conception. Conception, Judgment, and Reasoning, are in reality only various applications of the same simple faculty, that of Comparison or Judgment. I have endeavoured to show, that concepts are merely the results, rendered permanent by language, of a previous process of comparison ; that judgment is nothing but comparison, or the results of comparison, in its immediate or simpler form ; and, finally, that reasoning is nothing but comparison in its mediate or more complex application.[a] It is, therefore, altogether erroneous to maintain, as is commonly done, that a reasoning or syllogism is a more decompound whole, made up of judgments ; as a judgment is a compound whole, made up of concepts. This is a mere mechanical mode of cleaving the mental phœnomena into parts ; and holds the same relation to a genuine analysis of mind which the act of the butcher does to that of the anatomist. It is true, indeed, that a

a See above, pp. 116, 117.—ED.

syllogism can be separated into three parts or propositions; and that these propositions have a certain
meaning, when considered apart, and out of relation
to each other. But when thus considered, they lose
the whole significance which they had when united
in a reasoning; for their whole significance consisted
in their reciprocal relation,—in the light which they
mutually reflected on each other. We can certainly
hew an animal body into parts, and consider its
members apart; but these, though not absolutely void
of all meaning, when viewed singly and out of relation
to their whole, have lost the principal and peculiar
significance which they possessed as the coefficients
of a one organic and indivisible whole. It is the same
with a syllogism. The parts which, in their organic
union, possessed life and importance, when separated
from each other, remain only enunciations of vague
generalities, or of futile identities. Though, when
expressed in language, it be necessary to analyse a
reasoning into parts, and to state these parts one after
another, it is not to be supposed that in thought one
notion, one proposition, is known before or after
another; for, in consciousness, the three notions and
their reciprocal relations constitute only one identical
and simultaneous cognition.

The logicians have indeed all treated the syllogism
as if this were not the case. They have considered
one proposition as naturally the last in expression,
and this they have accordingly called the *conclusion*;
whilst the other two, as naturally going before the
conclusion, they have styled the *premises*, forming
together what they call the *antecedent*. The two
premises they have also considered as the one the
greater (*major*), the other the less (*minor*) by exclu-

sive reference to the one quantity of extension. All
this, however, is, in my view, completely erroneous.
For we may, in the theory of Logic, as we actually
do in its practical applications, indifferently enounce
what is called the *conclusion* first or last. In the
latter case, the conclusion forms a thesis, and the
premises its grounds or reasons ; and instead of the
inferential *therefore* (*ergo*, ἄρα), we would employ
the explicative *for*. The whole difference consists in
this,—that the common order is synthetic, the other
analytic ; and as, to express the thought, we must
analyse it, the analytic order of statement appears
certainly the most direct and natural.ᵃ On the subordinate matter of the order of the premises, I do not
here touch.

But to speak of the process in general :—Without
the power of reasoning we should have been limited
in our knowledge, (if knowledge of such a limitation
would deserve the name of knowledge at all),—I say
without reasoning we should have been limited to a
knowledge of what is given by immediate intuition ;
we should have been unable to draw any inference
from this knowledge, and have been shut out from
the discovery of that countless multitude of truths,
which, though of high, of paramount importance, are
not self-evident. This faculty is, likewise, of peculiar utility in order to protect us, in our cogita-
tions, from error and falsehood, and to remove these
if they have already crept in. For every, the most
complex, web of thought may be reduced to simple
syllogisms ; and when this is done, their truth or falsehood, at least in a logical relation, flashes at once into
view.

a Aristotle's *Analytics* are synthetic.

LECT.
XV.

2. Terms by
which the
process of
Reasoning
is denomi-
nated.

Reasoning.
Ratiocina-
tion.

Discourse.

Argumenta-
tion.
Argument.

Of the terms by which this process is denominated, *Reasoning* is a modification from the French *raisonner*, (and this a derivation from the Latin *ratio*), and corresponds to *ratiocinatio*, which has indeed been immediately transferred into our language under the form *ratiocination*. *Ratiocination* denotes properly the process, but, improperly, also the product of reasoning ; *Ratiocinium* marks exclusively the product. The original meaning of *ratio* was *computation*, and from the calculation of numbers it was transferred to the process of mediate comparison in general. *Discourse* (*discursus*, διάνοια) indicates the operation of comparison, the running backwards and forwards between the characters or notes of objects, (*discurrere inter notas*, διανοεῖσθαι) ; this term may, therefore, be properly applied to the Elaborative Faculty in general, which I have thus called the Discursive. The terms *discourse* and *discursus*, as διάνοια, are, however, often, nay generally, used for the reasoning process, strictly considered, and *discursive* is even applied to denote mediate, in opposition to intuitive, judgment, as is done by Milton.[a] The compound term *discourse of reason*[β] unambiguously marks its employment in this sense. *Argumentation* is derived from *argumentari*, which means *argumentis uti; argument* again, *argumentum*,—what is assumed in order to argue something,—is properly the middle notion in a reasoning,—that through which the conclusion is established ; and by the Latin Rhetoricians it was defined,—" pro-

---

a *Paradise Lost*, v. 486,—

    " Whence the soul
Reason receives, and reason is her being,
Discursive or intuitive ; discourse
Is oftest yours."

        —Ed.

β Shakespeare, *Hamlet*, act 1,

sc. 2,—

" —— A beast, that wants discourse of
    reason,
Would have mourned longer."

Hooker, *E. P.*, iii. 8, 18 : " By Discourse of reason, aided with the influence of divine grace."—Ed.

babile inventum ad faciendam fidem." [a]   It is often, LECT.
XV.
however, applied as coextensive with *argumentation.*
Inference or *illation,* (from *infero*), indicates the carry- Inference.
ing out into the last proposition what was virtually
contained in the antecedent judgments. *To conclude* To con-
clude.
(*concludere*), again, signifies the act of connecting and
shutting into the last proposition the two notions
which stood apart in the two first. A *conclusion* Conclusion.
(*conclusio*) is usually taken, in its strict or proper signification, to mean the last proposition of a reasoning ;
it is sometimes, however, used to express the product
of the whole process. *To syllogise* means to form syl- To syllo-
gise,
logisms. *Syllogism* (συλλογισμὸς) seems originally, Syllogism.
like *ratio,* to have denoted a *computation,*—an *adding
up,*—and, like the greater part of the technical terms
of Logic in general, was borrowed by Aristotle from
the mathematicians.[β] This primary meaning of these
two words favours the theory of those philosophers who,
like Hobbes[γ] and Leidenfrost,[δ] maintain that all reasoning, that all thought is in fact at bottom only a calculation, a reckoning. Συλλογισμὸς may, however, be
considered as expressing only what the composition of
the word denotes,—*a collecting together;* for συλλογίζεσθαι comes from συλλέγειν, which signifies *to collect.*[ε]

a Cicero, *Oratoriæ Partitiones,* c. 2. Cf. *Discussions,* p. 149.—ED.

β [See Piccartus, *Org. Arist.,* pp. 467, 468 ; Ammonius, *In Quinque Voces,* f. 1 ; Philoponus, *In An. Prior.,* f. 17 b ; Pacius, *Comm. in Org.,* pp. 118, 122 ; Bertius, *Log. Perip.,* p. 119. But see Waitz, *Organon,* i. p. 384.] [Schulze, *Logik,* § 70, p. 101. *Discussions,* p. 667, note.—ED.]

γ *Leviathan,* Pt. I. c. 5 ; *Computatio sive Logica,* c. 1. Cf. Stewart, *Elements,* P. ii. c. ii. § 3 ; *Works,* vol. iii. p. 132 *et seq.*—ED.

δ *De Mente Humana,* c. viii. §§ 4, 10, pp. 112, 118, ed. 1793.—ED.

ε Eugenios, Λογικὴ, p. 405, et ibi Blemmidas : [Καὶ τὸ μὲν ὄνομα, ὅτι συλλογή τις ἐστὶ λόγων πλειόνων ἐν αὐτῷ . . . 'Ο δὲ Βλεμμίδ. ἐν 'Επιτομ. Λογ. κεφ. λδ, "Ποτὲ δὲ καὶ αὐτὸ τὸ συμπέρασμα καλεῖται (φησὶ) συλλογισμός . . . ὡς συλλέγον τὴν ἐν πᾶσι τοῖς ὅροις διεσπαρμένην ἀπόδειξιν."
—Cf. Zabarella, *In Anal. Post.,* L. 1, *Opera Logica,* p. 640 : "Συλλογισμός, non συλλογὴ τῶν λόγων, sed quasi συλλογὴ τοῦ λόγου, *collectio rationis ;* ratio autem colligi dicitur, dum con-

LECT.
IV.
———
Collectio.

The general
conditions
of syllogism.

Finally, in Latin, a syllogism is called *collectio*, and to reason *colligere*. This refers to the act of collecting in the conclusion the two notions scattered in the premises.

"From what has already been said touching the character of the reasoning process, it is easy to see what are the general conditions which every syllogism supposes. For, as the essential nature of reasoning consists in this,—that some doubt should be removed by the application to it of some decisive general rule, there are to every syllogism three, and only three requisites necessary; 1°, A doubt, which of two contradictory predicates must be affirmed of a certain subject,—the problem or question, (problema, quæsitum); 2°, The application of a decisive general rule to the doubt; and, 3°, The general rule itself. But these requisites, when the syllogism is constructed and expressed, change their places; so that the general rule stands first, the application of it to the doubt stands second, and the decision in regard to the doubt itself stands last. Each of these necessary constituents of a syllogism forms by itself a distinct, though a correlative, proposition; every syllogism, therefore, contains three propositions, and these three propositions, in their complement and correlation, constitute the syllogism."[a] It will be proper, however, here to dictate a paragraph, expressive of the denominations technically given to the parts, which proximately make up the syllogism.

Par. LIV.
Denominations of the parts which proximately make up the syllogism.

¶ LIV. A Reasoning or Syllogism is composed of two parts,—that which determines or precedes, and that which follows or is determined. The

clusio infertur; quare a conclusione est syllogismus."—Ed.)
potius, quam a propositionibus dictœ   a *Esser, Logik*, § 83, p. 156.

one is called the *Antecedent* (*antecedens*); the
other, the *Consequent* (*consequens*). The Antecedent comprises the two propositions, the one
of which enounces the general rule, and the other
its application. These, from their naturally preceding the Consequent, are called the *Premises*
(*propositiones præmissæ, sumptiones, membra
antecedentia,* λήμματα). Of the premises, the
one which enounces the general rule, or the relation of the greatest quantity to the lesser, is
called the *Major Premise,* or *Major Proposition,*
or the *Proposition* simply, (*propositio major, propositio prima, propositio, sumptum, sumptio major, sumptio, thesis, expositio, intentio,* πρόσληψις,
πρότασις ἡ μείζων, λῆμμα τὸ μεῖζον). The other
premise, which enounces the application of the general rule, or the relation of the lesser quantity to
the least, is called the *Minor Premise,* the *Minor
Proposition,* the *Assumption,* or the *Subsumption,*
(*propositio minor, propositio altera, assumptio,
subsumptum, subsumptio, sumptio minor,* πρότασις
ἡ ἐλάττων, λῆμμα τὸ ἔλαττον). It is manifest
that, in the counter quantities of Breadth and
Depth, the two premises will hold an opposite
relation of major and minor, of rule and application. The Consequent is the final proposition, which enounces the decision, or the relation
of the greatest quantity to the least, and is called
the *Conclusion* (*conclusio, conclusum, propositio
conclusa, collectio, complexio, summa, connexio,
illatio, intentio,* and, in Greek, συμπέρασμα, τὸ
συναγόμενον,[a] τὸ ἐπιφερόμενον). This part is
usually designated by the conjunction, *Therefore*

LECT.
XV.

(*ergo*, ἄρα), and its synonyma. The Conclusion
is the *Problem* (*problema*), *Question* (*quæstio*,
quæsitum), which was originally asked, stated
now as a decision.[a] The Problem is usually omitted in the expression of a syllogism; but is one
of its essential parts. The whole nomenclature
of the syllogistic parts, be it observed, has reference to the one-sided views of the logicians in
regard to the process of reasoning.[β]

**Explica-
tion.
Antecedent
and Conse-
quent.**

The Syllogism is divided into two parts, the Antecedent and the Consequent :—the antecedent comprehending the two propositions, in which the middle
notion is compared with the two notions we would
compare together; and the consequent comprising the
one proposition, which explicitly enounces the relation
implicitly given in the prior of these two notions to
each other.

Premises.

The two propositions which constitute the antecedent are called, among other names, the *Premises*. Of
these the proposition expressing the relation of whole
which one of the originally-given notions holds to the
assumed or middle notion as its part, is called, among

Major.

other appellations, the *Major Proposition*, the *Major
Premise*, or *The Proposition*, κατ᾽ ἐξόχην. The other
proposition of the antecedent enouncing the relation of
whole, which the assumed or middle notion holds to
the other of the given notions as its part, is called,

Minor.

among other appellations, the *Minor Proposition*, the

a [See Alex. Aphrodisiensis, *In
Anal. Prior.*, l. c. 4, f. 17 b; Boethius, *In Topica Ciceronis*, L. i., *Opera*,
p. 764.]

β [See R. Agricola, *De Inventione
Dialectica*, L. ii. c. xiv. pp. 401, 417,
420; Vives, *Opera*, [t. i., *De Cen-*

sura Veri, L. ii. p. 606 *et sq.*, ed.
1555.—Ed.]; Bachmann, *Logik*, p.
184; Facciolati; Sextus Empiricus.
[Facciolati, *Rudimenta Logica*, c. iii.
p. 83, ed. 1750; Sextus Empiricus,
Hypotyposes, L. ii. p. 86 *et alibi.*—
Ed.]

Minor Premise, the *Assumption*, or the *Subsumption*. These, as terms of relation, vary, of course, with the relation in the counter quantities. The one proposition which constitutes the consequent is called, among other appellations, the *Conclusion.* Perhaps the best names for these three relative propositions of a syllogism would be *Sumption, Subsumption, Conclusion,* as those which express most briefly and naturally the nature and reciprocal dependence of the three judgments of a syllogism. In the first place, the expressions *Sumption* and *Subsumption* are appropriate logical expressions, in consequence of their both showing that Logic considers them, not as absolutely, but only as hypothetically true; for Logic does not warrant the truth of the premises of a syllogism, it only, on the supposition that these premises are true, guarantees the legitimacy of the inference,—the necessity of the conclusion. It is on this account that the premises have, by the Greek logicians, been very properly styled λήμματα,[a] corresponding to the Latin *sumptiones;* and were there any necessity to resort to Greek, the Major Proposition, which I would call *Sumption (sumptio)*, might be well denominated *Lemma* simply; and the Minor Proposition, which I would call the *Subsumption (subsumptio)*, might be well denominated the *Hypolemma.* In the second place, though both premises are sumptions or lemmata, yet the term *sumption*, as specially applied to the Major Premise, is fully warranted both by precedent and by principle. For, in like manner, the major proposition,—the major lemma, has always obtained both from the Greek and Latin logicians the generic term;—it has been called, *The Proposition, The*

[margin notes:]

LECT. XV.

Sumption, Subsumption, and Conclusion.

Grounds of their adoption as best names for the three propositions of a syllogism.

Lemma.

Hypolemma.

Assump-
tion.

Lemma, (*propositio, ἡ πρότασις, τὸ λῆμμα*); and as this is the judgment which includes and allows both the others, it is well entitled, as the principal proposition, to the style and title of *the proposition, the lemma, the sumption* by pre-eminence.[a] In the third place, the term *subsumption* is preferable to the term *assumption*, as a denomination of the Minor Premise; for the term *subsumption* precisely marks out its relation of subordination to the major premise, whereas the term *assumption* does not. *Assumption* would indeed, in contrast to *subsumption*, have been an unexceptionable word by which to designate the major proposition, had it not been that logicians have very generally employed it to designate the minor, so that to reverse its application would be productive of inevitable confusion. But for this objection, I should certainly have preferred the term *assumption* to that of *sumption*, for the appellation of the major proposition; not that in itself it is a preferable expression, but simply because *assumption* is a word of familiar usage in the English language, which *sumption* and *subsumption* certainly are not.

Objections
to the deno-
minations of
the Proposi-
tions of the
Syllogism
in ordinary
use.

Major Pro-
position and
Premise.

Minor Pro-
position and
Premise.

The preceding are reasons why the relative terms *sumption* and *subsumption* ought to be employed, as being positively good expressions; but the expediency of their adoption becomes still more manifest, when they are compared and contrasted with corresponding denominations in ordinary use. For the terms *major proposition* and *major premise, minor proposition* and *minor premise*, are exposed to various objections. In the first place, they are complex and tedious expres-

---

[a] See Cicero, *De Div.*, ii. 53: "Sed . . . . . assumptio tamen, quam demus tibi istas duas *assumptiones, ea* πρόσληψιν Iidem vocant, non debitur."—ED.

sions, whereas *sumption* and *subsumption* are simple
and direct. In the second place, the abbreviations in
common use, (the major proposition being called the
major, the minor proposition being called the *minor*,)
are ambiguous, not only in consequence of their vagueness in general, but because there are two other parts
of the syllogism to which these expressions, *major* and
minor, may equally apply. For, as you will soon be
informed, the two notions which we compare together
through a third, are called the *major* and the *minor
terms* of the syllogism; so that when we talk of
majors and minors in reference to a syllogism, it remains uncertain whether we employ these words to
denote the propositions or the terms of a reasoning.
Still more objectionable are the correlative terms, *Proposition* and *Assumption*, as synonyms for the major
and minor premises. The term *proposition* is a word
in too constant employment in its vague and general
sense, to be unambiguously used in a signification so
precise and special as the one in question; and, in
consequence of this ambiguity, its employment in this
signification has been in fact long very generally aban-
doned. Again, the term *assumption* does not express
the distinctive peculiarity of the minor premise,—
that of being a subordinate proposition,—a proposition
taken or assumed under another; this word would
indeed, as I have noticed, have been applied with far
greater propriety, had it been used to denote the major
in place of the minor premise of a syllogism.

These are among the reasons which have inclined
me to employ, at least along with the more ordinary
denominations, the terms *sumption* and *subsumption*.
Nor is it to be supposed, that this usage is destitute
of precedent, for I could adduce in its favour even the

LECT.
XV.

high authority of Boethius.[a] In general, and without reference to Logic, it appears marvellous how, in
English philosophy, we could so long do without the
noun *subsumption*, and the verb *to subsume*, for these
denote a relation which we have very frequently occasion to express, and to express which there are no
other terms within our reach. We have already in
English *assumption* and *assume*, *presumption* and
presume, *consumption* and *consume*, and there is no
imaginable reason why we should not likewise enrich
the language, to say nothing of *sumption*, by the analogous expressions *subsumption* and *subsume*.

The Conclu-
sion.

In regard to the proposition constituting the consequent of a syllogism, the name which is generally
bestowed on it,—the *Conclusion*,—is not exposed to
any serious objections. There is thus no reason why
it should be superseded, and there is in fact no other
term entitled to a preference.—So much in reference
to the terms by which the proximate parts of a syllogism are denoted.

I now proceed to state to you in general the Division of Syllogisms into Species determined by these
parts, and shall then proceed to consider these several
species in detail. But I have first of all to state to
you a division of Syllogisms, which, as comprehending, ought to precede all others. It is that of Syllogisms into Extensive and Comprehensive.

Par. LV.
First Divi-
sion of Syl-
logisms into
Extensive
and Com-
prehensive.

¶ LV. The First Division of Syllogisms is
taken from the different kinds of quantity under
which the reasoning proceeds. For while every

---

[a] "Quoniam enim omnis syllogismus ex propositionibus texitur,
prima vel propositio, vel *sumptum*
vocatur; secunda vero *assumptio*."—
Boethius, *De Syllogismo Hypothetico*,
lib. i.—Ed.

syllogism infers that the part of a part is a part
of the whole, it does this either in the quantity
of Extension,—the Predicate of the two notions
compared in the Question and Conclusion being
the greatest whole, and the Subject the smallest
part ; or in the counter quantity of Comprehension,—the Subject of these two notions being the
greatest whole, and the Predicate the smallest
part.

After what I have already stated in regard to
the nature of these opposite quantities, under the
doctrine of Concepts and Judgments,[a] and after the
illustrations I have given of the possibility of conducting any reasoning in either of these quantities
at will,[b] — every syllogism in the one quantity
being convertible into a syllogism absolutely equivalent in the other quantity,—it will be needless to
enlarge here upon the nature of this distinction in
general.   This distinction comprehends all others ;
its illustration, therefore, supposes that the nature
of the various subordinate classes of syllogisms should
be previously understood.   It will, therefore, be expedient, not at present to enter on any distinct consideration of this division of reasonings, but to show, when
treating of syllogisms under their various subaltern
classes, how each is capable of being cast in the mould
of either quantity, and not, as logicians suppose, in
that of extensive quantity alone.

The next distinction of Syllogisms is to be sought
for either in the constituent elements of which they
are composed, or in the manner in which these are
connected.   The former of these is technically called

*Matter and
form of syl-
logisms.*

a See above, p. 140 et seq.—Ed.   b See above, p. 272 et seq.—Ed.

the *matter* of a syllogism, the latter its *form*. You must, however, observe that these terms are here used in a restricted meaning. Both matter and form under this distinction are included in the form of a syllogism, when we speak of form in contrast to the empirical matter which it may contain. This, therefore, is a distinction under that form with which Logic, as you know, is exclusively conversant; and the matter here spoken of should be called, for distinction's sake, the *formal or necessary matter* of a syllogism. In this sense, then, the matter of a syllogism means merely the propositions and terms of which every syllogism is necessarily made up;[a] whereas, otherwise, the form of a syllogism points out the way in which these constituents are connected.[β] This being understood, I repeat that the next distinction of syllogisms is to be sought for either in their matter or in their form.

Their form,
the ground
of the next
grand dis-
tinction of
Syllogisms.
"Now in regard to their matter, syllogisms cannot differ, for every syllogism, without exception, requires the same constituent parts,—a question, the subsumption of it under a general rule, and the sumption of the general rule itself; which three constituents, in the actual enunciation of a syllogism, change, as I have already noticed, their relative situation;"[γ]—what was first in the order of thought being last in the order of expression.

"The difference of Syllogisms can, therefore, only be sought for in their different forms; so that their distinctions are only formal. But the form of a syllo-

---

a Proximate and remote matter.— *Marginal Jotting.* [See Hurtado de Mendoza, *Disput. Phil., Disp. Logi-ca*, t. i. d. x. § 48, p. 405 : "Materia (syllogismi) alia est proxima, alia remota. Remota sunt termini

propositionum, proxima vero sunt propositiones ipsæ, quibus conficitur syllogismus."—ED.]

β Krug, *Logik,* § 72, Anm., L—ED. [Cf. Fries, *Logik,* § 44.]

γ Esser, *Logik,* § 85, p. 159.—ED.

gism, considered in its greatest generality, is of a LECT.
twofold kind, viz. either an Internal and Essential, ——
or an External and Accidental. The former of these
depends on the relations of the constituent parts of
the syllogism to each other, as determined by the nature of the thinking subject itself; the latter depends
on the external expression of the constituent parts
of the syllogism, whereby the terms and propositions
are variously determined in point of number, position,
and consecution. We must, therefore, in conformity
to the order of nature, first of all, consider what classes
of syllogism are given by their internal or essential
form; and thereafter inquire what are the classes
afforded by their external or accidental modifications.
First, then, in regard to the Internal or Essential Form
of Syllogism.

" A Syllogism is only a syllogism when the conclusion follows from the premises with an absolute
certainty; and as this certainty is determined by a
universal and necessary law of thought, there must,
consequently, be as many kinds of Syllogism as there
are various kinds of premises affording a consequence
in virtue of a different law. Between the premises
there is only one possible order of dependency, for it
is always the sumption,—the major premise, which, as
the foundation of the whole syllogism, must first be
taken into account. And in determining the difference
of syllogisms, the sumption is the only premise which
can be taken into account as affording a difference of
syllogism; for the minor premise is merely the subsumption of the lesser quantity of the two notions,
concerning whose relation we inquire, under the
question, and this premise always appears in one
and the same form,—in that, namely, of a catego-

rical proposition. The same is, likewise, the case in
regard to the conclusion, and, therefore, we can no
more look towards the conclusion for a determination of the diversity of syllogism than towards the
subsumption. We have thus only to inquire in
regard to the various possible kinds of major proposition."[a]

Syllogisms
to be divided
according to
the charac-
ter of their
sumptions
and the law
regulating
the connec-
tion between
premises
and conclu-
sion. Now as all sumptions are judgments, and as we
have already found that the most general division of
judgments, next to the primary distinction of intensive and extensive, is into simple and conditional, this
division of judgments, which, when developed, affords
the classes of categorical, disjunctive, hypothetical,
and hypothetico-disjunctive propositions, will furnish
us with all the possible differences of major premises.
" It is also manifest that in any of these aforesaid propositions, (categorical, disjunctive, hypothetical, and
hypothetico-disjunctive,) a decision of the question,
—which of two repugnant predicates belongs to a
certain subject,—can be obtained according to a
universal and necessary law. In a categorical sumption, this is competent through the laws of Identity
and Contradiction ; for what belongs or does not
belong to the superordinate notion, belongs or does
not belong to the subordinate. In disjunctive sumptions, this is competent through the law of Excluded
Middle ; since of all the opposite determinations one
alone belongs to the object ; so that if one is affirmed
the others must be, conjunctively, denied, and if one
is denied the others must be, disjunctively at least,
affirmed. In hypothetical sumptions, this is competent
through the law of Reason and Consequent ; for where
the reason is, there must be the consequent, and where

a Essay, Logik, § 85.—ED.

the consequent is, there must be the reason."[a] There
are thus obtained three or four great classes of Syllogisms, whose essential characteristics I shall comprise
in the following paragraph :—

¶ LVI. Syllogisms are divided into different
classes, according as the connection between the
premises and conclusion is determined by the
different fundamental laws, 1°, Of Identity and
Contradiction ; 2°, Of Excluded Middle ; 3°, Of
Reason and Consequent ; these several determinations affording the three classes of *Categorical*,
of *Disjunctive*, and of *Hypothetical Syllogisms*.
To these may be added a fourth class, the *Hypothetico-disjunctive* or *Dilemmatic Syllogism*, which
is determined by the two last laws in combination.

Par. LVI. Second grand division of Syllogisms—according to the law regulating the inference.

Before proceeding to a consideration of these several syllogisms in detail, I shall, first of all, give you
examples of the four species together, in order that
you may have, while treating of each, at least a general notion of their differences and similarity.

Examples of the four species of syllogism.

1.—OF A CATEGORICAL SYLLOGISM.

1. Categorical.

Sumption ....*All matter is created ;*
Subsumption.....*But the heavenly bodies are material ;*
Conclusion........*Therefore, the heavenly bodies are created.*

a See *Essay, Logik,* § 66, p. 161.
This classification of syllogisms cannot be regarded as expressing the
Author's final view ; according to
which, as before observed, the principle of Reason and Consequent is
not admitted as a law of thought.
See above, p. 86, note a. In a note
by Sir W. Hamilton, appended to
Mr Baynes's *Essay on the New An-*
alytic of Logical Forms, the Author's
later view is expressed as follows :
" All *Mediate* inference is one—
that incorrectly called *Categorical ;*
for the *Conjunctive* and *Disjunctive*
forms of *Hypothetical* reasoning are
reducible to immediate inferences."
Compare *Discussions,* p. 651 *et seq.*
—ED.

LECT.
XV.   2.—OF A DISJUNCTIVE SYLLOGISM.

2. Disjunc- Sumption.........*The hope of immortality is either a rational ex-*
tive.   *pectation or an illusion;*
          Subsumption......*But the hope of immortality is a rational expec-*
                           tation;
          Conclusion........*Therefore, the hope of immortality is not an illusion.*

3. Hypo-   3.—OF AN HYPOTHETICAL SYLLOGISM.
thetical.
          Sumption.........*If Logic do not profess to be an instrument of*
                           invention, the reproach that it discovers nothing
                           is unfounded;
          Subsumption.....*But Logic does not profess to be an instrument of*
                           invention;
          Conclusion........*Therefore, the reproach that it discovers nothing*
                           is unfounded.

4. Hypo-   4.—OF THE DILEMMA OR HYPOTHETICO-DISJUNCTIVE SYLLOGISM.
thetico-dis-
junctive.
          Sumption.........*If man were suited to live out of society, he would*
                           either be a god or a beast;
          Subsumption.....*But man is neither a god nor a beast;*
          Conclusion........*Therefore, he is not suited to live out of society.*

LECTURE XVI.

STOICHEIOLOGY.

SECTION II.—OF THE PRODUCTS OF THOUGHT.

III.—DOCTRINE OF REASONINGS.

SYLLOGISMS.—THEIR DIVISIONS ACCORDING TO INTERNAL FORM.

A. SIMPLE—CATEGORICAL.—I. DEDUCTIVE IN EXTENSION.

IN our last Lecture, I entered on the Division of Syllogisms. I first stated to you the principles on which this division must proceed; I then explained the nature of the first great distribution of Reasonings into those of Intensive and those of Extensive Quantity; and, thereafter, that of the second great distribution of reasonings into Simple and Conditional, the Simple containing a single species,—the Categorical; the Conditional comprising three species, —the Disjunctive, the Hypothetical, and Hypothetico-disjunctive.[a] These four species, I showed you, were severally determined by different fundamental Laws of Thought: the Categorical reposing on the laws of Identity and Contradiction; the Disjunctive on the law of Excluded Middle; the Hypothetical on the law of Reason and Consequent; and the Hypothetico-disjunctive on the laws of Excluded Middle and Reason and Consequent in combination.

LECT.
XVI.

Recapitulation.

a Compare above, p. 236.—ED.

LECT.
XVI.
I. Simple
Syllogism.
The Cate-
gorical.
I now go on to the special consideration of the first
of these classes of Syllogism — viz. the Syllogism
which has been denominated *Categorical*. And in
regard to the meaning and history of the term *categorical*, it will not be necessary to say anything in
addition to what I have already stated in speaking of
judgments.* As used originally by Aristotle, the term
categorical meant merely *affirmative*, and was opposed
to *negative*. By Theophrastus it was employed in the
sense of absolute,—simple,—direct, and as opposed to
conditional; and in this signification it has continued
to be employed by all subsequent logicians, without
their having been aware that Aristotle never employed
it in the meaning in which alone they used it.

¶ LVII. A Categorical Syllogism is a reasoning
whose form is determined by the laws of Identity
and Contradiction, and whose sumption is thus a
categorical proposition. In a Categorical Syllogism there are three principal notions, holding
to each other the relation of whole and part;
and these are so combined together, that they
constitute three propositions, in which each principal notion occurs twice. These notions are
called *Terms* (*termini*, ὅροι), and according as the
notion is the greatest, the greater, or the least, it
is called the *Major*, the *Middle*, or the *Minor
Term.*β The Middle Term is called the *Argument*
(*argumentum*, λόγος, πίστις); the Major and

---

a See above, p. 234 et seq.—ED.

β [On principle of name of Major
and Minor terms, see Alex. Aphrodisiensis, *In An. Prior.*, L. i. cc. iv.
v.; Philoponus, *In An. Prior.*, L. i.
f. 23 b; Fonseca, *Instit. Dialect.*, L.

vi. c. xii. p. 343; Hurtado de Mendoza, p. 469.] [*Disput. Philosophiae*, t. i.; *Disp. Logica*, d. x. § 50 et
seq. Tolosæ, 1617. See also *Discussions*, p. 666 et seq.—ED.]

Minor Terms are called *Extremes (extrema, ἄκρα).*
If the syllogism proceed in the quantity of Extension, (and this form alone has been considered by logicians,) the predicate of the conclusion is the greatest whole, and, consequently, the Major Term ; the subject of the conclusion, the smallest part, and, consequently, the Minor Term. If the syllogism proceed in the quantity of Comprehension, the subject of the conclusion is the greatest whole, and, consequently, the Major Term ; the predicate of the conclusion, the smallest part, and, consequently, the Minor Term. In either quantity, the proposition in which the relation of the major term to the middle is expressed, is the *Sumption* or *Major Premise,* and the proposition in which is expressed the relation of the middle term to the minor, is the *Subsumption* or *Minor Premise.* The general forms of a Categorical Syllogism under the two quantities are consequently the following :—

AN EXTENSIVE SYLLOGISM.	AN INTENSIVE SYLLOGISM.
B is A	C is B
C is B	B is A
C is A	C is A
All man is mortal ;	*Caius is a man ;*
But Caius is a man ;	*But all man is mortal ;*
Therefore, Caius is mortal.	*Therefore, Caius is mortal.*

In these examples, you are aware, from what has
previously been said,[a] that the copula in the two different quantities is precisely of a counter meaning ; in the quantity of extension, signifying *is contained under ;* in the quantity of comprehension, signifying

a See above, p. 274.—Ed.

contains in it. Thus, taking the several formulæ, the Extensive Syllogism will, when explicitly enounced, be as follows :—

> *The Middle term B is contained under the Major term A ;*
> *But the Minor term C is contained under the Middle term B ;*
> *Therefore, the Minor term C is also contained under the Major term A.*

Or, to take the concrete example :—

> *The Middle term all men is contained under the Major term mortal.*
> *But the Minor term Caius is contained under the Middle term all men ;*
> *Therefore, the Minor term Caius is also contained under the Major term mortal.*

On the contrary, the Intensive Syllogism, when explicated, is as follows :—

> *The Major term C contains in it the Middle term B ;*
> *But the Middle term B contains in it the Minor term A ;*
> *Therefore, the Major term C also contains in it the Minor term A.*

Or, in the concrete example :—

> *The Major term Caius contains in it the Middle term man ;*
> *But the Middle term man contains in it the Minor term mortal ;*
> *Therefore, the Major term Caius also contains in it the Minor term mortal.*

Thus you see that by reversing the order of the two premises, and by reversing the meaning of the copula, we can always change a categorical syllogism of the one quantity into a categorical syllogism of the other.[*]

In this paragraph is enounced the general nature of a categorical syllogism, as competent in both the quantities of extension and comprehension, or, with more propriety, of comprehension and extension ; for comprehension, as prior to extension in the order of

[*] Not in Inductive Syllogisms.—*Jotting.* [See below, p. 323.—ED.]

nature and of knowledge, ought to stand first. But
as all logicians, with the doubtful exception of Aristotle, have limited their consideration to that process
of reasoning given in the quantity of extension, to the
exclusion of that given in the quantity of comprehension, it will be proper, in order to avoid misapprehension, to place some of the distinctions expressed in
this paragraph in a still more explicit contrast.

In the reasonings under both quantities, the words
expressive of the relations and of the things related
are identical. The things compared in both quantities
are the same in nature and in number. In each there
are three notions, three terms, and three propositions,
combined in the same complexity; and, in each
quantity, the same subordination of a greatest, a
greater, and a least. The same relatives and the
same relations are found in both quantities. But
though the relations and the relatives be the same,
the relatives have changed relations. For while the
relation between whole and part is the one uniform
relation in both quantities, and while this relation is
thrice realised in each between the same terms ; yet,
the term which in the one quantity was the least, is
in the other the greatest, and the term which in both
is intermediate, is in the one quantity contained by
the term which in the other it contained.

Now, you are to observe that logicians, looking
only to the reasoning competent under the quantity
of extension, and, therefore, looking only to the possibility of a single relation between the notions or terms
of a syllogism, have, in consequence of this one-sided
consideration of the subject, given definitions of these
relatives, which are true only when limited to the
kind of reasoning which they exclusively contem-

LECT.
XVI.

The reason-
ing in Com-
prehension
and that in
Extension
explicitly
compared
and con-
trasted.

Narrow and
erroneous
definitions
by logicians
of the Ma-
jor, Middle,
and Minor
terms.

LECT. XVI. plated. This is seen in their definitions of the Major, Middle, and Minor Terms.

1. Major. In regard to the first, they all simply define the Major term to be the predicate of the conclusion. This is true of the reasoning under extension, but of that exclusively. For the Major term, that is, the term which contains both the others, is, in the reasoning of comprehension, the subject of the conclusion.

2. Minor. Again, the Minor term they all simply define to be the subject of the conclusion; and this is likewise true only of the reasoning under extension : for, in the reasoning under comprehension, the Minor term is the

3. Middle. predicate of the conclusion. Finally, they all simply define the Middle term as that which is contained under the predicate, and contains under it the subject of the conclusion. But this definition, like those of the two other terms, must be reversed as applied to the reasoning under comprehension. I have been thus tediously explicit, in order that you should be fully aware of the contrast of the doctrine I propose, to what you will find in logical books ; and that you may be prepared for the further development of this doctrine,—for its application in detail.

Nomenclature of Major, Minor, and Middle terms. In regard to the nomenclature of Major, Minor, and Middle terms, it is not necessary to say much. The expression *term* (*terminus*, ὅρος) was first employed by Aristotle, and, like the greater part of his logical vocabulary, was, as I have observed, borrowed from the language of mathematics.[a] You are aware that the word *term* is applied to the ultimate constituents both of propositions and of syllogisms. The terms of a proposition are the subject and predicate. The terms

a See Scheibler, [*Opera Logica,* 279, note β.—ED.] Pars. iii. c. 2, p. 398, and above, p.

of a syllogism are the three notions which in their
threefold combination form the three propositions of
a syllogism. The major and minor terms Aristotle,
by another mathematical metaphor, calls the *extremes*
(ἄκρα), the *major* and *minor extremes;* and his definition of these and of the middle term is, unlike those
of the subsequent logicians, so general, that it will
apply with perfect propriety to a syllogism in either
quantity. " I call," he says, " the middle term that
which is both itself in another and another in it; and
which, by its position, lies in the middle; the extremes
I call both that which is in another and that in which
another is."* And in another place he says, " I define
the major extreme that in which the middle is; the
minor extreme that which is subordinated to the
middle."β

I may notice that the part of his definition of the
middle term, where he describes it as " that which, by
its position, lies in the middle," does not apply to the
mode in which subsequent logicians enounce the syllogism. For let A be the major, B the middle, and C
the minor term of an Extensive Syllogism, this will
be expressed thus :—

Sumption.............B *is* A, i. e. B *is contained under* A.
Subsumption.........C *is* B, i. e. C *is contained under* B.
Conclusion.............C *is* A, i. e. C *is also contained under* A.

In this syllogism the middle term B stands first
and last in the premises, and, therefore, Aristotle's
definition of the middle term, not only as middle by
nature, containing the minor and contained by the
major, but as middle by position, standing after the
major and before the minor, becomes inept. It will
apply, however, completely to the reasoning in com-

LECT. XVI.

Aristotle's definition of the terms of a syllogism.

His definition of the Middle term, as middle by position, not applicable to the mode in which subsequent logicians enounce the syllogism.

But quite applicable to the reasoning in Comprehension.

α *Anal. Prior.,* L. L., c. 4, § 3.   β *Ibid.,* § 8.

LECT.
XVI.

prehension; for the extensive syllogism given above being converted into an intensive, by reversing the two premises, it will stand as follows :—

Sumption...........C is B, i. e. C *contains in it* D.
Subsumption......B is A, i. e. D *contains in it* A.
Conclusion..........C is A, i. e. C *also contains in it* A.

It does not, however, follow, that Aristotle contemplated exclusively the reasoning in comprehension, or that he contemplated the reasonings in both quantities.

It does not, however, follow from this, that Aristotle either contemplated exclusively the reasoning in comprehension, or that he contemplated the reasonings in both quantities; for it is very easy to state a reasoning in extension, so that the major term shall stand first, the middle term second, and the minor last. We can state it thus :—

Sumption...........A is B, i. e. A *contains under it* B.
Subsumption......B is C, i. e. B *contains under it* C.
Conclusion..........A is C, i. e. A *contains under it* C.

This is as good a syllogism in extension as the first, though it is not stated in the mode usual to logicians. We may also convert it into a comprehensive syllogism, by reversing its premises and the meaning of the copula, though here also the mode of expression will be unusual.

Sumption...........B is C, i. e. B *is contained in* C.
Subsumption......A is B, i. e. A *is contained in* B.
Conclusion..........A is C, i. e. A *is contained in* C.

From this you will see, that it is not to the mere external arrangement of the terms, but to the nature of their relation, that we must look in determining the character of the syllogism.

Most convenient mode of stating a syllogism in an abstract form.

Before leaving the consideration of the terms of a syllogism, I may notice that the most convenient mode of stating a syllogism in an abstract form is by the letters S, P, and M,—S signifying the subject, as P the predicate, of the conclusion, and M the middle term of the syllogism. This you will be pleased to recollect, as we shall find it necessary to employ this notation in showing the differences of syllogisms from the different arrangement of their terms.

I have formerly stated that categorical syllogisms are regulated by the fundamental laws of Identity and Contradiction ; the law of Identity regulating Affirmative, the law of Contradiction, Negative, Categoricals. As, however, the laws of Identity and Contradiction are capable of certain special applications, these will afford the ground of a division of Categorical Syllogisms into a corresponding number of classes. It has been already stated, that all reasoning is under the relation of whole and part, and, consequently, the laws of Identity and Contradiction will find their application to categorical syllogisms only under this relation. *Categorical Syllogisms divided into special classes according to the applications of the laws of Identity and Contradiction under the relation of whole and part.*

But the relation of whole and part may be regarded in two points of view ; for we may either look from the whole to the parts, or look from the parts to the whole. This being the case, may we not apply the principles of Identity and Contradiction in such a way that we either reason from the whole to the parts, or from the parts to the whole ? Let us consider :—Looking at the whole and the parts together on the principle of Identity, we are assured that the whole and all its parts are one,—that whatever is true of the one is true of the other,—that they are only different expressions for the different aspects in which we may contemplate what in itself is absolutely identical. On the principle, therefore, that the whole is only the sum of the parts, I am entitled, on the one hand, looking from the whole to its parts, to say with absolute certainty,—What belongs to a whole belongs to its part ; *The relation of whole and part may be regarded in two points of view, and thus affords two classes of Reasonings.*

LECT.
XVI.

and what does not belong to a whole does not belong to its part: and on the other, looking from the parts to their whole, to say,—What makes up all the parts constitutes the whole ; and what does not make up all the parts does not constitute the whole.   Now, these two applications of the principles of Identity and Contradiction, as we look from one term of the relation of whole and part, or from the other, determine two different kinds of reasoning.   For if we reason downwards from a containing whole to a contained part, we shall have one sort of reasoning which is called the *Deductive;* whereas, if we reason upwards, from the constituent parts to a constituted whole, we shall have another sort of reasoning, which is called the *Inductive.*   This I briefly express in the following paragraph :—

Par. LVIII.
Categorical
Syllogisms
divided into
Deductive
and Induc-
tive.

¶ LVIII. Categorical Syllogisms are *Deductive*, if, on the principles of Identity and Contradiction, we reason downwards, from a containing whole to a contained part; they are *Inductive*, if, on these principles, we reason upwards, from the constituent parts to a constituted whole.

I. Deduc-
tive Cate-
gorical Syl-
logisms.

This is sufficient at present to afford you a general conception of the difference of Deductive and Inductive Categoricals.   The difference of these two kinds of reasoning will be properly explained, when, after having expounded the nature of the former, we proceed to consider the nature of the latter.   We shall now, therefore, consider the character of the deductive process,—the process which has been principally, and certainly most successfully, analysed by logicians ; for though their treatment of deductive reasoning has

been one-sided and imperfect, it is not positively LECT.
XVI.
erroneous; whereas their analysis of the inductive
process is at once meagre and incorrect. And, first,
of the proximate canons by which Deductive Categoricals are regulated.

¶ LIX. In Deductive Categoricals the uni- Par. LIX.
versal laws of Identity and Contradiction take Deductive Categori-
two modified forms, according as these syllo- cals,—their
gisms proceed in the quantity of Comprehension, or in that of Extension. The peculiar
canon by which Intensive Syllogisms of this
class are regulated, is, — What belongs to the
predicate belongs also to the subject; what is
repugnant to the predicate is repugnant also to the
subject. The peculiar canon by which Extensive
Syllogisms of this class are regulated, is,—What
belongs to the genus belongs to the species and
individual; what is repugnant to the genus is
repugnant to the species and individual. Or,
more briefly, What pertains to the higher class,
pertains also to the lower.

Both these laws are enounced by Aristotle,[a] and Explica-
both, from him, have passed into the writings of tion.
subsequent logicians. The former, as usually expressed, is,—*Prædicatum prædicati est etiam prædicatum subjecti;* or, *Nota notæ est etiam nota rei ipsius.*
The latter is correspondent to what is called the
Dicta de Omni et de Nullo; the *Dictum de Omni,*
when least ambiguously expressed, being,—*Quicquid
de omni valet, valet etiam de quibusdam et singulis;*—
and the *Dictum de Nullo* being,—*Quicquid de nullo*

a Categ., c. 3. Anal. Prior., i. 1.—Ed.

LECT.
XVL
valet, nec de quibusdam nec de singulis valet. But as
logicians have altogether overlooked the reasoning in
Comprehension, they have, consequently, not perceived
the proper application of the former canon ; which,
therefore, remained in their systems either a mere
hors d'œuvre, or else was only forced into an unnatural connection with the principle of the syllogism of extension.

*Connection
of the pro-
positions
and terms
of the Cate-
gorical Syl-
logism illus-
trated by
sensible
symbols.*

Before stating to you how the preceding canons are
again, in their proximate application to categorical
syllogisms, for convenience sake, still more explicitly
enounced in certain special rules, it will be proper to
show you the method of marking the connection of the
propositions and terms of a categorical syllogism by
sensible symbols. Of these there are various kinds,
but, as I formerly noticed, the best upon the whole,
because the simplest, is that by circles. According
to this method, syllogisms with affirmative and negative conclusions would be thus represented [β] :—

AFFIRMATIVE.

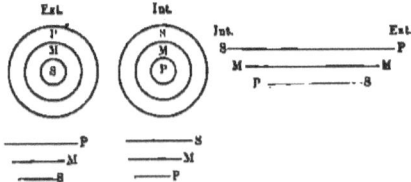

α [An objection to the mode of
syllogistic notation by circles is,
that we cannot, by this mode, show
that the contained exhausts the containing; for we cannot divide the
area of a circle between any number
of contained circles, representing in
extension all co-ordinate species, in
comprehension all the immediate
attributes.] [For the Author's final
scheme of notation, see Tabular
Scheme at end of Volume II.—ED.]

β See above, p. 250. Cf. Krug,
Logik, § 79, p. 245.—ED.

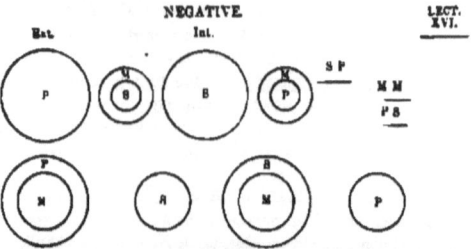

You are now prepared for the statement and illus- *Proximate Rules of Categorical Syllogisms. I. Extensive.*
tration of the various proximate rules by which all
categorical syllogisms are regulated. 'And, first, in
regard to these rules in relation to the reasoning of
Extension.

"Aldrich," says Dr Whately, "has given twelve
rules, which I find might be more conveniently reduced to six. No syllogism can be faulty which
violates none of these rules."[a] This reduction of the
syllogistic rules to six is not original to Dr Whately;
but had he looked a little closer into the matter, he
might have seen that the six which he and other
logicians enumerate, may, without any sacrifice of
precision, and with even an increase of perspicuity, be
reduced to three. I shall state these in a paragraph,
and then illustrate them in detail.

¶ LX. An Extensive Categorical Syllogism, *Par. LX. The Three Rules of the Extensive Categorical Syllogism.*
if regularly and fully expressed, is governed by
the three following rules :—

I. It must have three, and only three, Terms,
constituting three, and only three, Propositions.

a *Elements of Logic*, B. II. c. iii. § 2, p. 85, 8th edit.—En.

II. Of the premises, the Sumption must in quantity be Definite (*i. e.* universal or singular), and the Subsumption in quality Affirmative.

III. The Conclusion must correspond in Quantity with the Subsumption, and in Quality with the Sumption.[a]

*Illustration.
First Rule.*

These three simple laws comprise all the rules which logicians lay down with so confusing a minuteness.[β] The first is :—A categorical syllogism, if regular and perfect, must have three, and only three, propositions, made up of three, and only three, terms. "The necessity of this rule is manifest from the very notion of a categorical syllogism. In a categorical syllogism the relation of two notions to each other is determined through their relation to a third; and, consequently, each must be compared once with the intermediate notion, and once with each other. It is thus manifest that there must be three, and cannot possibly be more than three, terms; and that those three terms must, in their threefold comparison, constitute three, and only three, propositions. It is, however, to be observed, that it may often happen as if, in a valid syllogism, there were more than three principal notions, —three terms. But, in that case, the terms or notions are only complex, and expressed by a plurality of words. Hence it is, that each several notion extant in a syllogism, and denoted by a separate word, is not on that account to be viewed as a logical term or

*What is
properly to
be regarded
as a logical
term.*

a Krug, *Logik*, § 80.—Ed. [Cf. Alexander Aphrodisiensis, *In An. Prior.*, L. L, f. 17, Ald. ; Derodon, *Logica Restituta*, p. 639 *et seq.* ; Hoffbaner, *Anfangsgründe der Logik*, § 317, p. 164 ; Uschmann, *Logik*, § 122, p. 187 ; Esser, *Logik*, §§ 88, 89.

Schulze, *Logik*, § 79 ; Fries, *Logik*, § 55, p. 224.]

β See Scheibler, *Opera Logica*, pars. iv., p. 516 ; Keckermann, *Systema Logicæ Minus, Opera*, t. L. p. 239.—Ed.

terminus, but only those which, either singly or in
connection with others, constitute a principal momen-
tum of the syllogism."[a]   Thus, in the following syllogism, there are many more than three several notions
expressed by three several words, but these, we shall
find, constitute in reality only three principal notions
or logical terms :—

Sumption.........*He who conscientiously performs his duty is a*
truly good man ;
Subsumption.....*Socrates conscientiously performs his duty ;*
Conclusion.......*Therefore, Socrates is a truly good man.*

Here there are in all seven several notions denoted
by seven separate words :—1. *Conscientiously*, 2. *Performs*, 3. *Duty*, 4. *Truly*, 5. *Good*, 6. *Man*, 7. *Socrates ;*
but only three principal notions or logical terms,—viz.,
1. *Conscientiously performs his duty*, 2. *Truly good
man*, 3. *Socrates.*

"When, on the other hand, the expression of the
middle term in the sumption and subsumption is used
in two significations, there may, in that case, appear
to be only three terms, while there are in reality four ;
or, as it is technically styled in logic, a *quaternio terminorum*.[b]   On this account, the syllogism is vicious
in point of form, and, consequently, can afford no inference, howbeit that the several propositions may, in
point of matter, be all true.   And why ?—because there
is here no mediation, consequently no connection between the different terms of the syllogism.   For example :—

The animals are void of reason ;
Man is an animal ;
Therefore, man is void of reason.

Quaternio
termino-
rum.

a Krug, *Logik* § 80, p. 246 ; Anm.
1.—Ed.

β [Cf. Fonseca,] [*Instit. Dial.*, L.
vi. c. 20, p. 359.—Ed.]

" Here the conclusion is invalid, though each proposition, by itself, and in a certain sense, may be true. For here the middle term *animal* is not taken in the same meaning in the major and minor propositions. For in the former it is taken in a narrower signification, as convertible with *brute;* in ¦the latter in a wider signification, as convertible with *animated organism.*" [a]

Second
Rule.
The second rule is :—Of the premises, the sumption must in quantity be definite, (universal or singular), the subsumption must in quality be affirmative.—The sumption must in reference to its quantity be definite ; because it affords the general rule of the syllogism. For if it were indefinite, that is, particular, we should have no security that the middle term in the subsumption comprised the same part of the sphere which it comprised in the sumption. Thus :—

Some M *are* P ;
All S *are* M ;
All S *are* P.

Or, in a concrete example :—

Some works of art are cubical ;
All pictures are works of art ;
Therefore, all pictures are cubical.

In regard to the subsumption, this is necessarily affirmative. The sumption is not limited to either quality, because the proposition enouncing a general rule may indifferently declare *All* M *is* P, and *No* M *is* P. The assumption is thus indeterminate in regard to quality. But not so the proposition enouncing the application of a general rule. For it must subsume,

a Krug, *Logik,* p. 247.—ED.

that is, it must affirm, that something is contained LECT. XVI. under a condition ; and is, therefore, necessarily affirmative. We must say S *is* M. But in respect of quantity it is undetermined, for we can either say *All* S *is* M, or *Some* S *is* M. If the subsumption is negative, there is no inference ; for it is not necessary that a genus should contain only things of a certain species. This is shown in the following example :—

All men are animals ;
No horse is a man ;
Therefore, no horse is an animal.

Or, as abstractly expressed,—

All M *are* P ;
But no S *is* M ;

No S *is* P.

Thus it is, that in a regular extensive categorical syllogism, the sumption must be always definite in quantity, the subsumption always affirmative in quality.ₐ

I have, however, to add an observation requisite to Misconception in regard to definiteness of sumption in extensive categoricals, how obviated. prevent the possibility of a misconception. In stating it as a rule of extensive categoricals, that the sumption must be definite (*i.e.* universal or singular), if you are at all conversant with logical books, you will have noticed that this rule is not in unison with the doctrine therein taught, and you may, accordingly, be surprised that I should enounce as a general rule what is apparently contradicted by the fact that there are syllogisms,—valid syllogisms,—of various forms, in which the sumption is a particular, or the subsumption a negative, proposition. In explanation of this, it is enough at present to say, that in these syllogisms the premises are trans-

ₐ Krug, *Logik,* p. 248. Bachmann, *Logik,* § 124.—ED.

The mere
order of
enunciation
does not
constitute
the sump-
tion or sub-
sumption
in a reason-
ing.
posed in the expression. You will, hereafter, find that
the sumption is not always the proposition which
stands first in the enunciation, as the conclusion is not
always the proposition which stands last. Such trans-
positions are, however, only external accidents, and
the mere order in which the premises and conclusion
of a syllogism are enounced, no more changes their
nature and their necessary relation to each other, than
does the mere order in which the grammatical parts
of a sentence are expressed, alter their essential character and reciprocal dependence. In the phrases *vir
bonus* and *bonus vir*,—in both, the *vir* is a substantive
and the *bonus* an adjective. In the sentence variously
enounced,—*Alexander Darium vicit*,—*Alexander
vicit Darium*,—*Darium Alexander vicit*,—*Darium
vicit Alexander*,—*Vicit Alexander Darium*,—*Vicit
Darium Alexander*:—in these, a difference of order
may denote a difference of the interest we feel in the
various constituent notions, but no difference of their

What truly
constitutes
the sump-
tion and
subsump-
tion in a
reasoning.
grammatical or logical relations. It is the same with
syllogisms. The mere order of enunciation does not
change a sumption into a subsumption, nor a subsumption into a sumption. It is their essential relation and correlation in thought which constitutes the
one proposition a major, and the other a minor premise. If the former precede the latter in the expression of the reasoning, the syllogism is technically
regular; if the latter precede the former, it is technically irregular or transposed. This, however, as you
will hereafter more fully see, has not been attended
to by logicians, and in consequence of their looking
away from the internal and necessary consecution of
the premises to their merely external and accidental
arrangement, the science has been deformed and per-

plexed by the recognition of a multitude of different forms, as real and distinct, which exist only, and are only distinguished, by certain fortuitous accidents of expression. This being understood, you will not marvel at the rule in regard to the quantity of sumptions in extensive syllogisms, (which, however, I limit to those that are regularly and fully expressed),—that it must be definite. Nor will you marvel at the counter canon in regard to the quality of sumptions in intensive syllogisms,—that it must be affirmative.[a]

The necessity of the last rule is equally manifest as that of the preceding. It is :—The conclusion must correspond in quantity with the subsumption, and in quality with the sumption. "This rule is otherwise enounced by logicians :—The conclusion must always follow the weaker or worser part,—the negative and the particular being held to be weaker or worser in relation to the affirmative and universal. The conclusion, in extensive categoricals (with which we are at present occupied) is made up of the minor term, as subject, and of the major term, as predicate. Now, as the relation of these two terms to each other is determined by their relation to the middle term, and as the middle term is compared with the major term in the sumption ; it follows that the major term must hold the same relation to the minor in the conclusion which it held to the middle in the sumption. If then the sumption is affirmative, so likewise must be the conclusion ; on the other hand, if the sumption be negative, so likewise must be the conclusion. In the subsumption, the minor term is compared with the

Third Rule.

a [See Bachmann, *Logik,* § 124, pp. 192, 194, Anm. 3 ; Drobisch, *Logik,* § 73, p. 65, §§ 42, 44, pp. 34, 36 ; Schulze, *Logik,* § 79, p. 114 ; Krug, *Logik,* § 82, p. 249 ; Cf. § 83, p. 264, and § 109, p. 362 ; Facciolati, *Rudimenta Logica,* P. iii. c. iii. p. 91.]

middle; that is, the minor is affirmed as under the middle. In the conclusion, the major term cannot, therefore, be predicated of more things than were affirmed as under the middle term in the subsumption. Is the subsumption, therefore, universal, so likewise must be the conclusion; on the contrary, is the former particular, so likewise must be the latter." [a]

a Krug, *Logik*, § 80, p. 250-51.—ED.

LECTURE XVII.

STOICHEIOLOGY.

SECTION II.—OF THE PRODUCTS OF THOUGHT.

III.—DOCTRINE OF REASONINGS.

SYLLOGISMS.—THEIR DIVISIONS ACCORDING TO INTERNAL FORM.

A. SIMPLE.—CATEGORICAL—II. DEDUCTIVE IN COMPRE-HENSION—III. INDUCTIVE IN EXTENSION AND COM-PREHENSION.—B. CONDITIONAL.—DISJUNCTIVE.

IN my last Lecture, after terminating the consideration of the constituent elements of the Categorical
Syllogism in general, whether in the quantity of Comprehension or of Extension, I stated the subdivision
of Categorical Syllogism into Deductive and Inductive,— a division determined by the difference of
reasoning from the whole to the parts, or from the
parts to the whole. Of these, taking the former,—the
Deductive,—first into consideration, I was occupied,
during the remainder of the Lecture, in giving a view
of the laws which, in their higher or lower universality,
—in their remoter or more proximate application,
govern the legitimacy and regularity of Deductive
Categorical Syllogisms. Of these laws, the highest
are the axioms of Identity and Contradiction, by which
all Categorical Syllogisms are controlled. These, when

proximately applied to the two forms of Deductive
Categoricals, determined by the two quantities of
Comprehension and Extension, constitute two canons,
—the canon of the Intensive Syllogism being,—What
belongs to the predicate belongs also to the subject,—
what is repugnant to the predicate is repugnant also
to the subject ;—the canon of the Extensive Syllogism
being,—What belongs to the genus belongs also to
the species and individual,—what is repugnant to the
genus is repugnant also to the species and individual.
Each of these, however, in its more proximate application, is still further developed into a plurality of
more explicit rules. In reference to Extensive Syllogism, the general law, or the *Dictum de Omni et de
Nullo* (as it is technically called), is evolved into a
series of rules, which have been multiplied to twelve,
are usually recalled to six, but which, throwing out
of account irregular and imperfect syllogism, may be
conveniently reduced to three. These are, I. An Extensive Categorical Deductive Syllogism must have
three, and only three, terms, constituting three, and
only three, propositions. II. The sumption must in
quantity be definite, (*i. e.* universal or singular) ; the
subsumption must in quality be affirmative. III. The
conclusion must correspond in quantity with the subsumption, and in quality with the sumption. The
Lecture concluded with an explanation of these rules
in detail.

2. The In-
tensive
Categorical
Deductive
Syllogism. We have next to consider into what rules the law
of Intensive or Comprehensive Syllogism is developed,
in its more proximate application. Now, as the intensive and extensive syllogisms are always the coun-
terparts of each other, the proximate rules of the
two forms must, consequently, be either precisely

the same, or precisely the converse of each other. Accordingly, taking the three rules of extensive syllogisms, we find that the first law is also, without difference, a rule of intensive syllogisms. But the second and third, to maintain their essential identity, must be externally converted; for to change an extensive syllogism into an intensive, we must transpose the order or subordination of the two premises, and reverse the reciprocal relation of the terms. The three general rules of an Intensive Categorical Deductive Syllogism will, therefore, stand as follows:—

¶ LXI. An Intensive Categorical Deductive Syllogism, that is, one of Depth, if regularly and fully expressed, is governed by the three following rules. Par. LXI. Rules of the Intensive Categorical Deductive Syllogism.

I. It must have three, and only three, Terms, constituting three, and only three, Propositions.

II. Of the premises, the Sumption must in quality be Affirmative, and the Subsumption in quantity Definite, (that is, universal or singular).

III. The Conclusion must not exceed the Sumption in Quantity, and in Quality must agree with the Subsumption.

In regard to the first of these rules,—the rule which is identical for syllogisms whether extensive or intensive,—it is needless to say anything; for all that I stated in regard to it under the first of these forms, is valid in regard to it under the second. Explication. First Rule.

I proceed to the second, which is,—The sumption must in quality be affirmative, the subsumption must in quantity be definite, (that is, universal or singular). Second Rule.

And, here, we have to answer the question,—Why in
an intensive syllogism must the sumption be affirmative in quality, the subsumption definite in quantity ?
Let us take the following syllogism as explicated :—

> S *comprehends* M ;
> M *does not comprehend* P ;
> *Therefore,* S *does not comprehend* P.

> *Prudence comprehends virtue ;*
> *But virtue does not comprehend blameworthy ;*
> *Therefore prudence does not comprehend blameworthy.*

Here all goes on regularly. We descend from the
major term *prudence* to the middle term *virtue,* and
from the middle term *virtue* to the minor term *blame-
worthy.* But let us reverse the premises. We at once
see that though there is still a discoverable meaning,
it is not directly given, and that we must rectify and
restore in thought what is perverse and preposterous
in expression. In the previous example, the sumption
is affirmative, the subsumption negative. Now let us
take a negative sumption :—

> S *does not comprehend* M ;
> *But* M *comprehends* P.

Here there is no conclusion competent, for we can
neither say S *comprehends* P, nor S *does not comprehend* P. Or to take a concrete example,—

> *Prudence does not comprehend learning ;*
> *But learning comprehends praiseworthy.*

We can draw, it is evident, no conclusion ; for we
can neither say, from the relation of the two propositions, that *Prudence comprehends praiseworthy,* nor
that *Prudence does not comprehend praiseworthy.*

Grounds of
the rules
regarding
The reason why an extensive syllogism requires a
universal sumption, and an intensive syllogism an

affirmative, and why the one requires an affirmative
and the other a definite subsumption, is the following.
The condition common to both syllogisms is that the
sumption should express a rule. But in the extensive
syllogism this law is a universal rule, that is, a rule
to which there is no exception; but then it may be
expressed either in an affirmative or in a negative
form, whereas in the intensive syllogism this law is
expressed as a position,—as a fact, and, therefore,
admits only of an affirmative form, but, as it is not
necessarily universal, it admits of limitations or exceptions. This opposite character of the sumptions
of the two forms of syllogisms is correspondent to
the opposite character of their subsumptions. In the
extensive syllogism, the subsumption is, and can only
be, an affirmative declaration of the application of
the sumption as a universal rule. In the intensive
syllogism, the subsumption is either an affirmation or
a negation of the application of the sumption as a
positive law. Hence it is that in an intensive syllogism the major premise is necessarily an affirmative,
while the minor may be either an affirmative or a
negative proposition.

In regard to the second clause of the second rule,
the reason why the subsumption in an intensive syllogism must be definite in quantity, is because it would
otherwise be impossible to affirm or deny of each other
the minor and the major terms in the conclusion.
For example :—

Sumption........*Prudence is a virtue,* i. e. *Prudence comprehends
virtue ;*
Subsumption...*Some virtue is praiseworthy,* i. e. *Some virtue
comprehends praiseworthy.*

From these we can draw no conclusion, for the inde-

LECT.
XVII.

Sumption
and Sub-
sumption in
Extensive
and Com-
prehensive
Syllogisms.

finite *some virtue* does not connect the major term
prudence and the minor term *praiseworthy* into the
necessary relation of whole and part.

Third Rule.   In regard to the third rule—The conclusion must
be correspondent in quantity with the sumption, and
in quality with the subsumption—it is not necessary
to say anything.   Here, as in the extensive syllogism,
the conclusion cannot be stronger than the weakest
of its antecedents, that is, if any premise be negative
the conclusion cannot but be negative also; and if
any premise be particular, the conclusion cannot but
be particular likewise, and as a weaker quality is
only found in the subsumption and a weaker quantity
in the sumption, it follows that (as the rule declares)
the conclusion is regulated by the sumption in regard to its quantity, and by the subsumption in
regard to its quality.   It is, however, evident, that
though warranted to draw a universal conclusion from
a general sumption, it is always competent to draw
only a particular.

II. Induc-
tive Cate-
gorical Syl-
logisms.   So much for the proximate laws by which Categorical Deductive Syllogisms are governed, when considered as perfect and regular in external form.   We
shall, in the sequel, have to consider the special rules
by which the varieties of Deductive Categorical Syllogisms, as determined by their external form, are
governed; but at present we must proceed to the
general consideration of the other class of categorical
syllogisms afforded by their internal form,—I mean
those of Induction, the discussion of which I shall
commence by the following paragraph.

Par. LXII.
Inductive
Categorical   ¶ LXII. An Inductive Categorical Syllogism
is a reasoning in which we argue from the notion

of all the constituent parts discretively, to the
notion of the constituted whole collectively. Its
general laws are identical with those of the
Deductive Categorical Syllogism, and it may
be expressed, in like manner, in the form either
of an Intensive or of an Extensive Syllogism.

We shall, in the sequel, have to consider more
particularly the nature and peculiarities of Logical
Induction when we come to treat of the Figure of
Syllogism, and when we consider the nature of Logical or Formal, in contrast to Philosophical or Real Induction, under the head of Modified Logic. At present, I shall only say, that all you will find in logical
works of the character of logical induction is utterly
erroneous; for almost all logicians, except Aristotle,
consider induction, not as regulated by the necessary
laws of thought, but as determined by the probabilities
and presumptions of the sciences from which its matter
has accidentally been borrowed. They have not considered it, logically, in its formal, but only, extra-
logically, in its material conditions. Thus, logicians
have treated in Logic of the inductive inference from
the parts to the whole, not as exclusively warranted
by the law of Identity, in the convertibility of the
whole and all its parts, but they have attempted to
establish an illation from a few of these parts to the
whole; and this, either as supported by the general
analogies of nature, or by the special presumptions
afforded by the several sciences of objective existence.[a]

The views
of logicians
regarding
the nature
of Logical
Induction
erroneous.

Logicians, with the exception of Aristotle, who is,
however, very brief and unexplicit in his treatment of
this subject, have thus deformed their science, and

The charac-
ters of Logi-
cal or For-
mal, and of
Real or
Material,
Induction.

a Compare *Discussions*, p. 159.—ED.

perplexed the very simple doctrine of logical induction,
by confounding formal with material induction. All
inductive reasoning is a reasoning from the parts to
the whole ; but the reasoning from the parts to the
whole in the various material or objective sciences, is
very different from the reasoning from the parts to
the whole in the one formal or subjective science of
Logic. In the former, the illation is not simply
founded on the law of Identity, in the convertibility
of a whole and all its parts, but on certain presumptions drawn from an experience or observation of the
constancy of nature ; so that, in these sciences, the
inference to the whole is rarely from all, but generally
from a small number of, its constituent parts ; consequently, in them, the conclusion is rarely in truth an
induction properly so called, but a mixed conclusion,
drawn on an inductive presumption combined with a
deductive premise. For example, the physical philosopher thus reasons :—

This, that, and the other magnet attract iron ;
But this, that, and the other magnet represent all magnets ;
Therefore, all magnets attract iron.

Now, in this syllogism, the legitimacy of the minor
premise, *This, that, and the other magnet represent all
magnets*, is founded on the principle, that nature is
uniform and constant, and, on this general principle,
the reasoner is physically warranted in making a few
parts equivalent to the whole. But this process is
wholly incompetent to the logician. The logician
knows nothing of any principles except the laws of
thought. He cannot transcend the sphere of necessary, and pass into the sphere of probable, thinking ;
nor can he bring back, and incorporate into his own
formal science, the conditions which regulate the

procedure of the material sciences. This being the
case, induction is either not a logical process different
from deduction, for the induction of the objective
philosopher, in so far as it is formal, is in fact deductive; or there must be an induction governed by
other laws than those which warrant the induction
of the objective philosopher. Now, if logicians had
looked to their own science, and not to sciences with
which, as logicians, they had no concern, they would
have seen that there is a process of reasoning from
the parts to the whole, as well as from the whole to
the parts, that this process is governed by its own
laws, and is equally necessary and independent as
the other. The rule by which the Deductive Syllogism is governed is,—What belongs, or does not
belong, to the containing whole, belongs, or does not
belong, to each and all of the contained parts. The
rule by which the Inductive Syllogism is governed
is,—What belongs, or does not belong, to all the
constituent parts, belongs, or does not belong, to the
constituted whole. These rules exclusively determine all formal inference; whatever transcends or
violates them, transcends or violates Logic. Both are
equally absolute. It would be not less illegal to infer,
by the deductive syllogism, an attribute belonging
to the whole of something it was not conceived to
contain as a part; than, by the inductive, to conclude
of the whole what is not conceived as a predicate of
all its constituent parts. In either case, the consequent is not thought as determined by the antecedent; the premises do not involve the conclusion.[a]

To take the example previously adduced, as an

Canons of the Deductive and Inductive Syllogisms,—equally formal.

---

a [Cf. Krug, *Logik*, §§ 166, 167;   *Honalis*, §§ 477, 478; *Scotus*,] [*Quæs-*
Sanderson, Compendium Log. Artis,   *tiones in An. Prior.*, L. ii. q. viii. p.
L. iii. c. x. p. 112; Wolf, *Phil. Ra-*   316, ed. 610.—Ed.]

VOL. I.   X

illustration of a material or philosophical induction, it would be thus expressed as a formal or logical induction :—

> *This, that, and the other magnet attract iron;*
> *But this, that, and the other magnet are all magnets;*
> *Therefore, all magnets attract iron.*

Here the inference is determined exclusively by a law of thought. In the subsumption it is said—*This, that, and the other magnet are all magnets.* This means, *This, that, and the other magnet are,* that is, *constitute,* or rather, *are conceived to constitute, all magnets,* that is, *the whole—the class—the genus magnet.* If, therefore, explicitly enounced, it will be as follows :—*This, that, and the other magnet are conceived to constitute the whole class magnet.* The conclusion is—*Therefore, all magnets attract iron.* This, if explicated, will give—*Therefore the whole class magnet is conceived to attract iron.* The whole syllogism, therefore, as a logical induction, will be :—

> *This, that, and the other magnet attract iron;*
> *But this, that, and the other magnet are conceived to constitute the genus magnet;*
> *Therefore, the genus magnet attracts iron.*

It is almost needless to advert to an objection, which, I see, has misled Whately among others. It may be said, that the minor, *This, that, and the other magnet are all magnets,* is manifestly false. This is a very superficial objection. It is very true that neither here, nor indeed in almost any of our inductions, is the statement objectively correct,—that the enumerated particulars are really equivalent to the whole or class which they constitute, or in which they are contained. But as an objection to a logical syllogism, it is wholly incompetent, as wholly extralogical. For the logician has a right to suppose any material impossibility, any LECT. XVII. material falsity ; he takes no account of what is objectively impossible or false, and has a right to assume what premises he please, provided that they do not involve a contradiction in terms. In the example in question, the subsumption—*This, that, and the other magnet are all magnets*—has been already explained to mean not that they really are so, but merely that they are so thought to be. It is only on the supposition of *this, that, and the other magnet* being conceived to constitute the class *magnet*, that the inference proceeds, and, on this supposition, it will not be denied that the inference is necessary. I stated Formula for Inductive Syllo- that an inductive syllogism is equally competent in gism in Compreben- comprehension and in extension. For example, let us Compreben- suppose that x, y, z represent parts, and the letters sion and Extension. A and B wholes, and we have the following formula of an inductive syllogism in Comprehension :—

> x, y, z *constitute* A ;
> A *comprehends* B ;
> *Therefore,* x, y, z *comprehend* B.

This, if converted into an extensive syllogism, by transposing the premises and reversing the copula, gives :—

> A *is contained under* B ;
> x, y, z *constitute* A ;
> *Therefore,* x, y, z *are contained under* B.

But in this syllogism, it is evident that the premises are in an unnatural order. We must not, therefore, here transpose the premises, as we do in converting a deductive categorical of comprehension into one of extension. We may obtain an inductive syllogism in two different forms, and in either comprehension or extension, according as the parts stand for the major, or for the middle term. If the minor term is formed of the parts, it is evident there is no induction; for in this case they only constitute that quantity of the syllogism which is always a part, and never a whole. Let x, y, z represent the parts; where not superseded by x, y, z, S will represent the major term in a comprehensive, and the minor term in an extensive, syllogism; P will represent the major term in an extensive, and the minor term in a comprehensive, syllogism; and M the middle term in both. I shall, first, take the Inductive Syllogism of Comprehension.

FIRST CASE,—(The parts holding the place of the major term S).	SECOND CASE,—(The parts holding the place of the middle term).
x, y, z constitute M ;	S comprehends x, y, z;
M comprehends P ;	x, y, z constitute P;
Therefore, x, y, z comprehend P.	Therefore, S comprehends P.

Again, in the Inductive Syllogism of Extension :—

FIRST CASE,—(The parts holding the place of the major term P).	SECOND CASE,—(The parts holding the place of the middle term).
x, y, z constitute M ;	x, y, z are contained under P ;
S is contained under M ;	x, y, z constitute S ;
Therefore, S is contained under x, y, z.	Therefore, S is contained under P.

Whately and others erroneously make the Inductive Syllogism Deductive

Before leaving this subject, I may notice that the doctrine of logical induction maintained by Whately and many others, diverges even more than that of the older logicians from the truth, inasmuch as it makes this syllogism a deductive syllogism, of which the sumption, which is usually understood and not expressed, is always substantially the same—viz. " What belongs (or does not belong) to the individuals we have examined belongs (or does not belong) to the whole class under which they are contained." This doctrine was first, I think, introduced by Wolf,[a] for the previous logicians viewed the subsumption as the common, and, therefore, the suppressed premise, this premise always stating that the individuals or particulars enumerated made up the class under which they were severally contained.[β] For example, in the instance from the magnet we have already taken, the subsumption would be—*This, that, and the other magnet and so forth, are the whole class magnet.* This doctrine of the older logicians is correct as far as it goes; and to make it absolutely correct, it would only have been necessary to have established the distinction between the logical induction as governed by the *a priori* conditions of thought, and philosophical induction as legitimated by the *a posteriori* conditions of the matter about which the inquiry is conversant. This, however, was not done, and the whole doctrine of logical induction was corrupted and confounded by logicians introducing into their science the consideration of various kinds of matter, and admitting as logical an induction supposed imperfect, that is, one in which there was inference to the whole from some only of the constituent parts. This Imperfect Induction they held in contingent matter to be contingent,—

Correct as
far as it
goes.

Doctrine of
Imperfect
Induction.

a [Cf. Wolf, *Philosophia Rationalis*, § 470, first ed. 1728. So, before Wolf, Schramm, *Aristot. Philos. Principia*, p. 27, ed. Helmst., 1718: " Inductione ex multis singularibus colligitur universale supposito loco majoris propositionis hac canone :—Quicquid competit omnibus partibus, hoc competit toti, in isto (Enthymemate) vel major vel minor praemissarum, in hoc (Inductione) semper major propositio subintelligitur." Refers as follows—" *De Inductione, Philos. Altorf.*, Disp. xxiv. p. 252 et seq." See also Crakanthorpe, *Logica*,

c. xx. p. 217, ed. 1677.] [Cf. *Discussions*, p. 170, note.—Ed.]

β [On Induction in general, see Zabarella, *Tabula in An. Prior.*, p. 170 et seq., *Opera Logica*, (Appendix) ; Molinæus, *Elementa Logica*, L. i. c. ii. p. 99 ; Isendoorn, *Cursus Logicus*, L. iii. q. ii. p. 201 ; Crellius, *Isagoge*, L. iii. c. xx. p. 254 ; Keckermann, *Opera*, t. i. pp. 259, 733 ; Lambert, *Neues Organon*, L. § 296, 297, p. 183 ; Eugenics, *Λογική*, p. 410 ; Jo. Fr. Picus Mirandulanus,] [*Opera, Examen Doct. Vanit. Gent.*, L. v. p. 746 et seq.—Ed.]

LEUT.
XVII.

Bacon at
fault in his
criticism of
Aristotle's
doctrine of
Induction.

in necessary matter to be necessary; as if a logical inference were not in all cases necessary, and only necessary as governed by the necessary laws of thought. This misapprehension of the nature of logical or formal induction, and of its difference from philosophical or material induction, has been the reason why Bacon is at fault in his criticism of Aristotle's doctrine. For, looking only at the doctrine of the inductive syllogism given by Aristotle in the *Organon*, and not perceiving that the question there was only concerning the nature of induction as governed by the laws of thought, he forthwith assumed that this was the induction practised by the Stagirite in his study of nature, and, in the teeth both of the precept and of the practice of the philosopher, condemned the Aristotelic induction in the mass, as flying at once to general principles from the hasty enumeration of a few individual instances. Induction, as I mentioned, will, however, once and again, engage our attention in the sequel; but I have thought it proper to be somewhat explicit, that you might carry with you a clearer conception of the nature of this process, as contrasted with the process of the Deductive Syllogism.

B. Condi-
tional Syllo-
gisms.
I. Disjunc-
tive.

Having terminated the general consideration of Categorical Syllogisms, Deductive and Inductive, I now proceed to the next class of Reasonings afforded by the internal form; I mean the class of Disjunctive Syllogisms.

Par. LXIII.
A Disjunc-
tive syllo-
gism, —
what.

¶ LXIII. A Disjunctive Syllogism is a reasoning, whose form is determined by the law of Excluded Middle, and whose sumption is accordingly a disjunctive proposition, either of Contradiction (as, A *is either* B *or not* B)—or of

Contrariety (as, A *is either* B, *or* C, *or* D). In
such a judgment it is enounced, that B *or not*
B, or that B, C, *or* D, as opposite notions taken
together and constituting a totality, are each of
them a possible, and one or other of them a
necessary, predicate of A. To determine which
of these belongs, or does not belong to A, the
subsumption must either affirm one of the predicates, and the conclusion, *eo ipso*, consequently,
deny the other or others; or it must deny one
or more of them, and thus necessitate in the conclusion, either the determinate affirmation of the
other, or the indeterminate affirmation of the
others. A Disjunctive Syllogism is thus either
Affirmative, constituting the *Modus ponens*, or
Modus ponendo tollens, or Negative, constituting
the *Modus tollens*, or *Modus tollendo ponens*.

In each of these modes there are two cases,
which I comprehend in the following mnemonic
verses :—

(A) AFFIRMATIVE, or MODUS PONENDO TOLLENS :—
    1. *Falleris aut fallor ; fallor ; non falleris ergo.*
    2. *Falleris aut fallor ; tu falleris ; ergo ego nedum.*
(B) NEGATIVE, or MODUS TOLLENDO PONENS :—
    1. *Falleris aut fallor ; non fallor ; falleris ergo.*[a]
    2. *Falleris aut fallor ; non falleris ; ergo ego fallor.*

In illustration of this paragraph, I have defined a
disjunctive syllogism, one whose form is determined
by the law of Excluded Middle, and whose sumption
is, accordingly, a disjunctive proposition. I have not,
as logicians in general do, defined it directly,—a syllogism whose major premise is a disjunctive proposition.
For though it be true that every disjunctive syllogism

Explica-
tion.

A syllogism
with dis-
junctive
major pre-
miss is not
necessarily a
disjunctive
reasoning.

a This line is from Purchot. The others are the Author's own.—
Instit. Philos. Logica, t. i. p. 184. ED.

has a disjunctive major premise, the converse is not
true; for every syllogism that has a disjunctive
sumption is not, on that account, necessarily a disjunctive syllogism. For a disjunctive syllogism only
emerges, when the conclusion has reference to the
relation of reciprocal affirmation and negation subsisting between the disjunct members in the major premise,—a condition not, however, contained in the
mere existence of the disjunctive sumption.[a] For
example, in the syllogism :—

> D *is either* C *or* D ;
> But A *is* B ;
> *Therefore,* A *is either* C *or* D.

This syllogism is as much a reasoning determined,
not by the law of Excluded Middle, but solely by the
law of Identity, as the following :—

> B *is* C.
> A *is* B.
> *Therefore,* A *is* C.

For in both we conclude,—C (in one, C or D) *is an
attribute of* B ; *but* B *is an attribute of* A ; *therefore,*
C (C *or* D) *is an attribute of* A,—a process, in either
case, regulated exclusively by the law of Identity.[β]

This being premised, I proceed to a closer consideration of the nature of this reasoning, and shall,
first, give you a general notion of its procedure; then,
secondly, discuss its principle ; and, thirdly, its constituent parts.

1°. General
view of the
Disjunctive
Syllogism.
　　1°. The general form of the Disjunctive Syllogism
may be given in the following scheme, in which you

α Cf. Scheibler, *Opera Logica,*
Pars iv. p. 553 : "Neque enim syllogismus disjunctus semper est, cum
propositio est disjunctiva, sed cum
tota quæstio disponitur in proposi-
tione."—En.

β Sigwart, pp. 154, 157. [*Hand-
buch zur Vorlesungen über die Logik,*
von H. C. W. Sigwart, 3d ed., Tubingen, 1835, §§ 245, 248.—En.]

will observe there is a common sumption to the negative and affirmative modes :—

A is either B or C.

AFFIRMATIVE, or MODUS PON-ENDO TOLLENS—	NEGATIVE, or MODUS TOLLENDO PONENS—
Now A *is* B ;	*Now* A *is not* B ;
Therefore, A *is not* C.	*Therefore,* A *is* C.

a. Formula for a Syllogism with two disjunct members.

Or, in a concrete example :—

Sempronius is either honest or dishonest.

AFFIRMATIVE, or MODUS PON-ENDO TOLLENS—	NEGATIVE, or MODUS TOLLENDO PONENS—
Now Sempronius is honest ;	*Now Sempronius is not honest ;*
Therefore, Sempronius is not dishonest.	*Therefore, Sempronius is dishonest.*

"This formula is, however, only calculated for the
case in which there are only two disjunct members,
that is, for the case of negative or contradictory opposition ; for if the disjunct members are more than
two, that is, if there is a positive or contrary opposition, there is then a twofold or manifold employment
of the *Modus ponendo tollens* and *Modus tollendo
ponens*, according as the affirmation and negation is
determinate or indeterminate. If, in the *Modus ponendo tollens,* one disjunct member is determinately
affirmed, then all the others are denied ; and if several
disjunct members are indeterminately affirmed except
one, then only that one is denied. If, in the *Modus
tollendo ponens,* a single member of the disjunction be
denied, then some one of the others is indeterminately affirmed ; and if several be denied, so that one
alone is left, then this one is determinately affirmed." [a]
This will appear more clearly from the following formulæ. Let the common Sumption both of the *Modus
ponendo tollens* and *Modus tollendo ponens* be :—

b. Formula for a Syllogism with more than two disjunct members.

a Esser, *Logik,* § 93, p. 180.—ED.

A *is either* B *or* C *or* D.

I. THE MODUS PONENDO TOLLENS—

First Case.   A *is either* B *or* C *or* D ;
                Now A *is* B ;
                Therefore, A *is neither* C *nor* D.

Second Case.   A *is either* B *or* C *or* D ;
                Now A *is either* B *or* C ;
                Therefore, A *is not* D.

II. THE MODUS TOLLENDO PONENS.

First Case.   A *is either* B *or* C *or* D ;
                Now A *is not* B ;
                Therefore, A *is either* C *or* D.

Second Case.   A *is either* B *or* C *or* D ;
                Now A *is neither* B *nor* C ;
                Therefore, A *is* D.

Or, to take these in concrete examples, let the Common Sumption be :—

The ancients were in genius either superior to the moderns, or inferior, or equal.

I. THE MODUS PONENDO TOLLENS.

First Case.   *The ancients were in genius either superior to the
                moderns, or inferior, or equal ;
                Now the ancients were superior ;
                Therefore, the ancients were neither inferior nor
                equal.*

Second Case.   *The ancients were in genius either superior to the
                moderns, or inferior, or equal ;
                Now the ancients were either superior or equal ;
                Therefore, the ancients were not inferior.*

II. THE MODUS TOLLENDO PONENS.

First Case.   *The ancients were in genius either superior to the
                moderns, or inferior, or equal ;
                Now the ancients were not inferior ;
                Therefore, the ancients were either superior or equal.*

Second Case.   *The ancients were in genius either superior to the
                moderns, or inferior, or equal ;
                Now the ancients were neither inferior nor equal ;
                Therefore, the ancients were superior.*

Such is a general view of its procedure. Now, 2°, LECT. XVII. for its principle.

2°. The principle of the Disjunctive Syllogism.

" If the essential character of the Disjunctive Syllogism consist in this,—that the affirmation or negation, or, what is a better expression, the position or sublation, of one or other of two contradictory attributes follows from the subsumption of the opposite;—there is necessarily implied in the disjunctive process, that, when of two opposite predicates the one is posited or affirmed, the other is sublated or denied; and that, when the one is sublated or denied, the other is posited or affirmed. But the proposition,—that of two repugnant attributes, the one being posited, the other must be sublated, and the one being sublated, the other must be posited,—is at once manifestly the law by which the disjunctive syllogism is governed, and manifestly only an application of the law of Excluded Middle. For the *Modus ponendo tollens* there is the special rule,—If the one character be posited, the other character is sublated; and for the *Modus tollendo ponens* there is the special rule,—If the one character be sublated, the other character is posited. The law of the disjunctive syllogism is here enounced, only in reference to the case in which the members of disjunction are contradictorily opposed. An opposition of contrariety is not of purely logical concernment; and a disjunctive syllogism with characters opposed in contrariety, in fact, consists of as many pure disjunctive syllogisms as there are opposing predicates." [a]

3°. I now go on to the third and last matter of consideration,—the several parts of a Disjunctive Syllogism. 3°. The several parts of a Disjunctive Syllogism.

a Esser, *Logik*, § 94.—Ed.

" The question concerning the special laws of a disjunctive syllogism, or, what is the same thing, what is the original and necessary form of a disjunctive syllogism, as determined by its general principle or law,—this question may be asked, not only in reference to the whole syllogism, but likewise in reference to its several parts. The original and necessary form of a disjunctive syllogism consists, as we have seen, in the reciprocal position or sublation of contradictory characters, by the subsumption of one or other. Hence it follows, that the disjunctive syllogism must, like the categorical, involve a threefold judgment— viz. 1°, A judgment in which a subject is determined by two contradictory predicates; 2°, A judgment in which one or other of the opposite predicates is subsumed, that is, is affirmed, either as existent or non-existent; and, 3°, A judgment in which the final decision is enounced concerning the existence or non-existence of one of the repugnant or reciprocally exclusive predicates. But in these three propositions, as in the three propositions of a categorical syllogism, there can only be three principal notions—viz. the notion of a subject, and the notion of two contradictory attributes, which are generally enounced in the sumption, and of which one is posited or sublated in the subsumption, in order that in the conclusion the other may be sublated or posited. The case of contrary opposition is, as we have seen, easily reconciled and reduced to that of contradictory opposition." [a]   The laws of the several parts of a disjunctive syllogism, or more properly the original and necessary form of these several parts, are given in the following paragraph :—

a Esser, *Logik*, § 95.—ED.

¶ LXIV.—1°, A regular and perfect Disjunctive Syllogism must have three propositions, in
which, if the sumption be simple and the disjunction purely logical, only three principal notions
can be found.

2°, The Sumption, in relation to its quantity
and quality, is always uniform, being Universal
and Affirmative ; but the Subsumption is susceptible of various forms in both relations.

3°, The Conclusion corresponds in quantity
with the subsumption, and is opposed to it in
quality.[a]

The first rule is,—A regular and perfect disjunctive
syllogism must have three propositions, in which, if
the sumption be simple and the disjunction purely
logical, only three principal notions can be found.
" Like the categorical syllogism, the disjunctive consists of a sumption, constituting the general rule ; of
a subsumption, containing its application ; and of a
conclusion, expressing the judgment inferred. Disjunctive syllogisms are, therefore, true and genuine
reasonings ; and if in the sumption the disjunction
be contradictory, there are in the syllogism only three
principal notions. In the case of contrary disjunc-
tions, there may, indeed, appear a greater number
of notions ; but as such syllogisms are in reality
composite, and are made up of a plurality of syllogisms with a contradictory disjunction, this objection
to the truth of the rule is as little valid as the circumstance, that the subject in the sumption is sometimes twofold, threefold, fourfold, or manifold ; as, for
example, in the sumption—*John, James, Thomas, are*

a Esser, l. c. Krug, *Logik*, § 88.—Ed.

either virtuous or vicious. For this is a copulative proposition, which is composed of three simple propositions—viz., *John is,* &c. If, therefore, there be such a sumption at the head of a disjunctive syllogism, it is in this case, likewise, composite, and may be analysed into as many simple syllogisms with three principal notions, as there are simple propositions into which the sumption may be resolved."[a]

The second rule is,—The sumption is, in relation to its quantity and quality, always uniform,—being universal and affirmative; but the subsumption is susceptible of different forms in both relations. If we look, indeed, to the subject alone, it may seem to be possibly equally general or particular; for we can equally say of *some,* as of *all* A that they are either B or C. But as all universality is relative, and as the sumption is always more extensive or more comprehensive than the subsumption, it is thus true that the sumption is always general. Again, looking to the predicate, or, as it is complex, to the predicates alone, they, as exclusive of each other, appear to involve a negation. But in looking at the whole proposition, that is, at the subject, the copula, and the predicates in connection, we see at once that the copula is affirmative, for the negation involved in the predicates is confined to that term alone.[β]

In regard to the third rule, which enounces,—That the conclusion should have the same quantity with the subsumption, but an opposite quality,—it is requisite

---

a Krug, *Logik,* l. c.—Ed.
β See Krug, *Logik,* § 86, Anm. 2.—Ed. [Bachmann, *Logik,* § 141, p. 354. *Contra:*—Twesten, *Logik,* § 127, ed. 1825, p. 119. *Esser, Logik,* § 95. Derodon, *Logica Restituta,* p.

676.] ["Propositio Disjunctiva sullam habet quantitatem nisi suarum partium . . . sicut Propositio Hypothetica habet tantum quantitatem suarum partium." See above, p. 247, and p. 248, note a.—Ed.]

to say nothing, as the first clause is only a special
application of the rule common to all syllogisms that
the conclusion can contain nothing more than the
premises, and must, therefore, follow the weaker part;
and the second is self-evident, as only a special application of the principle of Excluded Middle, for, on this
law, if one contradictory be affirmed in the subsumption, the other must be denied in the conclusion, and
if one contradictory be denied in the subsumption,
the other must be affirmed in the conclusion.

The Disjunctive, like every other species of syllogism, may be either a reasoning in the quantity of
Comprehension, or a reasoning in the quantity of Extension. The contrast, however, of these two quantities is not manifested in the same signal manner in
the disjunctive as in the categorical deductive syllogism, more especially of the first figure. In the categorical deductive syllogism, the reasonings in the two
counter quantities are obtrusively distinguished by a
complete conversion, not only of the internal significance, but of the external appearance of the syllogism.
For not only do the relative terms change places in
the relation of whole and part, but the consecution of
the antecedents is reversed ; the minor premise in
the one syllogism becoming the major premise in the
other. This, however, is not the case in disjunctive
syllogisms. Here the same proposition is, in both
quantities, always the major premise ; and the whole
change that takes place in converting a disjunctive
syllogism of the one quantity into a disjunctive syllogism of the other, is in the silent reversal of the copula
from one of its meanings to another. This, however,
as it determines no apparent difference in single propositions, and as the disjunctive sumption remains

The Dis-
junctive
Syllogism
of Compre-
hension and
Extension.

always the same proposition, out of which the subsumption and the conclusion are evolved, in the one
quantity as in the other,—the reversal of the sumption, from extension to comprehension, or from comprehension to extension, occasions neither a real nor
Examples. an apparent change in the syllogism. Take, for example, the disjunctive syllogism :—

> *Plato is either learned or unlearned ;*
> *But Plato is learned ;*
> *Therefore, Plato is not unlearned.*

Now let us explicate this into an intensive and into
an extensive syllogism. As an Intensive Syllogism it
will stand :—

> *Plato comprehends either the attribute learned or the attribute*
> *unlearned ;*
> *But Plato comprehends the attribute learned ;*
> *Therefore, &c.*

As an Extensive Syllogism it will stand :—

> *Plato is contained either under the class learned, or under the*
> *class unlearned ;*
> *But Plato is contained under the class learned ;*
> *Therefore, &c.*

From this it appears, that, though the difference of
reasoning in the several quantities of comprehension
and extension obtains in disjunctive, as in all other
syllogisms, it does not, in the disjunctive syllogism,
determine the same remarkable change in the external
construction and consecution of the parts, which it
does in categorical syllogisms.

LECTURE XVIII.

STOICHEIOLOGY.

SECT. II.—OF THE PRODUCTS OF THOUGHT.

III.—DOCTRINE OF REASONINGS.

SYLLOGISMS.—THEIR DIVISIONS ACCORDING TO INTERNAL FORM.

B. CONDITIONAL.—HYPOTHETICAL AND HYPOTHETICO-DISJUNCTIVE.

HAVING now considered Categorical and Disjunctive Syllogisms, the next class of Reasonings afforded by the difference of Internal or Essential Form is the Hypothetical ; and the general nature of these syllogisms is expressed in the following paragraph :— LECT. XVIII.

¶ LXV. An Hypothetical Syllogism is a reasoning whose form is determined by the law of Reason and Consequent. It is, therefore, regulated by the two principles of which that law is the complement,—the one,—With the reason, the consequent is affirmed ; the other,—With the consequent, the reason is denied : and these two principles severally afford the condition of its Affirmative or Constructive, and of its Negative or Destructive, form (*Modus ponens et Modus tollens*). The sumption or general rule in such a syllogism is necessarily an hypothetical proposition (*If* A *is, then* B *is*). In such a proposition

Par. LXV.
5. Hypothetical syllogism,—its general character.

VOL. I.   Y

it is merely enounced that the prior member (A)
and the posterior member (B) stand to each other
in the relation of reason and consequent, if existing, but without it being determined whether
they really exist or not. Such determination
must follow in the subsumption and conclusion ;
and that, either by the absolute affirmation of the
antecedent in the subsumption, and the illative
affirmation of the consequent in the conclusion (the
modus ponens) ; or by the absolute negation of
the consequent in the subsumption, and the illative negation of the antecedent in the conclusion
(the *modus tollens*).[a] The general form of an hypothetical syllogism[β] is, therefore, the following :—

Common Sumption—*If* A *is, then* B *is;*

1,	2,
Modus Ponens :	Modus Tollens :
But A *is;*	*But* B *is not;*
Therefore, B *is.*	*Therefore,* A *is not.*

Or,

        A   B

1) Modus Ponens—*Si poteris possum; sed tu potes; ergo ego possum.*

        B   A

2) Modus Tollens—*Si poteris possum; non possum; nec potes ergo.*[γ]

Explica-
tion.

In illustrating this paragraph, I shall consider, 1°,
This species of syllogism in general ; 2°, Its peculiar
principle ; and, 3°, Its special laws.

[a For use of terms *ponens* and
tollens, see Boethius, *De Syllogismo
Hypothetico, Opera,* p. 611 ; Wolf,
Phil. Rat., § 400-410. Mark Duncan uses the terms " a positione ad
positionem," and " a remotione ad
remotionem." [*Institutiones Logicæ,*
L. iv. c. 6, § 4, p. 240. Cf. p. 243,
Salmurii, 1612.—Ed.]

β [On the Hypothetical Syllogism
in general, see Ammonius, *In de Interp., Procem.,* L. 3, Venetiis, 1546 ;
Philoponus, *In Anal. Prior.,* i. c.

23, f. 60, Venet., 1536 ; Magentinus,
In Anal. Prior., l. 16 b ; Alex.
Aphrodisiensis, *In Anal. Prior.,* ff.
87, 88, 109, 130, Ald., 1520 ; *In Topica,* f. 65, Ald., 1513 ; Anonymous
Author, *On Syllogisms,* f. 44, ed.
1536 ; Scheibler, *Opera Logica,* pars
iv. p. 548 ; Bolzano, *Wissenschaftslehre, Logik,* ii. p. 560 ; Waitz, *Organon, In An. Prior.,* L c. 23.]

γ These lines are the Author's
own.—Ed.]

1°, " Like every other species of simple syllogism
the Hypothetical is made up of three propositions,—
a sumption, a subsumption, and a conclusion. There
must, in the first place, be an hypothetical proposition
holding the place of a general rule, and from this proposition the other parts of the syllogism must be de-
duced. This first proposition, therefore, contains a
sumption. But as this proposition contains a relative
and correlative member,—one member, the relative
clause, enouncing a thing as conditioning ; the other,
the correlative clause, enouncing a thing as conditioned ; and as the whole proposition enounces merely
the dependency between these relatives, and judges
nothing in regard to their existence considered apart
and in themselves,—this enouncement must be made
in a second proposition, which shall take out of the
sumption one or other of its relatives, and categorically enounce its existence or its non-existence. This
second proposition contains, therefore, a subsumption ;
and, through this subsumption, a judgment is likewise
determined, in a third proposition, with regard to the
other relative. This last proposition, therefore, contains the conclusion proper of the syllogism.

" But as the sumption in an hypothetical syllogism
contains two relative clauses,—an antecedent and a
consequent,—it, therefore, appears double ; and as
either of its two members may be taken in the subsumption, there is, consequently, competent a twofold
kind of reasoning. For we can either, in the first place,
conclude from the truth of the antecedent to the truth
of the consequent ; or, in the second place, conclude
from the falsehood of the consequent to the falsehood
of the antecedent. The former of these modes of hypothetical inference constitutes what is sometimes called

the *Constructive Hypothetical*, but more properly the
Modus Ponens:—the latter what is sometimes called
the *Destructive Hypothetical*, but more properly the
Modus Tollens."[a] As examples of the two modes :—

Modus Ponens—*If Socrates be virtuous, he merits esteem ;*
     But Socrates is virtuous ;
     Therefore, he merits esteem.
Modus Tollens—*If Socrates be virtuous, he merits esteem ;*
     But Socrates does not merit esteem ;
     Therefore, he is not virtuous.[b]

So much for the character of the Hypothetical Syllogism in general. I now proceed to consider its
peculiar principle.

9°, Its pecu-
liar prin-
ciple,—the
law of Rea-
son and
Consequent. 2°, "If the essential nature of an Hypothetical
Syllogism consist in this,—that the subsumption
affirms or denies one or other of the two parts of a
thought, standing to each other in the relation of the
thing conditioning and the thing conditioned, it will
be the law of an hypothetical syllogism, that,—If the
condition or antecedent be affirmed, so also must
be the conditioned or consequent, and if the conditioned or consequent be denied, so likewise must be
the condition or antecedent. But this is manifestly

---

[a] Krug, *Logik*, § 81, Anm. 1, p.
254. Compare Esser, *Logik*, § 90,
p. 172.—Ed.

[b] [Nomenclature of Theophrastus,
Eudemus, and other Peripatetics, in
regard to Hypothetical Syllogism, in
contrast with that of the Stoics.

Προήγματα, ἑπόμενα, φανερά (Peripatetic), are called by the Stoics
respectively, τυγχάνοντα, ἐπόμενοι,
λεκτά.

Take this Hypothetical Syllogism :—

If it be day, the sun is on the earth ;
But it is day ;
Therefore, the sun is on the earth.

Here, *If it be day*, is called τὸ ἡγού-
μενον, both by Peripatetics and by
Stoics ; *the sun is on the earth*, is
called τὸ ἑπόμενον by Peripatetics, τὸ
λῆγον by Stoics. The whole, *If it be
day, the sun is on the earth*, is called
τὸ συνημμένον by Peripatetics, τὸ
τροπικὸν by Stoics : *But it is day*, is
μετάληψις to Peripatetics, πρόσληψις
to Stoics. *Therefore the sun is on
the earth* is συγκρίμεμα to Peripatetics, ἐπιφορὰ to Stoics. See Philoponus, *In Anal. Prior.*, L. i. c. 23, f.
60 a, ed. Venet. 1536 ; Brandis,
Scholia, p. 169. Cf. Anonymous
Author, *On Syllogisms*, f. 44.]

nothing else than the law of Sufficient Reason or of LECT.
Reason and Consequent."* The principle of this XVIII.
syllogism is thus variously enounced,—*Posita condi-* How
tione, ponitur conditionatum; sublato conditionato, enounced.
tollitur conditio. Or otherwise,—*A ratione ad ra-*
tionatum, a negatione rationati ad negationem ra-
tionis, valet consequentia. The one alternative of
either rule being regulative of the *modus ponens,* the
other of the *modus tollens.*β

"But here it may be asked, why, as we conclude Why we
from the truth of the antecedent to the truth of the cannot con-
consequent (*a ratione ad rationatum*), and from the the truth of
falsehood of the consequent to the falsehood of the truth of the
antecedent (*a negatione rationati ad negationem ra-* antecedent,
tionis), can we not conversely conclude from the truth the antece-
of the consequent to the truth of the antecedent, and falsehood of
from the falsehood of the antecedent to the falsehood the conse-
of the consequent? In answer to this question, it is
manifest that this could be validly done, only on the
following supposition—viz., if every consequent had
only one possible antecedent; and if, from an antecedent false as considered absolutely and in itself, it
were impossible to have consequents true as facts.

"Thus, in the first place, it is incompetent to conclude, that because B exists, that is, because the consequent member of the sumption, considered as an
absolute proposition, is true, therefore the supposed reason A exists, that is, therefore the alleged antecedent
member must be true; for B may have other reasons
besides A, such as C or D. In like manner, in the
second place, we should not be warranted to infer, that
because the supposed reason A is unreal, and the

α *Esser, Logik,* § 91, p. 174.— β See *Kant, Logik,* §§ 75, 76.
ED.   *Krug, Logik,* § 82.—ED.

antecedent member false, therefore the result B is also unreal, and the consequent member false; for the existence of B might be determined by many other reasons than A."[a]　For example :—

> If there are sharpers in the company we ought not to gamble;
> But there are no sharpers in the company;
> Therefore, we ought to gamble.

Here the conclusion is as false as if we conversely inferred, that *because we ought not to gamble, there are sharpers in the room.*

"Logicians have given themselves a world of pains in the discovery of general rules for the conversion of Hypothetical Syllogisms into Categorical.[b]　But, in the first place, this is unnecessary, in so far as it is applied to manifest the validity of an hypothetical syllogism ; for the hypothetical syllogism manifests its own validity with an evidence not less obtrusive than does the categorical, and, therefore, it stands in no need of a reduction to any higher form, as if it were of this a one-sided and accidental modification. With equal propriety might we inquire, how a categorical syllogism is to be converted into an hypothetical.　In the second place, this conversion is not always possible, and, therefore, it is never necessary. In cases where the sumption of an hypothetical syllogism contains only three notions, and where of these three notions one stands to the other two in the

---

a Krug, *Logik,* § 82, p. 256.—
Ed.

β [For the reduction of Hypotheticals, see Wolf, *Philos. Rat.,* § 412; Reusch, *Systema Logicum,* § 583; Molinæus, *Elementa Logica,* L. i. tract. iii. c. 1, p. 95 ; Keckermann, *Opera,* t. i. pp. 256, 767 ; Crellius, *Isagoge,* L. iii. c. 17, p. 243 ; Kiese-wetter, *Allgemeine Logik,* i. § 239, p. 115 ; Esser, *Logik,* §§ 99, 100. Against, see Krug, *Logik,* p. 356, and *Lexikon,* iii. p. 559 ; Fries, *Logik,* § 62, p. 257 ; Bachmann, *Logik,* § 89, Anm. 2 ; (In part), Aristotle, *Anal. Prior.,* L. i. c. 44, p. 374, ed. Pacii ; (In part), Pacius, *In Arist. Organon, loc. cit.,* p. 104.]

relation of a middle term,—in these cases, an hypothetical syllogism may without difficulty be reduced
to a categorical. Thus, when the formula, *If* A *is,
then* B *is,* signifies, *If* A *is* C, *then* A *is also* B,—
that is, A *is* B, *inasmuch as it is* C,—in this case
the categorical form is to be viewed as the original,
and the hypothetical as the derivative."[a]   For example:—

> *If Caius be a man, then he is mortal;
> But Caius is a man;
> Therefore, he is mortal.*

Here the notion *man* is regarded as comprehending
in it, or as contained under, the notion *mortal;* and
as being comprehended in, or as containing under it,
the notion *Caius:* it can, therefore, serve as middle
term in the categorical syllogism to connect the two
notions *Caius* and *mortal.*   Thus :—

> *Man is mortal;
> Caius is man;
> Therefore, Caius is mortal.*

"In such cases it requires only to discover the
middle term, in order to reduce the hypothetical
syllogism to a categorical form; and no rules are
requisite for those who comprehend the nature of the
two kinds of reasoning.

"But in those cases where the sumption of an
hypothetical syllogism contains more than three
notions, so that the formula, *If* A *is, then* B *is,*
signifies, *If* A *is* C, *then is* B *also* D,—in such cases
an easy and direct conversion is impossible, as a
categorical syllogism admits of only three principal
notions.   To accomplish a reduction at all, we must
make a circuit through a plurality of categorical syl-

a Krug. *Logik,* p. 258, Anm. 2.—E.D.

logisms before we can arrive at an identical conclusion,—a process which, so far from tending to simplify and explain, conduces only to perplex and obscure.[a]

Hypothetical syllogisms of one form easily convertible into that of another.

"On the other hand, we can always easily convert an hypothetical syllogism of one form into another,— the *modus ponens* into the *modus tollens*, the *modus tollens* into the *modus ponens*. This is done by a mere contraposition of the antecedent and consequent of the sumption. Thus, the Ponent or Constructive Syllogism :—

> *If Socrates be virtuous, then he merits esteem ;*
> *But Socrates is virtuous ;*
> *Therefore, he merits esteem,*

may thus be converted into a Tollent or Destructive Syllogism :—

> *If Socrates do not merit esteem, then he is not virtuous ;*
> *But he is virtuous ;*
> *Therefore, he merits esteem.*

"This latter syllogism, though apparently a Constructive syllogism, is in reality a Destructive. For *in modo ponente* we conclude from the truth of the antecedent to the truth of the consequent ; but here we really conclude from the falsehood of the consequent to the falsehood of the antecedent."[b] This latter syllogism, if fully expressed, would indeed be as follows :—

> *If Socrates do not merit esteem, he is not virtuous ;*
> *But Socrates is not not virtuous ;*
> *Therefore, he does not not merit esteem.*

3°, I now go on to a statement and consideration

a Compare Mark Duncan, *Instit. Log.*, L. iv., c. 6, § 4, p. 240 *et seq.* Derodon, *Logica Restituta, De Argumentatione*, § 106, p. 572.—ED.

[Bolzano, *Wissenschaftslehre, Logik*, ii. 266, p. 562.]

β Krug, *Logik*, p. 259-260.—ED.

of the special rules by which an hypothetical syllogism is governed.   ,

¶ LXVI. The special rules by which an Hypothetical Syllogism is regulated are the following :—

Par. LXVI.
3°, Special
Rules of
Hypotheti-
cal Syllo-
gism.

I. A regular and perfect hypothetical syllogism must have three propositions, in which, however, more than three principal notions may be found.

II. The Sumption is, in regard to quantity and quality, uniform, being always Definite and Affirmative ; whereas the Subsumption varies in both relations.

III. The Conclusion is regulated in quantity and quality by that member of the sumption which is not subsumed ; *in modo ponente*, they are congruent ; *in modo tollente*, they are opposed.[a]

"The question touching the special laws of the hypothetical syllogism, or, what is the same thing, the question touching the original and necessary form of the hypothetical syllogism as determined by its general principle,—the law of Reason and Consequent,—this question may be referred both to the whole reasoning and to its several parts. The original and necessary form of the hypothetical syllogism, as determined by its general principle, we have already considered. From this, as already noticed, it follows, as a corollary, that the hypothetical, like every other syllogism, must contain a threefold judgment : 1°, A judgment whose constituent members stand to each other in the relation of reason and consequent ; 2°, A judgment which subsumes as existent or non-

Explica-
tion.
First Rule.
This regu-
lates the
general
form of the
hypothetical
syllogism.

a Krug, *Logik*, § 83.—Ed.

346   LECTURES ON LOGIC.

LECT.
XVIII.

existent one or other of these constituent members, standing to each other in the relation of reason and consequent; and, 3°, Finally, a judgment decisive of the existence or non-existence of that constituent member which was not subsumed in the second judgment. In these three propositions,—sumption, subsumption, and conclusion,—there may, however, be found more than three principal notions; and this is always the case when the sumption contains more than three principal terms, as is exemplified in a proposition like the following :—*If God reward virtue, then will virtuous men be also happy.* Here, however, it must, at the same time, be understood, that this proposition, in which a larger plurality of notions than three is apparent, contains, however, only the thought of one antecedent and of one consequent; for a single consequent supposes a whole antecedent, how complex soever it may be, and a single antecedent involves in it a whole consequent, though made up of any number of parts. Both of these possibilities are seen in the example, now adduced, of an hypothetical judgment, in which there occur more than three principal notions. If, however, an hypothetical proposition involve only the thought of a single antecedent and of a single consequent, it will follow that any hypothetical syllogism consists not of more than three, but of less than three, capital notions; and, in a rigorous sense, this is actually the case."[a] On this ground, accordingly, some logicians of great acuteness have viewed the hypothetical syllogism as a syllogism of two terms and of two propositions.[β] This is, however,

(marginal note: Ground on which the Hypothetical Syllogism has been reported as having only two terms and two propositions.*)*

a Esser, *Logik,* § 92, p. 175-6.—Ed.

β See Kant, *Logik,* § 75. Kant's view is combated by Krug, *Logik,* §

43.—Ed. [A view similar to that of Kant is held by Weiss, *Logik,* §§ 210, 251; Herbart, *Logik,* § 65; Fischer, *Logik,* § 100, p. 137.]

erroneous; for, in an hypothetical syllogism, there _{LECT.}
are virtually three terms. "That under this form of _{XVIII.}
reasoning a whole syllogism can be evolved out of _{This view erroneous.}
not more than two capital notions depends on this,—
that the two constituent notions of an hypothetical
syllogism present a character in the sumption altogether different from what they exhibit in the subsumption and conclusion. In the sumption these
notions stand bound together in the relation of reason
and consequent, without, however, any determination
in regard to the reality or unreality of one or other;
if the one be, then the other is, is all that is enounced.
In the subsumption, on the other hand, the existence
or non-existence of what one or other of these notions
comprises is expressly asserted, and thus the concept
expressly affirmed or expressly denied manifestly
obtains in the subsumption a wholly different significance from what it bore when only enounced as a
condition of reality or unreality; and, in like manner,
that notion which the subsumption left untouched,
and concerning whose existence or non-existence the
conclusion decides, obtains a character altogether different in the end from what it presented in the
beginning. And thus, in strict propriety, there are
found only three capital notions in an hypothetical
syllogism—viz., 1°, The notion of the reciprocal dependence of subject and predicate; 2°, The notion of
the reality or unreality of the antecedent; and, 3°,
The notion of the reality or unreality of the consequent."[a] So much in explanation of the first special
law, or that regulative of the general form of the
hypothetical syllogism.

The second law states the conditions of these two

a Esser, loc. cit.—En.

premises,—that the sumption, in reference to its quantity and quality, is uniform, being always definite, that

is, singular or universal, and affirmative ; while the subsumption, in both relations, remains free.

That the
sumption
is always
definite to
be under-
stood in a
qualified
sense.
In regard to the sumption, when it is said that it is always definite, (that is, singular or universal,) and affirmative, this must be understood in a qualified sense. Touching the former, it may indeed be said that quantity may be altogether thrown out of account in an hypothetical syllogism.[a] For a reason being once supposed, its consequent is necessarily affirmed without limitation ; and, by the disjunction, the extension or comprehension of the subject is so defined, that the opposite determinations must together wholly exhaust it. It may, indeed, sometimes appear as if what was enounced in an hypothetical sumption, were enounced only of an indefinite number,—of some ; and it, consequently, then assumes the form of a particular proposition. For instance, *If some men are virtuous, then some other men are vicious.* But here it is easily seen, that such judgments are of an universal or exhaustive nature. In the proposition adduced the real antecedent is, *If some men (only) are virtuous,*—the real consequent is, *then all other men are vicious.* It would, perhaps, have been better had the relative totality of the major proposition of an hypothetical syllogism been expressed by another term than *universal.*[β] For the same reason it is, that the difference of extensive and comprehensive quantity determines no external change in the expression of an hypothetical syllogism ; for

a [See Alexander Aphrodisiensis, pp. 267, 344.—Ed.]
In Anal. Prior., f. 5 a. *Scholia,* ed.　β See above, p. 267. Compare
Brandis, p. 144. Derodon, *Logica*　Esser, *Logik,* § 92, p. 177.—Ed.
Restituta, p. 688.] [Compare above,

every hypothetical syllogism remains the same, whether LECT. XVIII. we read it in the one quantity or in the other.

In regard to the other statement of the rule,—that That the sumption is always affirmative. the sumption of an hypothetical syllogism must be always affirmative,—this likewise demands a word of illustration. It is true that the antecedent or the consequent of such a sumption may be negative as well as affirmative; for example, *If Caius be not virtuous, he is not entitled to respect; If the sun be not risen, it is not day.* But here the proposition, as an hypothetical judgment, is and must be affirmative. For the affirmative in such a judgment is contained in the positive assertion of the dependence of consequent or antecedent; and if such a dependence be not affirmed, an hypothetical judgment cannot exist.

In regard to what is stated in the rule concerning The subsumption. the conditions of the subsumption,—that this may either be general or particular, affirmative or negative,—it will not be requisite to say anything in illustration. For, as the subsumption is merely an absolute assertion of a single member of the sumption, and as such member may, as an isolated proposition, be of any quantity or any quality, it follows, that the subsumption is equally unlimited.

In reference to the third rule, which states that the Third Rule. conclusion is regulated in quantity and quality by that member of the sumption which is not subsumed, and this *in modo ponente* by congruence, *in modo tollente* by opposition, it will not be requisite to say much.

"In the conclusion, the latter clause of the sumption is affirmed *in modo ponente*, because the former is affirmed in the subsumption. In this case, the conclusion has the same quantity and quality as the

clause which it affirms. *In modo tollente* the antecedent of the sumption is denied in the conclusion;
because in the subsumption the *consequent* clause had
been denied. There thus emerges an opposition between that clause as denied in the conclusion, and
that clause as affirmed in the sumption. The conclusion is thus always opposed to the antecedent of the
sumption in quantity, or in quality, or in both together,
according as this is differently determined by the different constitution of the propositions. For example:—

> *If some men were omniscient, then would they be as Gods;*
> *But no man is a God;*
> *Therefore, some men are not omniscient, that is, no man is*
> *omniscient.*[a]

3. Hypothetico-disjunctive or Dilemmatic Syllogism.
I now proceed to the consideration of the last class
of syllogisms afforded by the Internal Form,—the
class of Dilemmatic or Hypothetico-disjunctive Syllogisms, and I comprise a general enunciation of their
nature in the following paragraph.

Par. LXVII. Hypothetico-disjunctive Syllogism or Dilemma.
¶ LXVII. If the sumption of a syllogism be at
once hypothetical and disjunctive, and if in the
subsumption the whole disjunction, as a consequent, be sublated, in order to sublate the antecedent in the conclusion;—such a reasoning is
called an *Hypothetico-disjunctive Syllogism*, or
a *Dilemma*. The form of this syllogism is the
following :—

> *If A exist, then either B or C exists;*
> *But neither B nor C exists;*
> *Therefore, A does not exist.*[β]

a Krug, *Logik,* § 83, p. 265.—Ed.
β Krug, *Logik,* § 67.—Ed. [Con-
tra, see Troxler, *Logik,* ii. p. 103 n°.
That the Dilemma is a negative induction, see Wallis, *Logica,* L. iii. c.
19, p. 218. Cf. Fries, *Logik,* § 60, p.
257; Aldrich, *Rudimenta Logicæ,* c.
iv. § 3, p. 107, Oxford, 1852; Platner, *Philosophische Aphorismen,* i. §
583, p. 250.]

We have formerly seen, that an hypothetical may
be combined with a disjunctive judgment; and if a
proposition of such a character be placed at the head
of a reasoning, we have the Hypothetico-disjunctive
Syllogism or Dilemma. This reasoning is properly an
hypothetical syllogism, in which the relation of the
antecedent to the consequent is not absolutely affirmed, but affirmed through opposite and reciprocally exclusive predicates. *If A exist, then either* B *or* C
exists. The sumption is thus at once hypothetical
and disjunctive. The subsumption then denies the
disjunctive members contained in the consequent or
posterior clause of the sumption. *But neither* B *nor*
C *exists.* And then the inference is drawn in the conclusion, that the reason given in the antecedent or
prior clause of the sumption must likewise be denied.
Therefore A does not exist.[a] For example :—

> *If man be not a morally responsible being, he must want either*
> *the power of recognising moral good (as an intelligent agent),*
> *or the power of willing it (as a free agent) ;*
> *But man wants neither the power of recognising moral good (as an*
> *intelligent agent), nor the power of willing it (as a free agent);*
> *Therefore, man is a morally responsible being.*

"An hypothetico-disjunctive syllogism is called the
dilemma or *horned syllogism* in the broader acceptation of the term (*dilemma, ceratinus, cornutus sc.*
syllogismus). We must not, however, confound the
cornutus and *crocodilinus* of the ancients with our
hypothetico-disjunctive syllogism. The former were
sophisms of a particular kind, which we are hereafter
to consider; the latter is a regular and legitimate
form of reasoning. In regard to the application of
the terms, it is called the *cornutus* or *horned syllogism*,

a Krug, *loc. cit.*—Ed.

because in the sumption the disjunctive members of
the consequent are opposed like horns to the assertion
of the adversary; with these we throw it from one
side to the other in the subsumption; in order to toss
it altogether away in the conclusion. If the disjunction has only two members, the syllogism is then
called a *dilemma* (*bicornis*) in the strict and proper
signification, literally *double sumption*. Of this the
example previously given is an instance. If it has
three, four, or five members, it is called *trilemma* (*tri-
cornis*), *tetralemma* (*quadricornis*), *pentalemma* (*quin-
quecornis*); if more than four, it is, however, usually
called *polylemma* (*multicornis*). But, in the looser
signification of the word, *Dilemma* is a generic expression for all or any of these." [a]

Rules for
sifting a
proposed
Dilemma.   "Considered in itself, the hypothetico-disjunctive
syllogism is not to be rejected, for in this form of
reasoning we can conclude with cogency, provided we
attend to the laws already given in regard to the
hypothetical and disjunctive syllogisms. It is not,
however, to be denied, that this kind of syllogism
is very easily abused for the purpose of deceiving,
through a treacherous appearance of solidity, and
from terrifying a timorous adversary by its horned
aspect. In the sifting of a proposed dilemma, we
ought, therefore, to look closely at the three following
particulars:— 1°, Whether a veritable consequence
subsists between the antecedent and consequent of
the sumption; 2°, Whether the opposition in the
consequent is thorough-going and valid; and, 3°,
Whether in the subsumption the disjunctive members are legitimately sublated. For the example of

a Krug, *loc. cit.* Anm. 2.—Ed. 268, 769.]
[Cf. Keckermann, *Opera*, t. i. pp.

a dilemma which violates these conditions, take the
following :—

> *If virtue were a habit worth acquiring, it must insure either*
> *power, or wealth, or honour, or pleasure;*
> *But virtue insures none of these;*
> *Therefore, virtue is not a habit worth attaining.*

" Here :—1°. The inference in general is invalid ; for
a thing may be worth acquiring though it does not
secure any of those advantages enumerated. 2°. The
disjunction is incomplete; for there are other goods
which virtue insures, though it may not insure those
here opposed. 3°. The subsumption is also vicious;
for virtue has frequently obtained for its possessors
the very advantages here denied." [a]

Before leaving this subject, it may be proper to
make two observations. The first of these is, that
though it has been stated that Categorical Syllogisms
are governed by the laws of Identity and Contradiction, that Disjunctive Syllogisms are governed by the
law of Excluded Middle, and that Hypothetical Syllogisms are governed by the law of Reason and Consequent,—this statement is not, however, to be understood as if, in these several classes of syllogism, no
other law were to be found in operation, except that
by which their peculiar form is determined. Such a
supposition would be altogether erroneous, for in all
of these different kinds of syllogism, besides the law
by which each class is principally regulated, and from
which it obtains its distinctive character, all the others
contribute, though in a less obtrusive manner, to allow
and to necessitate the process. Thus, though the laws
of Identity and Contradiction are the laws which pre-
eminently regulate the Categorical Syllogism,—still

The whole of the logical laws,— Identity, Contradiction, Excluded Middle, and Reason and Consequent,—are operative in each form of syllogism.

This illustrated. I. In Categorical Syllogisms.

a Krug, *Logik*, § 87, Anm. 3, p. 291.—Ed.

without the laws of Excluded Middle, and Reason and Consequent, all inference in these syllogisms would be impossible. Thus, though the law of Identity affords the basis of all affirmative, and the law of Contradiction the basis of all negative, syllogisms, still it is the law of Excluded Middle which legitimates the implication, that, besides affirmation and negation, there is no other possible quality of predication. In like manner, no inference in categorical reasoning could be drawn, were we to exclude the determination of Reason and Consequent. For we only, in deductive reasoning, conclude of a part what we assume of a whole, inasmuch as we think the whole as the reason —the condition—the antecedent—by which the part, as a consequent, is determined; and we only, in inductive reasoning, conclude of the whole what we assume of all the parts, inasmuch as we think all the parts as the reason—the condition—the antecedent—by which

The law of Identity formally the same with that of Reason and Consequent. the whole, as a consequent, is determined. In point of fact, logically or formally, the law of Identity and the law of Reason and Consequent in its affirmative form, are at bottom the same; the law of Identity constitutes only the law of Reason and Consequent,— the two relatives being conceived simultaneously, that is, as subject and predicate; the law of Reason and Consequent constitutes only the law of Identity, the two relatives being conceived in sequence, that is, as antecedent and consequent.[a] And as the law of Reason and Consequent, in its positive form, is only that of Identity in movement; so, in its negative form, it is only that of Contradiction in movement.

In Disjunctive Syllogisms, again, though the law of

a [Compare Köppen, *Darstellung et seq.*, Nürnberg, 1810.]
des Wesens der Philosophie, p. 102

Excluded Middle be the principle which bestows on them their peculiar form, still these syllogisms are not independent of the laws of Identity, of Contradiction, and of Reason and Consequent. The law of Excluded Middle cannot be conceived apart from the laws of Identity and Contradiction; these it implies, and, without the principle of Reason and Consequent, no movement from the condition to the conditioned, that is, from the affirmation or negation of one contradictory to the affirmation or negation of the other, would be possible.

Finally, in Hypothetical Syllogisms, though the law of Reason and Consequent be the prominent and distinctive principle, still the laws of Identity, Contradiction, and Excluded Middle are also there at work. The law of Identity affords the condition of Affirmative or Constructive, and the law of Contradiction of Negative or Destructive, Hypotheticals; while the law of Excluded Middle limits the reasoning to these two modes alone.

The second observation I have to make, is one suggested by a difficulty which has been proposed to me, in regard to the doctrine, that all reasoning is either from whole to part, or from the parts to the whole. The difficulty, which could only have presented itself to an acute and observant intellect, it gave me much satisfaction to hear proposed; and I shall have still greater gratification, if I should be able to remove it, by showing in what sense the doctrine advanced is to be understood. It was to this effect :—In Categorical Syllogisms, deductive and inductive, intensive and extensive, the reasoning is manifestly from whole to part, or from the parts to the whole, and, therefore, in regard to the doctrine in question, as relative to categorical reasoning, there was no difficulty. But this was not the case in regard to Hypothetical Syllogisms. These are governed by the law of Reason and Consequent, and it does not appear how the antecedent and consequent stand to each other in the relation of whole and part.

In showing how the reason and the consequent are to be viewed as whole and part, it is necessary, first, to repeat, that the reason or antecedent means the *condition*, that is, the complement of all without which something else would not be; and the consequent means the *conditioned*, that is, the complement of all that is determined to be by the existence of something else. You must further bear in mind, that we have nothing to do with things standing in the relation of reason and consequent, except in so far as they are thought to stand in that relation; it is with the *ratio cognoscendi*, not with the *ratio essendi*, that we have to do in Logic; the former is, in fact, alone properly denominated *reason* and *consequent*, while the latter ought to be distinguished as *cause* and *effect*. The *ratio essendi*, or the law of Cause and Effect, can indeed only be thought under the form of the *ratio cognoscendi*, or of the principle of Reason and Consequent; but as the two are not convertible, inasmuch as the one is far more extensive than the other, it is proper to distinguish them, and, therefore, it is to be recollected that Logic is alone conversant with the *ratio cognoscendi*, or the law of Reason and Consequent, as alone conversant with the form of thought.

This being understood, if the reason be conceived as that which conditions, in other words, as that which contains the necessity of the existence of the consequent, it is evident that it is conceived as containing the consequent. For, in the first place, a reason is LECT.
XVIII. only a reason if it be a sufficient reason, that is, if it comprise all the conditions, that is, all that necessitates the existence, of the consequent ; for if all the conditions of anything are present, that thing must necessarily exist, since, if it do not exist, then some condition of its existence must have been wanting, that is, there was not a sufficient reason of its existence, which is contrary to the supposition. In the second place, if the reason, the sufficient reason, be conceived as comprising all the conditions of the existence of the consequent, it must be conceived as comprising the consequent altogether ; for if the consequent be supposed to contain in it any one part not conceived as contained in the reason, it may contain two, three, or any number of parts equally uncontained in the reason, consequently it may be conceived as altogether uncontained in the reason. But this is to suppose, that it has no reason, or that it is not a consequent ; which again is contrary to the hypothesis. The law of Reason and Consequent, or of the Condition and the Conditioned, is only in fact another expression of Aristotle's law,—that the whole is necessarily conceived as prior to the part—*totum parte prius esse, necesse est.*[a] It is, however, more accurate ; for Aristotle's law is either inaccurate or ambiguous. Inaccurate, for it is no more true to say, that the whole is necessarily prior in the order of thought to

The Law of Reason and Consequent only another expression of Aristotle's law, that the whole is necessarily conceived as prior to the part.

Aristotle's law criticised.

a *Metaphysics*, iv. 11. Aristotle, however, allows a double relation. The whole, when conceived as actually constituted, must be regarded as prior to the parts ; for the latter only exist as parts in relation to the whole. Potentially, however, the parts may be regarded as prior ; for the whole might be destroyed as a system without the destruction of the parts. Where the whole is not conceived as actually constituted, this relation is reversed. Thus Aristotle's rule may be regarded as co-extensive with that given in the text. See the next note.—ED.

the parts, than to say that the parts are necessarily
prior in the order of thought to the whole. Whole
and parts are relatives, and as such are necessarily
coexistent in thought. But while each implies the
other, and the notion of each necessitates the notion
of the other, we may, it is evident, view either, in
thought, as the conditioning or antecedent, or as the
conditioned or consequent. Thus, on the one hand,
we may regard the whole as the prior and determining
notion, as containing the parts, and the parts, as the
posterior and determined notion, as contained by the
whole. On the other hand, we may regard the parts
as the prior and determining notion, as constituting
the whole, and the whole as the posterior and determined notion, as constituted by the parts.[a] In the
former case, the whole is thought as the reason, the
parts are thought as the consequent; in the latter, the
parts are thought as the reason, the whole is thought
as the consequent. Now in so far as the whole is
thought as the reason, there will be no difficulty in
admitting that the reason is conceived as containing
the parts. But it may be asked, how can the parts,
when thought as the reason, be said to contain the
whole? To this the answer is easy. All the parts
contain the whole, just as much as the whole contains
all the parts. Objectively considered, the whole does
not contain all the parts, nor do all the parts contain
the whole, for the whole and all the parts are precisely
equivalent, absolutely identical. But, subjectively

Whole and
Parts re-
spectively
may be
viewed in
thought
either as the
conditioning
or as the
conditioned.

a This is substantially expressed
by Aristotle, l. c., whose distinction
is applicable either to the order of
thought or to that of existence. Κατὰ
γένεσιν (i. e., regarded as a complete
system), the whole is actually, the
parts are only potentially, existent;
while, on the other hand, κατὰ
φθοράν (i. e., regarded as disorgan-
ised elements), the parts exist actually, the whole only potentially.
— ED.

considered, that is, as mere thoughts, we may either LECT.
think the whole by all the parts, or think all the parts XVIII.
by the whole. If we think all the parts by the whole,
we subordinate the notion of the parts to the notion
of the whole; that is, we conceive the parts to exist, as
we conceive their existence given through the existence
of the whole containing them. If we think the whole
by all the parts, we subordinate the notion of the
whole to the notion of the parts; that is, we conceive
the whole to exist, as we conceive its existence given
through the existence of the parts which constitute it.
Now, in the one case, we think the whole as conditioning or comprising the parts, in the other, the
parts as conditioning or comprising the whole. In
the former case, the parts are thought to exist, because
their whole exists; in the latter, the whole is thought
to exist, because its parts exist. In either case, the
prior or determining notion is thought to comprise
or to contain the posterior or determined. To apply *Application*
this doctrine :—On the one hand, every science is true, *of this doc-*
only as all its several rules are true; in this instance *trine to the*
solution of
the science is conceived as the determined notion, *the difficulty*
previously
that is, as contained in the aggregate of its constituent *stated.*
rules. On the other hand, each rule of any science is
true, only as the science itself is true ; in this instance
the rule is conceived as the determined notion, that
is, as contained in the whole science. Thus, every
single syllogism obtains its logical legitimacy, because
it is a consequent of the doctrine of syllogism ; the
latter is, therefore, the reason of each several syllogism,
and the whole science of Logic is abolished, if each
several syllogism, conformed to this doctrine, be not
valid. On the other hand, the science of Logic, as a
whole, is only necessary inasmuch as its complementary

doctrines are necessary; and these are only necessary inasmuch as their individual applications are necessary; if Logic, therefore, as a whole be not necessary, the necessity of the parts, which constitute, determine, and comprehend that whole, is subverted. In one relation, therefore, reason and consequent are as the whole and a contained part, in another, as all the parts and the constituted or comprised whole. But in both relations, the reason,—the determining notion, is thought as involving in it the existence of the consequent or determined notion. Thus, in one point of view, the genus is the determining notion, or reason, out of which are evolved, as consequents, the species and individual; in another, the individual is the determining notion or reason, out of which, as consequents, are evolved the species and genus.[a] In like manner, if we regard the subject as that in which the attributes inhere, in this view the subject is the reason, that is, the whole, of which the attributes are a part; whereas if we regard the attributes as the modes through which alone the subject can exist, in this view the attributes are the reason, that is, the whole, of which the subject is a part. In a word, whatever we think as conditioned, we think as contained by something else, that is, either as a part, or as a constituted whole; whatever we think as conditioning, we think either as a containing whole, or as a sum of constituting parts. What, therefore, the sumption of an hypothetical syllogism denotes, is simply this :— If A, a notion conceived as conditioning, and, therefore, as involving B, exist, then B also is necessarily conceived to exist, inasmuch as it is conceived as fully

---

a This is expressly allowed by   quoted from him by Sir W. Hamilton
Aristotle, *Metaph.*, iv. 25, and is   himself, *Discussions*, p. 173.—ED.

conditioned by, or as involved in, A. I am afraid that what I have now said may not be found to have removed the difficulty ; but if it suggest to you a train of reflection which may lead you to a solution of the difficulty by your own effort, it will have done better.

So much for Hypothetico-disjunctive syllogisms, the last of the four classes determined by the internal form of reasoning. In these four syllogisms,—the Categorical, the Disjunctive, the Hypothetical, and the Hypothetico-disjunctive, all that they exhibit is conformable to the necessary laws of thought, and they are each distinguished from the other by their essential nature ; for their sumptions, as judgments, present characters fundamentally different, and from the sumption, as a general rule, the validity of syllogisms primarily and principally depends.

LECTURE XIX.

STOICHEIOLOGY.

SECTION II.—OF THE PRODUCTS OF THOUGHT.

III.—DOCTRINE OF REASONINGS.

SYLLOGISMS.—THEIR DIVISIONS ACCORDING TO EXTERNAL FORM.

A. COMPLEX,—EPICHEIREMA AND SORITES.

LECT.
XIX.
——
Syllogisms.
—their Ex-
ternal Form. IN our treatment of Syllogisms, we have hitherto taken note only of the Internal or Essential Form of Reasoning. But besides this internal or essential form there is another,—an External or Accidental Form ; and as the former was contained in the reciprocal relations of the constituent parts of the syllogism, as determined by the nature of the thinking subject itself, so the latter is contained in the outer expression or enouncement of the same parts, whereby the terms and propositions are variously affected in respect of their number, position, and order of consecution. The varieties of Syllogism arising from their external form may, I think, be conveniently reduced to the three heads expressed in the following paragraph :—

Par. LXVIII.
Division of
Syllogisms
according
to External
Form. ¶ LXVIII. Syllogisms, in respect of their External Form, admit of a threefold modification. For while, as pure, they are at once *Simple*, and *Complete*, and *Regular*, so, as qualified, they are either *Complex*, or *Incomplete*, or *Irregular* : the two former of these modifications regarding the number of their parts, as apparently either too many or too few ; the last regarding the inverted order in which these parts are enounced.

I shall consider these several divisions in their order ; and, first, of the syllogisms which vary from the simple form of reasoning by their apparent complexity.

Explication.
A. Complex Syllogisms.

But before touching on the varieties of syllogism afforded by their complexity of composition, it may be proper to premise a few words in regard to the relation of syllogisms to each other. "Every syllogism may be considered as absolute and independent, inasmuch as it always contains a complete and inclusive series of thought. But a syllogism may also stand to other syllogisms in such a relation that, along with those correlative syllogisms, it makes up a greater or lesser series of thoughts, all holding to each other the dependence of antecedent and consequent. And such a reciprocal dependence of syllogisms becomes necessary, when one or other of the predicates of the principal syllogism is destitute of complete certainty, and when this certainty must be established through one or more correlative syllogisms."[a]   "A syllogism, viewed as an isolated and independent whole, is called a *Monosyllogism* (*monosyllogismus*), that is, a single reasoning ; whereas, a series of correlative syllogisms following each other in the reciprocal relation of antecedent and consequent, is called a *Polysyllogism* (*polysyllogismus*), that is, a multiplex or composite reasoning, and may likewise be denominated a *Chain of Reasoning* (*series syllogistica*). Such a chain,—

Relation of syllogisms to each other.

Classes and designations of related syllogisms. Monosyllogism.

Polysyllogism, or Chain of Reasoning.

a Esser, *Logik,* § 104.—Ed.

such a series, may, however, have such an order of
dependence, that either each successive syllogism is
the reason of that which preceded, or the preceding

This Ana-
lytic and
Synthetic.

syllogism is the reason of that which follows. In the
former case, we conclude analytically or regressively;
in the second, synthetically or progressively. That
syllogism in the series which contains the reason of

Prosyllo-
gism.

the premise of another, is called a *Prosyllogism* (*pro-
syllogismus*); and that syllogism which contains the

Episyllo-
gism.

consequent of another, is called an *Episyllogism* (*epi-
syllogismus*). Every Chain of Reasoning must, therefore, be made up both of Prosyllogisms and of Epi-
syllogisms."[a] "When the series is composed of more
than two syllogisms, the same syllogism may, in different relations, be at once a prosyllogism and an episyllogism; and that reasoning which contains the
primary or highest reason is alone exclusively a prosyllogism, as that reasoning which announces the last
or lowest consequent is alone exclusively an episyllogism. But this concatenation of syllogisms, as antecedents and consequents, may be either manifest, or
occult, according as the plurality of syllogisms may
either be openly displayed, or as it may appear only
as a single syllogism. The polysyllogism is, therefore,
likewise either manifest or occult. The occult polysyllogism, with which alone we are at present concerned, consists either of partly complete and partly
abbreviated syllogisms, or of syllogisms all equally
abbreviated. In the former case, there emerges the
complex syllogism called *Epicheirema*; in the latter,
the complex syllogism called *Sorites*."[b] Of these in
their order.

a Krug, *Logik*, § 111.—Ed.   Reusch, *Systema Logicum*, § 575, p.
b Esser, *Logik*, § 104.—Ed.   [Cf. 564, Iena, 1741.]

¶ LXIX. A syllogism is now vulgarly called an *Epicheirema* (ἐπιχείρημα), when to either of the two premises, or to both, there is annexed a reason for its support. As :—

> B is A;
> But C is B; for it is D;
> Therefore, C is also A.[a]
>
> Or,
>
> All vice is odious;
> But avarice is a vice; for it makes men slaves;
> Therefore, avarice is odious.[b]

In illustration of this paragraph, it is to be observed, that the Epicheirema, or Reason-rendering Syllogism, is either single or double, according as one or both of the premises are furnished with an auxiliary reason. The single epicheirema is either an epicheirema of the first or second order, according as the adscititious proposition belongs to the sumption or to the subsumption. There is little or nothing requisite to be stated in regard to this variety of complex syllogism, as it is manifestly nothing more than a regular episyllogism with an abbreviated prosyllogism interwoven. There might be something said touching the name, which, among the ancient rhetoricians, was used now in a stricter, now in a looser, signification.[γ] This, however, as it has little interest in a logical point of view, I shall not trouble you by detailing; and now proceed to a far more important and interesting subject,

a In full,—
  C is D;
  D is B;
  Therefore, C is B.
β In full,—
  What makes men slaves is a vice;
  But avarice makes men slaves;
  Therefore, avarice is a vice.
γ For some notices of these vari-

ations, see Quintilian, *Inst. Orat.*, v. 10, 2, v. 14, 5. Compare also Schweighæuser on Epictetus, i. 8 ; Trendelenburg, *Elementa Logicæ Aristotelicæ*, § 33 ; Facciolati, *Acroases, De Epichirremate*, p. 127 et seq. In Aristotle the term is used for a dialectic syllogism. See *Topics*, viii. 11.—ED.

— the second variety of complex syllogisms, — the Sorites.

¶ LXX. When, on the common principle of all reasoning, — that the part of a part is a part of the whole, — we do not stop at the second gradation, or at the part of the highest part, and conclude that part of the whole, — as *All* B *is a part of the whole* A, *and all* C *is a part of the part* B, *therefore all* C *is also a part of the whole* A, — but proceed to some indefinitely remoter part, as, D, E, F, G, H, &c., which, on the general principle, we connect in the conclusion with its remotest whole, — this complex reasoning is called a *Chain-Syllogism* or *Sorites*. If the whole from which we descend be a comprehensive quantity, the Sorites is one of Comprehension ; if it be an extensive quantity, the Sorites is one of Extension. The formula of the first will be :—

1) E *is* D ; that is, E *comprehends* D ;
2) D *is* C ; that is, D *comprehends* C ;
3) C *is* B ; that is, C *comprehends* B ;
4) B *is* A ; that is, B *comprehends* A ;
Therefore, E *is* A ; in other words, E *comprehends* A.

The formula of the second will be :—

1) B *is* A ; that is, A *contains under it* B ;
2) C *is* B ; that is, B *contains under it* C ;
3) D *is* C ; that is, C *contains under it* D ;
4) E *is* D ; that is, D *contains under it* E ;
Therefore, E *is* A ; in other words, A *contains under it* F.

These reasonings are both *Progressive*, each in its several quantity, as descending from whole to part. But as we may also, arguing back from part to whole, obtain the same conclusion, there is also competent in either quantity a *Regressive Sorites*. However, the formula of the Regressive Sorites in the one quantity, will be only that of the Progressive Sorites in the other.[a]

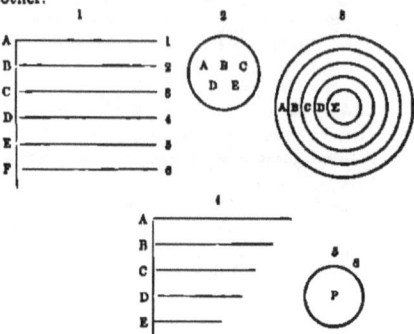

As a concrete example of these :—

I. PROGRESSIVE COMPREHENSIVE SORITES.

> *Bucephalus is a horse ;*
> *A horse is a quadruped ;*
> *A quadruped is an animal ;*
> *An animal is a substance ;*
> *Therefore, Bucephalus is a substance.*

[a] [On the Sorites in general, see Crakanthorpe, *Logica*, L. iii. c. 22, p. 219 ; Vella, *Dialect.*, L. iii. c. 54, fol. 38, ed. 1609 ; M. Duncan, *Instit. Log.*, L. iv. c. vii. § 6, p. 255 ; Facciolati, *Acroases, De Sorite*, p. 16 *et seq.* ; Melanchthon, *Erotem. Dial.*, L. iii. *De Sorite*, p. 743 ; Wolf, *Phil. Rat.*, § 466 *et seq.* ; Walch, *Lexikon*, s. "Sorites;" Fries, *Logik*, § 54.]

β Diagrams Nos. 1 and 2 represent the Affirmative Sorites in the cases in which the concepts are coextensive.—See above, p. 189, Diagram 2. Diagrams Nos. 3 and 4 represent the Affirmative Sorites in the case in which the concepts are subordinate.—See above, p. 189, Diagram 3. Diagram No. 5, taken in connection with No. 3, represents the Negative Sorites. Thus, to take the Progressive Comprehensive Sorites :— E is D, D is C, C is B, B is A, so A is P; therefore, no E is P.—ED.

Or as explicated :—

*The representation of the individual Bucephalus comprehends
or contains in it the notion horse ;*
The notion horse comprehends the notion quadruped ;
The notion quadruped comprehends the notion animal ;
The notion animal comprehends the notion substance ;
*Therefore, (on the common principle that the part of a part
is a part of the whole,) the representation of the individual, Bucephalus, comprehends or contains in it the
notion substance.*

II. REGRESSIVE COMPREHENSIVE SORITES.

An animal is a substance ;
A quadruped is an animal ;
A horse is a quadruped ;
Bucephalus is a horse ;
Therefore, Bucephalus is a substance.

Or as explicated :—

The notion animal comprehends the notion substance ;
The notion quadruped comprehends the notion animal ;
The notion horse comprehends the notion quadruped ; .
The representation, Bucephalus, comprehends the notion horse ;
*Therefore, (on the common principle, &c.) the representation,
Bucephalus, comprehends the notion substance.*

III. PROGRESSIVE EXTENSIVE SORITES, (which is, as enounced
by the common copula, identical in expression with the
Regressive Comprehensive Sorites, No. II.)

An animal is a substance ;
A quadruped is an animal ;
A horse is a quadruped ;
Bucephalus is a horse ;
Therefore, Bucephalus is a substance.

Or as explicated :—

The notion animal is contained under the notion substance ;
The notion quadruped is contained under the notion animal ;
The notion horse is contained under the notion quadruped ;

*The representation Bucephalus is contained under the notion
horse ;*

*Therefore, (on the common principle, &c.) the representation
Bucephalus is contained under the notion substance.*

IV. THE REGRESSIVE EXTENSIVE SORITES, (which is, as expressed
by the ambiguous copula, verbally identical with the
Progressive Comprehensive Sorites, No. I.)

> *Bucephalus is a horse ;*
> *A horse is a quadruped ;*
> *A quadruped is an animal ;*
> *An animal is a substance ;*
> *Therefore, Bucephalus is a substance.*

Or as explicated :—

*The representation Bucephalus is contained under the notion
horse ;*
The notion horse is contained under the notion quadruped ;
The notion quadruped is contained under the notion animal ;
The notion animal is contained under the notion substance ;
*Therefore, the representation Bucephalus is contained under
the notion substance.*

There is thus not the smallest difficulty either in
regard to the peculiar nature of the Sorites, or in regard to its relation to the simple syllogism. In the
first place, it is evident that the formal inference in
the Sorites is equally necessary and equally manifest
as in the simple syllogism, for the principle,—the part
of a part is a part of the whole,—is plainly not less
applicable to the remotest, than to the most proximate,
link in the subordination of whole and part. In the
second place, it is evident that the Sorites can be
resolved into as many simple syllogisms as there are
middle terms between the subject and predicate of the
conclusion, that is, intermediate wholes and parts between the greatest whole and the smallest part, which
the reasoning connects. Thus, the concrete example

*1. The for-
mal infer-
ence in Sori-
tes equally
necessary
as in simple
syllogism.*

*2. Sorites
resolvable
into simple
syllogisms.*

LECT.
XIX. of a Sorites, already given, is virtually composed of three simple syllogisms. It will be enough to show this in one of the quantities ; and, as the most perspicuous, let us take that of Comprehension.

This illus-
trated. The Progressive Sorites in this quantity was as follows, (and it is needless, I presume, to explicate it) :—

> *Bucephalus is a horse ;*
> *A horse is a quadruped ;*
> *A quadruped is an animal ;*
> *An animal is a substance ;*
> *Therefore, Bucephalus is a substance.*

Here, besides the major and minor terms, (*Bucephalus* and *substance*), we have three middle terms, —*horse*,—*quadruped*,—*animal.* We shall, consequently, have three simple syllogisms. Thus, in the first place, we obtain from the middle term *horse*, the following syllogism, concluding *quadruped* of *Bucephalus :*—

> I.—*Bucephalus is a horse ;*
> *But a horse is a quadruped ;*
> *Therefore, Bucephalus is a quadruped.*

Having thus established that *Bucephalus is a quadruped*, we employ *quadruped* as a middle term by which to connect *Bucephalus* with *animal.* We, therefore, make the conclusion of the previous syllogism (No. I.) the sumption of the following syllogism (No. II.)

> II.—*Bucephalus is a quadruped ;*
> *But a quadruped is an animal ;*
> *Therefore, Bucephalus is an animal.*

Having obtained another step, we, in like manner, make *animal*, which was the minor term in the preceding syllogism, the middle term of the following ; and the conclusion of No. II. forms the major premise of No. III.

III.—*Bucephalus is an animal ;*
But an animal is a substance;
Therefore, Bucephalus is a substance.

In this last syllogism, we reach a conclusion identical with that of the Sorites.

In the third place, it is evident that the Sorites is equally natural as the simple syllogism ; and, as the relation is equally cogent and equally manifest between a whole and a remote part, and a whole and a proximate part, that it is far less prolix, and, consequently, far more convenient. What is omitted in a Sorites is only the idle repetition of the same self-evident principle, and as this can without danger or inconvenience be adjourned until the end of a series of notions in the dependence of mutual subordination, it is plain that, in reference to such a series, a single Sorites is as much preferable to a number of simple syllogisms, as a comprehensive cipher is preferable to the articulate enumeration of the units which it collectively represents.

Before proceeding to touch on the logical history of this form of syllogism, and to comment on the doctrine in regard to it maintained by all logicians, I shall conclude what it is proper further to state concerning its general character.

¶ LXXI. A Sorites may be either Categorical or Hypothetical; and, in both forms, it is governed by the following laws :—Speaking of the Common or Progressive Sorites, (in which reasoning you will observe the meaning of the word *progressive* is reversed), which proceeds from the individual to the general, and to which the other form may be easily reduced :—1°. The number of the premises is unlimited. 2°. All the premises, with exception of the last, must be affirmative, and, with exception of the first, definite. 3°. The first premise may be either definite or indefinite. 4°. The last may be either negative or affirmative.

I have already given you examples of the categorical Sorites. The following is the formula of the hypothetical :—

PROGRESSIVE.	REGRESSIVE.
If D *is,* C *is;*	*If* D *is,* A *is;*
If C *is,* B *is;*	*If* C *is,* D *is;*
If B *is,* A *is;*	*If* D *is,* C *is;*
(In modo ponente),	(In modo ponente),
Now D *is;*	*Now* D *is;*
Therefore, A *is also.*	*Therefore,* A *is.*
(Or in modo tollente),	(Or in modo tollente),
Now A *is not;*	*Now* A *is not;*
Therefore, D *is not.*	*Therefore,* D *is not.*

Or to take a concrete example :—

PROGRESSIVE.

If Harpagon be avaricious, he is intent on gain;
If intent on gain, he is discontented;
If discontented, he is unhappy;
Now Harpagon is avaricious;
He is, therefore, unhappy.

REGRESSIVE.

If Harpagon be discontented, he is unhappy;
If intent on gain, he is discontented;
If avaricious, he is intent on gain;
Now Harpagon is avaricious;
Therefore, he is unhappy.

In regard to the resolution of the Hypothetical Sorites into simple syllogisms, it is evident that in this Progressive Sorites we must take the first two propositions as premises, and then in the conclusion connect the antecedent of the former proposition with the consequent of the latter. Thus :—

I.—*If Harpagon be avaricious, he is intent on gain ;*
If intent on gain, he is discontented ;
Therefore, if Harpagon be avaricious, he is discontented.

We now establish this conclusion, as the sumption of the following syllogism :—

II.—*If Harpagon be avaricious, he is discontented ;*
If discontented, he is unhappy ;
Therefore, if Harpagon be avaricious, he is unhappy.

In like manner we go on to the next syllogism :—

III.—*If Harpagon be avaricious, he is unhappy ;*
Now Harpagon is avaricious ;
Therefore, he is unhappy.

In the Regressive Sorites, we proceed in the same fashion ; only that, as here the consequent of the second proposition is the antecedent of the first, we reverse the consecution of these premises. Thus :—

I.—*If Harpagon be intent on gain, he is discontented ;*
If discontented, he is unhappy ;
Therefore, if Harpagon be intent on gain, he is unhappy.

We then take the third proposition for the sumption of the next, the second, syllogism, and the conclusion of the preceding for its subsumption :—

II.—*If Harpagon be avaricious, he is intent on gain ;*
If intent on gain, he is unhappy ;
Therefore, if Harpagon be avaricious, he is unhappy.

We now take this last conclusion for the sumption
of the last syllogism :—

> III.—*If Harpagon be avaricious, he is unhappy;*
> *Now Harpagon is avaricious;*
> *Therefore, he is unhappy.*

Disjunctive Sorites. But it may be asked, can there be no Disjunctive
Sorites? To this it may be answered, that in the
sense in which a categorical and hypothetical syllogism is possible,—viz., so that a term of the preceding
proposition should be the subject or predicate of the
following,—in this sense, a disjunctive sorites is impossible; since two opposing notions, whether as contraries or contradictories, exclude each other, and cannot, therefore, be combined as subject and predicate.
But when the object has been determined by two
opposite characters, the disjunct members may be
amplified at pleasure, and there follows certainly a
correct conclusion, provided that the disjunction be
logically accurate. As :—

> A *is either* B *or* C.
>
> Now,

B *is either* D *or* E;	C *is either* F *or* G;
D *is either* H *or* I;	F *is either* M *or* N;
E *is either* K *or* L.	G *is either* O *or* P.

Therefore, A *is either* H, *or* I, *or* K, *or* L, *or* M, *or* N, *or* O, *or* P.

Complex and inconceivable. Although, therefore, it be true that such a Sorites
is correct; still, were we astricted to such a mode
of reasoning, thought would be so difficult, as to
be almost impossible. But we never are obliged
to employ such a reasoning; for when we are once
assured that A *is either* B *or* C, and assured we are
of this by one of the fundamental laws of thought,

we have next to consider whether A is B or C, and
if A is B, then all that can be said of C, and if A is ——
C, then all that can be said of B, is dismissed as wholly
irrelevant.   In like manner, in the case of B, it must
be determined whether it is D or E, and in the case of
C, whether it is F or G; and this being determined,
one of the two members is necessarily thrown out of
account.   And this compendious method we follow in
the process of thought spontaneously, and as if by a
natural impulsion.

So much for the logical character of the Sorites.
It now remains to make some observations, partly
historical, partly critical, in connection with this subject.

In regard to the history of the logical doctrine of *Historical
notice of the
logical doc-
trine of
Sorites.*
this form of reasoning, it seems to be taken for granted,
in all the systems of the science, that both the name
Sorites, as applied to a chain-syllogism, and the
analysis of the nature of that syllogism, are part and
parcel of the logical inheritance bequeathed to us by
Aristotle.   Nothing can, however, be more erroneous. *Neither
name nor
doctrine
found in
Aristotle.*
The name Sorites does not occur in any logical treatise
of Aristotle; nor, as far as I have been able to discover, is there, except in one vague and cursory allusion, any reference to what the name is now employed
to express.[a]   Nay, further, the word *Sorites* is never,
I make bold to say, applied by any ancient writer
to designate a certain form of reasoning.   On the
contrary, *Sorites*, though a word in not unfrequent

a The passage referred to is probably *Anal. Prior.*, i. 25.   But there
was no need of a special treatment
of the Sorites, as it is merely a combination of ordinary syllogisms, and
subject to the same rules.—ED. [The
principle of the Sorites is to be found
in Aristotle's rule, *Categ.*, c. 2:
"Prædicatum prædicati est prædicatum subjecti." See also, *Anal.
Post.*, i. 23 *et seq.*   Cf. Pacius,
Comment., p. 159; Bertius, *Logica
Peripatetica*, L. iii. Appendix, p.
179.]

LECT.
XIX.

Sorites,
with ancient
authors,
used to de-
signate a
particular
kind of
sophism.

The nature
of this
sophism.

employment by ancient authors, nowhere occurs in any other logical meaning than that of a particular kind of sophism, of which the Stoic Chrysippus was reputed the inventor.[a] Σωρὸς, you know, in Greek, means a *heap* or *pile* of any aggregated substances, as sand, wheat, &c.; and *Sorites*, literally *a heaper*, was a name given to a certain captious argument, which in Latin obtained from Cicero the denomination of *acervalis*.[β] The nature of the argument was this:—You were asked, for example, whether a certain quantity of something of variable amount were large or small,—say a certain sum of money. If you said it was small, the adversary went on gradually adding to it, asking you at each increment whether it were still small; till at length you said that it was large. The last sum which you had asserted to be small, was now compared with that which you now asserted to be large, and you were at length forced to acknowledge, that one sum which you maintained to be large, and another which you maintained to be small, differed from each other by the very pettiest coin, or, if the subject were a pile of wheat, by a single corn. This sophism, as applied by Eubulides, (who is even stated by Laertius[γ] to be the inventor of the Sorites in general,) took the name of φαλακρὸς, *calvus, the bald.* It was asked,—was a man bald who had so many thousand hairs; you answer, No: the antagonist goes on diminishing and diminishing the number, till either you admit that he who

a Persius, *Sat.* vi. 80:
"Inventus, Chrysippe, tui finitor acervi."—ED.

[Cicero applies *Sorites* to an argument which we would call a *Sorites*, but it could also be a *Chrysippean.* *De Finibus,* L. iv. c. 18.]

β *De Divinatione*, ii. 4: "Quemadmodum Soriti resistas? quem, si necesse sit, Latino verbo liceat acervalem appellare." Cf. Facciolati, *Acervus*, p. 17 et seq.—ED.

γ L. ii. § 108.—ED.

was not bald with a certain number of hairs, becomes
bald when that complement is diminished by a single
hair; or you go on denying him to be bald, until
his head be hypothetically denuded. Such was the
quibble which obtained the name of *Sorites,—acervalis, climax, gradatio,* &c. This, it is evident, had no
real analogy with the form of reasoning now known
in logic under the name of *Sorites.*

But when was the name perverted to this, its Laurentius Valla the first to use Sorites in its present acceptation.
secondary signification? Of this I am confident,
that the change was not older than the fifteenth century. It occurs in none of the logicians previous
to that period. It is to be found in none of the
Greek logicians of the Lower Empire; nor is it to be
met with in any of the more celebrated treatises on
Logic by the previous Latin schoolmen. The earliest
author to whose writings I have been able to trace
it, is the celebrated Laurentius Valla, whose work
on *Dialectic* was published after the middle of the
fifteenth century. He calls the chain-syllogism—
" concervatio syllogismorum (quem Graeci σωρὸν vocant.) " [a] I may notice that in the *Dialectica* of his
contemporary and rival, George of Trebisond, the process itself is described, but, what is remarkable, no
appropriate name is given to it.[β] In the systems of
Logic after the commencement of the sixteenth century, not only is the form of reasoning itself described,
but described under the name it now bears.

I have been thus particular in regard to the history The doctrine of logicians regarding the Sorites illustrates
of the Sorites,—word and thing,—not certainly on
account of the importance of this history, considered

a *Dialecticæ Disputationes,* Lib.
iii. c. 12. See *Laurentii Vallæ Opera,*
Basileæ, 1540, p. 742.—ED.
β See *Georgii Trapezuntii De Re*

Dialectica Libellus, Coloniæ, 1533, f.
60 a. Cf. the Scholia of Neomagus,
ibid. f. 67 b.—ED.

their one-
sided view
of the
nature of
reasoning
in general.

in itself, but because it will enable you the better to
apprehend what is now to be said of the illustration
which the doctrine, taught by logicians themselves,
of the nature of this particular process, affords of the
one-sided view which they have all taken of the nature
of reasoning in general.

I have already shown, in regard to the simple syllogism, that all deductive reasoning is from whole to
part; that there are two kinds of logical whole and
two kinds of logical part,—the one in the quantity of
comprehension, the other in the quantity of extension;
and that there are consequently two kinds of reasoning corresponding to these several quantities. I further showed that logicians had in simple syllogisms
marvellously overlooked one, and that the simplest
and most natural, of these descriptions of reasoning,—
the reasoning in the quantity of comprehension; and
that all their rules were exclusively relative to the
reasoning which proceeds in the quantity of extension.
Now, in to-day's Lecture, I have shown that, as in
simple syllogisms, so in the complex form of the
Sorites, there is equally competent a reasoning in comprehension and in extension,—though undoubtedly,
in the one case as in the other, the reasoning in comprehension is more natural and easy in its evolution
than the reasoning in extension, inasmuch as the
middle term, in the former, is really intermediate in
position, standing between the major and the minor
terms, whereas, in the latter, the middle term is not
in situation middle, but occupies the position of one
or other of the extremes.

Now, if in the case of simple syllogisms it be marvellous that logicians should have altogether overlooked the possibility of a reasoning in comprehension,

it is doubly marvellous that, with this their prepossession, they should, in the case of the Sorites, have
altogether overlooked the possibility of a reasoning in
extension. But so it is.[a] They have all followed
each other in defining the Sorites, as a concatenated
syllogism in which the predicate of the proposition
preceding is made the subject of the proposition following, until we arrive at the concluding proposition,
in which the predicate of the last of the premises is
enounced of the subject of the first. This definition
applies only to the Progressive Sorites in comprehension, and to the Regressive Sorites in extension : but
that they did not contemplate the latter form at all is
certain, both because it is not lightly to be presumed
that they had in view that artificial and recondite
form, and because the examples and illustrations they
supply positively prove that they had not.

To the Progressive Sorites in extension, and to the
Regressive Sorites in comprehension, this definition is
inapplicable ; for in these, the subject of the premise
preceding is not the predicate of the premise following.
But the difference between the two forms is better
stated thus :—In the Progressive Sorites of comprehension and the Regressive Sorites of extension, the
middle terms are the predicates of the prior premises,
and the subjects of the posterior ; the middle term
is here in position intermediate between the extremes.
On the contrary, in the Progressive Sorites of extension and in the Regressive Sorites of comprehension,
the middle terms are the subjects of the prior pre-

---

a [Ridiger notices the error of
those who make Sorites only of
comprehensive whole. See his *De
Sensu Veri et Falsi*, L. ii. c. 10, §
5, p. 400. Cf. p. 343 n., § 6.] ["Er-
rant vulgo Peripatetici, et cum his
Gassendus, qui Soritem solum ad
prædicatum pertinere existimat."—
ED.]

mises and the predicates of the posterior ; the middle
term is here in position not intermediate between the
extremes.

Probable
reason why
logicians
overlooked,
in the case
of simple
syllogisms,
the reason-
ing in Com-
prehension.
To the question,—why, in the case of simple syllogisms, the logicians overlooked the reasoning in comprehension, and, in the case of the Sorites, the reasoning in extension,—it is perhaps impossible to afford a
satisfactory explanation. But we may plausibly conjecture what it is out of our power certainly to prove.
In regard to simple syllogisms, it was an original
dogma of the Platonic school, and an early dogma of
the Peripatetic, that philosophy,—that science, strictly
so called,—was only conversant with, and was exclusively contained in, universals ; and the doctrine of
Aristotle, which taught that all our general knowledge is only an induction from an observation of
particulars, was too easily forgotten or perverted by
his followers. It thus obtained almost the force of an
acknowledged principle, that everything to be known
must be known under some general form or notion.
Hence the exaggerated importance attributed to definition and deduction : it not being considered, that
we only take out of a general notion what we had
previously placed therein ; and that the amplification
of our knowledge is not to be sought for from above
but from below,—not from speculation about abstract
generalities, but from the observation of concrete particulars. But however erroneous and irrational, the
persuasion had its day and influence ; and it perhaps
determined, as one of its effects, the total neglect of
one half, and that not the least important half, of the
reasoning process. For while men thought only of
looking upwards to the more extensive notions, as the
only objects and the only media of science, they took

little heed of the more comprehensive notions, and
absolutely contemned individuals, as objects which
could neither be scientifically known in themselves,
nor supply the conditions of scientifically knowing
aught besides.   The logic of comprehension and of
induction was, therefore, neglected or ignored,—the
logic of extension and deduction exclusively cultivated, as alone affording the rules by which we might
evolve higher notions into their subordinate concepts.
This may help to explain why, subsequently to Aristotle, Logic was cultivated in so partial a manner;
but why, subsequently to Bacon, the logic of comprehension should still have escaped observation and
study, I am altogether at a loss to imagine.   But the
question,—why, when reasoning in general was viewed
only as in the quantity of extension, the minor form
of the Sorites should have been viewed as exclusively
in that of comprehension,—may perhaps be explained
by the following consideration : this form was not
originally analysed and expounded by the acuteness
of Aristotle.   But it could not escape notice that there
was a form of reasoning, of very frequent employment
both by philosophers and rhetoricians, in which a single
conclusion was drawn from a multiplicity of premises,
and in which the predicate of the foregoing premise
was usually the subject of the following.   Cicero, for
example, and Seneca, are full of such arguments ; and
the natural and easy evolution of the reasoning is
indeed peculiarly appropriate to demonstration.   Thus,
to prove that every body is movable, we have the
following self-evident deduction.   Every body is in
space ; what is in space is in some one part of space ;
what is in one part of space may be in another ; what
may be in another part of space may change its space ;

And why,
in the case
of the Sori-
tes, they
overlooked
the reason-
ing in Ex-
tension.

what may change its space is movable; therefore,
every body is movable. When, therefore, Valla, or
whoever else has the honour of first introducing the
consideration of this form of reasoning into Logic, was
struck with the cogency and clearness of this compendious argumentation, he did not attempt to reduce
it to the conditions of the extensive syllogism; and
subsequent logicians, when the form was once introduced and recognised in their science, were, as usual,
content to copy one from another, without subjecting
their borrowed materials to any original or rigorous
criticism.

> Ut nemo in sese tentat descendere ;—nemo !
> Sed præcedenti spectatur mantica tergo. [a]

Accordingly, not one of them has noticed, that the
Sorites of their systems proceeds in a different quantity
from that of their syllogisms in general,—that their
logic is thus at variance with itself; far less did any
of them observe, that this and all other forms of
reasoning are capable of being drawn in another
quantity from that which they all exclusively contemplated. And yet, had they applied their observation
without prepossession to the matter, they would easily
have seen that the Sorites could be cast in the quantity of extension, equally as common syllogisms, and
that common syllogisms could be cast in the quantity
of comprehension, equally as the Sorites. I have
already shown that the same Sorites may be drawn
either in comprehension or in extension; and in both
quantities proceed either by progression or by regres-
Example sion. But the example given may perhaps be viewed
of the Sori-
tes in Com- as selected. Let us, therefore, take any other; and

a Persius, iv. 23.—Ed.

the first that occurs to my recollection is the following
from Seneca,[a] which I shall translate :—

> *He who is prudent is temperate ;*
> *He who is temperate is constant ;*
> *He who is constant is unperturbed ;*
> *He who is unperturbed is without sorrow ;*
> *He who is without sorrow is happy;*
> *Therefore, the prudent man is happy.*

In this Sorites everything slides easily and smoothly
from the whole to the parts of comprehension. But,
though the process will be rather more by hitches, the
descent under extension will, if not quite so pleasant,
be equally rapid and certain.

> *He who is without sorrow is happy ;*
> *He who is unperturbed is without sorrow ;*
> *He who is constant is unperturbed ;*
> *He who is temperate is constant ;*
> *He who is prudent is temperate ;*
> *Therefore, the prudent man is happy.*

I do not think it necessary to explicate these two
reasonings, which you are fully competent, I am sure,
to do without difficulty for yourselves.

What renders it still more wonderful that the logicians did not evolve the competency of this process in
either quantity, and thus obtain a key to the opening
up of the whole mystery of syllogistic reasoning, is
this ;—that it is now above two centuries since the
Inverse or Regressive Sorites in comprehension was
discovered and signalised by Rodolphus Goclenius, a
celebrated philosopher of Marburg, in which university
he occupied the chair of Logic and Metaphysics.[β]

a *Epist.,* 85.—ED.
β *Goclenii Isagoge in Organum
Aristotelis,* Francof., 1598, p. 255.—

ED. [For the Goclenian Sorites before Goclenius, see Pacius, *Comment.
in Anal. Prior.,* i. 25, p. 159.]

LECT.
XIX.

This Sorites has from him obtained the name of *Goc-lenian ;* while the progressive Sorites has been called the common or Aristotelian. This latter denomination is, as I have previously noticed, an error ; for Aristotle, though certainly not ignorant of the process of reasoning now called *Sorites,* does not enter upon its consideration, either under one form or another. This observation by Goclenius, of which none of our British logicians seem aware, was a step towards the explication of the whole process ; and we are, therefore, left still more to marvel how this explication, so easy and manifest, should not have been made. Before terminating this subject, I may mention that this form of syllogism has been sometimes styled by logicians not only *Sorites,* but also *coacervatio, congeries, gradatio, climax,* and *de primo ad ultimum.* The old name before Valla, which the process obtained among the Greek logicians of the Lower Empire, was the vague and general appellation of *complex syllogism,* —συλλογισμὸς συνθετός.[a]

Epicheiro-
ma and
Sorites, as
polysyllo-
gisms, com-
paratively
simple, and
not pleon-
astic.

So much for the two forms of reasoning which may be regarded as composite or complex, and which logicians have generally considered as redundant. But here it is proper to remark, that if in one point, that is, as individual syllogisms, the Epicheirema and Sorites may be viewed as comparatively complex, in another, that is, as polysyllogisms, they may be viewed as comparatively simple. For resolve a Sorites into the various syllogisms afforded by its middle terms, and compare the multitude of propositions through which the conclusion is thus tediously evolved, with the short and rapid process of the chain-syllogism itself, and, instead of complexity, we should rather be

a [Blemmidas, *Epitome Logica,* c. 31.]

disposed to predicate of it extreme simplicity." In
point of fact, we might arrange the Epichcirema and
Sorites with far greater propriety under elliptical
syllogisms, than, as is commonly done by logicians,
under the pleonastic.   This last classification is,
indeed, altogether erroneous, for it is a great mistake
to suppose that in either of these forms there is aught
redundant.

a [See Leibnits, *Nouveaux Essais*,   ed. Raspe.]
L. iv. c. xvii. § 4, pp. 445, 446, 448.

LECTURE XX.

STOICHEIOLOGY.

SECT. II.—OF THE PRODUCTS OF THOUGHT.

III.—DOCTRINE OF REASONINGS.

SYLLOGISMS.—THEIR DIVISIONS ACCORDING TO EXTERNAL FORM.

B. DEFECTIVE,—ENTHYMEME.

C. REGULAR AND IRREGULAR,—FIGURE AND MOOD.

LECT.
XX.
———
B. Syllo-
gisms defec-
tive in Ex-
ternal Form.

I PROCEED now to the Second Class of Syllogisms,— those, to wit, whose External Form is defective. This class I give in conformity to the doctrine of modern logicians, whose unanimous opinion on the subject I shall comprehend in the following paragraph.

Par. LXXII.
The Enthy-
meme.

¶ LXXII. According to logicians in general, a defective syllogism is a reasoning in which one only of the premises is actually enounced. It is therefore, they say, called an *Enthymeme* (ἐνθύμημα), because there is, as it were, something held back in the mind (ἐν θυμῷ). But as it is possible to retain either the sumption or the subsumption, the Enthymeme is thus of two kinds:—an Enthymeme of the First, and an Enthymeme of the Second, Order. The whole distinction is, however, erroneous in principle, and even if not

erroneous, it is incomplete; for a Third Order of LECT.
XX.
Enthymemes is competent by the suppression of
the conclusion.

Such, as it is stated in the former part of the para- *Explica-*
graph, is the doctrine you will find maintained with *tion.*
singular unanimity by modern logicians; and, with *The common doctrine of the*
hardly an exception, this classification of syllogisms is *Enthymeme*
stated not only without a suspicion of its correctness, *futile, and erroneously*
but as a division established on the authority of the *attributed*
great father of logic himself. In both assertions they *to Aristotle.*
are, however, wrong, for the classification itself is
futile, and Aristotle affords it no countenance; while,
at the same time, if a distinction of syllogisms is to
be taken from the ellipsis of their propositions, the
subdivision of enthymemes is not complete, inasmuch as a syllogism may exist with both premises
expressed, and the conclusion understood.

I shall, therefore, in the first place, show that the
Enthymeme, as a syllogism of a defective enouncement, constitutes no special form of reasoning; in the
second, that Aristotle does not consider a syllogism of
such a character as such a special form; and, in the
third, that, admitting the validity of the distinction,
the restriction of the Enthymeme to a syllogism of
one suppressed premise cannot competently be maintained.

[a] I. In regard then to the validity of the distinction. *I. The En-*
This is disproved on the following grounds: First of *thymeme not a spe-*
all, the discrimination of the Enthymeme, as a syllo- *cial form of reasoning.*
gism of one suppressed premise, from the ordinary
syllogism, would involve a discrimination of the reasoning of Logic from the reasoning in common use;

a Compare *Discussions,* p. 153 *et seq.*—ED.

for, in general reasoning, we rarely express all the propositions of a syllogism, and it is almost only in the treatises on Abstract Logic, that we find examples of reasoning in which all the members are explicitly enounced. But Logic does not create new forms of syllogism, it merely expounds those which are already given; and while it shows that in all reasoning there are, in the mental process, necessarily three judgments, the mere non-expression of any of these in language, no more constitutes in Logic a particular kind of syllogism, than does the ellipsis of a term constitute in Grammar a particular kind of concord or government. But, secondly, Syllogism and Enthymeme are not distinguished as respectively an intralogical and an extralogical form; both are supposed equally logical. Those who defend the distinction are, therefore, necessarily compelled to maintain, that Logic regards the accident of the external expression, and not the essence of the internal thought, in holding that the Enthymeme is really a defective reasoning.[a]

It thus appears, that to constitute the Enthymeme as a species of reasoning distinct from Syllogism Proper, by the difference of perfect and imperfect, is of all absurdities the greatest.—But is this absurdity the work of Aristotle?—and this leads us to the second head.

II. Without entering upon a regular examination of the various passages of the Aristotelic treatises relative to this point, I may observe, in the first place, that Aristotle expressly declares in general, that a syllogism is considered by the logician, not in relation to its expression (οὐ πρὸς τὸν ἔξω λόγον), but

a [That Syllogism and Enthymeme are not properly distinct species of reasoning, see Derodon, *Logica Restituta*, Pars V. tract. i. c. 1, p. 602.]

exclusively as a mental process (ἀλλὰ πρὸς τὸν ἐν τῇ
ψυχῇ λόγον)." The distinction, therefore, of a class of
syllogisms as founded on a verbal accident, he thus of
course, implicitly and by anticipation, condemns. But
Aristotle, in the second place, does distinguish the
Enthymeme as a certain kind of syllogism,—as a syllogism of a peculiar matter,—as a syllogism from signs
and likelihoods.ᵝ Now if, having done this, it were
held that Aristotle over and above distinguished the
Enthymeme also as a syllogism with one suppressed
premise, Aristotle must be supposed to define the
Enthymeme by two differences, and by two differences
which have no mutual analogy; for a syllogism from
signs and likelihoods does not more naturally fall into
an elliptical form than a syllogism of any other matter.
Yet this absurdity has been and is almost universally
believed of the acutest of human intellects, and on
grounds which, when examined, afford not the slightest warrant for such a conclusion. On the criticism
of these grounds it would be out of place here to
enter. Suffice it to say, that the texts in the *Organon*
and *Rhetoric*, which may be adduced in support of the
vulgar opinion, will bear no such interpretation;—
that in one passage, where the word ἀτελὴς (*imperfect*) is applied to the Enthymeme, this word, if
genuine, need signify only that the reasoning from
signs and probabilities affords not a perfect or necessary inference; but that, in point of fact, the word
ἀτελὴς is there a manifest interpolation, made to
accommodate the Aristotelic to the common doctrine
of the Enthymeme, for it is not extant in the oldest
manuscripts, and has, accordingly, without any reference to the present question, been ejected from the

LECT.
XX.

The Enthy-
meme of
Aristotle,—
what.

a *Anal. Post.*, i. 10.—ED.   β *Anal. Prior.*, ii. 27; *Rhet.*, i. 2.—ED.

best recensions, and, among others, from the recent edition of the works of Aristotle by the Academicians of Berlin,—an edition founded on a collation of the principal manuscripts throughout Europe." It is not, however, to be denied that the term *Enthymeme* was applied to a syllogism of some unexpressed part, in very ancient times; but, along with this meaning, it was also employed by the Greek and Roman rhetoricians for a thought in general, as by Dionysius the Halicarnassian,[β] and the author of the *Rhetoric to Alexander*, attributed to Aristotle,[γ]—for an *acute dictum*, as by Sopater[δ] and Aulus Gellius,[ε]—for a reasoning from contraries or contradictories, as by Cicero.[ζ] Quintilian gives three meanings of the term; in one sense, signifying "*omnia mente concepta,*" in another, "*sententia cum ratione,*" in a third, "*argumenti conclusio, vel ex consequentibus vel ex repugnantibus.*"[η]

Applications of the term Enthymeme.
By Dionysius of Halicarnassus.
Author of Rhetoric to Alexander.
Sopater.
Aulus Gellius.
Cicero.
Quintilian.

a For a fuller history of this interpolation, see *Discussions*, p. 154.—ED. [For the correct doctrine of the Aristotelic Enthymeme, see Mariotte,) (*Essai de Logique*, P. ii. disc iii. p. 163, Paris, 1678.—ED.]

β *Epistola ad Cn. Pompeium de praecipuis Historicis*, c. 5: Τῆς μέντοι κολλικολογίας ἐκεῖνος καὶ τοῦ πλούτου τῶν ἐνθυμημάτων κατὰ πολὺ ὕστερος. The expression ἐνθυμημάτων κατὰ πολὺ ὕστερος is rendered by J. C. T. Ernesti, *Gedankra Fülle*; see his *Lexicon Technologiae Graecorum Rhetoricae*, v. ἐνθύμημα. The same sentence is repeated in nearly the same words by Dionysius, in his *Veterum Scriptorum Censura*, iii. 2.—ED.

γ The author of the *Rhetorica ad Alexandrum*, c. 8, classes the enthymeme among proofs (πίστεις), and, in c. 11, defines it as a proof drawn from any kind of opposition: Ἐνθυμή-

ματα δ' ἐστὶν οὐ μόνον τὰ τῷ λόγῳ καὶ τῇ πράξει ἐναντιούμενα, ἀλλὰ καὶ τοῖς ἄλλοις ἅπασιν. This work is attributed by Victorius to Anaximenes of Lampsacus, and this conjecture is adopted by the latest editor, Spengel.—ED.

δ *Sopatri Apamensis Prolegomena in Aristidem. Aristidis Op. Omn.*, ed. Jebb, vol. i. l. d 3: Καὶ τῇ τῶν ἐνθυμημάτων ἐναντότητι δημοτερίζοι. In Canter's *Prolegomena* this expression is rendered *sententiarum densitas*, and the word ἐνθυμημάτων in the same passage by *argutus in argumentis*. But compare *Discussions*, p. 157.—ED.

ε *Noctes Atticae*, vi. 13: "Quaerebantur autem non gravia nec reverenda, sed ἐνθυμήματα quaedam lepida et minuta."—ED.

ζ *Topica*, c. 13.—ED.

η *Inst. Orat.*, v. 10, 1.—ED.

Among the ancients, who employed the term for a syllogism with some suppressed part, a considerable number held, with our modern logicians, that it was a syllogism deficient of one or other premise, as Alexander the Aphrodisian, Ammonius Hermiæ, Philoponus,[a] &c. Some, however, as Pachymeres,[β] only recognised the absence of the major premise. Some, on the contrary, thought, like Quintilian,[γ] that the suppressed proposition ought to be the conclusion ;—nay, Ulpian the Greek commentator of Demosthenes, and the scholiast on Hermogenes the Rhetorician,[δ] absolutely define an Enthymeme—"a syllogism, in which the conclusion is unexpressed."[ε]

III. This leads us to the third head; for on no principle can it be shown, that our modern logicians are correct in denying or not contemplating the possibility of the reticence of the conclusion. The only principle on which a syllogism is competent, with one or other of its propositions unexpressed, is this,—that the part suppressed is too manifest to require enouncement. On this principle, a syllogism is not less possible with the conclusion, than with either of the premises, understood ; and, in point of fact, occurs quite as frequently as any other. The logicians, therefore,

LECT.
XX.

Dusted, with some of the ancients, a syllogism with some suppressed part.

The Aphrodisian.

Ammonius. Philoponus. Pachymeres.

Quintilian. Ulpian. Scholiast on Hermogenes.

III. Admitting the validity of the discrimination of the Enthymeme, is caused by restricted to a syllogism of one suppressed premiss.

a See Alexander, *In Topica*, pp. 6, 7, ed. Ald. 1513; Ammonius, *In quinque Voces Porphyrii*, f. 5 a, ed. Ald. 1546 ; Philoponus, *In Anal. Post.*, f. 4 a, ed. Ald. 1534. These authorities are cited in the Author's note, *Discussions*, p. 156. —ED.

β *Epitome Logices Aristotelis*, Oxon. 1866, p. 113. See also his *Epitome in Universam Aristotelis Dio- serendi Artem*, appended to Rasarius's translation of Ammonius on Porphyry, Lugd., 1547, p. 244.—ED.

γ *Inst. Orat.*, v. 14, 1.—ED.

δ Ulpian, *Ad Demosth. Olynth.*, ii. f. 7 b, ed. Ald., 1527. Anonymi ad Hermogenem, *De Inventione*, lib. iv. See *Rhetores Graeci*, ed. Ald. 1509, vol. ii. p. 371. In the same work, p. 365, the scholiast allows that either premiss or conclusion may be omitted.—ED.

ε An enlarged and corrected list of authorities on this question is given by the Author, *Discussions*, p. 157.—ED.

LECT.
XX.

to complete their doctrine, ought to have subdivided . the Enthymeme not merely into Enthymemes of the first and second, but also into Enthymemes of the third order, according as the sumption, the subsumption, or the conclusion is suppressed.[a] As examples of these various Enthymemes, the following may suffice :—

Examples of Enthymemes of the First, Second, and Third Order.

THE EXPLICIT SYLLOGISM.

Every liar is a coward ;
Caius is a liar ;
Therefore, Caius is a coward.

I. ENTHYMEME OF THE FIRST ORDER—(the Sumption understood.)

Caius is a liar ;
Therefore, Caius is a coward.

II. ENTHYMEME OF THE SECOND ORDER—(the Subsumption understood.)

Every liar is a coward ;
Therefore, Caius is a coward.

III. ENTHYMEME OF THE THIRD ORDER—(the Conclusion understood.)

Every liar is a coward ;
And Caius is a liar.

Epigrammatic example of Enthymeme with suppressed conclusion.

In this last, you see, the suppression of the conclusion is not only not violent, but its expression is even more superfluous than that of either of the premises. There occurs to me a clever epigram of the Greek Anthology, in which there is a syllogism with the conclusion suppressed. I shall not quote the original,

a [That the Enthymeme is of three orders is held by Victorinus, (in Cassiodorus, *Opera,* vol. ii. p. 536, ed. 1729 ; *Rhetores Pithœi,* p. 341, ed. 1599), or rather of four orders, for there may be an Enthymeme with only one proposition enounced. See Victorinus, as above.]

but give you a Latin and English imitation, which will serve equally well to illustrate the point in question.[*] The Latin imitation is by the learned printer Henricus Stephanus, and he applies his epigram to a certain Petrus, who, I make no doubt, was the Franciscan, Petrus a Cornibus, whom Buchanan, Beza, Rabelais, and others have also satirised.[β] It runs, as I recollect, thus :—

> " Sunt monachi nequam ; nequam non unus et alter :
> Præter Petrum omnes : est sed et hic monachus."

The English imitation was written by Porson upon Gottfried Hermann, (when this was written, confessedly the prince of Greek scholars,) who, when hardly twenty, had attacked Porson's famous canons, in his work *De Metris Græcorum et Romanorum.* The merit of the epigram does not certainly lie in its truth.

> " The Germans in Greek,
> Are sadly to seek ;
> Not five in five score,
> But ninety-five more ;
> All, save only Hermann,
> And Hermann's a German."

In these epigrams, the conclusion of the syllogism is suppressed, yet its illative force is felt even in spite

a The original is an epigram of Phocylides, preserved by Strabo, B. x. p. 467, ed. Casaubon, 1620. Compare *Anthologia Græca,* i. p. 54, ed. Brunck. Lips., 1794. *Poetæ Minores Græci,* ed. Gaisford, i. p. 444.

Καὶ τόδε Φωκυλίδεω· Λέριοι κακοί· οὐχ ὁ μέν, ὃς δ' οὔ·
πάντες, πλὴν Προκλέους· καὶ Προκλέης Λέριος.

For the Latin imitation by Stephanus, see *Thesd. Bezæ Poemata, item ex Georgio Buchanano, aliisque variis insignibus poetis excerpta carmina. Excudebat H. Stephanus, ex cujus etiam Epigrammatis Græcis et Latinis aliquot exteris adjecta sunt,* 1569, p. 217.

The parody by Porson is given in *A Short Account of the late Mr Richard Porson, M.A.,* p. 14, London, 1808. The original Greek, with Porson's imitation, is also given in Dr Wellesley's *Anthologia Polyglotta,* p. 433. — ED.

β See Buchanan, *Franciscanus,* l. 764 ; Beza, *Poemata,* p. 85, ed. 1569; Rabelais, L. iii. ch. 14. — ED.

LECT.
XX.
of the express exception; nay, in really conquering by implication the apparent disclaimer, consists the whole point and elegance of the epigram. To put the former into a syllogistic shape :—

Sumption—*The monks, one and all, are good-for-nothing varlets, excepting Peter;*
Subsumption—*But Peter is a monk.*

Now, what is, what must be, understood to complete the sense?—Why, the conclusion,—

Therefore, Peter is a good-for-nothing varlet like the rest.

There is recorded, likewise, a dying deliverance of the philosopher Hegel, the wit of which depends upon the same ambiguous reasoning. "Of all my disciples," he said, "one only understands my philosophy; and he does not." [a] But we may take this for an admission by the philosopher himself, that the doctrine of the Absolute transcends human comprehension.

What has now been said may suffice to show, not only that we may have enthymemes with any of the three propositions understood, but that the distinction itself of the enthymeme, as a species of syllogism, is inept.

C. Syllogisms, Regular and Irregular.
I now go on to the Third Division of Syllogisms, under the head of their External or Accidental form, —I mean the division of syllogisms into Regular and Irregular,—a distinction determined by the ordinary or extraordinary arrangement of their constituent parts. I commence this subject with the following paragraph :—

a See *Discussions*, p. 788.—ED.

¶ LXXIII. A syllogism is Irregular by relation,—1°. To the transposed order of its Propositions; 2°. To the transposed order of its
Terms; and, 3°. To the transposed order of both
its Propositions and Terms. Of these in their
order.

1°. A syllogism in extension is Regular, in the
order of its Propositions, when the subsumption
follows the sumption, and the conclusion follows
the subsumption. In this respect, therefore,
(discounting the difference of the quantities of
depth and breadth,) it admits of a fivefold irregularity under three heads,—for either, 1°. The
two premises may be transposed; or, 2°. The
conclusion may precede the premises, and here,
either the sumption or the subsumption may stand
last; or, 3°. The conclusion may be placed between the premises, and here either the sumption
or the subsumption may stand first. Thus, representing the sumption, subsumption, and conclusion by the letters A, B, C, we have, besides
the regular order, 1°. B, A, C,—2°. C, A, B,—3°.
C, B, A,—4°. A, C, B,—5°. B, C, A. (This doctrine of the logicians is, however, one-sided and
erroneous.)

2°. A syllogism is Regular or Irregular, in respect to the order of its Terms, according to the
place which the middle term holds in the premises. It is regular, in Comprehensive Quantity,
when the middle term is the predicate of the
sumption and the subject of the subsumption;—
in Extensive Quantity, when the middle term is
the subject of the sumption and the predicate
of the subsumption. From the regular order of

the terms there are three possible deviations, in
either quantity. For the middle term may occur,
1°. Twice as predicate; 2°. Twice as subject;
and, 3°. In Comprehensive Quantity, it may in
the sumption be subject, and in the subsumption
predicate; in Extensive Quantity, it may in the
sumption be predicate, and in the subsumption
subject. Taking the letter M to designate the
middle term, and the letters S and P to designate
the subject and predicate of the conclusion, the
following scheme will represent all the possible
positions of the middle term, both in its regular
and irregular arrangement. The Regular constitutes the First Figure; the Irregular order the
other Three.[a]

A.—In Comprehension.

I.	II.	III.	IV.
S *is* M.	S *is* M.	M *is* S.	M *is* S.
M *is* P.	P *is* M.	M *is* P.	P *is* M.
S *is* P.	S *is* P.	S *is* P.	S *is* P.

B.—In Extension.

I.	II.	III.	IV.
M *is* P.	P *is* M.	M *is* P.	P *is* M.
S *is* M.	S *is* M.	M *is* S.	M *is* S.
S *is* P.	S *is* P.	S *is* P.	S *is* P.

These relative positions of the middle term in
the premises, constitute, I repeat, what are called
the *Four Syllogistic Figures* (σχήματα, *figuræ*);
and these positions I have comprised in the two
following mnemonic lines:—

a Cf. Krug, *Logik*, § 104.—Ed.

FOR COMPREHENSION.

Præ sub; tum præ præ; tum sub sub; denique sub præ.

FOR EXTENSION.

Sub præ; tum præ præ; tum sub sub; denique præ sub.[a]

Of these two kinds of irregularity in the exter- Explica-tion. Irregular-ity in the external form of syl-logisms, aris-ing from transposi-tion of the Proposi-tions.
nal form of syllogisms, the former,—that of proposi-
tions,—is of far less importance than the latter,—that
of terms ; and logicians have even thrown it altogether out of account, in their consideration of Syllogistic Figure. They are, however, equally wrong
in passing over the irregular consecution of the propositions of a syllogism, as a matter of absolutely no
moment ; and in attributing an exaggerated importance to every variety in the arrangement of its terms.
They ought at least to have made the student of That a syllo-gism can be perspicu-ously ex-pressed by any of the five irregu-lar consecu-tions of its Proposi-tions.
Logic aware, that a syllogism can be perspicuously
expressed not only by the normal, but by any of the
five consecutions of its propositions which deviate
from the regular order. For example, take the following syllogism :—

> *All virtue is praiseworthy ;*
> *But sobriety is a virtue ;*
> *Therefore, sobriety is praiseworthy.*

This is the regular succession of sumption, subsumption, and conclusion, in a syllogism of extension ;
and as all that can be said, on the present question,
of the one quantity, is applicable, *mutatis mutandis,*
to the other, it will be needless to show articulately
that a syllogism in comprehension is equally suscep-

a This formula for Extension is   gic*, b. i c. iii. p. 169. The other
taken from Purchot, *Inst. Phil., Lo-*   line is the Author's own.—ED.

tible of a transposition of its propositions as a syllogism in extension.   Keeping the same quantity, to
wit, extension, let us first reverse the premises, leaving
the conclusion in the last place (B, A, C.)

> *Sobriety is a virtue ;*
> *But all virtue is praiseworthy ;*
> *Therefore, sobriety is praiseworthy.*

This, it will be allowed, is sufficiently perspicuous.
Let us now enounce the conclusion before the premises ; and, under this head, let the premises be first
taken in their natural order (C, A, B.)

> *Sobriety is praiseworthy ;*
> *For all virtue is praiseworthy ;*
> *And sobriety is a virtue.*

Now let the premises be transposed (C, B, A.)

> *Sobriety is praiseworthy ;*
> *For sobriety is a virtue ;*
> *And all virtue is praiseworthy.*

The regressive reasoning in both these cases is not
less manifest than the progressive reasoning of the
regular order.

In the last place, let us interpolate the conclusion
between the premises in their normal consecution
(A, C, B.)

> *All virtue is praiseworthy ;*
> *Therefore, sobriety is praiseworthy ;*
> *For sobriety is a virtue.*

Secondly, between the premises in their reversed
order (B, C, A.)

Sobriety is a virtue;
Therefore, sobriety is praiseworthy;
For all virtue is praiseworthy.[a]

In these two cases the reasoning is not obscure, though perhaps the expression be inelegant; for the judgment placed after the conclusion had probably been already supplied in thought on the enunciation of the conclusion, and, therefore, when subsequently expressed, it is felt as superfluous. But this is a circumstance of no logical importance.

It is thus manifest, that, though worthy of notice in a system of Logic, the transposition of the propositions of a syllogism affords no modifications of form yielding more than a superficial character. Logicians, therefore, were not wrong in excluding the order of the propositions as a ground on which to constitute a difference of syllogistic form : but we shall see that they have not been consistent, or not sufficiently sharp-sighted, in this exclusion; for several of their recognised varieties of form,—several of the moods of syllogistic figure,—consist in nothing but a reversal of the premises.

In reality, however, there is no irregular order of the syllogistic propositions, except in the single case where the conclusion is placed between the premises. For a syllogism may be either called *Synthetic*, in which case the premises come first, and the conclusion is last, (the case alone contemplated by the logicians); or it may be called *Analytic*, the proposition styled the conclusion preceding, the propositions called the premises following, as its reasons, (a case not contemplated by the

[a] Cf. Krug, *Logik*, § 104, Anmerk, i.—En.

logicians). The Analytic and Synthetic syllogisms may again be each considered as in the quantity of Extension, or as in the quantity of Comprehension ; in which cases we shall have a counter-order of the premises, but of which orders, as indeed of such quantities, one alone has been considered by the logicians.

The natural and transposed order of the Syllogistic Terms.

I now, therefore, go on to the second and more important ground of regularity and irregularity— the natural and transposed order of the Syllogistic Terms. The forms determined by the different position of the middle term by relation to the major and minor terms in the premises of a syllogism, are

Figures of Syllogism.

called *Figures* (σχήματα, *figuræ*),—a name given to them by Aristotle.[a] Of these the first is, on the prevalent doctrine, not properly a figure at all, if by figure be meant in Logic, as in Grammar and Rhetoric, a deviation from the natural and regular

Three figures distinguished by Aristotle.

form of expression. Of these figures the first three were distinguished by Aristotle, who developed their rules with a tedious minuteness sometimes obscure, and not always in the best order, but altogether with an acuteness which, if ever equalled, has certainly

Fourth Figure attributed to Galen, but on slender authority

never been surpassed. The fourth, which Whately, (at least in the former editions of his *Elements*,) and other recent Oxford logicians seem to suppose to be, like the others, of Aristotelic origin,— we owe perhaps to the ingenuity of Galen. I say *perhaps*, for though in logical treatises attributed without hesitation to the great physician, as if a doctrine to be found in his works, this is altogether erroneous. There is, I am certain, no mention of the fourth figure in any writing of Galen now extant, and

a *Anal. Prior.*, i. 4.—Ed. [Cf. Pacius, *Comment.*, pp. 118, 122.]

no mention of Galen's addition of that figure, by
any Greek or Latin authority of an age approximating to his own. The first notice of this Galenic
Figure is by the Spanish Arabian, Averroes of Cor-
dova, in his commentary on the *Organon.*[a] Averroes flourished above a thousand years posterior to
Galen; and from his report alone (as I have also
ascertained) does the prevalent opinion take its rise,
that we owe to Galen this amplification, (or corruption,
as it may be,) of the Aristotelic doctrines of logical
figure. There has been lately published from manuscript by Didot of Paris, a new logical treatise of
Galen.[β] In this work, in which the syllogistic figures
are detailed, there is no mention of a fourth figure.
Galen, therefore, as far as we know, affords no exception to the other authors upon Logic. In these circumstances, it is needless to observe how slender is the
testimony in favour of the report; and this is one of
many others in which an idle story, once told and
retailed, obtains universal credit as an established fact,
in consequence of the prevalent ignorance of the
futility of its foundation. Of the legitimacy of the
Fourth Figure I shall speak, after having shown you
the nature of its reasoning.

Before proceeding further in the consideration of
the Figure of Syllogism, it is, however, necessary
to state a complex modification to which it is
subject, and which is contained in the following
paragraph :—

¶ LXXIV. The Figure of Syllogism is modified by the Quantity and Quality of the proposi-

Marginal notes:

LECT.
XX.

First as-
cribed to
Galen by
Averroes.

Complex
modification
of the
Figure of
Syllogism.

Par. LXXIV.
Syllogistic
Moods.

---

a *Prior Analytics,* [B. i. ch. 8,—
ED.]

β Γαληνοῦ Εἰσαγωγὴ Διαλεκτικὴ—
ἐν Παρισίῳ ᾳωμδ' (1844).—ED.

tions which constitute the reasoning. As the
combination of Quantity and Quality affords
four kinds of propositions,—Universal Affirmative (A), Universal Negative (E), Particular
Affirmative (I), Particular Negative (O); and
as there are three propositions in each syllogism,
there are consequently in all sixty-four arrangements possible of three propositions, differing in
quantity and quality;—arrangements which constitute what are called the *Syllogistic Moods*,
(τρόποι, *modi*). I may interpolate the observation :—The Greek logicians after Aristotle, looking merely to the two premises in combination,
called these *Syzygies*, (συζυγίαι, *jugationes, con-
jugationes, combinationes*). Aristotle himself
never uses τρόπος for either mood or modality
specially; nor does he use συζυγία in any definite sense. His only word for mood is the vague
expression *syllogism*.

The greater number of these moods are, however, incompetent, as contradictory of the general
rules of syllogism; and there are in all only
eleven which can possibly enter a legitimate
syllogism. These eleven moods again are, for the
same reason, not all admissible in every figure,
but six only in each, that is, in all twenty-four;
and again of these twenty-four, five are useless,
and, therefore, usually neglected, as having a
particular conclusion where a universal is competent. The nineteen useful moods admitted by
logicians, may, however, by the quantification of
the predicate, be still further simplified, by super-
seding the significance of Figure.

In entering on the consideration of the various LECT.
Moods of the Syllogistic Figures, it is necessary that XX.
you recall to memory the three laws I gave you of the Explica-
Categorical Syllogism, and in particular the two clauses
of the second law,—That the sumption must be definite, (general or singular), and the subsumption affirmative,—clauses which are more vaguely expressed
by the two laws of the logicians,—that no conclusion
can be drawn from two particular premises,—and
that no conclusion can be drawn from two negative
premises. This being premised; you recollect that
the four combinations of Quantity and Quality, competent to a proposition, were designated by the four
letters, A, E, I, O,—A denoting a universal affirmative ;—E, a universal negative ;—I, a particular affirmative ;—O, a particular negative.

> Asserit A ; negat E ; verum universaliter ambæ :
> Asserit I ; negat O ; sed particulariter ambo.[a]
>
> A, it affirms of this, these, all ;
>   As E denies of any :
> I, it affirms, as O denies,
>   Of some, or few, or many.
> Thus A affirms what E denies,
>   And definitely either ;
> Thus I affirms what O denies,
>   But definitely neither.[β]

Now, as each syllogism has two premises, there are, The possible com-

a See above, p. 253.—Ed.
β [The following are previous
English metrical versions of these
lines :—

" A doeth affirme, E doeth denigh,
   which are bothe universall :
I doeth affirm, O doeth deuigh,
   whiche are particular call."

—Wilson, Rule of Reason, p. 27 a,
1551.

" A says and E denies ; both totally.
   I says and O denies ; both partially."

—Wallis, Institutio Logicæ, 1686, L.
ii. c. 4, p. 105.]

LECT.
XX.

binations of
premises.

consequently, sixteen different combinations possible
of premises differing in quantity and quality,—viz. :

1) A A.	2) E A.	3) I A.	4) O A.
A E.	E E.	I E.	O E.
A I.	E I.	I I.	O I.
A O.	E O.	I O.	O O.

How many
of these are
syllogisti-
cally valid.

Now the question arises,—are all of these sixteen
possible combinations of different premises valid towards a legitimate conclusion ? In answer to this,
it is evident that a considerable number of these are
at once invalidated by the first clause of the second
law of the categorical syllogism, in so far as recognised by logicians, by which all moods with two particular premises are excluded, as in these there is no
general rule. Of this class are the four moods, I I,
I O, O I, and O O. And the second clause of the
same law, in so far as recognised by logicians, invalidates the moods of two negative premises, as in
these there is no subordination. Of this class are the
four moods, E E, E O, O E, and O O. Finally, by
the two clauses of the second rule in conjunction, the
mood I E is said to be excluded, because the particular sumption contains no general rule, and the negative subsumption no subordination. (This, I think, is
incorrect.) These exclusions have been admitted to
be valid for every Figure ; there, consequently, remain
(say the logicians), as the possible modes of any legitimate syllogism, the eight following—A A, A E, A I,
A O, E A, E I, I A, O A ;* but some of these, as apparently contradictory of the second rule in its more definite assertions,—that the sumption must be general
and the subsumption affirmative,—I shall, after stating

* Cf. Bachmann, *Logik*, § 129.—ED.

to you the common doctrine of the logicians, show to LECT.
XX. be really no exceptions.

But whether each of the moods, though *a priori* Whether each mood possible, affords a proper syllogism in all the figures, that is a possible, affords a priori possible —this depends on the definite relations of the middle able affords term to the two others in the several figures. These, a proper syllogism in all therefore, require a closer investigation. I shall con- the figures. sider them, with the logicians, principally in the quantity of extension, but, *mutatis mutandis*, all that is true in the one quantity is equally true in the other.

Now if, in the first figure, we consider these eight First Figure. moods with reference to the general rules, we shall find that all do not in this figure afford correct syllogisms; but only those which are constructed in conformity to the following particular rules, which are, however, in this figure, identical with those we have already given as general laws of every perfect and regular categori- cal syllogism.

The symbol of the First Figure is,—

$$\left.\begin{matrix} \text{M P,} \\ \text{S M,} \end{matrix}\right\} \text{ for Extension; } \left.\begin{matrix} \text{S M,} \\ \text{M P,} \end{matrix}\right\} \text{ for Comprehension.}$$

The first rule is,—" The sumption must be univer- sal. Were it particular, and, consequently, the sub- sumption universal, as :—

> *Some* M *are* P ;
> *But all* S *are* M ;

we could not know whether S were precisely the part of M which lies in P, and it might be altogether out of P. In that case, an universal negative conclusion would be the correct ; but this cannot be drawn, as there is no negative premise, and though accidentally perhaps true, still it is not a necessary consequence of the premises."[a]

"The second rule is,—The subsumption must be affirmative. Were it negative, and consequently the sumption affirmative, in that case S would be wholly excluded from the sphere of M ; and, consequently, the general rule under which M stands would not be applicable to S.　Thus :—

> *All* M *are* P ;
> *No* S *is* M ;
> *No* S *is* P.
>
> *All colours are physical phænomena ;*
> *No sound is a colour ;*
> *Therefore, no sound is a physical phænomenon.*

"Here the negative conclusion is false, but the affirmative, which would be true,—*all sounds are physical phænomena,*—cannot be inferred from the premises, and, therefore, no inference is competent at all."[β]

Legitimate moods of First Figure.
Thus, in this figure, of the eight moods generally admissible, I A and O A are excluded by the first ; A E and A O by the second rule.　There remain, therefore, only four legitimate moods, A A, E A, A I, *Their symbols.* and E I.—The lower Greek logicians denoted them by the terms,—

> Γράμματα, Ἔγραψε, Γραφίδι, Τεχνικός ; [γ]

the Latin schoolmen by the terms—

> *Barbara, Celarent, Darii,* and *Ferio.*

α Bachmann, *Logik*, § 130, p. 203. —Ed. [So Hollmann, *Phil. Rationalis, quæ Logica vulgo dicitur,* § 461, Gottingæ, 1746 ; Lovanienses, *Commentaria in Isag. Porphyrii et in omnes Libros Arist. de Dialectica, Anal. Prior.,* L. i. p. 215, Lovanii, 1547 ; Ulrich, *Instit. Log. et Met.,* § 191, Ienæ, 1785 ; Fonseca, *Instit.*

Dial., L. vi. c. 21, p. 363.]
β Bachmann, as above.—Ed. [Cf. Derodon, *Logica Restituta,* P. iv. p. 618 ; Ulrich, as above ; Lovanienses, as above ; Hollmann, *Logica,* § 462.]
γ For an account of these mnemonics, see *Discussions,* p. 671, second edition.—Ed.

In the Latin symbols, which are far more ingenious and complete, and in regard to the history of which I shall say something in the sequel, the vowels are alone at present to be considered, and of these the first expresses the sumption, the second the subsumption, and the third the conclusion. The correctness of these is shown by the following examples and delineations.

"The first mood of this figure :—

I. BARBARA.

1. Barbara.

All M are P ;
All S are M ;
Therefore, all S are P.

All that is composite is dissoluble ;
All material things are composite ;
Therefore, all material things are dissoluble.

II. CELARENT.

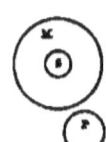

2. Celarent.

No M is P ;
All S are M ;
Therefore, no S is P.

No finite being is exempt from error ;
All men are finite beings ;
Therefore, no man is exempt from error.

III. DARII.

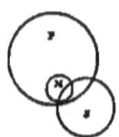

3. Darii.

All M are P ;
Some S are M ;
Therefore, some S are P.

All virtues are laudable
Some habits are virtues ;
Therefore, some habits are laudable.

" This diagram makes it manifest to the eye why

LECT.
IX.

the conclusion can only be particular.   As only a part of the 'sphere S lies in the sphere M, this part must lie in the sphere P, as the whole of M lies therein; but it is of this part only that any thing can be affirmed in the conclusion.   The other part of S can either lie wholly out of P, or partly in P but out of M; but as the premises affirm nothing of this part, the conclusion cannot, therefore, include it.

4. Ferio.

IV. FERIO.

No M *is* P ;
Some S *are* M ;
Therefore, some S *are not* P.

No virtue is reprehensible ;
Some habits are virtues ;
Therefore, some habits are not reprehensible.

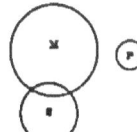 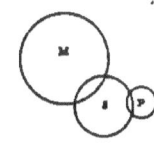

" The conclusion in this case can only be particular, as only a part of S is placed in the sphere of M.   The other part of S may lie out of P or in P.   But of this the premises determine nothing."[a]

Second Figure.

The symbol of the Second Figure is—

$${P\ M, \atop S\ M,}\Big\}\ \text{for Extension};\quad {S\ M, \atop P\ M,}\Big\}\ \text{for Comprehension}.$$

Its rules.

" This figure is governed by the two following rules. Of these the first is—One premise must be negative.[β] For were there two affirmative premises, as :—

a Bachmann, *Logik*, p. 204-206.—   β [See Derodon, *Logica Restituta*,
ED.   P. iv. p. 637; Hollmann, *Logica*, §§

All P are M ;
All S are M ;

All metals are minerals ;
All pebbles are minerals ;

the conclusion would be—*All pebbles are metals,* which would be false.

" The second rule is :—The sumption must be universal.[a] Were the sumption particular, the subsumption behoved to be universal ; for otherwise no conclusion would be possible. But in that case the sumption, whether affirmative or negative, would afford only an absurd conclusion.[β]

" If affirmative, as :—

> *Some P are M ;*
> *No S is M ;*
> *Therefore, some S are not P.*

> *Some animals lay eggs, i.e. are egg-laying things ;*
> *No horse lays eggs, i.e. is any egg-laying thing ;*
> *Therefore, some horses are not animals.*

" If negative, as :—

> *Some P are not M ;*
> *All S are M ;*
> *Therefore, some S are not P.*

> *Some minerals are not precious stones ;*
> *All topazes are precious stones ;*
> *Therefore, some topazes are not minerals.*

In both cases the conclusion is absurd.

403, 464; Lovanienses, *Com. in Arist. Anal. Prior.*, L. i. p. 219; Scotus,) [*Quæstiones in Anal. Prior.*, L. i. q. 20, f. 266.—ED.]

a See Hollmann, and Lovanienses, as cited above.—ED.

β [Cf. Fonseca, *Instit. Dial.*, L. vi. c. 21. p. 363.]

"There thus remain," say the logicians, "only the moods *Cesare, Camestres, Festino, Baroco.*

1. Cesare.

I. CESARE.

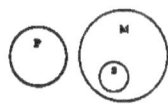

No P is M ;
All S are M ;
Therefore, no S is P.
Nothing material has free will ;
All spirits have free will ;
Therefore, no spirit is material.

2. Camestres.

II. CAMESTRES.

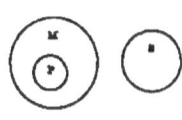

All P are M ;
No S is M ;
Therefore, no S is P.
All colours are visible ;
No sound is visible ;
Therefore, no sound is a colour.

3. Festino.

III. FESTINO.

No P is M ;	*No vice is praiseworthy ;*
Some S are M ;	*Some actions are praiseworthy ;*
Therefore, some S are not P.	*Therefore, some actions are not vices.*

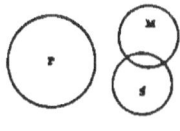 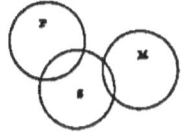

"The diagram here is alternative, for as the conclusion can only comprise a part of S, as it is only the consequence of a partial subordination of S to M, the other parts of S which are out of M may either lie within or without P. The conclusion can, therefore, only be particular.

IV. Baroco.

All P are M ;
Some S are not M ;
Therefore, some S are not P.

All birds are oviparous ;
Some animals are not oviparous ;
Therefore, some animals are not birds." [a]

---

[a] Bachmann, *Logik,* as above.—ED.

LECTURE XXI.

STOICHEIOLOGY.

SECTION II.—OF THE PRODUCTS OF THOUGHT.

III.—DOCTRINE OF REASONINGS.

SYLLOGISMS,—THEIR DIVISIONS ACCORDING TO EXTERNAL FORM.

FIGURE—THIRD AND FOURTH.

LECT. XXI.

Recapitulation.

IN our last Lecture, after terminating the general consideration of the nature of Figure and Mood in Categorical Syllogisms, we were engaged in a rapid survey of the nineteen legitimate and useful moods belonging to the four figures, according to the received doctrine of logicians, (consequently, exclusively in Extension) ; and I had displayed to you the laws and moods of the First and Second Figures.   Before, therefore, proceeding to any criticism of this doctrine, it behoves us to terminate the view of the two remaining figures.

Third Figure.

To each of the first two figures, logicians attribute four moods ; to the third they concede six ; and to the fourth five.   The scheme of the Third Figure, in Extension, is—

$$M \ P,$$
$$M \ S.$$

Its rules.

This figure (always in extension) is governed by

the two following laws :—the first is, " The subsumption must be affirmative." Were the minor premise
a negative, as in the syllogism,—

> All M are P ;   *All fiddles are musical instruments ;*
> No M is S ;   or,   *But no fiddle is a flute ;*

here the conclusion would be ridiculous,—*Therefore,
no S is P,—Therefore, no flute is a musical instrument.* For M and S can both exclude each other,
and yet both lie within the sphere of P.

" The second law is,—The conclusion must be particular, and particular although both premises are
universal.[β] This may be shown both in affirmative
and negative syllogisms. In the case of affirmative
syllogisms, as :—

> All M are P ;
> But all M are S ;

here, you will observe, M lies in two different spheres
—P and S, and these must in the conclusion be connected in a relation of subordination. But S and P
may be disparate notions,[γ] and, consequently, not to
be so connected ; an absurd conclusion would, therefore, be the result. For example,

> *All birds are animals with feathers ;*
> *But all birds are animals with a heart ;*
> *Therefore, all animals with a heart are animals*
> *with feathers.*

" Again," say the logicians, " in regard to negatives :
—In these only the sumption can be negative, as the

a [See Aristotle, *Anal. Prior.*, l.
6, §§ 8, 16; Hollmann, *Logica*, §
466; Lovanienses, *In Anal. Prior.*,
L. L p. 220.]

β [But see Hollmann, *Logica*, §§
332, 438; Lovanienses, *In Anal.*

Prior., L. i. p. 220.]

γ *Disparate notions, i.e.* co-ordinate parts of the comprehension of
their common subject M. See above,
p. 224.—Ed.

subsumption, (by the first rule), must be affirmative.
Thus :—

No M is P ;   No silver is iron ;
But all M are S ;   or, But all silver is a mineral.

"Here the conclusion—No S is P,—No mineral is
iron, would be false.

"Testing the eight possible moods in Extension by
these special rules, there remain for this figure six,
which by the Latin logicians have been named, Darapti, Felapton, Disamis, Datisi, Bocardo, Ferison.—
The first mood of this figure is :—

1. Darapti

I. DARAPTI [a]

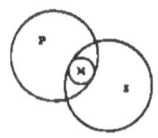

All M are P ;
But all M are S ;
Therefore, some S are P ;
or,
All gilding is metallic ;
All gilding shines ;
Therefore, some things that shine are
metallic.

"Here it is manifest that M cannot at once lie in
two different spheres, unless these partially involve,—
partially intersect each other.   But only partially ;
for as both P and S are more extensive than M, and
are both only connected through M, (i. e. through a
part of themselves), they cannot, except partially, be
identified with each other.

a [Some of the ancient logicians, among others Porphyry, have made two moods of Darapti, as Aristotle himself does in Cesare and Camestres, in Disamis and Datisi.   See Boethius, De Syllogismo Categorico, I. ii., Opera, p. 594 alibi.   Cf. Zabarella, Opera Logica, De Quarta Figura Syllog., pp. 119, 120 et seq.; Alex. Aphrodisiensis, In Anal. Prior., f. 5, ff. 23, 24, Ald. 1531 ; Philoponus, In Anal. Prior., L. i. c. 5, f. 25 b; Apuleius, De Habitud. Doct. Plat., L. iii., Opera, p. 37, 38, ed. Elmenhorst.]

" The second mood of this figure is,—

II. FELAPTON.[a]

No M *is* P ;
But all M *are* S ;
Therefore, some S *are not* P ;

OR,

No material substance is a moral subject ;
But all that is material is extended ;
Therefore, something extended is not a moral subject.

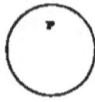 

" You will observe, that according to this diagram,
the conclusion ought to be—No S is P, because the
whole of S lies out of the sphere of P ; and as in the
concrete example, the notion *extended* is viewed as
out of the notion *moral subject*, we might conclude,—
Nothing extended is a moral subject. But this conclusion, though materially correct, cannot, however,
be formally inferred from the premises. In the sumption, indeed, the whole of M is excluded from the
sphere of P ; but in the subsumption M is included
in the sphere S, that is, we think that the notion M
is a part of the notion S. Now in the conclusion, S
is brought under P, and the conclusion of a categorical syllogism, in reference to its quantity, is, as you
remember, by the third general law regulated by the
quality of the subsumption. But as in the present
case the subsumption, notwithstanding the universality of the expression, only judges of a part of S ;

a [Aristotle gives Fapesmo, *Anal.
Prior.*, L. ii. c. 7, p. 169, Cantab.
Prior., L. 7. (Burgersdyck, *Instit.* 1647.)]

the conclusion can, in like manner, only judge of a
part of S. Of the other parts of S there is nothing
enounced in the premises. The relation between S
and P could likewise be as follows :—

No M is P;
But all M are S;
or,
No pigeon is a hawk;
But all pigeons are birds.

" Here the conclusion could not be a universal negative,—*Therefore, no S is P*—*Therefore, no bird is a
hawk*—for the sphere of S (*bird*) is greater than that
of either M (*pigeon*) or P (*hawk*) ; it may, however,
be a particular negative—*Therefore, some S are not P,*
(*therefore, some birds are not hawks*),—because the
sumption has excluded M and P (*pigeon* and *hawk*)
from each other's sphere, and, consequently, the part
of S which is equal to M is different from the part of
S which is equal to P.—But if this be the case when
the subsumption has an universal expression, the same,
a fortiori, is true when it is particular.

" The third mood of this figure is :—

3. *Disamis.*

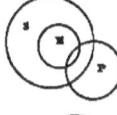

III. DISAMIS.

Some M are P ;
But all M are S ;
Therefore, some S are P ;

or,

Some acts of homicide are laudable ;
But all acts of homicide are cruel ;
Therefore, some cruel acts are laudable.

" The fourth mood of this figure is :—

IV. DATISI.

All M *are* P ;
But some M *are* S ;
Therefore, some S *are* P ;

or,

4. Datisi.

All acts of homicide are cruel ;
Some acts of homicide are laudable ;
Therefore, some laudable acts are cruel.

" This diagram makes it manifest that more than a single case is possible in this mood. As the subsumption is particular, the conclusion can only bring that part of S which is M into identity with P ; of the other parts of P there can be nothing determined, and these other parts, it is evident, may either lie wholly out of, or partly within, P.

" The fifth mood of this figure is :—

V. BOCARDO.

Some M *are not* P ;
But all M *are* S ;
Therefore, some S *are not* P ;

5. Bocardo.

or,

Some syllogisms are not regular ;
But all syllogisms are things important ;
Therefore, some important things are not things regular.

" The sixth mood of this figure is :—

VI. FERISON.

6. Ferison.

No M *is* P ;
But some M *are* S ;
Therefore, some S *are not* P ;

2 D

or,

No truth is without result ;
Some truths are misunderstood ;
Therefore, some things misunderstood are not without result.

 or,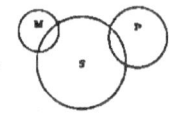

" Here, as in the premises, only that part of S which
is M is excluded from P, consequently the other parts
of S may either likewise lie wholly out of P, or partially in P." [a]

So much for the moods of the third figure.

Fourth Figure.   " The formula of the Fourth Figure is :—

P M
M S.

Its laws.   " This figure is regulated by three laws.

" I. Of these the first is—If the sumption be affirmative, the subsumption must be universal.   The
necessity of this law is easily seen.   For if we had the
premises—

All P are M ;
But some M *are* S ;

in this case, M might, or might not, be a notion superior to P.   On the former alternative, if M be higher
than P, and likewise higher than S, then the whole of
S might be contained under P.—In this case, the
proper conclusion would be a universal affirmative ;
which, however, cannot follow from the premises, as

a Bachmann, *Logik*, § 132, p. 211-213.—ED.

the subsumption, *ex hypothesi*, is particular. On the
latter alternative, even if M were not superior to S,
still since P is only a part of M, we could not know
whether a part of S were contained under P or not.
For example :—

> *All men are animals ;*
> *But some animals are amphibious.*

From these premises no conclusion could be drawn.

"II. The second rule by which this figure is governed
is—If either premise be negative, the sumption must
be universal.

"Suppose we had the premises—

> *Some P are not M ;*
> *But all M are S ;*
> *Therefore, some S are not P ;*
>
>   or,
>
> *Some animals are not feathered ;*
> *But all feathered animals are birds ;*
> *Therefore, some birds are not animals ;*

in this case, the whole of S lies within the sphere
of P; there cannot, therefore, follow a particular
negative conclusion, and if not that, no conclusion
at all. The same would happen were the sumption a
particular affirmative, and the subsumption a universal negative.

"III. The third rule of the fourth figure is—If the
subsumption be affirmative, the conclusion must be
particular. This (the logicians say) is manifest. For
in this figure S is higher than M, and higher than P,
consequently only a part of S can be P.

"If we test by these rules the eight possible moods,
there are in this figure five found competent, which,
among sundry other names, have obtained the fol-

lowing: *Bramantip, Camenes, Dimaris, Fesapo, Fresison.*

"Of these moods the first is :—

1. Brama-
tip.

I. BRAMANTIP, otherwise BAMALIP, &c.

All P are M ;
All M are S ;
Therefore, some S are P ;

or,

All greyhounds are dogs ;
But all dogs are quadrupeds ;
Therefore, some quadrupeds are greyhounds.

"The second mood is called :—

2. Camenes.

II. CAMENES, CALEMES, or CALENTES, &c.

All P are M ;
But no M is S ;
Therefore, no S is P ;
or,
All ruminating animals have four
stomachs ;
But no animal with four stomachs is carnivorous ;
Therefore, no carnivorous animal ruminates.

"The third mood in the fourth figure is variously denominated :—

Dimaris.

III. DIMARIS, or DIMATIS, or DIBATIS, &c.

Some P are M ;
But all M are S ;
Therefore, some S are P ;
or,
Some practically virtuous men are neces-
sitarians ;
All necessitarians speculatively subvert the distinction of vice and
virtue ;
Therefore, some who speculatively subvert the distinction of vice
and virtue are practically virtuous men.

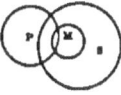

"The fourth mood of this figure is :—

IV. FESAPO.

No P is M ;
All M are S ;
Therefore, some S are not P ;
or,
No negro is a Hindoo ;
But all Hindoos are blacks ;
Therefore, some blacks are not negroes.

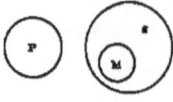 or,

"According to the first of these diagrams, all S is excluded from P, and thus the conclusion would seem warranted that—*No S is P.* This conclusion cannot, however, be inferred ; for it would violate the third rule of this figure. For while we, in the sumption, have only excluded M, that is, a part of S, from P, and as the other parts of S are not taken into account, we are, consequently, not entitled to deny these of P. The first diagram, therefore, which sensualises only a single case, is not coadequate with the logical formula, and it is necessary to add the second in order to exhaust it. The second diagram is, therefore, likewise a sensible representation of Fesapo ; and that diagram makes it evident that the conclusion can only be a particular negative.

"The fifth and last mood is :—

V. FRESISON.

No P is M ;
But some M are S ;
Therefore, some S are not P.

or,

No moral principle is an animal impulse ;
But some animal impulses are principles of action ;
Therefore, some principles of action are not moral principles.

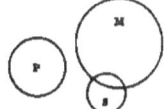
or,
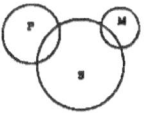

"The demonstration is here the same as in the former
mood. Since the subsumption only places a part of
M in the sphere of S, the conclusion, whose quantity
is determined by the subsumption, can only deny P
of that part of S which is likewise a part of M." [a]

Mood and
Figure in
Compre-
hension.

Having thus concluded the exposition of the various
Figures and Moods of Syllogisms, as recognised by
logicians, in reference to Extensive Quantity, it will
not be necessary to say more than a word in general,
touching these figures and moods in reference to Comprehensive Quantity. Whatever mood and figure is
valid and regular in the one, is valid and regular in
the other ; and every anomaly is equally an anomaly
in both. The rules of the various figures which we
have considered in regard to syllogisms in Extension,
are all, without exception or qualification, applicable
to syllogisms in Comprehension, with this single pro-
viso, that, as the same proposition forms a different
premise in the several quantities, all that is said of the
sumption in extension, should be understood of the
subsumption in comprehension, and all that is said of
the sumption in comprehension, should be understood
of the subsumption in extension. What, therefore,

a Bachmann, *Logik,* § 133, p. 218-223. — Ed.

has hitherto been, or may hereafter be, stated of the LECT.
XXI.
mood and figure of one quantity, is to be viewed as
applicable, *mutatis mutandis*, to the other. This being
understood, I proceed, in the first place, to show you Criticism of
the forego-
that the complex series of logical forms which I have ing doctrine
of logical
enumerated, may be considerably diminished, and the forms.
doctrine of syllogism, consequently, reduced to a higher
simplicity. In doing this I shall consider, first, the
Figures, and, secondly, their Moods.

Now, as regards the number of the Figures, you are I. The
Figures.
aware, from what I formerly stated, that Aristotle
only contemplated the first three, and that the fourth, The Fourth.
which is, by those who do not mistake it for an Aristotelic form, referred with little probability to Galen,
was wholly unnoticed until the end of the twelfth or
the beginning of the thirteenth century, when it was
incidentally communicated, as an innovation of the
physician of Pergamus, by the celebrated Averroes, in
his commentary on the *Prior Analytics* of Aristotle,
but by Averroes himself rejected as an illegitimate
novelty.[a] The notice of this figure by the commentator was, however, enough ; and though repudiated
by the great majority of the rigid Aristotelians, the
authority of Scotus, by whom it was defended,[β] secured
for it at last, if not an universal approval, at least a

a *In Anal. Prior.*, L 8. *Opera
Aristotelis*, t. L L 78, Venetiis, 1560.
—Ed.

β This statement is marked as
doubtful in the Author's Common-
place Book. Scotus [*Quæst. in Anal.
Prior.*, L q. 34) expressly rejects the
Fourth Figure. He says, "Solam
tribus medis potest fieri debita ordi-
natio respecto extremorum secundum
subjectionem et predicationem ; igi-
tur tres erunt figuræ et non plures
. . . . quia per solam transpositio-

nem non pervenit diversitas alicujus
præmissæ nec conclusionis : per consequens nec diversitas figuræ."
The Fourth Figure is, however,
said by Ridiger, (*De Sensu Veri et
Falsi*, p. 337), to have been introduced by Galen and Scotus. Hos-
pinianus (*De Controversiis Dialecti-
cis*, c. xix.) attributes (erroneously)
the invention of this figure to Scotus.
Compare also Noldius, *Logica Recognita*, c. xiii. § 4, p. 277.—Ed.

very general toleration, as a legitimate though an
awkward form.   The arguments indeed by which it
was attempted to evince the incompetency of this
figure, were not of a character calculated to enforce
assent ; for its inference is not less valid than that of
any other,—however tortuous and perverse it may be
felt to be.   In fact, the logicians, in consequence of
their exclusive recognition of the reasoning in extension, were not in possession of the means of showing,
that this figure is a monster undeserving of toleration,
far less of countenance and favour.   I shall not, therefore, trouble you with the inconclusive reasoning on
the part either of those who have assailed, or of those
who have defended this figure, but shall at once put
you in possession of the ground on which alone, I
think, its claim to recognition ought to be disallowed.

Grounds on
which the
Fourth
Figure
ought to bo
disallowod.
In the first place, then, you are aware that all reasoning is either in the quantity of comprehension, or
in the quantity of extension.   You are aware, in the
second place, that these quantities are not only different, but, as existing in an inverse ratio of each other,
opposed.   Finally, in the third place, you are aware
that, though opposed, so that the maximum of the
one is the minimum of the other, yet the existence of
each supposes the existence of the other ; accordingly,
there can be no extension without some comprehension,—no comprehension without some extension.

A cross
inference
possible
from Exten-
sion to Com-
prehension
and vice
versa.
This being the case, it is evident that, besides the
definite reasoning from whole to part, and from parts
to whole, within the several quantities and in their
perpendicular lines, there is also competent an indefinite inference across from the one quantity to the
other.   For if the existence of the one quantity be
only possible under the condition of the other, we may

always, it is self-evident, in the first place, from the affirmation of anything in extension, indefinitely affirm it in comprehension, as, reciprocally, from the affirmation of anything in comprehension, we may indefinitely affirm it in extension ; and, in the second place, from the negation of anything in extension, we may absolutely deny it in comprehension, as reciprocally, from the negation of anything in comprehension, we may absolutely deny it in extension.

LECT. XXI.

Now, what has not been observed, such is exclusively the inference in the Fourth Figure ; its two last rules are in fact nothing but an enunciation of these two conditions of a cross inference from the one quantity to the other ; and the first rule will be hereafter shown to be only an error, the result of not observing that certain moods are only founded on the accident of a transposed order of the premises, and, therefore, constitute no subject for a logical legislation.

This the nature of the inference in the Fourth Figure.

To prove this statement of the nature of the inference in the fourth figure, it is only necessary to look at its abstract formula. In extension this is :—

Proved and illustrated.

$$P \ is \ M \ ;$$
$$M \ is \ S \ ;$$
$$\overline{S \ is \ P.}$$

Here in the premises P is contained under M, and M is contained under S ; that is, in the premises S is the greatest whole and P the smallest part. So far, this syllogism in extension is properly a syllogism in comprehension, in which the subject of the conclusion is the greatest whole, and its predicate the smallest part. From such premises we, therefore, expect, that the conclusion carrying out what was established in

LECT.
XXL

the antecedent, should affirm P as the part of S.—In this, however, our expectation is disappointed; for the reasoning suddenly turns round in the conclusion, and affirms S as a part of P. And how, it may be asked, is this evolution in the conclusion competent, seeing that it was not prepared, and no warrant given for it in the premises? To this the answer is prompt and easy. The conclusion in this figure is solely legitimated by the circumstance, that from an identity between the two terms in one quantity, we may always infer some identity between them in the other, and from a non-identity between them in one quantity, we can always infer a non-identity in the other. And that in this figure there is always a transition in the conclusion from the one quantity, is evident; for that notion which in the premises was the greatest whole, becomes in the conclusion the smallest part; and that notion which in the premises was the smallest part, becomes in the conclusion the greatest whole. Now how is this manœuvre possible?—how are we entitled to say that because A contains all B, therefore, B contains some A? Only it is clear, because there is here a change from the containing of the one quantity to the containing of the other; and because, each quantity necessarily implying the indefinite existence of the other, we are consequently permitted to render this necessary implication the ground of a logical inference.

This hybrid inference is, 1. Unnatural.

It is manifest, however, in the first place, that such a cross and hybrid and indirect reasoning from the one quantity to the other, in the fourth figure, is wholly of a different character and account from the reasoning in the other three figures, in which all inference, whether upwards or downwards, is equable

and homogeneous within the same quantity. The
latter in short is natural and easy; the former unnatural and perverse.

In the second place, the kind of reasoning competent in the fourth figure, is wholly useless. The
change from the one quantity to the other in the
course of a syllogism, is warranted by no necessity, by
no expediency. The reasoning in each quantity is
absolute and complete within itself, and all that can
be accomplished in the one process can equally well
be accomplished in the other. The jumping, therefore,
from extension to comprehension, or from comprehension to extension, in the conclusion of the fourth
figure, is a feat about as reasonable and useful in
Logic, as the jumping from one horse to another would
be reasonable and useful in the race-course. Both are
achievements possible; but, because possible, neither
is, therefore, a legitimate exercise of skill.

We may, therefore, on the ground that the fourth
figure involves a useless transition from one quantity
to another, reject it as a logical figure, and degrade it
to a mere logical caprice.

But, in the third place, there is a better ground;
the inference, though valid in itself, is logically,—is
scientifically, invalid. For the inference is only legitimated by the occult conversion of the one quantity
into the other, which takes place in the mental process.
There is thus a step taken in the reasoning, which is
not overtly expressed. Were the whole process stated
in language, as stated it logically ought to be, instead
of a simple syllogism with one direct conclusion, we
should have a complex reasoning with two conclusions;
one conclusion direct and immediate, (the inference,
to wit, of conversion), and from that immediate con-

LECT.
XXI.

clusion another mediate and indirect, but which, as it
stands, appears as the one sole and exclusive conclusion from the premises.   This ground, on which I
think the fourth figure ought to be specially abolished,
is stated with the requisite details in the Logical
Appendix contained in the second edition of my *Discussions on Philosophy.*[a]

a P. 663.—ED.

LECTURE XXII.

STOICHEIOLOGY.

SECTION II.—OF THE PRODUCTS OF THOUGHT.

III.—DOCTRINE OF REASONINGS.

SYLLOGISMS.—THEIR DIVISIONS ACCORDING TO EXTERNAL FORM.

C. REGULAR AND IRREGULAR.

FIGURE—REDUCTION.

IN my last Lecture, after terminating the view of the nineteen Moods of the Four Syllogistic Figures, according to the doctrine of logicians, I entered on the consideration,—how far their doctrine concerning the number and legitimacy of these various figures and moods was correct. In the conduct of this discussion, I proposed, first, to treat of the Figures, and, secondly, to treat of the Moods. Commencing, then, with the Figures, it is manifest that no exception can possibly be taken to the first, which is, in point of fact, no figure at all, but the one regular,—the one natural form of ratiocination. The other three figures divide themselves into two classes. The one of these classes comprehends the fourth; the other, the second and third figures. The fourth figure stands, on the common doctrine of the logicians, in a more unfavourable situation than the second and third. It was not

LECT.
XXII.

Recapitula-
tion.

recognised by Aristotle; it obtained admission into
the science at a comparatively recent period; it has
never in fact been universally recognised; and its
progress is manifestly more perverse, circuitous, and
unnatural, than that of any other.

In regard to this fourth figure, I stated that the
controversy among logicians touching its legitimacy,
had been without result; its opponents failing to show
that it ought to be rejected; its defenders failing to
show that it was deserving of recognition. I then
stated that the logicians, in their one-sided view of
the reasoning process, had let slip the one great principle on which the legitimacy of this figure was to be
determined. I then explained to you that the peculiarity of the fourth figure consists in this,—that the
premises are apparently the premises of a syllogism
in one kind of quantity, while its conclusion is the
converted conclusion of a syllogism in the other. It
is thus in every point of view contorted and preposterous. Its premises are transposed, and the conclusion follows from these, not directly, but through the
medium of a conversion. I showed how, and how far,
this kind of reasoning was competent, and that though
the inference in the fourth figure is valid, it is incon-
venient and useless, and, therefore, that the form itself,
though undoubtedly legitimate, is still only a legitimate monster. Herewith the Lecture terminated.

General
character of
the Second,
Third, and
Fourth Fig-
ures.
Now, looking superficially at the matter, it might
seem, from what has now been said, that the fourth
ought to be at once expunged from the series of
logical figures. But a closer examination will show
us that this decision would be rash. In point of fact,
all figure properly so called, that is, every figure, with
the exception of the first, must be rejected equally

with the fourth, and on the following ground,—that they do not, in virtue of their own expressed premises, accomplish their own inference, but that this is done by the mental interpolation of certain complementary steps, without which no conclusion in these figures could be drawn. They are thus in fact reasonings apparently simple, but in reality complex; and when the whole mental process is expressed, they are found to be all only syllogisms in the first figure, with certain corollaries of the different propositions intermingled.[a] This doctrine corresponds with that of the logicians, in so far as they, after Aristotle, have allowed that the three last figures are only valid as reducible to the first; and, to accomplish this reduction, they have supplied us with a multitude of empirical rules, and lavished a world of ingenuity in rendering the working of these complex rules more easy. From Whately and the common books on Logic, you are of course acquainted with the import of the consonants in the cabalistical verses, *Barbara, Celarent*, &c.;[b] and it must be confessed that, taking these verses on their own ground, there are few human inventions which display a higher ingenuity. Their history is apparently altogether unknown to logicians. They were, in so far as they relate to the three first or Aristotelic figures, the invention of Petrus Hispanus, who died in 1277 Pope John XXII., (or as he is reckoned by some the XXI., and by others the XX). He was a native of Lisbon. It is curious that the corresponding Greek mnemonics were, so far as I can discover, the invention of his contemporary Nicephorus Blemmidas, who

---

a This doctrine of Figure, which is developed in paragraph lxxv., is mainly taken from Kant. See his Essay *Die falsche Spitzfindigkeit der* *vier syllogistischen Figuren*, 1762; *Werke*, l. p. 55, ed. Rosenkranz and Schubert.—Ed.

β See *Discussions*, p. 660.—Ed.

was designated Patriarch of Constantinople.[a] Between them, these two logicians thus divided the two highest places in the Christian hierarchy; but as the one had hardly begun to reign when he was killed by the downfall of his palace,[β] so the other never entered on his office, by accepting his nomination, at all. The several works of the Pope and the Patriarch were for many centuries the great text-books of Logic,—the one in the schools of the Greek, the other in the schools of the Latin church.

The Greek
symbols less
ingenious
than the
Latin.
The Greek symbols are far less ingenious than the Latin, as they mark only the consecution, quantity, and quality of the different propositions of the various moods of the three generally admitted figures, without showing to what mood of the first the moods of the other two figures are to be reduced, far less by what particular process this is to be done. All this is accomplished by the symbols of the Roman Pontiff. As to the relative originality, or the priority in point of date, of these several inventions, I am unable to speak with certainty. It is probable, however, that the Blemmidas was the first, both because his verses are the simpler and ruder, and because it is not known that he was acquainted with the writings of the Western logicians; whereas I find that the *Summulæ* of Hispanus are in a great measure taken, not indeed from the treatise of Blemmidas upon *Dialectic*, but from the *Synopsis of the Organon* of his somewhat earlier contemporary Michael Psellus.[γ]

a But see *Discussions*, p. 672.—Ed.

β See Platina, [*Historia de Vitis Pontificum Romanorum*, p. 181, ed. 1572. See also Brucker, *Hist. Phil.*, vol. iii. p. 816.—Ed.]

γ The reverse is probably the truer account; the work which goes by the name of Psellus being in all probability a translation from Hispanus, the mnemonics, with one exception, being omitted. See *Discussions*, p. 128.—Ed.

But the whole of the rules given by logicians for the Reduction of Syllogisms are unphilosophical, for they are merely the empirical statements of the operation of a principle in detail, which principle itself has been overlooked, but which, when once rationally explicated, supersedes the whole complex apparatus of rules for its mechanical application.

The Rules of logicians for the Reduction of Syllogisms unphilosophical.

If I succeed, therefore, in explaining to you how the three last Figures are only the mutilated expressions of a complex mental process, I shall not only subvert their existence as forms of reasoning not virtually identical with the first figure,—I shall not only relieve you from the necessity of studying the tedious and disgusting rules of their reduction, but in fact vindicate the great principles of reasoning from apparent anomaly. For, in the first place, if the three last figures are admitted as genuine and original forms of reasoning, the principle that all reasoning is the recognition of the relation of a least part to a greatest whole, through a lesser whole or greater part, is invalidated. For, in the three latter figures, the middle term does not really hold the relation of an intermediate whole or part to the subject and predicate of the conclusion ; for either, in the second figure, it contains them both, or, in the third, is contained by them both, or, in the fourth, at once contains the greatest whole, (that is, the predicate in extensive, the subject in comprehensive, quantity), and is contained by the smallest part, (that is, the subject in extensive, the predicate in comprehensive, quantity). In the second place, if these three figures are admitted as independent and legitimate forms, the second general rule I gave you for categorical syllogisms, is invalidated in both its clauses. For it will not hold true, that every cate-

The last three Figures only the mutilated expressions of a mental process, and virtually identical with the first.

LECT.
XXII.

gorical syllogism must have an universal sumption
and an affirmative subsumption. The law of the
universal quantity of the sumption is violated, in the
third figure by Disamis and Bocardo, in the fourth
by Dimaris; the law of the affirmative quality of
the subsumption is violated, in the second figure by
Camestres and Baroco, and in the fourth by Camenes.
I, therefore, proceed to reconcile all these anomalies by
the extinction of the three last figures, as more than
accidental modifications of the first, and commence
with the following paragraph :—

Par. LXXV.
The Second,
Third, and
Fourth Fig-
ures only
accidental
modifica-
tions of the
First.

¶ LXXV. The three last (that is, Second, Third,
Fourth) Figures are merely hybrid or mixed reasonings, in which the steps of the process are
only partially expressed. The unexpressed steps
are, in general, conversive inferences, which we
are entitled to make, 1°, From the absolute negation of a first notion as predicated of a second,
to the absolute negation of the second notion as
predicated of the first—*if no A is B, then no
B is A*; 2°, From the total or partial affirmation
of a lesser class or notion of a greater, to the
partial affirmation of that greater notion of that
lesser—*if all (or some) A is B, then some B
is A.*

Moods of
Second
Figure.
1. Cesare.

Taking the figures and moods in their common
order; in the Second Figure the first mood is Cesare,
of which the formula is :—

No P is M ;
But all S are M ;
Therefore, no S is P.

Here the ostensible or expressed sumption, *No P is*

M, is mentally converted into the real sumption by
the inference,—*Then no* M *is* P.   The other propositions follow regularly,—viz.:

> *But all* S *are* M ;
> *Therefore, no* S *is* P.

The real syllogism, fully expressed, is thus :—

> Real Sumption,.......*No* M *is* P ;
> Subsumption,.........*But all* S *are* M ;
> Conclusion,...........*Ergo, no* S *is* P.

To save time, I shall henceforward state the complementary propositions which constitute the real and
proximate parts of the syllogism, by the name of *real,
proximate,* or *interpolated* sumption, subsumption, or
conclusion ; and those who take notes may simply
mark these, by placing them within brackets.   To
avoid confusing the conversive inference with the
ostensible conclusion of the syllogism, I shall mark
the former by the illative conjunction *then ;* the latter
by the illative conjunction *therefore.*   I shall take the
concrete examples which I chanced to give in illustration of the various moods.   In Cesare the concrete
example was :—

Ostensible Sumption,............	*Nothing that is material has free will ;*
Real, Interpolated, Sumption,...	*(Then, nothing that has free will is material ;)*
Subsumption,.....................	*But all spirits have free will ;*
Conclusion,......................	*Therefore, no spirit is material.*

Throwing out of account the ostensible sumption,
and considering the syllogism, in its real nature, as
actually evolved out of the sumption mentally understood ; we have thus, instead of a syllogism in Cesare
of the second figure, a syllogism in Celarent of the

first. The seeming irregularity is thus reduced to real order.

2. Cam-
estres.
The second mood of the second figure, viz. Cam-estres,[a] is rather more irregular, and, therefore, the process of redressing it, though equally easy, is somewhat more complex. The formula is :—

All P *are* M ;
But no S *is* M ;
Therefore, no S *is* P.

In reality
Celarent.
Here, in the first place, the premises are transposed, for you remember by the second general law of syllogisms, the sumption must in extension be universal, and the subsumption affirmative. By a preliminary operation, their apparent consecution must, therefore, be accommodated to their real. The premises being restored to order, there is yet a further intricacy to unravel. The sumption and the conclusion are neither of them proximate ; for we depart from a conversive sumption, and primarily obtain a conclusion which only gives us the ostensible conclusion, in the second instance, through an inference. Thus :—

Ostensible Sumption,....................*No* S *is* M ;
Proximate or Real Sumption,........(*Then, no* M *is* S ;)
Subsumption,..............................*All* P *are* M ;
Proximate or Real Conclusion,......(*Therefore, no* P *is* S ;)
Ostensible Conclusion,................*Therefore, no* S *is* P.

The concrete example given was :—

All colours are visible ;
But no sound is visible ;
Therefore, no sound is a colour.

---

a [That Cesare and Camestres are   *Opera Logica, De Quarta Figura*
the same syllogism with acciden-   *Syllog.*, p. 111, and authorities cited
tal order of premises, see Zabarella,   above, p. 414, note.]

Reversing the premises, we have :—

Apparent Sumption,.... ....*No sound is visible ;*
Proximate or Real Sumption,...*(Then, nothing visible is a sound ;)*
Subsumption,........................*All colours are visible ;*
Proximate or Real Conclusion,...*(Therefore, no colour is a sound ;)*
which gives, as a conversive
inference, the
Expressed Conclusion,............*Then, no sound is a colour.*

Thus it is evident that Camestres, in the second figure, is only a modification of Celarent, in the first.[a]

The third mood of the Second Figure, Festino, presents no difficulty. We have only to interpolate the real sumption, to which the subsumption and conclusion proximately refer. Thus :—

Festino. Is reality Ferio.

Expressed Sumption,............*No P is M ;*
Real or Proximate Sumption,...*(Then, no M is P ;)*
Subsumption,.......................*But some S are M ;*
Conclusion,............................*Therefore, some S are not P.*

Our concrete example was :—

Expressed Sumption,.......*No vice is laudable ;*
              Some actions are laudable ;
              Therefore, some actions are not vices.

Here we have only to interpolate as the real sumption :—

        Nothing laudable is a vice.

Festino, in the second figure, is thus only Ferio in the first, with its sumption converted.

a Cf. Krug, *Logik,* § 100, p. 308; Mark Duncan, *Instit. Logicæ,* L. iv. c. 4, p. 222.—Ed. [Derodon, *Logica Restit.,* Pars iv. p. 648. Reusch, *Systema Logicum,* § 439, p. 615].

The fourth mood, Baroco, is more troublesome. In fact, this mood and Bocardo, in the third figure, have been at once the *cruces* and the *opprobria* of logicians. They have, indeed, succeeded in reducing these to the first figure by what is called the *reductio ad impossibile*, that is, by circuitously showing that if you deny the conclusion in these syllogisms, the contradictory inference is absurd ; but as of two contradictories one or other must be true, it, therefore, remains that the original conclusion shall be admitted. This process is awkward and perplexing : it likewise only constrains nascent, but does not afford knowledge ; while at the same time we have here a syllogism with a negative subsumption, which, if legitimate, invalidates the universality of our second general rule. Now, on the principle I have proposed to you, there is no difficulty whatever in the reduction of this or of any other mood. Here, however, we do not, as in the other moods of the second figure, find that the syllogism proximately departs from an unexpressed sumption, but that the proximate subsumption and the proximate conclusion have been replaced by two derivative propositions. The formula of Baroco is :—

All P *are* M ;
But some S *are not* M ;
Therefore, some S *are not* P.

But the following is the full mental process :—

Sumption,.....	*All* P *are* M ;
Real Subsumption,..............	(*Some not-*M *are* S ;)
which gives the	{ *Then, some* S *are not-*M ;
Expressed Subsumption,.......	{ Or, *some* S *are not* M ;
Real Conclusion, ...	(*Therefore, some not-*P *are* S ;)

which gives the Expressed Conclusion,...............	{ *Then, some* S *are not-*P ; *Or, some* S *are not* P.

Or, to take our concrete example :—

> *All birds are oviparous ;*
> *But some animals are not oviparous ;*
> *Therefore, some animals are not birds.*

Of this the explicated process will stand as follows :—

Sumption,........................	*All birds are oviparous ;*
Real Subsumption,...............	{ *(Some things not oviparous are animals ;)*
which gives the Expressed Subsumption, ...	{ *Then, some animals are not-oviparous ;* *Or, are not oviparous ;*
Real or Proximate Conclusion,	{ *(Therefore, some things not birds are animals ;)*
which gives the Expressed Conclusion,............	{ *Then, some animals are not-birds ;* *Or, are not birds.*

Now, in this analysis of the process in Baroco, we
not only resolve the whole problem in a direct and
natural and instructive way ; but we get rid of the
exception which Baroco apparently affords to the
general rule, that the subsumption of a categorical
must be affirmative. Here you see how the real subsumption is affirmative, and how, from having a
negative determination in its subject, it by conversion
assumes the appearance of a negative proposition, the
affirmative proposition,—*some things not-birds are
animals,* being legitimately converted, first into,—
some animals are not-birds, and this again being legitimately converted into,—*some animals are not birds.*
You recollect that, in the doctrine of Propositions,[a] I
showed you how every affirmative proposition could

a See above, p. 253.—Ed.

LECT.
XXII.

be adequately expressed in a negative, and every negative in an affirmative form; and the utility of that observation you now see, as it enables us simply to solve the problem of the reduction of Baroco, and, as we shall also see, of Bocardo. Baroco is thus directly reduced to Darii of the first figure, and not, as by the indirect process of logicians in general, to Barbara.[a] On this doctrine the name Baroco is also improper, and another, expressive of its genuine affinity, should be imposed.

Third Figure.

We proceed now to the Third Figure. You will observe that, as in the Second Figure, with the ex-

a There seems to be an error in the text here. The syllogism, as finally reduced, is not in Darii, nor in any legitimate mood; and its natural reduction, according to the method adopted by the Author, is not to Darii, but to Ferio, by means of an unexpressed assumption. Thus:—

All P are M;
Then no not-M are P;
Some S are not-M;
Therefore, some S are not P.

This is the method adopted by the following logicians, referred to by the Author in his Common-Place Book, viz.:— Noldius, who calls Baroco, Facrono, *Logica Recognita,* cap. xii. § 12, p. 300, 1666; Reusch, (who follows Noldius), *Systema Logicæ,* § 539, p. 611, 2d ed., 1741; Wolf, *Phil. Rationalis,* § 384; Hochmann, *Logik,* § 133, Anm., i. p. 224. Before any of the above-mentioned writers, Mark Duncan gives the reduction of Camestres to Celarent, and of Baroco to Ferio, by counter-position. He adds, with special reference to the reduction of Baroco to Ferio by this method,—"Hanc reductionis speciem existimo a scholasticis perspectam fuisse: sed despec-

tam; quia in prima figura propositio minor affirmans attributi infiniti, quam primo intuitu videatur esse negans, formæ evidentiam obscurat: atqui syllogismorum reductio comparata est non ad formæ bonitatem obscurandam, sed illustrandam." *Institutiones Logicæ,* L. iv. c. 3, § 4, p. 230. Salmurii, 1612.

The syllogism of the text may also be exhibited more circuitously, as Darii, by retaining the affirmative quality in the converted proposition. Thus:—

All not-M are not-P;
Some S are not-M;
Therefore, some S are not-P.

This is the method of reduction employed by Derodon, who, in the same way, would reduce Camestres to Barbara, *Logica Restituta,* P. iv. tract. i. c. 2, art. 6, p. 648. The error here noticed seems to have originated in a momentary confusion of the reduction of Baroco with that of Bocardo; which, however, could not be rectified without greater alterations in the text than the Editors consider themselves justified in making.—Ed.

ception of Baroco, it was the sumption of the two
promises which was affected by the conversion, so in
the third it is the subsumption. For in Camestres of
the second, and in Disamis and Bocardo of the third,
figure, the premises are transposed. This understood
subsumption is a conversive inference from the expressed one, and it is the proximate antecedent from
which the real conclusion is immediately inferred.

In the first mood of this figure, Darapti, the subsumption is an universal affirmative; its conversion
is, therefore, into a particular affirmative. Its formula is—

Sumption,............................*All* M *are* P;
Expressed Subsumption,............*But all* M *are* S;
which gives the
Really Proximate Subsumption,...(*Then, some* S *are* M;)
from which directly flows
The Conclusion,........................*Therefore, some* S *are* P.

Our concrete example was :—

Sumption,........................... *All gilding is metallic;*
Expressed Subsumption,........ *But all gilding shines;*
which gives, as a conversion,
the
Real Subsumption,................. { *Then, some things that shine are gilding;* }
and from this last imme-
diately proceeds the
Conclusion,........................ { *Therefore, some things that shine are metallic.* }

Thus, Darapti, in the third figure, is nothing but a
one-sided derivative of Darii in the first.[a]

The second mood of the Third Figure is Felapton.
Its formula—

a [Reusch, *Systema Logicum*, § 539, p. 614.]

Sumption,..........................*No* M *is* P ;
Expressed Sumption,........*All* M *are* S ;
The Real Subsumption,......(*Then, some* S *are* M ;)
from which
The Conclusion,..............*Therefore, some* S *are not* P.

Our example was—

Sumption,........................ | *Nothing material is a free agent ;*
Expressed Subsumption,........ { *But everything material is extended ;*
Of which the Real Subsumption } (*Then, something extended is material ;*)
is the converse,................
From which the Conclusion, ... { *Therefore, something extended is not a free agent.*

Felapton, in the third Figure, is thus only a modification of Ferio in the first.

3. Disamis. The third mood in this figure is Disamis. Its formula—

> *Some* M *are* P ;
> *But all* M *are* S ;
> *Therefore, some* S *are* P.

Is really Darii. Here the premises are transposed. Their order being rectified :—

Sumption,........................ *All* M *are* S ;
Expressed Subsumption,......... *But some* M *are* P ;
Which, by conversive inference, gives the Proximate } (*Then, some* P *are* M ;)
Subsumption, ...
From which proceeds the Real } (*Therefore, some* P *are* S ;)
Conclusion,.....................
Which, by conversion, gives the } *Then, some* S *are* P.
Expressed Conclusion,..... ...

Our example was (the reversal of the premises being rectified) :—

Sumption,........................ *All acts of homicide are cruel ;*
Expressed Subsumption,........ { *But some acts of homicide are laudable ;*

Which gives, as a conversive inference, the Proximate Subsumption,........................	*(Then, some laudable acts are acts of homicide ;)*	LECT. XXII.
From this Proximate Conclusion,	*(Therefore, some laudable acts are cruel ;)*	
Which again gives, as its converse, the Expressed Conclusion,....	*Therefore, some cruel acts are laudable ;*	

Thus Disamis in the third, is only Darii in the first figure.

The fourth mood of the Third Figure is Datisi, which is only Disamis, the premises not being reversed, and the conclusion not a conversive inference. It requires, therefore, only to interpolate the proximate subsumption. Thus— *4. Datisi.*

In reality Darii.

Sumption,............................	*All M are P ;*
Expressed Subsumption,.........	*But some M are S ;*
Giving by conversion,............	*(Then, some S are M ;)*
From which last the Conclusion,	*Therefore, some S are P.*

Sumption,............................	*All acts of homicide are cruel ;*
Expressed Subsumption,.........	*But some acts of homicide are laudable ;*
Which gives, by conversion, the Proximate Subsumption,......	*(Then, some laudable acts are acts of homicide ;)*
From which the Conclusion,.....	*Therefore, some laudable acts are cruel.*

Thus, Datisi likewise is only a distorted Darii.

The fifth mood of the Third Figure is the famous mood Bocardo, which, as I have mentioned, with Baroco, but far more than Baroco, was the opprobrium of the scholastic system of reduction. So intricate, in fact, was this mood considered, that it was looked upon as a trap, into which if you once got, it was no easy matter to find an exit. Bocardo was, during the middle ages, the name given in Oxford to the Aca- *5. Bocardo.*

444 LECTURES ON LOGIC.

XXII.

demical Jail or Carcer,—a name which still remains as a relique of the ancient logical glory of that venerable seminary. Rejecting, then, the perplexed and unsatisfactory reduction by the logicians of Bocardo to Barbara by an apagogical exposition, I commence by stating, that Bocardo is only Disamis under the form of a negative affirmative; its premises, therefore, are transposed. Removing the transposition, its formula is—

> *All* M *are* S ;
> *But some* M *are not* P ;
> *Therefore, some* S *are not* P.

which is thus explicated, like Baroco :—

Sumption,............................	*All* M *are* S ;
Expressed Subsumption,.........	*Some* M *are not* P ;
Which gives, by conversive inference, ...	*(Then, some not*-P *are* M ;)
From this Real Subsumption proceeds the Proximate Conclusion, ...	*(Therefore, some not*-P *are* S ;)
Which again gives, by conversion, the Expressed Conclusion,....	*Then, some* S *are not*-P ;
Whence again,......................	*Some* S *are not* P ;

Our concrete example was (the order of the premises being redressed) :—

Sumption,............................	*All syllogisms are important ;*
Expressed Subsumption,.........	*But some syllogisms are not regular ;*
From which, by conversive inference, ...	*(Then, some things not regular are syllogisms ;)*
And from this Proximate Subsumption proceeds the Proximate Conclusion,...............	*Therefore, some things not regular are important ;*
From whence, by conversion, the Expressed Conclusion,.........	*Then, some important things are not-regular ;*
Whence, ...	*Whence, some important things are not regular ;*

Bocardo is thus only a perverted and perplexed Darii.[a]

LECT.
XXII.

The last mood of the Third Figure is Ferison, which is without difficulty,—it only being required to interpolate the real subsumption, from which the conclusion is derived. Its formula is—

a. Ferison.

In reality
Ferio.

Sumption,.............................	*No M is* P ;
Expressed Subsumption,.........	*But some* M *are* S ;
Which gives, by conversive inference, the Subsumption, ...	*Then, some* S *are* M ;
From which immediately flows the Conclusion, ...	*Therefore, some* S *are not* P.
Sumption,.............................	*No truth is without result ;*
Expressed Subsumption,.........	*But some truths are misunderstood ;*
The Conversive Inference from which is,..........................	*Then, some things misunderstood are truths ;*
And from this Implied Subsumption immediately proceeds the Conclusion,......................	*Therefore, some things misunderstood are not without result.*

Ferison[β] is thus only Ferio, fringed with an accident of conversion.

The Fourth Figure is distinguished from the two former in this,—that in the Second and Third Figures one or other, but only one or other, of the premises requires the interpolation of the mental inference; whereas, in the Fourth Figure, either both the premises require this, or neither, but only the conclusion. The three first moods, (Bamalip, Calemes, Dimatis,) need no conversion of the premises; the two last, Fesapo and Fresison, require the conversion of both.

The result of the foregoing discussion is that, in

Fourth
Figure.

a [See Noldius, *Log. Rec.*, c. xii. § 12, p. 301. Bocardo is called Docamroc by Noldius. Cf. Reusch, *Syst. Log.*, § 539, p. 611.)

β [Scotus says that Ferison, Bocardo, and Felapton, are useless, as concluding indirectly. *Quæstiones, In Anal. Prior.*, I. i. q. 24.]

The First
Figure the
only simple
and inde-
pendent
form of
reasoning.

rigid truth, no figure is entitled to the dignity of a simple and independent form of reasoning, except that which has improperly been termed the First; the three latter figures being only imperfect or elliptical expressions of a complex process of inference, which, when fully enounced, is manifestly only a reasoning in the first figure. There is thus but one figure, or, more properly, but one process of categorical reasoning; for the term *figure* is abusively applied to that which is of a character regular, simple, and essential.

Figure of
Hypotheti-
cal, Dis-
junctive,
and Hypo-
thetico-Dis-
junctive
Syllogisms.

Having, therefore, concluded the treatment of figure in respect of Categorical Syllogisms, it remains to consider how far the other species of Simple Syllogisms,— the Hypothetical, the Disjunctive, and the Hypothetico-disjunctive,—are subject to this accident of form. In regard to the Hypothetical Syllogism, this kind of reasoning is not liable to the affection of figure. It is true indeed that we may construct a syllogism of three hypothetical propositions, which shall be susceptible of all the figures incident to a categorical reasoning; but this is itself in fact only a categorical syllogism hypothetically expressed. For example :—

> *If A is, then B is;*
> *But if S is, then A is;*
> *Therefore, if S is, then B is.*

This syllogism may certainly be varied through all the figures, but it is not an hypothetical syllogism, in the proper signification of the term, but manifestly only a categorical; and those logicians who have hence concluded, that a hypothetical reasoning was exposed to the schematic modifications of the categorical, have only shown that they did not know how to discriminate these two forms by their essential differences.

In regard to the Disjunctive Syllogism the case is different; for as the disjunctive judgment is, in one point of view, only a categorical judgment whose predicate consists of logically opposing members, it is certainly true that we can draw a disjunctive syllogism in all the four figures.

I shall use the letters P, M, and S; but as the disjunction requires at least one additional letter, I shall, where that is necessary, take the one immediately following.

Figure I.

M *is either* P *or* Q;
S *is* M;
Therefore, S *is either* P *or* Q.

Figure II.

First case—

P *is either* M *or* N;
S *is neither* M *nor* N;
Therefore, S *is not* P.

Second case—

P *is neither* M *nor* N;
S *is either* M *or* N;
Therefore, S *is not* P.

Figure III.

M *is either* P *or* Q;
M *is* S;
Therefore, some S *is either* P *or* Q.

Figure IV.

First case—

P *is either* M *or* N;
Both M *and* N *are* S;
Therefore, some S *is* P.

Second case—

> P *is either* M *or* N ;
> *Neither* M *nor* N *is* S ;
> *Therefore,* S *is not* P.[a]

Figure of Composite Syllogisms. Of Composite Syllogisms,—I need say nothing concerning the Epicheirema, which, it is manifest, may be in one figure equally as in another. But it is less evident that the Sorites may be of any figure; and logicians seem, in fact, from their definitions, to have only contemplated its possibility in the first figure. It is, however, capable, by a little contortion, of all the four schematic accidents; but as this at best constitutes only a logical curiosity, it is needless to spend any time in its demonstration.[β]

So much for the Form of reasoning, both Essential and Accidental, and for the Divisions of Syllogisms which are founded thereon.

---

a See Chr. J. Braniss, *Grundriss der Logik*, § 394, p. 146. Compare Krug, *Logik*, p. 387 *et seq.*

β For this development of the Sorites, see Appendix X. For other developments of the Sorites in different figures, see Herbart, *Lehrbuch zur Einleitung in die Philosophie*, § 70; Drobisch, *Neue Darstellung der Logik*, §§ 80-84. — ED.

LECTURE XXIII.

STOICHEIOLOGY.

SECTION II.—OF THE PRODUCTS OF THOUGHT.

III.—DOCTRINE OF REASONINGS.

SYLLOGISMS.—THEIR DIVISIONS ACCORDING TO VALIDITY.

FALLACIES.

ALL the varieties of Syllogism, whose necessary laws and contingent modifications we have hitherto considered, are, taken together, divided into classes by reference to their Validity ; and I shall comprise the heads of what I shall afterwards illustrate, in the following paragraph. LECT. XXIII.

¶ LXXVI. Syllogisms, by another distribution, are distinguished, by respect to their Validity, into *Correct* or *True* and *Incorrect* or *False*. The Incorrect or False are again (though not in a logical point of view) divided, by reference to the intention of the reasoner, into *Paralogisms*, or *Faulty Reasonings*, and *Sophisms*, or *Deceptive Reasonings*. The Paralogism (*paralogismus*) is properly a syllogism of whose falsehood the employer is not himself conscious ; the Sophism (*sophisma, captio, cavillatio*) is properly a false Par. LXXVI. Syllogisms, — Correct and Incor- rect.

syllogism, fabricated and employed for the purpose of deceiving others.   The term *Fallacy* may
be applied indifferently in either sense.   These
distinctions are, however, frequently confounded ;
nor, in a logical relation, are they of account.
False Syllogisms are, again, vicious, either in
respect of their form or of their matter, or in
respect of both form and matter.[a]

Explica-
tion.

Logical and
absolute
truth dis-
criminated.

In regard to the first distinction contained in this
paragraph,—of Syllogisms into Correct or True and
Incorrect or False,—it is requisite to say a few words.
It is necessary to distinguish logical truth, that is, the
truth which Logic guarantees in a reasoning, from the
absolute truth of the several judgments of which a
reasoning is composed.   I have frequently inculcated
that Logic does not warrant the truth of its premises,
except in so far as these may be the formal conclusions of anterior reasonings,—it only warrants (on
the hypothesis that the premises are truly assumed)
the truth of the inference.   In this view the conclusion may, as a separate proposition, be true, but if this
truth be not a necessary consequence from the premises, it is a false conclusion, that is, in fact no conclusion at all.   Now on this point there is a doctrine
prevalent among logicians, which is not only erroneous,
but, if admitted, subversive of the distinction of
Logic as a purely formal science.   The doctrine in
question is in its result this,—that if the conclusion
of a syllogism be true, the premises may be either true
or false, but that if the conclusion be false, one or
both of the premises must be false ; in other words,
that it is possible to infer true from false, but not

a Krug, *Logik*, § 115. ED.

false from true. As an example of this I have seen
given the following syllogism :—

> *Aristotle is a Roman;*
> *A Roman is a European;*
> *Therefore, Aristotle is a European.*

The inference, in so far as expressed, is true; but I
would remark that the whole inference which the
premises necessitate, and which the conclusion, therefore, virtually contains, is not true,—is false. For the
premises of the preceding syllogism gave not only the
conclusion, *Aristotle is a European*, but also the conclusion, *Aristotle is not a Greek;* for it not merely
follows from the premises, that Aristotle is conceived
under the universal notion of which the concept *Roman*
forms a particular sphere, but likewise that he is conceived as excluded from all the other particular spheres
which are contained under that universal notion. The
consideration of the truth of the premise, *Aristotle
is a Roman*, is, however, more properly to be regarded as extralogical; but if so, then the consideration
of the conclusion, *Aristotle is a European*, on any
other view than a mere formal inference from certain
given antecedents, is, likewise, extralogical. Logic is
only concerned with the formal truth,—the technical
validity,—of its syllogisms, and anything beyond the
legitimacy of the consequence drawn from certain
hypothetical antecedents, it does not profess to vindicate. Logical truth and falsehood are thus contained
in the correctness and incorrectness of logical inference; and it was, therefore, with no impropriety
that we made a true or correct, and a false or incorrect syllogism convertible expressions.[a]

a Cf. Esser, *Logik,* § 109.—Ed.

LECT.
XXIII.

The distinc-
tion of In-
correct Syl-
logisms into
Paralogisms
and So-
phisms not
of logical
import.

In regard to the distinction of Incorrect Syllogisms into Paralogisms and Sophisms, nothing need be said. The mere statement is sufficiently manifest; and, at the same time, it is not of a logical import. For Logic does not regard the intention with which reasonings are employed, but considers exclusively their internal legitimacy. But while the distinction is one, in other respects, proper to be noticed, it must be owned that it is not altogether without a logical value. For it behoves us to discriminate those artificial sophisms, the criticism of which requires a certain acquaintance with logical forms, and which, as a play of ingenuity and an exercise of acuteness, are not without their interest, from those paralogisms which, though not so artificial, are on that account only the more frequent causes of error and delusion.

Formal and
Material
Fallacies.

The last distinction is, however, logically more important, viz., of reasonings, 1°, Into such as are materially fallacious, that is, through the object-matter of their propositions; 2°, Into such as are formally fallacious, that is, through the manner or form in which these propositions are connected; and, 3°, Into such as are at once materially and formally fallacious. Material Fallacies lie beyond the jurisdiction of Logic. Formal Fallacies can only be judged of by an application of those rules in the exposition of which we have hitherto been engaged.

Ancient
Greek
Sophisms.

The application of these rules will afford the opportunity of adducing and resolving some of the more capital of those Sophisms, which owe their origin to the ingenuity of the ancient Greeks. " Many of these sophisms appear to us in the light of a mere play of wit and acuteness, and we are left to marvel at the interest which they originally excited, at the celebrity

which they obtained, and at the importance attached
to them by some of the most distinguished thinkers
of antiquity. The marvel will, however, be in some
degree abated, if we take the following circumstances
into consideration.

"In the first place, in the earlier ages of Greece the
method of science was in its infancy, and the laws of
thought were not yet investigated with the accuracy
and minuteness requisite to render the detection of
these fallacies a very easy matter. Howbeit, therefore, men had an obscure consciousness of their fallacy, they could not at once point out the place in
which the error lay; they were thus taken aback,
confounded, and constrained to silence.

"In the second place, the treatment of scientific
subjects was more oral and social than with us; and
the form of instruction principally that of dialogue
and conversation. In antiquity, men did not isolate
themselves so much in the retirement of their homes;
and they read far less than is now necessary in the
modern world : consequently, with those who had a
taste for science, the necessity of social communication
was greater and more urgent. In their converse on
matters of scientific interest, acuteness and pro-
fundity were perhaps less conducive to distinction
than vivacity, wit, dexterity in questioning and in
the discovery of objections, self-possession, and a
confident and uncompromising defence of bold, half-
true, or even erroneous assertions. Through such
means a very superficial intellect can frequently, even
with us, puzzle and put to silence another far acuter
and more profound. But, among the Greeks, the
Sophists and Megaric philosophers were accomplished
masters in these arts.

    " In the third place, as we know from Aristotle and
Diogenes Laertius,[a] it was the rule in their dialogical
disputations, that every question behoved to be answered by a yes or a no, and thus the interrogator
had it in his power to constrain his adversary always
to move in a foreseen, and, consequently, a determinate, direction. Thus the Sophisms were somewhat
similar to a game at forfeits, or like the passes of a
conjuror, which amuse and astonish for a little, but
the marvel of which vanishes the moment we understand the principle on which they are performed."[β]

    As the various fallacies arise from secret violation
of the logical laws by which the different classes of
syllogisms are governed, and as syllogisms are Categorical, or Hypothetical, or Disjunctive, or Hypothetico-disjunctive, we may properly consider Fallacies
under these four heads, as transgressions of the syllogistic laws in their special application to the several
kinds of syllogism.

Par. LXXVII.
Fallacies,—
their divi-
sion and
classifica-
tion.
    ¶ LXXVII. The Syllogistic Laws determine, in
reference to all the classes of Syllogism, the three
following principles ; and all Fallacies are violations of one or other of these principles, in relation to one or other class of syllogism.

    I. If both the Logical Form and the Matter of
a syllogism be correct, then is the Conclusion
true.

    II. If the syllogism be Materially Correct, but
Formally Incorrect, then the Conclusion is not (or
only accidentally) true.

a Arist. *Soph. Elench.*, c. 17 ; La-   β Bachmann, *Logik*, § 384, p.
ertius, L. ii. c. 18, § 133. The refer-   513.
ences are given by Bachmann.—Ed.

III. If the syllogism be Formally Correct, but
Materially Incorrect, then the Conclusion is not
(or only accidentally) true.

Fallacies, as violations of these principles in
more immediate reference to one or other of the
Four Classes of Syllogism, must again be vicious
in reference either to the form, or to the matter,
or to both the form and matter of a syllogism.
Fallacies are thus again divided into *Formal* and
Material, under which classes we shall primarily
arrange them.

      ⸀ LXXVIII. Of Formal Fallacies, the Catego-
rical are the most frequent, and of these, those
whose vice lies in having four in place of three
terms (*quaternione terminorum*) ; for this, in
consequence of the ambiguity of its expression,
does not immediately betray itself.   Under this
genus are comprised three species, which are
severally known under the names of, 1°, *Fallacia
sensus compositi et divisi* ; 2°, *Fallacia a dicto
secundum quid ad dictum simpliciter*, et vice
versa ; 3°, *Fallacia figuræ dictionis.*

"That in a categorical syllogism only three terms
are admissible, has been already shown.   A categorical syllogism with four capital notions has no connection ; and is called, by way of jest, the *logical
quadruped* (*animal quadrupes logicum*).   This vice
usually occurs when the notions are in reality different, but when their difference is cloaked by the verbal identity of the terms ; for, otherwise, it would be
too transparent to deceive either the reasoner himself
or any one else.   This vice may, however, be of various

kinds, and of these there are, as stated, three principal species.

1. Fallacia
sensus com-
positi et
divisi.

"The first is the *Fallacia sensus compositi et divisi*,— the *Fallacy of Composition and Division*." This arises when, in the same syllogism, we employ words now collectively, now distributively, so that what is true in connection, we infer must be also true in separation, and *vice versa*; as, for example:—*All must sin; Caius sins; therefore, Caius must sin.*" Here we argue, from the unavoidable liability in man to sin, that this particular sin is necessary, and for this indi-

Modes of
this Fallacy.

vidual sinner. "This fallacy may arise in different ways. 1°, It may arise when the predicate is joined with the subject in a simple and in a modal relation. For example,— *White can be* (i. e. *become*) *black, therefore white can be black.*—2°, It may arise from the confusion of a copulative and disjunctive combination. Thus,—*9 consists or is made up of 7 + 2, which are odd and even numbers, therefore 9 is odd and even.*—3°, It may arise, if words connected in the premises are disjoined in the conclusion. Thus,—*Socrates is dead, therefore Socrates is.*"

An example of the first of these contingencies,— that which is the most frequent and dangerous,— occurs when, from its universality, a proposition must be interpreted with restriction. Thus, when our Saviour says, *The blind shall see,—The deaf shall hear*, he does not mean that the blind, as blind, shall see,—

---

a [See Fonseca, *Instit. Dial.*, L. viii. c. v. p. 106, Ingolstadii, 1604.]

β Krug, *Logik*, § 118, p. 420.— ED. [On the distinction of *Sensus Compositi et Divisi*, so famous in the question of foreknowledge and liberty, see its history in Itzix, *Commentarii ex Disputationes, de Scientia*,

de Ideis, de Veritate, ac de Vita Dei, Disp. xxxiii. p. 261 et sq. Alvarez, in Gala, *Philosophia Generalis*, L. iii. c. iii. sect. 2, § 8, p. 466.]

γ [Denzinger,] *Die Logik als Wissenschaft der Denklunst*, dargestellt, § 538, Bamberg, 1836. — ED.]

that the deaf, as deaf, shall hear, but only that those who had been blind and deaf should recover the use of these senses. To argue the opposite would be to incur the fallacy in question.

The second fallacy is that *A dicto secundum quid ad dictum simpliciter*, and its converse, *A dicto simpliciter ad dictum secundum quid.* The former of these,—the fallacy *A dicto secundum quid ad dictum simpliciter,*— arises when from what is true only under certain modifications and relations, we infer it to be true absolutely. Thus, if from the fact that some Catholics hold the infallibility of the Pope, we should conclude that the infallibility of the Pope is a tenet of the Catholic Church in general. The latter, the fallacy *a dicto simpliciter ad dictum secundum quid*, is the opposite sophism, where from what is true absolutely we conclude what is true only in certain modifications and relations,—as, for example, when from the premise that *Man is a living organism*, we infer that *A painted or sculptured man is a living organism.*[a]

The third fallacy,—the *Sophisma figuræ dictionis*,— arises when we merely play with the ambiguity of a word. The well-known syllogism, *Mus syllaba est ; Mus caseum rodit ; Ergo, syllaba caseum rodit*,[β] is an example ; or,

> *Herod is a fox ;*
> *A fox is a quadruped ;*
> *Therefore, Herod is a quadruped.*

To this fallacy may be reduced what are called the *Sophisma equivocationis*, the *Sophisma amphiboliæ*, and the *Sophisma accentus*,[γ] which are only con- temptible modifications of this contemptible fallacy.

2. *Fallacia a dicto secundum quid ad dictum simpliciter, and its conversa.*

a Cf. Denzinger, *Logik*, § 564. — ED.   γ On these fallacies, see Denzinger,
β Seneca. *Epist.*, 48.—ED.   *Logik*, §§ 559, 560, 561.—ED.

¶ LXXIX. Of Material Fallacies, those are of
the most frequent occurrence, where from a premise which is not in reality universal, we conclude
universally; or from a notion which is not in
reality a middle term, we infer a conclusion.
Under this genus there are various species of
fallacies, of which the most remarkable are, 1°,
the *Sophisma cum hoc (vel post hoc), ergo propter hoc*; 2°, *Sophisma pigrum*, or *ignava ratio*;
3°, *Sophisma polyzeteseos*; and 4°, *Sophisma heterozeteseos.*[a]

Explica-
tion.
Fallacies of
an Unreal
Universal-
ity, and of
an Illusive
Reason.

In this paragraph you will observe that there are
given two genera of Material Fallacies,—those of
an Unreal Universality (*sophismata ficta universalitatis*), and those of an Illusive Reason (*sophismata
falsi medii*, or *non causa ut causa*). I must first
explain the nature of these, considered apart; then
show that they both fall together, the one being
only the categorical, the other only the hypothetical
expression of the same vice; and, finally, consider
the various species into which the generic fallacy is
subdivided.

"Our decisions concerning individual objects, in so
far as they belong to certain classes, are very frequently fallacies of the former kind; that is, conclusions from premises of an unreal universality. For
example:—*The Jews are rogues—The Carthaginians,
faithless—The Cretans, liars—The French, braga-
docios—The Germans, mystics—The rich, purse-
proud—The noble, haughty—Women, frivolous—
The learned, pedants.*—These and similar judgments,
which in general are true only of many,—at best only

a Cf. Krug. *Logik*, § 117.—Ed.

of the majority, of the subjects of a class, often con-

stitute, however, the grounds of the opinions we form
of individuals; so that these opinions, with their
grounds, when expressed as conclusion and premises,
are nothing else than fallacies of an unreal generality,
—*sophismata fictæ universalitatis.* It is impossible,
however, to decide by logical rules, whether a proposition, such as those above stated, is or is not universally
valid ; in this, experience alone can instruct us. Logic
requires only, in general, that every sumption should
be universally valid, and leaves it to the several
sciences to pronounce whether this or that particular
sumption does or does not fulfil this indispensable
condition."[a] The *sophisma fictæ universalitatis* is
thus a fallacious syllogism of the class of categoricals.

But the second kind of material fallacies, the

sophisms of Unreal Middle, are not less frequent than
those of unreal universality. When, for example, it
is argued, (as was done by ancient philosophers), that
the magnet is animated, because it moves another
body, or that the stars are animated, because they
move themselves;—here there is assumed not a true,
but merely an apparent, reason, there is, consequently,
no real mediation, and the *sophisma falsi medii* is
committed. For, in these cases, the conclusion in the
one depends on the sumption,—*If a body moves another body, it is animated ;* in the other, on the sumption,—*If a body moves itself, it is animated,* but as
the antecedent and consequent in neither of these
sumptions are really connected as reason and consequent,—or as cause and effect,—there is, therefore,
no valid inference of the conclusion.[β] The *sophisma*

a Krug, *Logik,* § 117, Anm., p.
422.—Ed.

β Cf. Krug, *Logik,* p. 423. —
Ed.

LECT.
XXIII.

The fallacies
of Unreal
Reason and
of Unreal
Univer-
sality co-
incide.

non causæ ut causæ is thus an hypothetical syllogism ;
but, as it may be categorically enounced, this fallacy
of unreal reason will coincide with the categorical fallacy of unreal universality. Thus, the second example
above alleged—

If the stars move themselves, they are animated ;
But the stars do move themselves ;
Therefore, the stars are animated ;

is thus expressed by a categorical equivalent :—

All bodies that move themselves are animated ;
But the stars move themselves ;
Therefore, the stars are animated.

In the one case, the sumption ostensibly contains the
subsumption and conclusion, as the correlative parts
of a causal whole ; in the other, as the correlative
parts of an extensive whole, or, had the categorical
syllogism been so cast, of an intensive whole. The
two genera of sophisms may, therefore, it is evident,
be considered as one,—taking, however, in their particular manifestation, either a categorical or an hypothetical form.

Fallacy of
Unreal
Reason as
dangerous
in its nega-
tive as in
its positive
form.

I may notice that the sophism of Unreal Generality
or Unreal Reason, is hardly more dangerous in its positive than in its negative relation. For we are not
more disposed lightly to assume as absolutely universal, what is universal in relation to our experience,
than lightly to deny as real, what comes as an exception to our factitious general law. Thus it is that
men having once generalised their knowledge into a
compact system of laws, are found uniformly to deny
the reality of all phænomena which cannot be comprehended under these. They not only pronounce the
laws they have generalised as veritable laws of nature,

which, haply, they may be, but they pronounce that there are no higher laws; so that all which does not at once find its place within their systems, they scout without examination as visionary and fictitious. So much for this ground of fallacy in general; we now proceed to the species.

Now, as unreal reasons may be conceived infinite in number, the minor species of this class of sophisms cannot be enumerated; I shall, therefore, only take notice of the more remarkable, of those which, in consequence of their greater notoriety, have been honoured with distinctive appellations.

The first is the *Sophisma cum hoc (vel post hoc),* *ergo propter hoc.* This fallacy arises, when, from the contingent consecution of certain phænomena in the order of time, we infer their mutual dependence as cause and effect. When, for example, among the ancient Romans, a general, without carefully consulting the augurs, engaged the enemy, and suffered a defeat; it was inferred that the cause of the disaster was the unfavourable character of the auspices. In like manner, to this sophism belongs the conclusion, so long prevalent in the world, that the appearance of a comet was the harbinger of famine, pestilence, and war. In fact, the greater number of the hypotheses which constitute the history of physics and philosophy, are only so many examples of this fallacy. But no science has exhibited, and exhibits, so many flagrant instances of the sophism *cum hoc, ergo propter hoc,* as that of medicine; for, in proportion as the connection of cause and effect is peculiarly obscure in physic, physicians have only been the bolder in assuming that the recoveries which followed after their doses, were not concomitants but effects. This sophism is, in

practice, of great influence and very frequent occurrence; it is, however, in theory, too perspicuous to
require illustration.

**b. 'Ignava
Ratio.**
The second fallacy is that which has obtained the
name of *Ignava ratio*, or *Sophisma pigrum*,—in Greek,
ἀργὸς λόγος.[a] The excogitation of this argument is
commonly attributed to the Stoics, by whom it was
employed as subsidiary to their doctrine of fate. "It
is an argument by which a man endeavours to vindicate his inactivity in some particular relation, by the
necessity of the consequence. It is an hypothetico-
Example. disjunctive syllogism, and, when fully expressed, is
as follows :—

Sumption,........ *If I ought to exert myself to effect a certain event,
                    this event either must take place or it must
                    not ;*

Subsumption,...... *If it must take place, my exertion is superfluous ;
                    if it must not take place, my exertion is of no
                    avail ;*

Conclusion,........ *Therefore, on either alternative, my exertion is
                    useless.*"[b]

Cicero, in the twelfth chapter of his book, *De Fato*,
thus states it :—

*If it be fated that you recover from your present disease, whether
you call in a doctor or not, you will recover ; again, if it be
fated that you do not recover from your present disease,
whether you call in a doctor or not, you will not recover ;
But one or other of the contradictories is fated ;
Therefore, to call in a doctor is of no consequence.*

Others have enounced the sumption in various forms,
for example :—*If it be impossible but that you recover*

a See Menage on Diogenes Laertius, L. II. p. 123.—ED. [Facciolati,
Arrouon, v. p. 55. Gassendi, Opera,

t. I. *De Log. Orig. et Var.*, L. i. c.
8, p. 81.]
β Krug, *Logik*, § 117, p. 424.—ED.

from the present disease, &c.,—or—If it be true that LECT.
you will recover from this disease,—or—If it be decreed XXIII.
by God that you will not die of this disease, and so Its various
likewise in different manners, according to which like- designa-
wise the question itself has obtained various titles as
*Argument De Fato — De Possibilibus — De Libero
Arbitrio — De Providentia — De Divinis Decretis —
De Futuris Contingentibus — De Physica Praedeter-
minatione,* &c. No controversy is more ancient,
none more universal, none has more keenly agitated
the minds of men, none has excited a greater influence upon religion and morals; it has not only
divided schools, but nations, and has so modified not
only their opinions but their practice, that whilst the
Turks, as converts to the doctrine of Fate, take not
the slightest precaution in the midst of pestilence,
other nations, on the contrary, who admit the contin-
gency of second causes, carry their precautionary
policy to an opposite excess.

The common doctrine, that this argument is an Its history.
invention of the Stoics, and a ground on which they
rested their doctrine of the physical necessitation of
human action, is, however, erroneous, if we may
accord credit to the testimony of Diogenes Laertius,
who relates, in the Life of Zeno, the founder of this
sect, that he bestowed a sum of two hundred minæ
on a certain dialectician, from whom he had learned
seven species of the argument called the λόγος θερί-
ζων, *metens,* or *reaper,*—which differs little, if at all,
from the *ignava ratio.*[a] For how this sophism is constructed, and with what intent, I find recorded in the
commentary of Ammonius on the book of Aristotle

a See Laertius, vii. 25. The ob- cidati, *Armoires,* v. p. 57, ed. 1750.
servation in the text is from Fac- —ED.

Περὶ Ἑρμηνείας.[a] Of the same character, likewise, is the argument called the λόγος κυριεύων, the *ratio dominans*, or *controlling reason*, the process of which Arrian describes under the nineteenth chapter of the second book of the sayings of Epictetus.[b] *The lazy reason,—the reaper,—*and *the controlling reason*, are thus only various names for the same process.

The vice of this sophism. In regard to the vice of this sophism, "it is manifest that it lies in the sumption, in which the disjunct members are imperfectly enounced. It ought to have been thus conceived—If I ought to exert myself to effect a certain event, which I cannot, however, of myself effect, this event must either take place from other causes, or it must not take place at all. It is only under such a condition that my exertion can on either alternative be useless, and not if the event depend wholly or in part for its accomplishment on my exertion itself, as the *conditio sine qua non*."[γ] It is plain, however, that the refutation of this sophism does not at all affect the doctrine of necessity; for this doctrine, except in its very absurdest form,— the *Fatum Turcicum*,—makes no use of such a reasoning.

c. Sophisma polyteleseos. "The third fallacy is the *Sophisma polyzeteseos* or *quæstionis duplicis,—the sophism of continuous questioning*, which attempts, from the impossibility of assigning the limit of a relative notion, to show by continued interrogation the impossibility of its determination at all. There are certain notions which are

---

a F. 91 b, ed. Ald. Venet., 1546. —Ed.

β The purpose of this sophism may be gathered from Arrian, but not the nature of the argument itself. It is also mentioned, though not explained, by Lucian, *Vit. Auct.* s. 22; Plutarch, *Sympos.*, i. 1, 5; Gellius, *N.A.*, i. 2. Compare Facciolati, *Acroases*, v. p. 87.—Ed.

γ Krug, *Logik*, p. 424.—Ed.

only conceived as relative,—as proportional, and whose limits we cannot, therefore, assign by the gradual addition or detraction of one determination. But there is no consequence in the proposition, that, if a notion cannot be determined in this manner, it is incapable of all determination, and, therefore, absolutely inconceivable and null."[a] Such is the Sorites, the nature of which I have already explained to you. This reasoning, as applied to various objects, obtained various names, as, besides the Sorites or Accrvus, we have the *crescens*,[β]—the φαλακρός or *calvus*,[γ]—the ὑπερθετικός, *superpositus* or *superlativus*,[δ]—the ἡσυχάζων or *quiescens*, &c. &c.[ε] The Sorites is well defined by Ulpian,[ζ] a sophism in which, by very small degrees, the disputant is brought from the evidently true to the evidently false. For example, I ask, Does one grain of corn make up a heap of grain ? My opponent answers,—No. I then go on asking the same question of two, three, four, and so on *ad infinitum*, nor can the respondent find the number at which the grains begin to constitute a heap. On the other hand, if we depart from the answer,—that a thousand grains make a heap, the interrogation may be continued downward to unity, and the answerer be unable to determine the limit where the grains cease to make up a heap. The same process may be performed, it is

---

a Krug, *Logik*, § 117.—Ed.

β Wyttenbach, *Ad Plutarch. De Sera Num. Vind.*, p. 559 ; *Præcepta Phil. Log.*, p. iii. c. 9, § 4.—Ed.

γ Diog. Laert., ii. 108. Cf. Gassendi, *De Log. Orig.*, c. 3.—Ed.

δ Epictetus, *Dissert.*, lib. 2, 2. As interpreted by Gassendi, *De Log. Orig.*, c. 6. But the true reading is probably ὑπερβατικός. See Schweighæuser's note.—Ed.

ε Cicero, *Acad.*, ii. 29. Epictetus, *Dissert.*, ii. 19, 18.—Ed.

ζ Lege, 177. *De Verb. Signif.* : "Natura cavillationis, quam Græci σωρείτην appellarunt, hæc est, ut ab eo ab evidenter veris per brevissimas mutationes disputatio ad ea quæ evidenter falsa sunt perducatur." Quoted by Gassendi, *De Log. Orig. et Var.*, c. 3, *Opera*, t. i. p. 41, and by Menage, *Ad. Laert.* ii. 108.—Ed.

manifest, upon all the notions of proportion, in space and time and degree, both in continuous and discrete quantity.[a]

d. Sophis-
ma hetero-
zeteseos.

The fourth and last fallacy of this class is the *sophisma heterozeteseos,* or *sophism of counter-questioning,*[β] and, as applied to various objects, it obtained,

Its various
names.

among the ancients, the names of *the Dilemna,*[γ]—the *Cornutus,*[δ]—*the Litigiosus,—the Achilles,*[ε]—*the Mentiens,*[ζ]—*the Fallens,*[η]—*the Electra,*[θ]—*the Obvelatus,*[ι]—*the Reciprocus,*[κ]—*the Crocodilinus,*—*the οὖτις;*[λ]—*the Inductio imperfecta;*[μ] and to this should also be re-

Its charac-
ter.

ferred the Ass of Buridanus.[ν] " It is a hypothetico-disjunctive reasoning, which rests on a certain supposition, and which, through a reticence of this supposition, deduces a fallacious inference. To take, for an example of this fallacy, the κεράτινος or Cornutus :—it is asked ;—Have you cast your horns ?—If you answer, I have ; it is rejoined, Then you have had horns : if you answer, I have not, it is rejoined, Then you have them still.[ξ]—To this question, and to the inferences from it, the disjunctive proposition is supposed,—A certain subject has either had horns or has them still. This disjunction is, however, only correct

---

a Krug, *Logik,* § 117.—Ed.

β [See Gassendi, *Opera,* t. i. *De Log. Orig. et Var.,* c. 6, p. 51.]

γ Hermogenes, *De Invent.,* L. iv., and *Proleg. ad Hermogenem.* See Walz's *Rhetores Graeci,* vol. iii. p. 167, iv. p. 14.—Ed.

δ Seneca, *Epist.,* 45. Menage, *Ad Diog. Laert.,* L. ii. 108.—Ed.

ε Diog. Laert., L. ix. 23. Aristotle, *Phys.,* vi. 9. *Soph. Elench.,* 24.—Ed.

ζ Menage, *Ad Diog. Laert.,* L. ii. 108. Cicero, *Acad.,* ii. 29.—Ed.

η Diog. Laert., ii. 108.—Ed.

θ Lucian, *Vit. Auct.,* § 22. Cf.

Menage, *Ad Diog. Laert.,* L. ii. 108. —Ed.

ι Menage, *ibid.*—Ed.

κ Aulus Gellius, *N. A.,* I. v. c. 10, 11.—Ed.

λ Lucian, *l. c.* Quintilian, *Inst. Orat.,* i. 10, 5. Cf. Menage, *Ad Diog. Laert.,* L. ii. 108.—Ed.

μ Ammonius, *Ad Arist. Categ.,* f. 58. Cf. Menage, *loc. cit.*—Ed.

ν Cicero, *De Inventione,* L. i. c. 31.—Ed.

ξ See Denzinger, *Logik,* § 571, from whom these designations are taken. *Krug's Works,* p. 238.—Ed.

ο Diog. Laert., vii. 187.—Ed.

if the question is concerning a subject to which horns
previously belonged. If I do not suppose this, the
disjunction is false ; it must, consequently, thus run :
—a certain subject has either had or not had horns.
In the latter case they could not of course be cast.
The alternative inferences (*then you have had them*, or
then you have them still) have no longer ground or
plausibility." [a]   To take another instance in the *Liti-* The *Litigiosus or Reciprocus*. Of the history of this famous
dilemma there are two accounts, the Greek and the
Roman. The Roman account is given us by Aulus
Gellius,[β] and is there told in relation to an action
between Protagoras, the prince of the Sophists, and The case of Protagoras and Euathlus, a young man, his disciple. The disciple had Euathlus.
covenanted to give his master a large sum to accom-
plish him as a legal rhetorician ; the one half of the
sum was paid down, and the other was to be paid on
the day when Euathlus should plead and gain his
first cause. But when the scholar, after the due
course of preparatory instruction, was not in the same
hurry to commence pleader, as the master to obtain
the remainder of his fee, Protagoras brought Euathlus
into court, and addressed his opponent in the following reasoning :—Learn, most foolish of young men,
that however matters may turn up,—(whether the
decision to-day be in your favour or against you),—
pay me my demand you must. For if the judgment
be against you, I shall obtain the fee by decree of the
court, and if in your favour, I shall obtain it in terms
of the compact, by which it became due on the very
day you gained your first cause. You thus must
fail, either by judgment or by stipulation. To this
Euathlus rejoined :—Most sapient of masters, learn

a Krug, *Logik*, p. 425.—Ed.   β L. v. c. 10.

LECT.
XXIII.

from your own argument, that whatever may be the finding of the court, absolved I must be from any claim by you. For if the decision be favourable, I pay nothing by the sentence of the judges, but if unfavourable, I pay nothing in virtue of the compact, because, though pleading, I shall not have gained my cause. The judges, says Gellius, unable to find a *ratio decidendi*, adjourned the case to an indefinite day, and ultimately left it undetermined. I find a parallel story told, among the Greek writers, by Arsenius, by the Scholiast of Hermogenes, and by Suidas,[a] of the rhetorician Corax (*anglicè* Crow) and his scholar Tisias. In this case the judges got off by delivering a joke against both parties, instead of a decision in favour of either. We have here, they said, the plaguy egg of a plaguy crow, and from this circumstance is said to have originated the Greek proverb, κακοῦ κόρακος κακὸν ᾠόν.

Parallel case of Corax and Tisias.

Herewith we terminate the First Great Division of Pure Logic,—Stoicheiology or the Doctrine of Elements.

a [Prolegomena to Hermogenes, in Walz's *Rhetores Græci*, tom. iv. pp. 13, 14. Arsenii Violetum, edit. Walz, Stuttgard, 1832, pp. 313, 314; quoted by Sigwart, *Logik*, § 331, p. 211, 3d edit. Suidas, quoted by Schottus, *Adagia Græcorum*, p. 450, 1612.]